PENGUIN BOOKS
HUÉ CITY

Claire Betita de Guzman is a Filipina writer based in Singapore and author of five novels: *Sudden Superstar*, *Miss Makeover*, *Budget is the New Black*, *Girl Meets World*, and *No Boyfriend Since Birth*, which was adapted into a TV series. A former journalist, she started as a reporter for the broadsheet *Today* before becoming a lifestyle editor for international and local magazines including *Cosmopolitan Philippines* and *Harper's Bazaar Singapore*. She works closely with the Migrant Writers of Singapore and has led talks and panels at literary events, including the Singapore Writers Festival and Poetry Festival Singapore. She studied Journalism and graduated cum laude from the University of the Philippines. She has taken writing courses at the University of Oxford in England and has been a fellow in literary workshops in Europe and Asia, including Miradoux, France, Bali, Indonesia, and Tbilisi, Georgia. She is co-author of a poetry collection, *Dreaming of the Divine Downstairs* and is co-editor of *Get Luckier*, an anthology of Philippine–Singaporean writings. Find her online at www.clairebetita.com.

Also by Claire Betita de Guzman

Sudden Superstar (2023)

Huế City

Claire Betita de Guzman

PENGUIN BOOKS

An imprint of Penguin Random House

PENGUIN BOOKS

Penguin Books is an imprint of the Penguin Random House group of
companies whose addresses can be found at
global.penguinrandomhouse.com

Published by Penguin Random House SEA Pte Ltd
40 Penjuru Lane, #03-12 Block 2,
Singapore 609216

First published in Penguin Books by Penguin Random House SEA 2024

ISBN 9789815144277

Typeset in Garamond by MAP Systems, Bengaluru, India

www.penguin.sg

To those who've dared, and to those who dream of starting over

Part One

Typhoon Yolanda

CARMEN

He grew up in Andalusia, the driest region in Spain, so Carmen told him the typhoon story.

'The roof of our home was the first to go,' she began, 'and we ran from house to house trying to find one that wouldn't get blown away.'

Typhoon Yolanda hit Tacloban at 7.47 p.m. one night in November, three months ago, with pounding rain and winds going at 300 kilometres per hour and storm surges reaching seven metres high. Their modest bungalow by the sea, Carmen continued, was demolished by the tsunami-like waves.

She paused, watching as Luis took a slow sip from an amber-coloured bottle and stroked his beard, which was matted and dirty-blond. He sat across from her, silent but rapt. And he was sipping, rather than gulping, because the beer was warm, like the noontime sun beating on the glass walls of Kabayan Café where they were comfortably ensconced in a booth: Carmen next to Auntie Swan, Luis next to his Canon DSLR and The North Face backpack, a beat-up carabiner dangling from a strap. Carmen liked that they were protected from the heat, from Taft Avenue's traffic-clogged streets and its harried lunch crowd. The waiters, too many for such a place, had mercifully drawn the blinds.

Carmen wasn't comfortable talking about Yolanda, about the typhoon. But she steeled herself to offer more information, things she felt Luis ought to know: how, after the typhoon, she'd been left with nothing but the clothes on her back; how, the morning after, she and Uncle Amado and Auntie Swan went back and found their house gone, save for the cement floor and a concrete pillar; how she salvaged a cherished photograph of her mother, dry and intact, tucked between the flattened bushes. A small miracle in the midst of the catastrophe that befell them.

She told Luis all this, thinking of Uncle Amado, who knew the waiters here. He would be coming any minute now, in this casual Filipino restaurant with orange plastic chairs and loud pop music, favoured by yuppies who worked in the nearby offices and students who went to college at the De La Salle. Kabayan Café was packed and busy enough for one to easily blend in, remain anonymous and undisturbed, with cheap Filipino food—oily, fried pork dishes like *lechon kawali* and *sisig* and, of course, San Miguel beer. Luis had told them earlier that he wanted a local experience.

'Carmen now sleeps on the sofa downstairs,' Auntie Swan volunteered, the words sliding easily off her mouth, as they always did during these meetings. Auntie Swan had worked abroad for more than a decade; she was good at speaking English, at speaking up. 'She prefers it to her own bedroom on the second floor.' She picked up the menu and scanned it for a moment, before looking back at Luis.

'Rain frightens me,' Carmen interjected. 'Especially at night, when it drums loudly on the roof.' She tried her best to affect a shudder.

'Is that so?' Luis asked, concern clouding his face. He reached across the table and gave the top of her hand a soft, reassuring pat. Carmen shot him a small, grateful smile; she expected this and she had learned, after all this time, not to recoil. Later, she could swear there were tears in Luis's eyes. There was already a sympathetic droop in his eyebrows, a marked softening in his voice, when he said: 'Is that why you decided to relocate to Manila?'

Carmen nodded. 'Yes, we had to get away from . . .' Her voice trailed off. She thought of her mother, of the picture she said she'd found in the bushes after the storm. 'Yes,' she said, again. 'Manila is our home now.'

That was what she'd told him earlier at Luneta Park. Carmen had been going to this park for years, always with Uncle Amado and Auntie Swan, sometimes with Max and once, a long time ago, with her mother. That last bit about her mom was true, though she'd been reluctant to share it. Thankfully, talk turned mostly to the typhoon, even though the sky over Luneta that morning was a slab of bright blue chalcedony, with clouds like delicate daubs of white paint. Luneta Park was a sprawling fifty-eight-hectare space, one of Manila's largest urban parks but Carmen had always favoured this spot. The daily vendors had already come with their carts strung with candy, snacks, plastic basketballs, and mobile cases underneath bunches of loudly-coloured balloons and gaudy kites. A few tourists were there too, early birds ready to brave the humidity, looking dutiful with their backpacks and water bottles and small cameras as if they were on a school field trip. Most were headed to see the site of Jose Rizal's 1896 execution by a firing squad, where a monument now stood.

Luis, when Carmen first spotted him, had been sitting cross-legged on a bench near *La Madre Filipina*, a mother-and-children sculpture in white plaster that was her favourite among all the statues in the park. Luis had his head bent down low, left hand grasping a pencil moving rapidly in sure, practised strokes on the surface of a small sketch pad on his lap. His khaki Bermuda shorts appeared wrinkly, his faded red sando, a sleeveless T-shirt that tourists favoured to combat Manila's heat, looked loose yet oddly chic against his meaty arms. When he looked up, as if to take a break, Carmen saw that his face was open and friendly and slightly hopeful as his eyes scanned the people trickling in from the street.

So, she had gone over, tapping his shoulder lightly before stepping back. 'Hi,' she said with a tentative smile and a playful wave of her phone, wondering for a moment if she looked just like another girl wanting to post something on Facebook. She looked the same as always: bare-faced except for a light dusting of face powder she'd inherited from Auntie Swan, hair pulled back in a low ponytail, a clean T-shirt, jeans from yesterday, and sneakers. She always wore sneakers— never mind if they were scuffed and ugly; they are shoes she could run in. Auntie Swan herself had on a pair of flat slides.

Luis had steadied his eyes on her. 'Hi,' he said, his bearded face breaking into an amiable, expectant smile. Carmen thought he looked relieved.

'Can you please take a picture of my aunt and me?' She had handed him her phone, murmuring that it was new and had been a birthday gift. Looking pleased, she beckoned Auntie Swan to come closer. And then, she stood back, put on her best smile, and wrapped an arm around her aunt, who made a cheesy V-sign with her fingers then cried *Mabuhay!* as Luis snapped them against *La Madre*. At this, they all laughed. Carmen joked that Auntie Swan had been watching too many lunchtime shows on TV.

'Mabuhay?' Luis had said, still chuckling as he closed his sketchbook and stuffed it inside his backpack. 'Is that Tagalog? I know I've heard it before. What does it mean?'

'Long live!' Auntie Swan had replied, pertly. She cocked her head and flashed Carmen a smug look as if to say, *See, I'm smart.*

They had exchanged names afterwards and drifted towards the Japanese gardens, seeking shade. Luis told them he was staying in a small hotel in nearby Ermita and was just starting his tour of the Philippine capital. So far, he'd visited the Cultural Center of the Philippines, wanting to see its infamous Brutalist design. He was a fan of the famous Le Corbusier he said, a name Carmen wasn't familiar with. And then he had gone to see the wrought-iron, Spanish-inspired façade of the Manila Hotel, which he said reminded him of home. He was an architect-turned-artist who'd just had a small exhibition in Barcelona and dabbled in photography. Carmen noted the heavy, long-lensed camera slung over his shoulder.

'We're from the province,' Carmen had told him, as they reached the potted bonsai trees lining the perimeter of the gardens. 'Tourists in our own country,' she added with a rueful chuckle. She told him that Auntie Swan and she had just moved from Tacloban City in the south, an hour's plane ride away. Tacloban City was in the eye of super-typhoon Yolanda that had been reported on CNN, BBC, Al Jazeera, and every other international news channel. Like him, Carmen told Luis, they were seeing the sights of Manila up close and for the first time. And yes, her aunt and she also thought Manila was congested and polluted. 'But it's a respite from Tacloban's traumatic experience,'

Carmen said, taking Auntie Swan's hand into her own. 'Manila, for typhoon victims like us, is . . . a change of scene.'

Luis had nodded vehemently, his face solemn. He understood or at least, was determined to. He may not have gone through the same trauma, he said, but he too had fled his hometown in Almeria along the Andalusian coast of Spain because life had become stultifying.

'Everything was dry and brown,' he had said of Almeria's landscape. 'A literal desert.' It became a sad reflection of his daily life. He decided to quit his job and sell everything—his apartment, his car, and all his possessions—to embark on a tour of the other side of the world. Southeast Asia first, then Australia, then South America. He told them that he had just come from Thailand, where he said he didn't spend much money. 'Everyone was smiling,' he said. Manila was his second stop.

They had reached the end of the gardens, along the path that led them out back towards Kalaw Street and came to a stop under a lone, anaemic fire tree. They gazed out across the traffic-lined avenue where a cornucopia of stores and stalls were haphazardly lined up: a McDonald's, a laundry shop, a tourist agency, a Western Union, a few small hotels.

'I'm hungry,' Auntie Swan had said, after a minute. She turned to the tourist. 'Luis, why don't you join us for lunch?' She glanced at Carmen, her smile benign. 'After we've eaten something, we can visit the Bellevue, the old Art Deco theatre along Pedro Gil street and just a jeepney ride away from where my parents—bless them—used to go. A good architect like you would appreciate the design for sure.'

'My aunt has diabetes,' Carmen had said, apologetically. 'She can't go hungry or else her blood sugar will drop. So please, do eat with us and try Filipino food.'

Luis had said yes without hesitation. He hoisted his backpack higher on his shoulder and took Auntie Swan's elbow, as if afraid she might collapse any moment.

'My treat, okay?' Auntie Swan had said, smiling softly and patting Luis's shoulder. Tough Auntie Swan, suddenly demure. It always threw Carmen off. She glanced quickly at the foreigner.

Luis had only laughed and waved an arm dismissively. His face took an eager and earnest quality while steering them both across the street, as if he knew where to go and which parts of Manila to avoid. They led him to Kabayan Café on the next street, which, they told him, served tasty Filipino food, and where they always ate. 'My Uncle Amado, he'll join us—yes?' Carmen said. 'He knows the waiters there.'

And so here they were, talking about Typhoon Yolanda. And about Luis, too: where exactly he was staying (Red Planet Hostel), how many days he'd be exploring Manila (four days), which countries he planned to visit next (Huế City in Vietnam, Siem Reap in Cambodia, with a stopover in Singapore and KL in Malaysia). Auntie Swan peppered him with questions, and he seemed only too happy to answer. He didn't ask whether any of them had been to Spain or any country in Europe, and that was all right because they hadn't. Carmen noticed that he was more of a talker than a listener. He was animated, bending his vowels and extending his consonants as he spoke to them in his Spanish accent. The coolness of Kabayan's air-con, a relief from the midday humidity, was relaxing as was being with a group. It was tiring to be alone, Carmen knew, as she watched his face carefully. It was a mottled mix of red, pale, and brown, as if the tan couldn't decide where to settle.

And then, Uncle Amado burst through the door, though no one in the crowded restaurant seemed to notice, except Carmen. She stood up to receive her uncle's peck on the cheek, announcing, 'Luis, this is my favourite uncle!' and smiling her first real smile of the day. Uncle Amado thrust his hand out, smiling widely. There was a chip in his front tooth, but no one ever seemed to notice that. It was Uncle Amado's eyes, bright and alert, that always held people's attention. 'So nice of you to join my girls for lunch!' He crowed, shaking Luis's hand, then standing by the booth for a moment. 'What an honour. Come, come, let's all have a round of beer! On me!'

Uncle Amado grabbed another chair and sat down. He signalled to the waiter, and it was as if the food came all at once: plates of *chicharon bulaklak*, deep-fried pork intestines, along with skewers of barbecued pork, mounds of fried rice, a piping-hot, aromatic bowl of *bulalo*, Uncle Amado's favourite boiled beef soup where pieces of marrow floated to the broth's already greasy top. 'This is true Filipino food!' he boomed, pushing the intestines towards Luis. The Spaniard promptly took one and popped it gaily inside his mouth. Even as he chewed, he gave Uncle Amado an elated, exaggerated thumbs-up sign.

When the beer arrived, warm and in half-litre bottles, Uncle Amado poured a glass for Luis and dropped two big chunks of ice in before handing it to him. 'Come, *hijo*, you better have your drink cold. It's so hot outside!'

Carmen quickly looked at Luis, but he'd matched her uncle's smile and was now taking a long, glorious sip. He said nothing about the ice in his San Miguel beer, though she knew some would have balked at this. She also knew that Luis was now unable to resist Uncle Amado's charms: his unabashed friendliness, his sweeping gestures, his jokes, his booming voice, his crazy laugh, and the way he listened. Because, yes, Uncle Amado always listened. And he took care of everyone, even tourists they had just met.

Auntie Swan had been placing spoonfuls of sisig—fried, finely-chopped pieces of pig's ears and face, looking crisp and still steaming—on Luis's plate. Luis didn't protest. Then, she served a tender piece of beef bulalo on top of Carmen's rice, along with a piece of green lettuce. 'Go on,' she said, in her good, well-enunciated English. 'Carmen dear, eat some.'

Carmen took a bite but found it hard to swallow. There was a lump in her throat. All week, there had been a disturbing feeling in her throat that she'd been trying to ignore. But she caught sight of Luis's face and it was eager, not anxious or tense. In fact, there was no trace of anxiety at all. Instead, there was a greediness to the way he laughed and nodded at Uncle Amado's words. Maybe even a smugness. A kind of excitement and impatience that, Carmen imagined, was how he'd be when talking to folks back home, to fellow travellers he'd eventually meet. I know Manila, he'd say. I've mingled with the locals. I know their stories. One family even had their home blown away by a typhoon. Imagine that!

She felt a sharp intake of her own breath as Uncle Amado dropped another piece of ice in Luis's drink. The tourist only chuckled and downed it without reservation. He was already tipsy, Carmen could tell, but not drunk. He won't be: Luis was strong and robust, and judging from the way he'd consumed glass after glass of the San Miguel, an avid drinker.

But he would regret this. Carmen knew it. Luis Sobrepeña of Andalusia, Spain, would never forget this day. He would remember her and the name she had given him, which was Camille, not Carmen. Camille from Tacloban in south-eastern Philippines, a thousand kilometres away, though she had never stepped outside Manila.

Pimp

HAI

He wished there was a special entrance for the prostitutes. He was convinced that he broke out in a light sweat every time he saw those girls—terrifyingly overdone with their thick, fake lashes, spindly stilettos, and jewel-toned cocktail shifts that stopped an inch or two below the crotch—walking with such purpose across the stuffy lobby of his hotel. They walked with a swagger he could not really define and never carried purses like Sinh or any girl he knew. Instead, they had a wolfish look, a kind of smugness that said, I don't need to be in the streets anymore.

They always headed to where he was standing: behind the reception counter at Minh Thanh Hotel, where he worked six nights a week. It was he, after all, who would call them up. He, who had their numbers. Months ago, when he'd first entered their digits into his phone, he'd carefully typed 'CV' at the end of their names—short for *ca ve*, what he and his friends in Huế City called the bony girls in tiny blouses who sized them up with sullen eyes and who waited behind the ragged trees in Thuy Thien Park. Some of these prostitutes paced the shadowy length of the bridge at Truong Tien, where traffic usually slowed in the evenings. The rest came out after midnight on their motorbikes, wearing fancy bike helmets that weren't really helmets, bantering with their pimps, targeting the stray drunken foreigners who slurped bún bò huế—Hai's favourite beef noodle and a definite wake-upper—at the roadside stalls. '*Khong nguoi tay map*,' the girls shrieked and cowered behind their pimps whenever they spotted a heavyset

11

man who looked interested. *No fat foreigners.* The girls—his girls—often told him that, too.

Now, these working girls didn't need to go out to get a customer. Vietnam was wired and they had Facebook pages, Instagram accounts, LINE, and WhatsApp installed on their Samsungs or iPhones. All it took was a text or an online message.

So, when he wasn't checking-in guests or assigning them rooms, Hai called a ca ve for them. He perused a Facebook page called Cave VIP and took note of the girls, screening them for his guests. His guests complained that everything in Huế rudely shut down at 9 p.m.—including the air-con in the lobby of Minh Thanh. By 10 p.m., the lobby would be deserted save for Hai, Quang the security guard, a bellboy, and a few male guests asking for girls. Mr Mark, the yellow-haired engineer with the potbelly and nicotine-stained teeth—who flew to Huế from Saigon every month and once handed him a crisp, twenty-dollar bill—usually asked for two.

He couldn't exactly remember when he became a sort of unofficial *bao ke,* a pimp. 'Night manager', was what he normally told people when they asked about his work in Minh Thanh Hotel. 'Marketing' was what he called his other job running after tourists at the bus terminal, pleading for them to book a twelve-dollar room at the hostel he worked for part-time. It sounded better than 'tout'. Hai liked these euphemisms, though he hadn't yet figured out a classy term for pimp.

Bao ke would do for now.

The girls would arrive twenty minutes after the call, never heading down to the basement to park their motorbikes. Instead, they would smartly hand them to Quang at the front driveway before bursting into Minh Thanh's high-ceilinged lobby, already made warm by the absence of air conditioning.

It was this moment that made Hai nervous, when they crossed the vast space between the lobby doors and his spot at reception or the elevators leading to the rooms. He was painfully aware of the security cameras and sometimes he wished the girls would use the money to dress more elegantly.

It was a ridiculous thought, he knew, and one he'd already abandoned. Some of these girls had whole families to feed, extended clans in the countryside who thought their daughters or nieces were in Huế City working as waitresses, seamstresses, or receptionists in four-star hotels, just like Hai. And who was he to judge how they wore their clothes? His girlfriend, Sinh, always complained that he dressed so sloppily himself.

But when their spiky heels made that annoying click-clack as they made their way to the elevators or when they opened their heavily-rouged mouths and spoke in a pitch that belonged more to the confounding stalls of Dong Ba Market than in his four-star lobby, Hai would feel his armpits grow damp.

'Hello, *Anh* Hai,' they'd coo, using the respectful term for older brother, when they were early and hung out in the lobby. As if Dieu, the petite one with the palest skin and the thickest lashes, hadn't just called him a stupid fool in all caps twenty minutes earlier, when they'd argued about the price—her price—over text. He'd texted her that his guest, being a bi-weekly regular, had asked for a discount.

And then, they were gone, disappearing behind the steel doors of the elevator, armed with room numbers and their best English phrases. This was when Hai could breathe easier in the airless lobby and allow himself, finally, to think of his tips. This was when he could stretch out on the threadbare folding bed behind the reception counter, text Sinh the good night message he knew she expected and wait for morning to come.

Accomplice

MARINA

Everyone wants a lover but what they really need is an accomplice. Someone who thinks you're not crazy for doing something random, like standing in front of a closed museum in the dark, waiting for a stranger you've just met. Waiting for him to pick you up, to bring you to a hotel, where, as he promised, you would learn the language of the Vietnamese.

Someone like Vinh, maybe, who'd come up with this silly, secret code for sex—for what else was there to do inside a hotel room? It was Marina who told him, earlier that evening, about wanting to learn Vietnamese. But it was he who instructed her to take a taxi from her five-star resort, travel the forty-minute distance, and alight in front of Huế's Royal Museum of Antiquities along Le Truc. Wait for him, he'd said, and he would come. She stood under a busted street lamp, hidden in the shadows, despite which she felt exposed, vulnerable, a little unsafe. It was already ten o'clock and the streets in this part of Huế City were deserted and she was supposed to be somewhere else or in bed because god knows how her forty-two-year-old body needed that sleep.

But, never mind all that. Never mind that she had only met Vinh that very day. She had said yes because she had been looking for an accomplice all her life.

* * *

Vinh was her tour guide and he emerged from somewhere along that dark sidewalk, grinning and relaxed, hands shoved in the pocket of his jeans. 'Ready?' he asked, as if they were meeting for something

15

benign, like a cup of coffee. The night felt warm and airless. Soon, he was leading her into a spartan room in a flaking, four-story building called Elegant Hotel. The air-con, they would discover later, was not working. The carpet, too, was threadbare, sticky and rough—though Marina only realized this at the end, after they put their clothes back on, when she pulled up her jeans and it caught at the carpet burns on her knees.

But, in that moment, when it was only just the beginning, Marina found herself simply marvelling at the smallness of the room, at the vastness of the possibilities. 'This is nice,' she breathed, fingering the bed's thin, greying blanket. A little rectangle of a window, glazed with a gossamer layer of grime, looked out on the now-empty boulevard that ran along Huế's Perfume River.

She sat by the headboard and smiled at Vinh, who, she realized, had been smiling the whole time. Vinh's teeth were startlingly even and white, his skin caramel, his black teardrop-shaped eyes, impish. A tiny mole, looking like it had been drawn on by a Sharpie, sat delicately in the middle of his chin.

She had met him that morning, noticed him right away when he had hopped inside the van in faded jeans, scruffy Adidas sneakers, and a baseball cap. '*Xin chao!*' He had boomed, his face split into a wide smile as he proceeded to collect everyone's names. 'Marina, Marina!' he had sung, to the tune of Santana's famous ballad, after she told him hers. She remembered how she'd felt flattered, then a little embarrassed.

Then, she'd felt glad that she'd chosen to go. She'd been to a lot of press trips—fifteen years of working for magazines had let her experience all sorts in random cities all over the world—she had almost not gone to this one. No one at *Parcours*, the magazine where she edited seventeen pages of the lifestyle section every month, had seemed interested in this strange-sounding city that was only a little more than two hours' flight away from Singapore. No, most of the editorial staff including her boss, Giselle, went for the big ones: press trips to Lake Como, Tasmania, Hokkaido, Sao Paolo, the Hebrides or any of the Scandinavian countries. And there was no shortage of it at *Parcours*, which Giselle always asserted would soon be Singapore's preferred magazine, when people are tired of *Travel+Leisure* and *Condé Nast Traveler*.

But when Marina had received the email invitation two weeks ago, there was something hopeful and old-fashioned about the itinerary: three nights at a new five-star resort called The Nam Hai, a dinner at the chef's table, a Vietnamese coffee shop crawl, a tour of the city of Huế, and flights care of SilkAir, who organized this whole thing because they had opened up a new direct route from Singapore to Huế City. It sounded more like a mediocre travel agency's tour package than a media trip for the Singapore press meant to promote the airline and the destination.

And then Marina had recalled a memory, one that seemed so important years ago—twelve years ago—of when she just arrived in Singapore from Manila. It was about starting over in a new city, one that wasn't yet marred by pain. Also, she'd seen flimsier press itineraries, and so she went.

* * *

It was her first time in Huế, in Central Vietnam—'Vietnam's belly', Vinh called it as part of his tour guide spiel that morning. The phrase sounded oddly familiar, and a quick check on Google on her phone revealed a Wikitravel piece that said the exact same thing. She wondered if the other journalists noticed or even the bloggers who were always bent over their phones and iPads, legit-looking cameras slung around their necks, for they were also their own photographers.

Still, Marina listened raptly as the van trundled through narrow streets and tree-lined avenues, and Vinh continued to talk, in a voice that she found charming and melodious, about Vietnam's imperial kings. 'They never wanted to repeat a dish,' Vinh said with conspiratorial glee, as if the Nguyen dynasty, Huế's last ruling family, were just his unruly, next-door neighbours. She watched him as he twisted his broad shoulders to face them from the front seat. 'In Huế, one was guaranteed three hundred sixty-five dishes,' Vinh concluded, as the van came to a slow stop in front of a faded citadel. 'A dish for each day of the year.'

She wondered how it would feel to repeat the same spiel over and over again, if tour guides like Vinh made a conscious effort to make it sound as fresh and natural every time or if it came instinctively. She wondered if they were pleased at how easily it all clicked inside their brains, how comfortably it rolled off their tongues. Did it really delight or did it depress them—to have to master all this information? She wondered if they felt freed or simply trapped by the thought that in this life, they would always know just this one thing by heart.

* * *

Vinh's cheeriness made the tour part of the press trip seem less like work and more of an outing with friends. He cracked charming jokes and constantly checked on the journalists. Was everyone comfortable? Had everyone secured their souvenirs? Had they all visited the happy house—the toilet? At this, everyone laughed. Vinh took their pictures with an adroit hand and made sure he took multiple shots. 'Another one? For safety?' he always asked. The grin never left his face.

They went to the ruins of Mỹ Sơn, built on a flat, grassy plain where the only obstacles were overgrown weeds and a few loose rocks. They darted through the crumbling temples, feeling a lot like children playing hide-and-seek. Vinh then brought them to Huế's imperial citadels, blithely strolling along the paths where emperors of the Nguyen dynasty used to tread and stopping last at Tử Cấm Thành, the Purple Forbidden City where, a thousand years ago, the same noble kings beheaded those who trespassed.

When they arrived back at The Nam Hai, Marina hung back. She always found a way to extend the connection—it must have been built into her. This time, she was convinced that she needed more information for her article. She was sure that there were a handful of Vietnamese words Vinh had mentioned earlier that were tricky to spell, and Marina didn't want to make a mistake.

'I need to ask you a few more questions,' she told him, as the other journalists drifted off in the direction of their villas.

'Of course,' he had said, as if it wasn't already almost seven, and they hadn't been tearing across Central Vietnam for ten hours. 'Sure.' His voice sounded so friendly.

He led her to a padded bench in an innocuous corner of the lobby where she rattled off her queries, which, to her dismay, sounded simple and unnecessary even as she was saying them.

But Vinh grinned and answered each question with thoughtful ease. He wrote down a few words in Vietnamese so that she got the spelling right, his handwriting a graceful curlicue.

And then, she murmured about wanting to learn Vietnamese. At this, he threw back his head and laughed. 'You want to learn our language?' His black eyes narrowed and curved up. 'This is not the place for it.'

'Oh?' Marina watched his smirk turn sheepish as he glanced towards the reception counter. 'Where, then?' As with all her questions, this sounded naïve.

'In a hotel.'

They exchanged numbers, and she had to feign a stomach ache to escape that evening's requisite press dinner with the chef. She had to wait in front of a darkened museum, as Vinh had instructed her to do. It was only for ten minutes, after which he appeared, seemingly out of nowhere, beaming as he walked towards her.

And now she was here, and he was sliding beside her, catching her lips and running his tongue over her front teeth.

* * *

There must be someone, Marina had always believed, who could accept the rawest of your desires, the ugliest of your thoughts, the oddest, most trivial of your requests. Everyone has these in varying degrees, don't they?

Some think they've found it—this elusive, precious accomplice: in a husband, a boyfriend, a best friend. She wouldn't really know. She had neither husband nor boyfriend nor even a best friend. Not anymore.

So, she looked for it in her lovers. Those, she had. Will he be the one, she would always think after sex, after they would part—will he be the one who thought there was nothing wrong with her ideas? Or with her?

* * *

It was only six when she woke up, blinking against the sun shining persistently through the hotel room's dirty windows. There was a steady drone of motorcycles below, faint voices from the street drifting above. The Vietnamese are early risers—she had read that somewhere or was that part of Vinh's spiel yesterday? Marina glanced at Vinh's sleeping form beside her, the sheet tucked chastely under a tanned, muscled arm, and wondered if it had been a bad idea to spend the night.

'I need to go,' she said, just as Vinh began to stir. She clambered naked out of the bed and pulled open the shower's flimsy accordion-style door. 'I have a breakfast meeting.' In truth, she had merely planned to join the other journalists for breakfast. She didn't want to be missed again. Her excuses last night had sounded unconvincing, even to her ears.

When she emerged from the shower, skin still tender from the warm spray of water, she was surprised to see her things neatly arranged on the narrow dresser by the window: her necklace and earrings laid out on the table, her blouse, jeans, and underwear draped cleanly on the chair, her clunky sneakers looking obsessively aligned on the floor, just waiting for her to slip her feet back in.

'See?' Vinh was back to his smiling self, already dressed in his blue long-sleeved shirt and jeans. He made a sweeping gesture at the table. 'Everything's ready for you. You don't have to worry.' Marina thought he looked more hopeful than proud. Later, she would marvel at how the Vietnamese made everything sound so simple.

But, in that moment, Marina found herself rooted on the spot, still dripping in her towel, astonished at how neatly her possessions had been laid out.

'Oh,' she said, finally. 'Thanks.' This was not her first time in Vietnam, and Vinh, certainly not the first almost-stranger she'd gone to bed with. But there was something both jarring and touching in the act. An act of intrusion but also of intimacy. Jarring in its novelty, moving in its candid intimacy.

She stepped back and turned her head. She didn't want Vinh to see how her eyes had bloomed hot and red.

* * *

Vinh deposited her in a taxi, saying that it would be interesting for her to see the locals having their morning coffee right on the street. Marina wasn't sure she liked how he sounded as if he simply picked up from where he had left off from yesterday's tour. She remembered how he had stroked the inside of her thighs the previous night. This didn't seem to be the same person.

She thought of the damp, crumpled sheets at Elegant Hotel. Of the sweat they'd left behind, the fluids that escaped their bodies, bit by bit, as they pressed and slid against each other under the malfunctioning air-con. She remembered how, afterwards, Vinh had fallen asleep immediately, lying peaceful and supine beside her, his hands resting like an angel on his stomach. Without meaning to, Marina had found herself gazing at his round, sleeping face for a good half hour, spent but frustratingly alert because of the vigorous sex.

Her villa at The Nam Hai was cool and silent when she returned at seven, revelling in how her bones felt heavy, how the insides of her thighs felt sore, at the secrets she told herself. She realized that she'd forgotten to turn off the lights; the jewel-toned Vietnamese lamps in the ceiling glowed quiet but fierce as if betrayed. The four-poster mahogany bed, perched solidly on a raised platform in the middle of the room, remained as pristine and untouched as the night before.

But now, back in the soothing calm of The Nam Hai, she hummed as she soaped her skin with a coconut-scented bar at her villa's open-air shower, overcome with a peculiar calm at the possibilities. Once she returned to Singapore, they would exchange messages, whisper into their phones, overuse FaceTime. They would visit each other, travel and have sex in brand new places like lovers or old buddies. Like accomplices.

Later, she would wish that she had etched that moment in her head—when she was all happy and heady from the soap and the steam and the fact that she could see the sky and the tops of the coconut trees, tall and unapologetic and bulging with hard fruit. She would wish that she had been more in that moment, had lived it and kept it. Because there would be no more messages or calls or anything at all from Vinh in the next seven days or ever again.

Kabayan Café

CARMEN

They knew it was time when he started staggering towards the toilet.

They had watched Luis polish off the last of his beer, pop the last morsel of chicharon into his mouth, and announce in an almost unintelligible slur that it was time to go. But instead of Kabayan's glass-fronted entrance, he lurched towards the back, into the direction of a wooden door painted the same dull cream as the walls, the space surrounding the metal doorknob scuffed with grimy hand marks. It was marked 'CR'—short for 'comfort room', someone at the table had explained to Luis, and he had joked about it when he wasn't yet in this wasted state.

'I hope he doesn't pass out in there,' Carmen whispered into Auntie Swan's ear. Her voice caught; she was tired from all the talking. More tired than usual, though she knew better than to tell the group, because things were only just starting. She looked across the table at Uncle Amado who hadn't eaten much and whose beer remained warm. He, too, was gazing intently in the direction of the toilet, the folds behind his neck twisted and thick, like doughnuts. At the next table, another addition to their little group: Max, Uncle Amado's grandson, had joined them earlier and was fiddling with the snap-on lid of a plastic ketchup bottle.

'Pass out? No.' Auntie Swan shook her head, firm and dismissive, annoyance tinging her voice. Sometimes Carmen wished she was like Auntie Swan, who was always so sure.

'Another hour, yes,' Uncle Amado said. His tone was calm, almost reassuring.

Auntie Swan's stony face softened, too, but only for a split second. 'Don't worry,' she said. 'I checked—'

'Help him up, Max,' Uncle Amado cut in, nodding towards the other man, who immediately got up.

He nodded knowingly at Carmen pointing to the toilet. 'Sure, "*Lo*,"' he said, his voice almost drowned by the din of the place. Carmen liked how Max always called Uncle Amado *lolo*, the respectful term for grandfather.

'Don't let him hit his head,' Uncle Amado added, eyes sweeping across the busy restaurant, 'or bother anyone.' Uncle Amado was considerate like this.

Max, as planned, made his entrance at exactly 3 p.m., just as Luis was downing his fourth glass of iced beer. 'Hola! Who's this?' Luis asked, the words tumbling over each other.

'My grandson,' Uncle Amado told Luis, almost apologetically, when Max reached them. This, too, was what they'd agreed upon.

'Luis from Spain!' Max cried, pumping Luis's hand after introductions were made. 'I don't want to miss out on this fun! We're all family, you know?' And, of course, Luis was only too happy to invite him to join them. How can he say no to more locals, and—as Max had so fervently said—to family?

* * *

It was already 5.30 in the evening and beginning to get dark. Traffic along Taft Avenue was at a standstill. Without looking out, Carmen knew that the traffic enforcers were at their places at the intersections, furiously signalling and redirecting—a valiant effort to untangle the pulsing rows of bumper-to-bumper cars. She knew that the sidewalks were already crawling with people on their way home, some in shockingly-long queues that stretched to a kilometre just to board the MRT, LRT, the buses and jeepneys, even the more costly commuter vans. Commuting in Manila, just like many things in this city, was a battle in itself. And this was how her people fought through the rush-hour commute: they waited patiently in long queues, stood in line on pedestrian stairs and bridges, after which they endured hours on the road, squeezed against each other in tightly-packed jeepneys and standing butt-to-butt in trains, coaxing air out of its stuffy confines or staving the leftover afternoon heat with makeshift cardboard fans. In Kabayan Café, the dinner crowd was growing: chattering, fresh-faced college students oblivious to anything else, employees in corporate attire hunched over their smartphones consumed by Facebook and thoughts of the long commute home.

Carmen cast a silent glance in the direction of the toilet, where Max was now standing guard, shifting from one loafer-clad foot to the other. She caught a movement by her side—just her reflection, it turns out, on one of Kabayan's glass walls; a faint image of her that she didn't need to see to already know she had tired, droopy eyes, a tense jaw, and a face that looked bloated because she's been holding her breath on and off. Her hair, as always, was pulled back and tied in a messy bun, with a wispy fringe she kept long enough to hide her eyes. Her little group told her she was like this all the time: tight and secretive, hard and wound-up. 'Not in a good way,' Auntie Swan had said, with that loud cluck of her tongue that no one really liked, 'in a sad, sad way.' Max, who'd once caught Carmen's shoulders and jokingly attempted a massage, said her shoulder blades were like rocks.

'He's taking a long time,' Carmen said now, unable to stop herself. She glanced at the time on her phone, then again at Uncle Amado. He always knew what to do. 'Do you think . . .' Her voice trailed. It was common for them to go to the toilet; the others did too, before, but this was longer than usual.

Uncle Amado gave her a slight nod. 'We'll ask Max to take him out,' he said. He beckoned for Max to go.

Auntie Swan was frowning. 'You haven't eaten.' She pursed her lips over Carmen's barely-touched plate. 'Are you ill?'

Carmen's gaze swivelled towards Auntie Swan. 'No,' she said, simply. She just wanted it to be over.

Uncle Amado was twisting around to look for the waiter who had served them the food and beer. When he came with the bill, they watched as Uncle Amado ran his thick fingers on the handwritten receipt. It amounted to 755 pesos. *Just eleven euros,* Carmen thought, as she usually did, for a meal and drinks that fed all five people. She knew Uncle Amado was thinking the same thing. Loose change, he always said.

'Thanks, boss.' The waiter cooed, as Uncle Amado slipped an extra five-hundred under the receipt.

'Have yourself a nice cup of coffee,' Uncle Amado replied, smiling. He always said things like 'enjoy a coffee' or 'get a snack' whenever he gave a tip. Carmen had never met a waiter who didn't like him.

They started gathering Luis's things and distributed it among themselves: Uncle Amado with Luis's blue North Face, Carmen with his bulky professional Canon, which was heavier than it looked. Auntie Swan plucked Luis's faded green Knicks cap from the table and twirled it around her finger, wrinkling her nose.

'Let's go.' Uncle Amado gave a brisk nod, ushering them both outside. Once out, the evening's humidity and traffic fumes hit Carmen's face like a slap. Even from the sidewalk, they could see the toilet door open and then Luis, leaning heavily on the doorway, looking like he was to about to crumple on the floor. And then they saw Max swoop in to grab him by the armpits, draping the foreigner's gangly arm around his shoulder as they slowly and carefully wended their way together, as if conjoined at the hip, through Kabayan's crowded tables. Carmen checked to see if anyone was staring, but only a couple of people turned their heads. It was not unusual for people to get drunk—or look like they were drunk—in this kind of place.

'He just peed, he didn't puke,' Max reported, brisk and matter-of-fact, when they made it outside. Luis's head drooped. 'And no,' he added, pointedly shaking his head at Uncle Amado, 'he didn't hit his head.'

'We've been here for too long.' Uncle Amado looked grim. 'I don't know how we can move with all this traffic.' He scanned the length of Taft Avenue, then pointed to the corner where it turned into an alley that led to the next street. 'We'll get a pedicab and go through there.'

Auntie Swan nodded, immediately spotting one that had just dropped a passenger in front of a Dunkin' Donuts three buildings away. She plopped Luis's green cap on her head and extended a flabby arm in an exaggerated wave.

'Camille.'

It was Luis, still leaning on Max. The men and Auntie Swan ignored him; they didn't even turn. 'Camille,' Luis said again. A pitiful croak, which came out as 'kuhmml.' He was struggling to open his eyes, but his face was drawn, mottled, pasty, and pale despite his tan and the macho full-on beard. His legs started to buckle underneath him, and Max, quick as lightning, hoisted him back up by the armpits.

Carmen looked at the foreigner under the yellow lights of the street lamp but said nothing. She wanted to tell him that they won't take his things, his camera, his phone, his Knicks cap, or even the expensive laptop that she knew was in the heavy backpack. No, they were not thieves like that.

Authentic

HAI

It was incredible how stingy they were. He had always imagined them in impressively clean, stately mansions, driving flashy top-downs, throwing snowballs at each other in a white winter wonderland, and then coming home to a big pile of bow-tied gifts under a massive, twinkling Christmas tree—just like in HBO movies.

So, it confused him when, one morning in December, a tall, blonde man in high-tech hiking shoes and a backpack as big as his torso, shook his head with a vengeance and declared Hai's offer of an eleven-dollar room as 'too expensive'.

'There's air-con and a swimming pool, sir!' Hai panted, struggling to match the man's strong, clipped pace. It was his first day working at the bus terminal as a part-time employee of Phong Nha Hostel. His job, according to Phong Nha's owner Madame Beo, was to persuade as many tourists as he could to book a room at the hostel. And this man, though he was hurrying purposefully towards the street, looked to Hai like he didn't yet have a place to stay.

The man looked straight ahead and said nothing. There was a busy crowd at the bus terminal that morning, but no one had taken up Hai's offer of cheap rooms. 'I can give you a free lift to the hostel on my motorbike,' Hai pressed on, trying to keep his voice light. He had caught on and was now briskly walking with him side-by-side. But a wayward jostle from a sudden stream of arriving passengers caused him to thrust Phong Nha's filmy brochures into the man's face with more force than he'd wanted—prompting an angry swat and another vicious 'No!'

Hai stopped in his tracks, staring in shock and disbelief at the man's back, already rapidly retreating. He had expected this foreigner's face to break into a look of epiphany, of welcome pleasure at the thought of such an irresistible deal: a perfectly decent room for (he was told, by Madame Beo) the price of a cocktail in his own country. Instead, what did he get? A blatant rejection and a scowl that was so obviously venomous, though the guy had stubbornly avoided meeting his eyes.

He tried again. He walked away from the offensive backpacker and loped back towards the crowded terminal, where he'd already spotted a small bus skittering to a stop. Hai knew it was from the tiny postcard town of Hội An, where backpackers usually spent a night or two before continuing on to Huế.

A ragtag group was spilling out, decked out in floppy hats and brightly-coloured clothing. Hai spied a lone, heavyset woman in sandals and shorts, and he moved towards her as she stepped off the rickety bus. Her round, jowly cheeks and the fond way she'd grinned at the kid who'd squeezed past her reminded him of his aunt in Saigon. *She,* he was convinced, would be more agreeable.

But he'd barely taken a few steps when the woman started chanting loudly, like a possessed shaman, even as he was only approaching.

'No, no, no, no, no, no, no, *no!*'

She looked and sounded ridiculous, of course; Hai hadn't yet even uttered a word. Then, she looked at him straight in the eye, put up a large hand with all five fingers spread out, and boomed: 'Nope! You— whatever it is, just *no!*'

Hai slunk back trembling towards one of the terminal's tented café stalls and ordered a cà phê đen đá, only to spill his coffee on the brochures.

* * *

That was years ago. Now, he knew better. Now, he knew that it wasn't personal when tourists brushed him off or yelled, 'Go away!' as if he had the season's deadly virus. Now, it was okay if they insulted or ignored him, even if he was standing right there, saying a proper hello. Now, it was okay if they said no—even if he'd been waiting and running and fighting all morning amid the bus terminal's oily fumes, steeping in its rotting-papaya-and-diesel smell.

He had learned to tune all that out. He had learned to take it easy, to strike gently, to make conversation. He had learned to joke. 'No money, no honey!' he had told a guy, an Australian, who'd cheekily asked him why he was doing this kind of job.

This job, the Australian had said. Hai remembered how this tourist, with his shiny, silver watch and spiffy Nike sneakers, had been careful not to say 'tout'—as if it were something offensive.

But it didn't matter. Hai had learned all these things and then some. He still worked as a tout for Phong Nha in the mornings, but he'd also gotten himself another job. Minh Thanh Hotel was classified as four-star accommodation; his position there as night receptionist was, therefore, a four-star job. More befitting, he was convinced, and it gave him a kind of status he felt he rightfully deserved.

It was in Minh Thanh that he'd finally learned what tourists really wanted—needed—and that was an 'authentic experience'. Oh, how he'd heard that phrase uttered again and again in his four-star lobby. Every foreigner seemed to be in desperate search for something authentic—foolishly thinking it could be found in Vietnam, in Huế, in the ruins of this city.

He had learned not to blame them; he himself had been naïve once. He still remembered the day when he'd been so gullible, thinking there was something left in this world that was truly genuine.

'I *need* a real and authentic Vietnamese experience,' a German guest had told him years ago, when Hai used to moonlight as a tour guide.

The guest had wanted to see Huế's countryside on a motorbike and Hai remembered how they'd ridden through the dirt roads on his beat-up Honda, to see the rice paddies and gum trees in Quảng Bình, then the tunnels of Vịnh Mốc. But a sudden September downpour caught them when they were in the open fields, and Hai called an uncle who lived nearby, asking if they can stop by until the rains let up.

When they had arrived, Hai was surprised to find that his uncle and his wife had prepared a semi-elaborate lunch of sticky bánh xèo cakes and steaming bowls of bún bò huế, laid out like a feast on the bare floor. His uncle had ordered cans of Huda beer from the store next door, offered the German guy his own cigarettes, and made stirring toasts to family, Germany, and Vietnam. Hai had felt warm and fortunate and content and thought of his parents who lived a hundred kilometres away in Quảng Trị.

The tourist, who had said he was from Dresden, had been visibly touched and taken so many pictures of them and the cornucopia of food on the floor, that his camera battery ran out.

And then the rains had let up. Hai already donned his helmet, ready to wheel his motorbike out through the door when his uncle pulled him aside and asked for the money.

'Did you enjoy the meal?' Hai had asked the German afterwards, forcing himself to make conversation as they turned into the main road towards Huế City.

'Spectacular,' the tourist had replied, giving Hai's shoulder a satisfied pat. 'Now, *that* was a real and local Vietnamese experience. Don't you agree?'

'Yes,' Hai whispered, thinking of his uncle and the two million dong—his entire tour guide fee—that had just left his pocket. 'Authentic.'

Minh Thanh

MARINA

It was uncanny how every Vietnamese had started looking like him: the gangly man in black pyjama pants pedalling on a bicycle along Le Loi street, whose skin she thought was the same golden shade as Vinh; the broad-shouldered guy in a blue shirt—the very same one, it seemed, that Vinh had worn that night in Elegant Hotel—dawdling behind the counter at the corner shop that peddled mobile phones; a random guest she spotted loitering in the lobby, whose blinding grin looked familiar. At one point during those three days of silence after their meeting, days without a text or an email from Vinh, Marina thought she saw him among the tall, dusky waiters who served her thick, sweet coffee every day until her last morning at The Nam Hai.

Even the bellman at Minh Thanh Hotel, where Marina was to stay for three more days after checking out of The Nam Hai, bore a convenient resemblance to Vinh in the way he stood ramrod straight and alert.

She bid goodbye to the media group that morning, with blithe promises to keep in touch. The Nam Hai launch was done, and she, like several of the other lifestyle journalists, had managed their schedules to allow a few more days overseas to do extra work for their publications. The media team from Korea was doing a fashion–lifestyle shoot with Vietnamese designers based in Hanoi, the ones from Malaysia, a beach summer special in Nha Trang. The writer from Indonesia was travelling by motorbike from Huế to Sapa in the north as part of a travel feature for their next issue.

Marina's extended itinerary included an interview with Amanda Ho, a Singaporean socialite-turned-entrepreneur who ran a clothing boutique in the old tourist town of Hội An three hours away. The other interview was with a Singaporean-French chef helming the kitchens of La Residence, the oldest of the three five-star hotels in Huế. Profile features were a main part of the lifestyle section of *Parcours*. Amanda and the chef were adequate content, quintessential examples of how Singaporeans could thrive outside of their tiny island state, sharing their journey of success with the world. That was the pitch. *Le parcours* meant 'route', after all, and showing the way to its readers had always been its theme and mission.

Marina wished she could say that she came up with these contacts, but she hadn't. Her editor, Giselle, had always wanted to include the globe-trotting Amanda in the magazine—'for optics', Giselle had said, 'just find a lifestyle angle'—and La Residence had been tossed to her by the advertising team because the hotel had just booked a three-month, full-page ad contract with *Parcours*. A magazine was a business and even if Marina did have her own contacts, the profit-generating strategies of her superiors came first.

They had just put the latest issue to bed before she left for Huế, so this was the precious one-week window where the editorial staff, including her, had a little breathing space. Marina had looked at her schedule just before she moved and checked-in at Minh Thanh, everything she'd written on her pocket-size Moleskin neatly and clearly laid out.

'You're so old-fashioned,' she could almost hear Cecile, her managing editor at *Parcours* who was prone to gentle chiding, saying. She hadn't been talking about the way Marina still kept and carried around a notebook for notes and schedules, instead of just logging it into her phone or some app. Cecile was talking about going paperless, getting information online, doing interviews via email or video, without ever even meeting your subject in person. Email interviews, even for big, lengthy features, were normalized. This she felt more and more every time she was immersed in her usual cycle of writing, editing, attending media launches and events. But Marina had been working with magazines since the early noughties; back then, email interviews were deemed sloppy, a follow-up for extra information, sometimes used as a last resort. True, it was now 2015 and hard to imagine that there was a time when people felt that way. Still, Marina believed that meeting Amanda Ho, or any of her interviewees for that matter, in person produced a more nuanced story. This was her process, had always been. She wasn't about to change that now.

Despite these neat arrangements, she had allowed herself a messy, disruptive night with Vinh and now it hung onto her, faint but persistent, like the smell of grease on clothes. She had been attracted to him, yes. She hated to admit it, even to herself, but she had foolishly wanted something more. She was prone to this, she knew—always asking 'what if' and 'could this be the one?'—increasingly, it seemed, at the most inopportune times. There was always the possibility, wasn't there? These encounters—they were foolish and risky and could be dangerous. But, Marina had to remind herself, this had not been her first time doing this—casual sex, one-night stands, sex with strangers, fuck-buddies—she was supposed to be used to this. Sex, the physical act of it, felt good to her. It may have felt awkward when she was in her twenties—slutty, they would call it nowadays—but she had learned to make it into something discreet, forthright, and sometimes satisfying. Most of all, it was unapologetic. She was forty-two years old, unmarried, financially independent. Free and untethered, in a way.

One thing still connected her to the Philippines: her mother in Manila. Lolita Bellosillo, now almost eighty, had refused to live with her in Singapore. Marina had suggested this purely out of obligation, though she knew this was another dangerous possibility; even if her mother was pushing eighty, Marina wasn't sure she'd like to live with the same person she'd spent her whole life running away from. She was relieved when her mother said no, when she insisted on staying in their small, rented apartment that, eventually, Marina managed to buy, years after she moved to Singapore. Besides, how would her mother react to the men she brought home to her flat in Serangoon? To her not coming home some nights or shuffling in at five in the morning? How would that even work out?

Marina had moved to Singapore twelve years ago to start a new life and that she did. She'd like to believe that she'd finally learned to compartmentalize her life. She'd also discovered, to her dismay, that old habits die hard, and sometimes, she just gave in. Now, it bewildered her to find herself in the lobby of a completely different hotel, the latest lover out of sight, unable to stop herself from thinking about him. It had been a one-night stand, something she had done many times, with men who were probably better than Vinh. What was different now? And what, really, had she been hoping for? That it would be the last one? That this would be different? That she had finally found someone?

It was still about that.

There had been lovers but there had never been someone. The last time she'd had someone was fifteen years ago. Now she was forty-two, Singapore was turning fifty.

She hated it when she was like this. When she was overcome with yearning, then confusion, then desperation. But she felt helpless against it, and more palpably, alone. Yes, that was it. She felt alone.

* * *

The bellman who looked like Vinh was struggling with her heavy suitcase. They were on the way up to her room on the third floor but only one elevator was working, and he had invited her to take the stairs.

'Troi oi, that elevator,' the bellman said, shaking his head good-naturedly as if tolerating a naughty but harmless toddler. It reminded Marina of the people in the Philippines. Marina watched him square his already-straight shoulders, before hoisting her aluminium Rimowa on them and mounting determinedly up the stairs. 'A little exercise is good. Right, madam?' His voice echoed through the fire exit.

Marina paused behind him and nodded absently, her mind still flitting between Vinh, her mother, and her immediate surroundings. Minh Thanh Hotel was a decent four-star hotel, but it was a contrast to the expansive resort that was The Nam Hai. With its lush, sprawling grounds and airy, well-appointed villas, the latter was every inch a luxe resort, while Minh Thanh was all done up in dark wood, marble floors and gold finishes that made you feel ensconced in a shiny little palace. It sat well in between the Perfume River and the city centre, yet the price for each night still came up less than a restaurant dinner in Singapore.

'Madam? Follow me, please. Just one more floor.'

Marina looked up at the bellman, who'd paused on the landing and was now twirling her suitcase with a kind of hopeful pep that she knew was meant to coax a smile out of her. She nodded wordlessly and wiped a bead of sweat from her right temple, noting how her armpits had grown damp.

Focus on something else, she told herself. The work you need to do, the call you need to make to your mother. For the past twelve years, she had been sending her mother a monthly allowance, transferred from her bank in Singapore to her mother's account in Manila, every twentieth of the month. This month, she had not yet made the transfer. The monthly allowance that she'd been sending her mother for years would have to be delayed for a few days because of this trip. Today was a lull at work, and she needed to check her email.

* * *

She decided to go back down and walk around. The sidewalk looked more sedate and less complicated compared to Saigon and Hanoi. Maybe find a soup place; a tasty, spicy broth always seemed to somehow calm her insides. She'd been particularly taken with bún bò huế, Huế's local beef soup that she'd sampled at one of the buffets at The Nam Hai; it must be readily available on a sidewalk stall or at a casual restaurant near the hotel.

'Xin chao, *chi!*' The receptionist's voice sang out, a thin and automatic greeting that rose above the satisfying *whoosh* of the elevator doors just as Marina stepped out. She hadn't seen the girl when she had checked-in; the previous one must have ended her shift.

'Hi,' Marina gave a small smile, trying not to stare at the cake-y whiteness of the young girl's face, splitting open with a crooked set of teeth. It made her think of her own teeth, of the meticulous way she'd been taking care of them, seven years since she turned thirty-five and had broken an upper molar after an overenthusiastic bite into a biscotti.

She glanced at the thin man in a grey suit beside her, noticing how he drew himself up straighter.

'I'm sorry for my colleague,' he said, in a voice that was startlingly deep and incongruous with his built. A name plate shone on his left breast: 'Hai' it said in black lettering so thin and delicate it looked like it could be wiped off anytime with a determined thumb. 'She thought you were Vietnamese.'

Marina managed a close-lipped smile. 'Oh, yeah?' She gave a dismissive wave of her hand. 'It's okay.' It wasn't the first time she'd been called 'chị', the respectful term for an older woman or sister.

'Would you like an umbrella?' The receptionist called Hai spoke so formally. He was gesturing towards a lacquered holder in the corner, crammed with colourful, neatly-wound umbrellas.

Marina swung her head towards the glass walls of the lobby, which looked directly out on the street, noticing only now that it had turned translucent and wet. She hadn't even bothered to open the heavy drapes of her room.

'Oh, no,' she said, trying to sound light. She thought she saw the hazy outlines of a car and of splashing water as it zoomed by the street with a roar. Keeping dry amid the downpour suddenly seemed like too much work. She'd have to settle for tepid room service. Spicy, street-side bún bò huế would have to wait.

She turned back towards the elevators. The only working one was already open.

'Ma'am? I can call you a taxi!'

His voice echoed through the hallway, rounder and deeper and sounding as if she'd just walked through a tunnel. But she shook her head at her reflection, just as the elevator doors whooshed close.

* * *

She was opening drawers, trying to find the in-room dining brochure, when the phone rang.

'Hello, ma'am.'

'Yes?' Her hand was still inside the drawer, feeling for a piece of paper or plastic. She knew menus were sometimes just laminated paper.

'This is Hai, the receptionist.' She recognized the voice, pictured the loose suit.

'Yes, Mr Hai?' She frowned. 'What is it?' Had she forgotten something downstairs?

'Are you alone?'

She felt something inside her recoil. She thought of the group of Vietnamese chefs she'd met last week, who'd asked her age and chatted about their salaries as if they were talking about that evening's dinner. To Marina, it felt outrageous and blatant; it had taken her some time to digest that, in Vietnam, this was completely accepted. She pressed the phone to her ear, noted the sharp, sterile smell of rubbing alcohol. 'Why?'

'Would you like to drink beer with me?'

She glanced at the receiver, not sure if she had heard it right.

'Beer?' She ran her hand again through the dresser's empty drawer. 'Why?'

'I thought you might like some company.'

She paused. This was strange but also familiar. 'Where?'

'Here, in the lobby.'

She wondered why she didn't just say no.

Modus Operandi

CARMEN

As was often the case, nothing went as planned. For one, Luis's head was on her lap.

'Too much,' Auntie Swan was saying now, with that downward twist of her lip when things didn't go her way. She made that clear to them over and over earlier that evening as they waited for a taxi in front of Kabayan Café, with a barely-conscious Luis held up by Max, almost crumpling like a rag doll at one point when Max lost his grip.

'Mado,' Auntie Swan repeated, crossing her arms and glaring pointedly at the front seat. 'You gave him too much.' She pressed herself against the back seat door, as if to escape Luis's broad torso lying sideways on Carmen and her.

Uncle Amado, sitting shotgun with the driver up front, said nothing.

Carmen wished Max was here, but they couldn't all fit in the taxi. He was the one who could calm Auntie Swan or at least distract her with that silly way of his and still get things moving sans unpleasantness. But he'd taken the jeepney back to Uncle Amado's house in Barangay Bicutan where, as agreed, he would wait for them.

'Too much to drink, sir?' The taxi driver asked, with a quick turn of his head as he glanced at Uncle Amado, his cheek pulled back into a grin. The sir came out as 'sehr', in that funny way Filipinos often flattened their vowels. He was a narrow-shouldered guy with longish curls who couldn't be more than thirty, sporting a disinterested smile when they piled into his Toyota Vios, the three of them struggling with the bulk of a man who seemed dead to the world. Now, in the midst of traffic, he was curious but non-committal; this drunk white man wasn't his problem. He needed only to get through this slow-moving road, bring them from one place to the next. He was just making conversation, as everyone in this city did.

He'd taken in a lot of drunk passengers, the driver was saying now, especially in this part of Manila and at all times of the day, some in an even worse state than the passed-out man they had with them.

'You know these foreigners.' Uncle Amado made a wet clucking sound. 'How they love to drink, don't they?' Carmen watched as he shook his head, a rueful tilt. 'Don't get me wrong, *brod*,' he continued. 'Drinking is my only exercise. My type of weight-lifting.' He raised his arm high as if holding a mug of beer, up and down, flexing a barely-there bicep. Then, his shoulders started to shake with laughter.

The young driver chuckled along. 'It's more fun in the Philippines, as they say!'

Auntie Swan, listening to the exchange, glowered at the back of the car.

'Auntie,' Carmen said quietly, steeling her voice to sound more confident than she felt. 'Never mind all that.' She shifted uncomfortably, aware that her denim-encased thighs were starting to sweat under the weight of Luis's sleeping head. 'Let's just get this over with.'

Auntie Swan muttered something under her breath. She was unhappy, Carmen knew—they all were, in varying degrees—and not just because of today.

Because it was always like this, wasn't it? Something to get over with. A task to do as quickly and as cleanly as possible. Otherwise, it got messy. And then they were fucked. Those were Max's words, too.

More than anyone, *she* wanted to get this over with. What Carmen hadn't told Max was that there'd been an urgency in her lately, the kind that had her desperately wanting for things to speed up, her role played, the deed and her work, done.

She thought of how things had gone that afternoon. They were supposed to get out of that restaurant; it had been a bad idea to stay that long. It was already evening rush hour and they were supposed to disappear into the crowd or in the dark corners of the city; Manila, no matter how congested, still had some. They were supposed to walk Luis to the nearest ATM. That was what Auntie Swan had wanted. After all, they'd done it before.

But Luis, without meaning to, had other plans. It had taken several pours of beer and nearly three hours before he showed any sign of drowsiness—or even just plain drunkenness. The whole time they were eating and drinking at Kabayan, Luis was animated and alert. Tipsy for a long while but not weak or disoriented. They were prepared to wait, sure. They'd all talked about this, that you couldn't predict how a person's body responds and so they must be prepared for anything—whether it took waiting or changing the plan. They must adapt, go with what's presented to them. It was the only way they could get this done.

When it had finally hit Luis, it was like a light switched off. It completely knocked him out—collapsing as he did the moment he stumbled out of the toilet door. And then he could hardly stand back up, even though Max caught him right on time. They had taken too long. Usually, they were out by mid-afternoon, when there was a lull in the streets. Because it was rush hour, the jeepneys were full.

They had to bring him home.

She shouldn't have been surprised. They'd done it countless times.

The taxi was crawling along South Super Highway, already crammed with cars. Past the toll and turn left, and it would soon be Barangay Bicutan. Carmen willed the car to move forward.

The driver had turned on the radio without asking anyone. But even as the mournful, seductive strains of 'Ang Huling El Bimbo'—recognizable to every Filipino—and the whine of Ely Buendia's voice filled what little space was there in the car, Luis did not stir. Uncle Amado's and the cabbie's heads started swaying to the slow tune.

Carmen looked out the window at the other cars that were creeping along the highway. Where had she been when this song first came out? She was ten years old when she first heard it, that she knew for sure. And there were others: catchy, mushy songs in her language by the same band whose music she'd grown to love, just because her mother played them so often at home when she was younger. Her mother said she even met Ely himself at a gig at a bar in Makati when Carmen was too small to remember. Back then, she had a yaya, a nanny who did everything her mother couldn't, which was a lot of things.

The taxi had managed to inch its way towards the toll gate. The driver stopped and handed over a hundred peso bill to the woman perched some feet higher than them in her tiny, windowed stall. A small plastic electric fan stuck to the glass on one side whirred continuously, looking like a toy. The woman hardly glanced at any of them, much less Luis lying on their laps in the back seat.

'Thank you, miss.' Even without seeing his face, Carmen knew the driver had flashed her a flirtatious smile, lingering at the toll, not pressing the gas until an impatient beep from the car behind sent him roaring off and quickly turning onto the service road.

This was how her mother drove, too, Carmen thought, as her head tipped back against the backrest because of the sudden speed. Volatile and emotional, in fits and starts, braking suddenly or pressing on the gas seemingly with all her might when something annoyed her, or she had a fight—a discussion, she always said—with her father. Carmen gritted her teeth, caught herself. This was it. Another one of those times when she wanted things to be over. Except for this part, Max knew everything about her mother and her.

She cast a sidelong glance at Auntie Swan, now silent. There was rage boiling underneath her, Carmen knew. In every single one of them, she was sure. That was why they were all here, wasn't it? That was why they all did this.

Auntie Swan was fuming, for sure. What's with you, still thinking of your mother, she imagined Auntie Swan berating her. What's she got to do with all this?

She wondered if Auntie Swan would understand, even if Carmen ever told her. What would she tell her? Here she was in a taxi, cradling an unconscious man. Her mother had nothing and everything to do with this.

Hai's Lobby

HAI

There was a moment, as he was standing by the doors of Minh Thanh Hotel's one working elevator, when Hai felt himself waver, suddenly anxious about what he had just done: inviting a hotel guest to drink beer in the lobby. He had been so sure when he picked up the phone at reception to speak with the woman called Marina, right after he saw her go back to her room. He had asked her with such confidence, such assurance and perhaps even aplomb, that he wasn't surprised that she had said yes.

It lasted for less than a minute, this feeling; by then the elevator doors opened and there was Marina herself, standing in front of him once again. She had put on a pair of black, thick-rimmed eyeglasses, swapped the long, summer dress she'd worn earlier for a plain white T-shirt and a narrow skirt that stopped above her knees. The skirt looked like it had been fashioned by some ambitious tailor from an old pair of jeans.

Earlier, he had helped her check-in. Marina Bellosillo had a Singaporean passport, but she didn't sound like the other Singaporeans he'd met, though there weren't many. He noticed that she spoke with a different accent, in a slower voice and a lower register that he couldn't quite place. She had been alone when she walked in, rolling her luggage quietly across Minh Thanh's marble floor, and the first thing that struck him was the downcast expression on her face. Despite the expensive-looking dress, the sleek, handsome suitcase, the hair that looked light and dark in all the right places, the twinkling diamond studs on her ears—she had a worried, preoccupied look in her eyes and a slight but still-noticeable vertical furrow on her brow which, he was convinced,

45

wasn't really due to something as mundane as a delayed flight or a resigned tiredness caused by a harried day. He'd assumed she would be in her late twenties, but when he'd opened her bright red passport to log in the details into the computer, he'd been surprised to discover that she was already forty-two years old.

'Sign here, ma'am,' he had said, thrown off by his little discovery and suddenly conscious of his Vietnamese accent as he slid a pen and the hotel registration printout towards her.

She had taken them without looking up. He found himself mesmerized by the rapid movements of her hand as she marked the sheet with a controlled and confident sweep, a gold band with heart-shaped little diamonds that was not a wedding ring winking from her middle finger.

And then Tam the bellman had swooped in with a grin and broad-shouldered handsomeness, grabbing her silvery suitcase so effortlessly, as if it was packed with cotton. When Hai handed Marina the little booklet that contained the room keycard, she had said a feeble 'thank you,' but barely gave him another glance as she was led away by Tam towards the elevators.

'Have a pleasant stay, ma'am,' Hai murmured to the space in front of the counter, newly-empty save for a faint, lingering scent of expensive rose and musk.

* * *

He introduced himself again, just in case she had forgotten him. 'Good evening,' he said now, in what he hoped was his best voice. 'I'm Mr Hai. You can call me Hai.' He extended a hand, just as she stepped out of the elevator.

'Hello.' Her lips stretched into a sceptical smile. 'Again.' She shook his hand in a way that felt limp and cursory, as if she was just passing by and about to flee any moment. But she took a step beside him and they turned towards the lobby.

'Mr Hai?'

He swung his head towards her, slightly alarmed. 'What?' He was surprised to see a small, wry smile on her face. 'I mean—yes? What is it?'

'Did I really hear that right?' That low, deliberate voice again. The furrow on her brow reappeared. 'We're drinking beer? Here?'

He chose to ignore her disbelieving tone. 'Yes, yes,' he said, softly, giving her an assuring nod as he led her to a corner of the sprawling, high-ceilinged lobby already devoid of guests at 9 p.m.

'Please.' He motioned to a pair of nubby beige armchairs, high-backed and hulking and partially facing the floor-to-ceiling glass wall that looked out on the street. An inconspicuous spot. 'We can sit here.'

Marina paused before she lowered herself into the chair, carefully placing her knees together. Hai sat across from her and watched as she surveyed the six cans of Huda sweating on the solid-wood coffee table. He pressed the heel of his palm on his knee and leaned forward.

'You like beer?'

'It's okay.' She nodded and looked at the empty lobby. 'But is it really all right to drink *here?*'

Hai felt around his pocket for his Camels and the plastic lighter he always kept with him, aware that Marina's doubtful expression hadn't gone away. He quickly slid out a stick from the crumpled pack, noting that there were only five cigarettes left. Had he really almost finished the pack? He needed a stick when he was stressed, he needed one when he was relaxed. Right now, he couldn't decide if he was one or the other or both. He knew, though, that what Marina really wanted to ask was if it was it okay for *him* to be drinking here, in the middle of his shift.

He lit up. 'Yes, of course.' It was low season in November and the lobby was empty. Stuffy, too, because they turned off the air-con at nine every evening. Duc, his manager, was away for two weeks and probably singing karaoke, blind drunk, in Saigon's District 7 right that very minute. Besides, he didn't feel like he was doing anything wrong. It was already past nine o'clock; everything except the DMZ Bar was closed in Huế. He didn't know what the big deal was.

'What about her?'

Hai followed Marina's gaze. She was looking at Huong, who'd earlier foolishly addressed Marina as 'chi'. She was standing behind the reception counter, engrossed, as usual, with something on her phone. Hai had berated her that evening about her gaffe; he'd been working in hotels long enough to know that some foreigners didn't really like being mistaken for a local, even though Vietnamese women preferred to be called 'chi'. It was just more respectful. But of course Huong had only nodded distractedly, just as she had when he told her he was entertaining a guest in the lobby. All she cared about was being picked up by her boyfriend later at midnight.

'My colleague?' His head swung back to look at her.

'Yes.' Marina's brow furrowed again. 'Won't she be . . . disturbed? Or report you.'

'Don't worry,' he said. He realized he was smiling. 'This is Vietnam. It's no problem.' He sat back, relaxed for a moment, then reached over and popped open a can.

Marina looked at him, blinking her eyes pensively. 'Okay,' she said, after a few moments. She accepted the beer and took a sip.

'You smoke?' He threw a suggestive glance at his crumpled pack on the table, beside the ashtray he kept forgetting to use.

'Oh, no.' Marina's eyes followed the smoke as it curled from the tip of his cigarette and rose slowly in front of them.

'I know some people in Singapore,' he said.

'I'm not Singaporean,' she said.

'But your passport?' He remembered the bright red passport he had held earlier that day.

'I'm from the Philippines,' she said. 'I became a citizen a few years ago.'

'But you were born in Singapore?'

'What? No.' She traced the edge of the table with her forefinger. 'I moved to Singapore for work, then—'

'So you can do that? Become a citizen, easy?'

Marina looked nonplussed. 'You apply for permanent residency first, then you apply to become a citizen,' she said. 'I've lived in Singapore for twelve years, I thought that was a safe number.' She paused. 'It's a process.'

Hai took a deep drag. *How complicated*, he thought. Not that he was interested. No, not now. He had things to do here in Huế. He liked that Marina told him these things and that he had asked.

* * *

He went on with the usual questions. 'First time in Vietnam?' He asked it carefully, animatedly, and hopefully without sounding too pushy. This woman in front of him, who'd agreed to come down for beer, had something skittish and unsettled about her. One wrong question and she might bolt, retreat to the familiar comfort of her cool, air-conditioned room on the third floor.

'No, no,' she said, shaking her head and smiling a little. She didn't seem to want to talk more.

'How many days?'

'Oh,' she said, putting down the beer on the table. 'I was here for work. Just,' she hesitated, gazing at the green and white design of the Huda can she'd just been holding, 'a week.' Then, she looked up at him and straightened her back. 'Yes, a week. I stayed at The Nam Hai.' The furrow between her brows was back, and she pursed her lips, now devoid of the red paint she'd been wearing earlier.

The Nam Hai was Hué's most expensive hotel and cost no less than six hundred dollars a night. What did she do, to be able to spend all that money on that kind of hotel?

And then a long, drawn, high-pitched siren filled the lobby. When he turned towards the reception counter, he saw Huong drop her phone with a clatter on the counter, just as a pair of pyjama-clad women came bursting through the fire exit. In the next few minutes, couples and groups in their sleepwear, toting clothes, shoes, a bag or the other, appeared in the lobby looking sleepy, baffled and stricken.

It was the fire alarm, they would learn later, pressed by accident. Hai had to get up and speak to all of them, mostly in Vietnamese, telling them that they should calm down, that it was safe, and that they could go back to their rooms. It had been a mistake, he kept telling them, one big false alarm.

And then he had looked back at where Marina was still tucked into the huge armchair, looking like a queen even in thick glasses and a strange skirt. She was scrolling through her phone, unmoved and detached as if half of Minh Thanh's guests hadn't gone done in a rackety panic, and the whole fire alarm ruckus hadn't just happened.

It was then that he felt a stinging surge of irritation—at the hotel and its provinciality, at the guests and their cluelessness, at Huong and her uselessness. At the silly, unnecessary mess of it all. And then the next thought annoyed him even more because, he realized, all he could think of at that moment was, *fuck, don't let her leave just yet.*

Huda Beer

MARINA

He was asking her a lot of questions. Questions she thought she was used to, so she relaxed a little. She sat back against the stiff armchair and sipped her beer. The air-con didn't seem to be working or was turned off; there was a growing stuffiness about the room, the air threatening to turn sticky, warm. It felt awkward sitting in the lobby with a half-dozen cans of unopened beer in front of her, set so blatantly on a spindly coffee table that didn't look like it belonged there, even if Hai had assured her several times that everything was fine. His body language—the swift, practised way he arranged the small table, the careful appreciativeness with which he looked at her—suggested that there was nothing extraordinary about this except that she had said yes, that she was here with him. Still, a part of her kept expecting someone to walk in—a guest, Hai's boss, somebody—and accuse them that they were doing the wrong thing, or that they were in the wrong place.

No one did. It was only a little past nine o'clock, but the lobby was empty except for them and the other receptionist, Huong. There was an atmosphere of simply passing time, as if they were done for the night.

Marina was used to odd invitations from men, but this was different. She was still thinking of Vinh; she was, in truth, still desperate for a distraction. But she said yes because she was drawn to the strangeness of Hai's invitation. That it was so simple and ordinary and actually plausible only added to the mystery, the audacity. To drink beer on a slow night at the lobby of the hotel where you worked—why ever not?

51

Maybe it wouldn't have been so peculiar if Minh Thanh Hotel actually had a working bar or a café, as most hotels—at least the ones Marina had stayed in—did. Perhaps it would have been less strange if she was drinking with a fellow guest. But Minh Thanh only had a reception counter and a waiting area with a few armchairs and side tables, and the invitation had come from an employee in the middle of his shift. It was the first time someone had invited her to drink at his *actual* place of work, a receptionist about to turn the lobby of his hotel into his own personal bar. And so she had said yes, mostly fuelled by distraction and restlessness and also, curiosity. She was interested to see how a situation like this could be pulled off, negotiated. She wanted to participate first-hand.

'Are you sleepy?' Hai asked her now. The night had started on this note, with these kinds of questions and though they seemed jejune, Marina decided that after a week of *her* asking questions at work, it was good to be the one being asked, the one being listened to.

'No,' she replied, shaking her head. Her gaze fell again on the table, at the dented metal ashtray teetering on its edge, which Hai only sometimes used, and Hai's fingers, which looked graceful and slender. His nails were trimmed, except for a single, inch-long nail he'd left uncut on his right pinkie finger.

'Tired?'

'Ah, no.' She looked up. Had he caught her looking at his hands? She didn't want him to think she was attracted to him because she wasn't—especially with that long pinkie finger nail. It seemed important to him that she was *en forme*.

She had her own questions to ask. 'How long have you been working here?'

'Four years,' Hai said, promptly. He raised his chin, puffing up his thin chest. 'I worked in different hotels here in Huế, many jobs. I started as a bellboy, a long time ago.'

'And now you're a receptionist.'

'Night manager,' Hai said, rushing out the phrase. 'I'm in charge of the front desk from ten to six, every night.' There was another job, one he did in the mornings, for a backpacker hostel.

That was a clever term, night manager. And this man, Marina sensed, was someone who was unapologetic about using all the euphemisms he could, if they served him. She surveyed his face, which she hadn't paid much attention to earlier when he had been checking her in. Hai was still in his too-loose hotel uniform, his skin matte and smooth against the thick, grey fabric. He had a small, pointy face with a delicate but pronounced chin and a pert nose, features that gave him an almost feminine quality. He spoke in that forceful but modulated, almost electric voice that sometimes dropped to a clear whisper, whenever he seemed to be wanting to make a point. When he smiled, his face split open in a kind of helpless, watery grimace; a shapeless smile with the corners of his mouth pulled down and wide across his cheeks. Because he stared at her so openly, Marina let herself look at the way his lips puckered up as he drew from his cigarette. The way he was smoking, she knew she would still smell of cigarette smoke tomorrow.

Hai asked about her stay in Vietnam, then veered to questions about her citizenship. She's Singaporean, isn't she? But why didn't she speak like the Singaporeans, he asked. The question could come off as rude, but she understood what he wanted to know. Still, it startled her not because of its suddenness or even its bald directness, but because she realized she hadn't talked about her Singapore citizenship in months, maybe years.

Hai seemed surprised to learn that she was a Filipino who got Singaporean citizenship, then appeared defeated when she started telling him the details of the process. She didn't blame him. She had been like this too, once.

Hai was sitting across from her, leaning but not close enough. 'What is your job?'

'I'm a writer,' she said. 'An editor. For a magazine.'

'Is it here in Vietnam? Your magazine?'

'No.' She shook her head and gave him a tight-lipped smile. 'Just in Singapore.' He didn't ask the magazine's name or what kind of magazine it was, and she had no desire to elaborate. Sometimes it was hard to know what to say.

'What do you write about?'

'Lifestyle,' she replied, automatically.

'Life?' Hai asked, before she could continue. 'You write about life.' He nodded quickly, as if it all made sense.

'Ah, no.' Marina scratched at her brow and let out a rueful chuckle. 'I write about hotels, restaurants, places. People. Entrepreneurs. Artists.' She paused, unsure if she should go on, piqued by this little mix-up. For a moment, she wanted to close her eyes and pretend that she was indeed writing about 'life'—the version that Hai was talking about.

What she wanted to tell him was that to her it was completely different. Life was real, uncomfortable, sometimes ugly. What she wrote for *Parcours*—well, it was all styled and curated and so they were all supposed to appear beautiful. Writing about life was a completely different thing and all she did really, was write about what made something worthwhile and inspiring and because two-thirds of what appeared in the lifestyle section of *Parcours* were directives from advertising, she'd had to try hard to find the good in some of those things.

'A good job,' Hai said, approvingly. 'Good salary.'

Marina didn't say anything. When Hai said it like that, neat and conclusive, it was tempting to just accept it as true. But she'd known for a long time that it wasn't. Sure, it was a good job. It paid for her apartment in Singapore.

Now Hai was sitting hunched on his chair, arms draped in between his legs. He was looking at something on the floor beyond the table in front of them. He glanced up again at her and asked, 'Do you have a husband?'

'A husband?' Marina raised her eyebrows. But Hai sounded so plaintive, she doubted if there was even any malice to it. 'No, I'm not married.'

She picked up her half-consumed can and took a sip, surprised that she appreciated this earnest directness where she didn't feel pressed to elaborate. *When will you get married?* Was a question she was often asked, as if there was something wrong about being single in your forties. That was the message, had always been. She'd grown up, after all, watching sitcoms on TV where actors joked about the old maid teacher, who ultimately ended up derided for life.

Singapore was a relief. A Filipina colleague that she didn't have time to get to know better—she'd had to move to Sydney for work—told her that what she liked about moving to a new place was the anonymity. 'You can reinvent yourself.' It was true, Marina realized. In Singapore, no one knew her and so no one asked insensitive questions. There was no contrived intimacy. And no one, so far, had accused her of *still* being single in her forties.

'You should have children,' her mother had once said, which meant that she should find someone soon and get married, like everyone else. 'You might not have the chance when you get older.'

'You gave birth to me when you were thirty-nine,' Marina had retorted.

'So you're overdue.' Her mother seldom spoke about her birth, only that she had a Caesarean operation and that it had cost a lot.

'Now you want me to have kids,' Marina had said. '*Aber*, with whom?'

'Why, with someone who deserves you, of course,' her mother had answered, shrugging loftily. 'If not, who will take care of you when you get old?' But she refused to elaborate after that, busying herself with something else, a signal that the subject was closed, leaving Marina to wonder if her mother was referring to the husband or the child who would take care of her.

She wondered what her mother's reaction would be if she turned up pregnant.

* * *

Hai was telling her about his other job, the day job with the backpacker hostel. 'I do marketing,' he said, matter-of-fact and almost dismissive. 'And you? You travel often? How many countries?'

She knew this, she had counted using an online country counter. 'Forty-nine.'

'You've been to Hội An?'

'I'm going there tomorrow, for an interview.'

When he handed her another can, she asked, again: 'Do you do this often?'

'Drink beer in the lobby?'

Marina nodded, glancing at the reception counter where Huong was. 'By yourself? Or with someone?'

'No,' Hai said, his voice turning soft. 'This is my first time.'

'Then why did you invite me here?'

For half a minute, it seemed that Hai didn't move, his eyes intent on a spot Marina couldn't see beyond the glass wall. Then, he drew himself up. 'I thought you'd like some company.'

'Oh?' Was that it? She didn't know if it was disappointment she felt. Somehow, between Hai's call to her room and their shared time in this makeshift spot in the lobby she'd assumed a platonic closeness growing between them, and so she'd come to expect only the truth from him.

'You looked—'

'Lonely?' Her eyebrows shot up.

'No.' Hai gave her a small, patient smile that only made Marina feel as if he was softening the blow. 'Friendly,' he said, finally. 'I asked you, because you looked friendly.'

Call Me Camille

CARMEN

Max was the one who told her to use Camille.

'Camille'—they'd all agreed—is a typhoon victim, a lass from Leyte, east of the Philippines, studying to be a nurse, whose home in the outskirts of Tacloban City had been flattened by one of the world's strongest typhoons. A good story, Max always said, and so it was important to get it right.

Carmen knew about typhoons. They blew through the Philippines every wet season from July to October and with such regularity, there were times she didn't even know one was already making landfall, stirring up water surges and dismantling houses—in one of the islands down south or the cities up north, a mere five or six hours away from Manila. When she was nine or ten and still living with her mother, a typhoon meant chilly weather and staying home, mostly in bed wrapped in sweaters and blankets, the windows shut tight for hours because of the wind and rain. Schools were closed. Office employees, like her mother, were sent home. Going out was dangerous, unless you were foolish or desperate: debris flew from dislodged rooftops and broken trees, roads filled up with waist-length water, cars got stuck overnight on the highways. Sometimes their garage flooded with the continuous downpour, and her mother had to get help from the neighbours to lift their car up using the jack, a haphazard technique she learned from her father. It worked every time.

Carmen didn't know a thing about nurses. But sometimes she allowed herself to imagine being one—a real nurse, someone who got paid every month to help people. A nurse, Carmen believed, was someone who belonged to that lucky group that had always known what they wanted and had prepared their whole lives for their chosen profession. They were the ones who had proper degrees, who could now earn the minimum wage, or who could at least have a steady job, none of which Carmen had at the moment. What she had, now at twenty-five-years old, was just a high school diploma and barely a year in college: she had done two semesters of Business Administration at the Philippine Women's University, only to drop out before the school year ended. She told herself it was hard to stay motivated—doing group work or discussing business paradigms, say—when you couldn't pay the fees. Besides, the math subjects were too impenetrable: she'd failed her finals in Math I, could never make sense of the numbers no matter how many times her professor wrote the formulae on the board. She wasn't even sure if Business Administration was for her. She had only enrolled because it was a non-quota course and at the urging of Nanay Luisa, her aunt turned unofficial guardian, who'd always wanted her to go to college.

Beside PWU was St Paul's Hospital, and Carmen often bumped into groups of nursing students on her way to class, girls she thought looked elegant in their ironed, long-sleeved white blouses and black-and-white chequerboard skirts. They had neat hair that seemed to fall just right on their shoulders or, if not, they sported big, shiny, black clips securing the perfectly-formed buns at the nape of their necks. Sometimes she saw them in their nursing whites, looking official and brisk with stockings and caps. Her mother had dressed her up that way too, once, a long time ago, for a Halloween party, back when she still attended good schools, schools that could afford parties for every mundane occasion, like Halloween. Nowadays, she could only imagine these white-clad, newly-minted nurses finally stationed in the sterile, identical rooms of St Paul's, soothing and smiling at patients, making them feel better, for sure helping heal them. Sure, they were paid a pittance—as Max was so fond of reminding her—but that was still a monthly salary, wasn't it?

Someone who had that kind of job certainly didn't keep secrets about how she lived or made her money, Carmen always thought. 'Camille' the nurse, she imagined, knew exactly who she was and what she wanted, and so would talk a lot and candidly; she would be the type to easily make friends at work. She would not be a loner like Carmen nor would she ever find herself in Carmen's current state: unemployed and hard-up, flailing and directionless, and whose only real friend was Max, the one and only real friend she'd had since she arrived in Barangay Bicutan fourteen years ago. He'd been there right from the start, it was almost as if he didn't even count: a friend by default. Meanwhile, 'Camille' the nurse would have a whole circle of colleagues whom she would trade stories with on a daily basis, colleagues who would listen, work friends who would trust. Yes, they would trust her, and they would be right to do so. They would all know each other's lives, each other's hardships, each other's dreams.

'Camille' the nurse, she knew, would have nothing to hide.

Max had laughed when she told him this. Laughed so heartily—no, so *raucously*, with a hand pressing hard on his already-hard stomach and a derisive shake of his head—that it almost made her regret even bringing it up. They had gotten together as usual one late night last week, over the old standby bottle of Ginebra, cheap gin that was sold at every corner *sari-sari* store. She'd been using 'Camille' almost every week now, for months whenever there was a job. Max laughed because he was going out with an actual nurse named Patty who had told him that she'd had to administer an injection to herself as part of a practical exam.

'Is that what you want, Carms?' Max had teased. He grabbed the gin bottle and twisted the cap open. 'Poke yourself with a needle?'

She had watched him pour the clear liquid into a foggy glass, squeezing the juice of a calamansi over it, the tiny green lime almost disappearing in his fingers. He tipped in a teaspoon of white sugar, the thick granules of which almost always never melted but made the drink go down easier for Carmen. It was a concoction he'd been making for her since they were teenagers, when she was fourteen and Max was seventeen and he'd finally let her drink beer and 'the hard stuff' like gin with his friends and him. There was ready-made lime juice available by the bottle, but this method saved them a few pesos. Max himself often chased down his shot with water or beer.

Carmen had pursed her lips and frowned. 'Oh? Maybe she's just making it up,' she said, trying to employ the same kind of throwaway audacity she'd always known Max had loads of. People made things up all the time, she wanted to add, and she, of all people, knew that. But she had grown up with Max, was used to his remarks. When she was younger, she sometimes found herself unconsciously mimicking him. That hadn't lasted.

'It's true!' He had given the glass a quick, final stir, the sound of the metal teaspoon against glass bouncing sharply off the jalousie windows.

'Well,' she had shrugged now, wondering again how she could have withstood all those years of Max's teasing, 'it could be worse.'

'Indeed it can,' Max had been holding back another bubble of deep-throated laughter. 'When it was Patty's turn to inject herself on the inside of her elbow, she couldn't even find her vein!'

That had diffused the tension. Carmen felt her shoulders drop, her annoyance instantly dissipate as a corner of her mouth lifted up in a small, grudging smile even if a part of her didn't want it to. Max's kind of trivial humour was often enough used to make things right, though she would find it funnier when they were younger.

'You can go back to school, you know,' Max said now, a little more quietly. Casual and offhand, always. Well-meaning, Carmen was sure. Sometimes Carmen wished she was like him, someone who acted as if the whole world was within easy reach and didn't really care if he reached it.

'No,' she said. 'Not right now. I have other priorities.'

'I know you do.' He dropped his gaze and shook out a cigarette from a pack he produced among the various bits and bobs by the side of the table. Max only smoked while drinking, two sticks at most, and a sign that he was in a reflective mood. 'I know—'

Carmen nodded, a little too quickly. 'Still saving,' she said, alarmed as soon as the words got out that it sounded defensive.

'For . . .?' Max eyed her. 'Still?'

'Yup.' She didn't want to repeat herself, Max knew everything. She didn't need to tell him *again* that the priority was to put enough money, as long as she was able to, into The Savings. It wasn't just having enough money to get through the day, the week, the month. For three years now, she'd been stuffing whatever pesos she'd managed to earn here and there into a metal box buried at the very back of her cabinet, an old *aparador* from the 1960s inherited from Nanay Luisa. Locked, of course, and kept secret from everyone except for Max. This was her current priority, since she'd found the Facebook page of her mother three years ago. She's got a little more than thirty-thousand pesos right now, which she touched when she only needed it.

Max wasn't letting up. He grabbed her arm, poked it a couple of times with his forefinger. 'Well, so? Not going to nursing school, then?'

Carmen pulled her arm away. 'I'm scared of injections.' Also, it had been years since she'd been at PWU; she'd forgotten all those business strategies.

Max howled with laughter. 'Aha. That's so Carmen!'

'I just want . . .' Carmen swallowed, hard. 'Well, you know what I want.' She had told Max so many times about finding her mother, all these years. What she hadn't worked up the courage to say was—until that happened, she would still be waiting for her real life to start.

'What about that food stall you said you wanted to have someday? All the cooking you've been doing, even before . . . this. Don't you want to do it long-term?' Max leaned back. 'It's not too late to dream about being a small business owner. Maybe.'

This food stall business was something Max had brought up repeatedly ever since she'd mentioned it a few years back, not long after she'd dropped out of college. To help out with the expenses of Nanay Luisa, she'd had the idea of cooking fried snacks and selling them on a folding table in front of the house, which stood right by the alley: *qwek-qwek*, quail's eggs dipped and fried in batter, starchy, pseudo-fish balls and processed sausages called *kikiam* from a frozen package she purchased at the wet market. Then she'd told Max that she might want to open her own food stall someday. The moment the words came out, she wondered what made her say them. Maybe it was the pressure to come up with an answer or maybe it was Max, as self-designated older brother and best friend who had always told her to try everything, *anything.*

Carmen actually started getting into it, this food-selling business, as far as she could afford it. She started selling her snacks five times a week, when she could borrow from Max or have a little money left over from whatever odd job she'd taken on during the week.

And then it had to stop because Max told her about the group. About how it was easy and yet she could earn much, much more. And she did. And now she had thirty thousand tucked in The Savings. She didn't think she could have saved that much selling her rolls of *lumpia*, no matter how tasty they were. No, they—and Carmen, she believed this now—didn't stand a chance.

Forgetting

MARINA

Except for her suitcase, she owned nothing in this room. On her second day at Minh Thanh Hotel, Marina sat against the headboard of her unmade bed looking at the room's dull beige walls, the bare brightness of Huế's morning light seeping through the diaphanous curtains. Her gaze fell on the spare, marble-topped dresser and she realized that she liked being far away from the clutter of her flat in Singapore. It was 6 a.m. and she had her laptop open, about to dive into her email to go over some submissions—a couple of contributing writers had messaged to say they'd turned in their stories for the next issue—when she thought of her own quiet, two-bedroom cocoon in Serangoon. There, in the heartland of Singapore, was where she'd accumulated multiples of everything crammed in the many closets she'd had painstakingly installed: dresses, shoes, make-up, bags, books, all bursting and threatening to spill out of those boxy squares of neatness that composed her flat back home. She couldn't count how many lipsticks or shoes she had, and she was afraid to: it could very well be over a hundred. Not much for some people, but too much and a little ridiculous for such a small space like hers. She'd started putting heels in the guest bedroom, scarves in the kitchen cabinets. There were purses still with their tags on, stuffed in the laundry basket.

She held on to things; she was aware of this. Growing up poor in Manila had taught her to take anything and everything, to keep whatever she could; working in Singapore when she turned thirty led her to believe that if she found something good, why would she ever want it to stop? These were things that could make her better, things that could improve her life. And, she might not have the chance to have them again.

And now here she was in this quiet, nondescript hotel room, with just her well-worn Rimowa open in a corner, holding a week's worth of clothes, shoes, and toiletries. That she owned nothing else at this moment brought her back to her past, years and miles away at a different time and a different city. It was a moment, she realized, that she wanted to savour, was worth savouring. And then it brought her back to the present, to her current life in Singapore where, in the past few years, she had begun to suspect something that was starting to hold true: The things she'd surrounded herself with—things that she thought would lift her up—now felt like they were wearing her down.

Right now, she was away from all that. Here was where she could forget all that. This place, she'd decided, when she checked in last night, was where she could momentarily forget about her life in Singapore, her work, her family—or what was left of it. This was what she liked about her current surroundings: In the sparseness and the strangeness of an unfamiliar room, where soiled towels were replaced and sheets were religiously changed, she could even pretend she hadn't done what she'd done with Vinh, and all the others.

* * *

The articles that her writers had sent needed a lot of tightening, and so she filed it under her to-do folder for editing the next day. Right now, she wanted to focus on prepping for the interview with Amanda Ho scheduled at 5 p.m. that day. 'It's muggy in Hội An, especially when it's heaving with day tourists,' Amanda Ho had written in her email. 'Afternoons are much cooler, and Hội An is empty.' Marina mentally reviewed the steps she needed to take: hire a taxi to go down to Amanda's boutique for the interview, then a walk along some iconic Hội An streets where Amanda would point out her favourite spots. The *Parcours* formula for lifestyle, which wasn't exactly original, but it did the job. The photographer was Vietnamese, handpicked by Amanda herself and already cleared with Giselle and Pei Lin, *Parcours*'s art director.

Marina was flipping the pages of her notebook, looking for additional questions she'd jotted down, when her phone sounded.

'Are you awake?'

A text from Hai. Marina paused, a little startled to receive this kind of message so early that it felt so intimate, almost like an intrusion. But then, hadn't she felt the same way last night, when he called her room and invited her to drink beer at the lobby?

In all his inelegance, Hai had inadvertently pointed out what was maybe the true reason she was bumbling all over this city, falling into bed with people like Vinh. A truth or something close to it: Hai said he'd invited her because she seemed friendly. What he really meant, she knew—even though he'd never even uttered the word—was that she seemed lonely. Hai didn't know anything about her, of course, or what had happened with Vinh. But Marina had been around different people long enough to know that they could sense when things were amiss, and that they could be oblique, even if they didn't mean to.

* * *

'I have work,' was her text reply to Hai's invitation for coffee. It was only six-thirty and she was well aware that Amanda's interview was a full ten hours away. She paused, then deleted the letters, one by one. She'd spent too many years using work as an excuse.

'Sorry,' she typed again. 'Next time.'

She jumped into the shower after that, turning the knob to the coldest setting. She preferred cold showers, even on cold days. Hai had asked her last night how old she was, a question that perhaps should have offended her more than it surprised her. Surely he must have seen her date of birth stated clearly on her passport when she checked-in. When he told her he was thirty-three, almost a decade younger than her and born in the eighties, she wondered if he knew how much he could do with such a length of time stretched out before him.

She'd begun to feel a certain flabbiness and softness all over her edges: the top of her hips, the perimeter of her buttocks, the back of her arms, the undersides of her boobs, her jawline. Even her feet seemed suddenly uncomfortable in her own sneakers. And then there were the mammograms, the ob-gyn, the medical and dental checkups that were frightening at first, and then humbling. Growing up, no one told her that your body should be examined each year. What was there to check as long as you could walk, talk, breathe? People went to doctors when they had accidents or when they were in unbearable pain. With her parents, there had been no such thing as going to the doctor for 'just a check-up'. That was dangerous, according to her mother.

'You go in for one illness,' she had said, 'and you'll come home with a dozen you didn't know you had.' Besides, that money could be spent somewhere else, like food and electricity bills.

Marina's doctor in Singapore was younger than her, as was her dentist. There was the annual medical exam, the constant reminder that she was in her forties and that she should care about what she ate, how much she exercised. She'd begun to think that even expecting you would even live the next day was almost arrogant.

'At your age, you just have a five percent chance of getting pregnant,' her ob-gyn had told her, when she went for her pap smear and asked about changing her pills. If she had been undecided about having children, it wouldn't be long before time would be making the decision for her.

Yes, there was the issue of time. There were days when, while editing or working on her stories at the *Parcours* offices, she could feel it closing in on her: when it would only be morning and then suddenly it would be evening and time to go home. And then it was the next day, and the next. The day was over before she'd even had the chance to savour it, to enjoy it, to really *look* at it. When she turned forty-two, she realized that that was how she was: she wanted to look at things, to think everything over.

And then it hit her one day, while she was being rattled about inside a taxi by yet another rage-y Singaporean driver, as the car zipped across the city-state because she needed to make it to three launch parties in the space of one evening: she may only just have a mere, short twenty, twenty-five years to enjoy her life—to travel, to lift things, to climb hills, to really look at the world. To do the mundane things she had always taken for granted. And also, to meet someone.

Once, when she was still working for *Manila Guardian*, she was assigned to do a story on skydiving. She completed the two-day training with a licenced skydiver and was scheduled to jump from a plane flying above the flatlands of Pampanga, some two hours away from Manila. The day of the jump, her section editor sent her to attend the commencement exercise of an all-girls' university. Former Philippine president Cory Aquino was the keynote speaker and there was talk about an impending illness.

The Cory Aquino story made it to the front page. Marina did not make it to Pampanga. She sent a photographer instead, to take photos of the skydiver who had trained her. She never did the jump.

She gave little thought to it at that time; there were other writing assignments lined up, people to interview, press conferences to attend. And in Manila, getting yourself from one place to next was an energy-sapping experience, but it was necessary and Marina did this daily. In the years that followed, Marina often found herself wondering what could have been, if she'd gone through with it. A real skydiving experience, free-falling through air and then gliding through it, thanks to the nifty, life-saving invention that was the parachute. Her instructor had told her that all skydivers had two, in case the first one failed to deploy.

What could that feeling have been? Would it have made her braver? Less fearful? More open to taking risks? And wasn't she taking some risks now? It made her wonder how it felt, to let go of yourself like that. To willingly expose yourself to possible death. Because she would never do it now, not at this age.

She'd forgotten a lot of her newspaper stories from years ago, but at that moment in Minh Thanh's hotel room, she remembered skydiving. It was an experience that she could only imagine, editing and revising the moments that didn't even happen. She didn't want to feel that kind of regret again.

She stepped out of the shower, wrapped herself up in a fluffy towel. She unplugged her phone from the charger. 'Coffee, where?' It wasn't too late to change her mind.

'I'll take you on my motorbike,' came Hai's reply, less than a minute later.

Ativan Gang

CARMEN

It had been so unceremonious, the day she joined the group. The 'gang', people would say, but they weren't really a gang—much less called themselves so. They were a *family*, as Max liked to remind them every so often, as if that wasn't the whole point of everything. Max, well, he just had to be extra. 'You've got to feel it,' he always told them, mock-hugging Uncle Amado and air-kissing Auntie Swan in that hilarious way he always had. 'To make people believe that we're a real family, we must *feel* like one.'

To Carmen, he did the *mano*: he touched the back of her hand to his forehead, a Filipino way of showing respect, already a dying practice and often reserved for the very old. 'See?' he said, as he pressed her knuckles gently on his brow, his touch warm and lingering. 'Respect, like this. That goes a long way.' He grinned at her as he straightened up, dropping her palm. 'If not, *palpak*.' An utter failure.

They weren't really a family. No, of course they weren't—that had been clear right from the start. Carmen already knew that but she had been curious, then sceptical. People—well, the tourists they sought out—surely, must have seen through that. They must have seen how fake Auntie Swan was when she talked about being a housewife to Uncle Amado, they must have seen through Uncle Amado's quiet but steely act, Max's charm and humour—his ready compliments and jokes all meant to distract and disarm. But no, the tourists never expressed any doubt at all. They actually believed that Uncle Amado was her uncle, Auntie Swan her aunt, and Max, an older cousin. And Carmen looked—really looked, closely—at their faces, searching for that doubt, some disbelief, or at least a sort of tolerance. But no, they accepted the facts without question at all. Only after some weeks did she realize that these tourists were just too busy thinking about themselves to notice anything else: that something was amiss and that something didn't quite add up. They were busy talking, experiencing, doing what they believed was the 'untouristy' thing like talking to the locals—them.

They were friends, but not really. Uncle Amado, who used to work as a security guard in a mall, said he met Auntie Swan when she was caught shoplifting by one of the plainclothesmen assigned to the women's clothing section. He had been called up to the office, and he found her sitting in front of the department manager, looking defiant. There was a mound of dresses on the table.

Auntie Swan, who used to work in Hong Kong and Singapore as a domestic helper had been scammed herself by a recruitment agency whose rep ran away with her 25,000 pesos. She had worked as a domestic helper in Singapore for ten years, sent home by her employer when she got into a fight with another Filipina.

After that, she couldn't get back to Singapore again. It was even harder to get work in Hong Kong, with all the competition. She was completely on her own—separated from her husband, estranged from her kids. She said she wanted money so she could see her new grandchild.

Max met them both at Luneta Park, where he was picking pockets. And Max, well, Carmen had known him all her life. At least, that was what she thought, until the Ativan Gang.

* * *

It had a lot to do with Max but ultimately, it was about the money. And working with this group, she was promised plenty. That is, once they got the hang of it. Once they got past their conscience and the fear, Carmen always thought—the constant discomfort, the secret life that always somehow felt like the kind of life she'd be living forever. The Ativan Gang entailed a lot of role-playing, but it also felt natural.

She had tried working odd jobs here and there since she stopped studying at PWU, and way before she'd even started the food stall: waitress, clerk, sales staff at Metro Department Store. The sales staff gig was the most 'prestigious' of the lot, but it also paid the lowest—less than five hundred pesos a day, with half almost going into the lunch she bought daily at the cheap sidewalk eatery nearby, and the long commute from work in Mandaluyong to Barangay Bicutan. All were contractual and temporary and so she found herself out of a job every three or six months. She had also worked as an assistant for one of Max's contacts in a travel agency, but it had been another short-lived deal; after two months, the boss suddenly announced that they wanted someone who'd completed a college degree.

Carmen had broached this with Nanay Luisa, when she found herself out of work *again,* after the travel agency gig, and before she even found her mother on Facebook.

'What if I just work as a domestic helper?' she asked one morning as they sat around the flimsy folding table in the kitchen, drinking instant coffee. Carmen sat on a wobbly stool on one side, facing Nanay Luisa and Tito Clem, her live-in partner of fifteen years.

'You can't be serious,' Nanay Luisa said, a light trail of toasted flour lingering on her chin as she bit into a piece of *pandesal* bread. Tito Clem sipped his milky coffee and said nothing.

'At least I'll be working abroad,' Carmen said. 'And I can send you money every month.'

There was a time, when she was younger, when she had thought 'working abroad' only meant being a nurse in New York and London, restaurant manager in Singapore, dancer in Japan, or sales staff in Dubai. Now she knew it also meant being domestic helpers and caregivers in Hong Kong, Singapore, Saudi Arabia—everywhere, really—who could earn upwards of 500 dollars, just because they were abroad. Just because it wasn't the Philippines.

Her mother, too, had left this country to work abroad. What was it that her mother had said, right before she left? 'So you can have new toys, Carmen. So you can have everything that you want.'

Was it weird that she remembered that phrase clearly, from fourteen years ago, right here in Barangay Bicutan? Had she only dreamed it? If she had, then she had also dreamed the hopeful-turned-fraught phone calls of the years following, the wondering and the longing and finally, the loneliness.

Nanay Luisa shook crumbs off the tips of her fingers, her face now twisted in a rare scowl. 'You'll be a maid?' Nanay Luisa was fifty-three years old and washed clothes for some of the residents in the nearby subdivision. Tito Clem, who'd moved in just before Carmen arrived in Nanay Luisa's house, was a part-time mechanic at a nearby vulcanizing shop.

'An OFW,' Carmen corrected. Right, there was even an official ring to it. 'Not a maid. A helper.'

'Why—the horror stories,' Nanay Luisa said. 'Haven't we told you?' Nanay reached for a glass of water, wincing as she swallowed. 'You know it yourself—'

'Maybe it won't happen to me,' Carmen cut in. 'I might be good at it.' She was dismayed to note that she didn't sound convincing at all.

'Is this because you want to follow . . .' Nanay Luisa's eyes flicked sharply over to Tito Clem, as if asking for help.

'My mother?' Carmen kept her voice non-committal. She had expected this. 'No,' she said. 'Not at all. I don't even know where she is—she said the States, right? Anyway, haven't we all given up? That includes me.' She was rambling, as she tended to, whenever she or someone spoke of her mother. It was a habit that confused her, because it wasn't as if she hadn't completely processed it in her head, hadn't thought about what happened fourteen years ago, a thousand times. And at that time, when she spoke about working abroad, that thing about her mother was true: Carmen *had* given up, in a way.

'At least I'll have something,' Carmen repeated. 'Money, for one. And more, who knows?'

'Carmen, *anak*.' It was Tito Clem. 'It's better to have nothing.' He toyed with an empty packet of instant coffee on the table. 'Do you want to eat dinner standing up every night? Or sleep under the kitchen table?' They knew of someone, he said, who worked in Hong Kong who had to scavenge the day's trash just so she could have something to eat, another one who couldn't send money back to her family in the Philippines because her employers had kept her passport and salary for a year.

Carmen knew about this, too. How could she not? Auntie Swan herself said her first employer hit her with an iron, claiming it was an accident. She heard these stories everywhere, not just in Barangay Bicutan. It was on TV, in the tabloids, on YouTube. It was told over and over again.

She would have been a good maid, she was convinced of that. But then there came the Ativan Gang and she was good there, too.

* * *

She got in right away. She was a shoo-in because of Max, who seemed to have a hundred things going on at once: selling stolen mobile phones, shoplifting goods, some light pickpocketing. There was probably more but she knew better than to press. It wouldn't have made a difference, anyway: There was nothing Max could do that could make her stay angry for too long. She knew he hung out in the posh cafés in Makati, making bags disappear and discreetly swiping wallets or phones left unattended on cluttered tables. He'd brought her several times to these upscale places and she had marvelled at how he didn't look out of place among the customers: men with styled hair dressed in dapper shirts or brand-new-looking sneakers, women in complicated clothes she'd only seen in store windows or worn by those perky actresses in lunchtime TV shows. *Mestizos* and *mestizas,* people who looked half-Filipino like Max, who sat as if they had always belonged there and spoke in straight, well-enunciated English among themselves or toyed with their thin, silver laptops and paid more than three hundred pesos for something that was poured in a tall, logoed paper cup. Max moved with ease among them, confidently striding the brief space between door and counter from where shiny, hissing espresso makers were lined up and the people behind who took your order looked as spiffy as their customers.

But they was no match for Max. He knew the blind spots of the CCTVs. Even better, he scouted out those places that didn't have these cameras. He brought along one or two accomplices who hung out on the fringes. Sometimes he went alone. 'Distract people when they least expect it' was one of his favourite adages. 'Just ask these folks what time it is and see what happens,' he'd say, jokingly, without contempt. 'You'd be surprised at how these folks never pay attention.'

'So why do you need me then?'

'Because *you* pay attention.' Max grinned. 'And also, because you listen—something these old folks seem to have forgotten.' He looked at her with those rheumy eyes. 'Besides, you're not doing anything right now, are you?'

What he meant was that she needed the money to go look for her mother.

He brought her to Uncle Amado's house one afternoon, where he said they were waiting.

'This is Carmen,' Max said. They were in the *sala* downstairs. 'She can be your daughter. *Mas* okay, isn't it? This way, we're all more believable.'

Uncle Amado was agreeable, looking as if he had already expected this. Auntie Swan was curt and eyed her suspiciously at first. 'Are you sure you're up to the job?' she asked, eyes narrowing. 'Are you used to talking with foreigners? With strangers? You might get scared and give up on the first try. That would mess up everything.'

'No, no,' Max said, shaking his head. 'Carmen's made of tougher stuff. She can do it.'

'It's hard operating with two men,' Uncle Amado said. 'Too threatening. Carmen . . .' He turned to Auntie Swan. 'She might be a good addition.'

'You need to smile a lot,' Auntie Swan said. 'Friendly, but not too friendly.'

'We do Luneta Park and Manila Bay,' Uncle Amado said. 'We befriend foreigners, the ones who travel solo. Say we have one, an American tourist—doesn't matter where they're from, really. Important thing is to ask him if he's travelling alone. Where is his hotel? How long is he staying in the Philippines?'

'It's important to size him up,' Auntie Swan said. 'Ask him what his plans are, what kind of travelling does he do—because that's our way of finding out if he's got the money or if he's just some shoestring tourist out for a dirt-cheap deal while combing through Asia.'

'Remember, Carmen,' Max said. 'Ask the questions gently, inquisitively. Just always think that you're part of a Filipino family from the province who's simply curious, inexperienced, and eager to get to know someone not from their own country.'

Auntie Swan was nodding. 'Right, Max! Who could say no to a wholesome Filipino family, simply wanting to share the local experience with a foreigner?'

* * *

Max brought her to the jeepney stop after that. 'Don't worry. I'll be working with you.'

Carmen took her seat at the edge of the jeepney. It was still empty. 'How long have you been doing this for?'

'Not long.' Max was vague. 'It's so simple, really.'

'Is it safe, this drug?'

'Nothing's safe. We could die right now.'

'Max!' Carmen looked at him. 'I mean, it won't kill people, will it?'

Max laughed. 'Ativan? No! These meds, they're just anti-anxiety pills. Like sleeping pills. Auntie Swan said she was given those when she had an operation in Singapore. She knows the right dose.'

Phong and Beer

HAI

The stall where they drank beer on Ngo Hien Street looked just like the others in Huế: nondescript, its façade wall worn and patched-up in unfinished paint primers, as if someone tried painting then gave up and left. It sat on the end of a busy street near the train station, but appeared empty when Hai arrived, the usual low plastic tables in bright blue and a smattering of red stools, shiny and unoccupied, still neatly arranged on whatever was left of the sidewalk. He would have wanted to hang out here, with the view of the street and passers-by but Phong preferred drinking beer inside. The motorbikes distracted him, Phong said, but Hai knew his best friend tended to dominate these drinking sessions. He needed your full attention.

Hai went through the gaping accordion doors and found him sprawled in the middle of the room, on the only wooden chair with a generous backrest that Chi Hien, the stall owner, reserved for Phong. They've been drinking there for years, Phong perhaps more than him, hence the favouritism.

'*Chao anh*!' Phong called out loudly, as if he owned the place. A plastic table by his side, similar to the ones outside, held a can of beer and a dull, squat glass. Phong raised a lazy hand, not moving from his position: feet crossed, long, jean-clad legs extended in front of him. He had on a loose white shirt, open a few buttons lower than normal, exposing smooth, caramel-coloured skin.

Hai nodded to Chi Hien, who was in her usual spot behind the scuffed glass and metal shelf in a corner where she kept a modest display of iced tea and canned beer, and tiny clear-plastic square packets of peanuts and watermelon seeds.

'You're early,' Hai said, giving one last glance at the busy street, and his motorbike which he'd parked out front. He paused and stood by the entrance.

'You look different,' Phong said, smirking. 'You're all red in the face. Have you been drinking with Duong?' Hai watched Phong shift in his seat and noted once again how effortlessly good-looking his friend was. Phong had always been, even when they were teenagers running through the rubber tree fields in Quảng Trị.

'A beautiful man,' was what one foreign guest in Huế—clearly smitten by Phong's electric smile and cheerful, can-do demeanour—had once called him years ago when they were still working together as bellboys at the Lotus Huế Hotel. Phong was tall and lanky and kept his hair longish, the black curls falling just right on his forehead. He had a chin that jutted out—which he had been constantly teased for when they were young—but he had big, round eyes whose curly eyelashes were often a topic whenever they hung out with someone he was dating. Hai sometimes found Phong's smug confidence unbearable, but with women, he exuded a kind of insouciance that Hai supposed was attractive. At least, that was what the women he'd dated had said more than once.

'Nothing's different,' Hai muttered, moving quickly across the room. 'Everything's still shit.' He wasn't sure he meant that but that morning he'd almost forgotten to log in a phone reservation at Minh Thanh and that never happened unless he was preoccupied with something.

'You spoke with the building owner?' He was here to talk to Phong about something important, not get blind drunk like they used to when they were younger. The idea about the hotel had come years after they had both worked their way up from bellboys to waiters to receptionists. Tour guides, now and then. After six years of taking orders from managers who almost always thought their ideas were right, they realized they could manage their own small hotel. They just needed the money.

'No, forget the hotel—let's talk about this woman!' Phong was unstoppable. He sat up, blew gaily at the air in front of him and let out a derisive chuckle.

'The hotel's important, *anh.*' Hai arranged his face into what he hoped was something detached, business-like, as if he couldn't care less about what Phong said or about Marina for that matter—when actually he did, very much. He was here to talk about the partnership Phong and he had been planning: a small hotel of their own, one that they would manage and, hopefully, earn a profit from in a year. They were looking for a building to lease, a place that they could turn into something more than a cheap hostel. A two-star hotel.

Hai took off his shoes and settled on the stool, wondering if it had been a good idea to tell Phong about Marina Bellosillo when they had spoken earlier on the phone. But he couldn't help himself. When Phong called him that morning, he let slip that he had met someone, someone important at Minh Thanh.

'Now, anh,' Phong said now, his tone syrupy, as if he hadn't heard a word from Hai. He handed Hai a can of beer. 'Don't be stingy with the details.' The shirt he had on was new, Hai realized, one that he hadn't seen before.

Phong worked as a tour guide for a small travel agency and sometimes went along as an extra guide for bigger trips to Halong Bay or Dalat. He was good at English, using new words he'd encounter. And he was bolder with pronunciation, less self-conscious and so open for corrections that it endeared him to whichever English-speaking person he was with. They had studied the same course at Huế University, got their degrees in Tourism in the same year. Somehow, Phong did better in every subject and took to English so much easier than Hai, seemingly without even trying.

'I already told you about her,' Hai said. When they were younger, Phong's energy was contagious. Now, Hai only felt drained, a little lightheaded. 'What other details do you want?'

There were times he regretted saying things to Phong. When they both came to Huế City from Quảng Trị years ago, Phong had been his lifeline, the only person he could trust and someone who reminded him of his hometown. In Huế, they lived in the same boarding house tucked deep inside the winding alleys of the city, where they slept on a single mattress in a room with other male students. They worked first as waiters in small coffee shops in their first year then as bellboys when they graduated from Huế University. But Phong was different. His family was from Quảng Trị but they owned land. They were better off.

'This is the first time you've invited a hotel guest to . . . what was it? Drink beer in the lobby?' Phong took a slug from his can, his face breaking into a sly smile. 'Only you would do something weird like that.'

Hai frowned. 'Weird?' he asked sharply, surprised that he felt stung. 'Look who's talking.'

'Well, she didn't tell you how strange that was?'

Hai swallowed, the biting comeback he'd reserved for Phong already lost somewhere in his throat. At that moment, he was struck by this new thought: had he actually made a bad impression on Marina instead of what he'd thought was a friendly, welcoming move? For the first time since he'd invited Marina to come down to the lobby, he felt lame instead of victorious. And to think that he'd been congratulating himself for days for having the courage to step out of his comfort zone.

Hai looked at his friend. Phong was oblivious and, for a split second, Hai wished to be more like him—breezing through life with a laugh, jumping at risks and opportunities with hardly a thought about what would come next. Phong had all types of girlfriends, but they were all Vietnamese.

But no—Hai had to be Hai, he had to be terrified, he had to overthink things.

'So, tell me,' Phong leaned forward, blithe and challenging, clasping his fingers together on his knees. 'Why did you invite a hot girl downstairs to drink beer in your pitiful lobby? And, was she really hot?'

'Shut up.' Hai bristled. Phong always spoke this way. Always said 'hot girl' instead of a beautiful girl, always said pussy and tits even when there were other people around.

'Does Sinh know?'

Hai wanted to strangle him. 'Of course not. Why do you even ask that question?'

'Thought so,' Phong sang out.

'Childish.' Hai tried to keep the anger out of his voice, but oddly, he found himself pleased that they were on the topic of Marina.

'So, tell me,' Phong leaned back into his chair. 'Let me understand why you've suddenly become all bold and asked a foreigner out.' He clasped his hands behind his head and gave Hai another smirk.

Hai rested his arms on his knees, recalling the surprising jolt of emotions he felt when the fire alarm sounded in Minh Thanh—just a false alarm and not the first time that it'd happened. People started filing into the lobby, interrupting his moment with Marina and then there it was: a sudden loathing for his city's backward ways, the regret about having to leave Marina by herself because he had to attend to his sleepy, disoriented guests.

'Well, she is a hot girl,' Hai said, softening. He would confront Phong later. Right now, all he wanted to do was think about the woman who'd agreed to come down and have a drink with him. 'Maybe not too bad in bed.'

'That's my boy.' Phong grinned. 'From the Philippines, you said?'

'Singapore,' Hai said, quickly. 'Filipina working in Singapore. But she's a Singapore citizen now.'

'Aha,' Phong said, 'so special.'

'Not really.'

Another knowing smile. 'Of all your guests in Minh Thanh, she's the one you've decided to fuck with?' Phong narrowed his eyes, looking comical. 'Or to just fuck.'

Hai tried not to show his surprise and dismay at Phong's remark, rankling because it was so close to the truth. What *had* he been thinking when Marina Bellosillo walked in at Minh Thanh that day? He felt a little embarrassed to admit that yes, he had wanted to fuck her at first—fuck a foreigner, that is, just because he'd never had. And Marina looked Vietnamese; she wouldn't feel so alien, he supposed, in bed.

Marina did not ask the usual touristy questions. She had asked him about himself and his work, instead of places she could visit in Huế. He didn't see in her that kind of greedy consumption of the sights. And she'd been oblivious, almost stoic, when the fire alarm went off on her first night at the hotel, as if she couldn't be bothered with the ordinary and mundane.

He thought it a neat kind of detachment, and one that he found comforting. Marina was different from the Vietnamese in this way, from all the local women he knew whose emotions readily, messily spilled out at the slightest provocation. *They* would have screamed and kicked and cried upon learning that the hotel was on fire. He'd witnessed his aunts wail and roll on the floor like possessed children when they discovered his uncles' affairs. Sinh had, too, once—though Hai had never had an affair. He'd slept with other women, but no, not the way his uncles did.

'What's she doing in Singapore?' Phong asked now.

'In the media or something.' Hai shrugged. 'She's a writer.'

He understood that she was some sort of boss in a magazine in Singapore, the name of which he couldn't pronounce properly and so he had not asked any more about it. She lived in the kind of first-world city that his colleagues and he had always talked about, where everything worked. He had looked at her hands: they were so smooth and supple-looking, it was hard to believe she was over forty as her passport had indicated.

It could only be, he was convinced, due to the regenerative the power of money. With money, you can do anything.

He had wanted to bring Marina to bed, yes. He had wanted to know how it was to fuck someone who was not goddamned Vietnamese. And God knows he knows the Vietnamese in bed. The girls he picked up, when Sinh was working overtime at the restaurant, lay there like a fish, expecting him to do all the work. Come to think of—even Sinh was like that most of the time.

So, he changed his mind. This will not be a short-lived fuck, as he had initially planned. This will be so much more. He wanted to fuck her, yes. But there was much more to be gained if he didn't. Not now. And it was up to him to try and make something of things. Hadn't it always been like this?

His phone buzzed; a message from Duong asking if he was coming to a former colleague's wedding that afternoon. In his absence, Duong had most likely gotten several tourists today to book at the hostel. Overeager Duong, who wore his heart on his sleeve, spoke English with that funny western accent, and never kept anything in.

But then he knew what he had to do. He finished his beer in one smooth swallow, slid another stick from his pack. There were still a number of buses coming in before noon, and Marina, thankfully, was still in Vietnam.

Amanda Ho

MARINA

An email was glowing in her inbox when Marina got back to Minh Thanh Hotel mid-afternoon: Amanda Ho had written asking to postpone the *Parcours* interview to tomorrow, instead of late that afternoon. And instead of doing it at her clothing boutique in the centre of Hội An, Amanda wrote: Wouldn't it be better if Marina interviewed her at home, so she could see how Amanda lived?

No one could know how one really lived, Marina thought, bristling as she typed back a reply, because no one really revealed how they lived—or didn't know how. She'd learned that much from all the interviews she'd done, all those feature articles she'd written. For profile interviews like these, it seemed to her that people were compelled to show up in what they believed was their best self. Magazines like *Parcours*, of course, preferred it. It was a little like tidying up before the cleaner comes, as Marina sometimes did. You are willing to show some of the mess but not all of it.

She had an early morning flight back to Singapore on Sunday, the day after all her interviews. It was Friday today and because Marina had another interview lined up on Saturday with the Singaporean-French chef at La Residence, now she would have to push that interview to a few hours later. La Residence had a three-month ad contract with *Parcours;* now that there were direct flights from Singapore to Huế, the advertising manager, Angela, was about to ask for the five-star hotel to up their spend. She wanted to talk to someone and let them know about the time adjustment.

Maybe Cecile was right, Marina thought, as she scrolled through her messages, trying to find the contact number of La Residence. And maybe she, Marina, was wrong in insisting on doing her interviews in person. 'Just email the questions or do FaceTime,' Cecile had urged when Marina told her she was doing a feature on Amanda Ho in the lifestyle section. 'Stalk her Insta,' Cecile had added. 'You'll probably get more information that way. With Amanda, you'll probably end up knowing what her before-bedtime fragrance is.'

And then: 'I should have known you weren't going the practical route.'

Cecile was always looking for ways to do something faster. 'Faster doesn't mean better,' Marina would tell her. Marina knew this because she once had Cecile's job as *Parcours*'s managing editor, briefly. She had taken over the position when Giselle had fired the previous editor, and in the interim, it left Marina the overwhelming task of line editing and proofreading all pages of the issue.

'Just get it done,' was another one of Cecile's favourite lines, which meant doing it just to get it over with. Marina wondered if this applied to everything else in Cecile's life.

* * *

The first thing that struck Marina was Amanda Ho's powerful handshake, though she couldn't exactly define the hard, finger-crushing grip that Marina was so sure would leave a bruise on her worn, middle-aged knuckles. Amanda was a little over five-feet tall but striking in a delicate way: all slim wrists and narrow shoulders, a small, heart-shaped face. She wore her hair in a pixie cut, as if it was an afterthought.

Marina didn't have trouble finding her house, which was nestled amid carefully-arranged kapok and frangipani trees, looking like a Balinese villa on a quiet corner road some dozen kilometres from Hội An. Amanda said in her email to walk right in through the gate, along the gravel driveway that led to the entrance. She passed a small but ornate fountain, catching sight of an Art Deco swimming pool at the side whose iridescent turquoise tiles, she would learn later, were by Carrara, ordered and shipped from Italy. To the right was an open garage with a black, macho Porsche and a more sedate greige Volvo, gleaming and silent.

And then there was Amanda at the front door, looking like she was on vacation in a geometric tan bra, a black-and-white batik-print open tunic and loose fisherman's pants. She was barefoot. For a split-second, Marina thought of all the others she had interviewed, and how it had not always been this way.

'Glad you made it.' Amanda said, giving her that bone-crushing handshake, her eyes meeting Marina's, dark and bright at the same time. 'I appreciate you coming out all the way here.' There was a formal graciousness about her that felt unexpected for someone who appeared so young; Amanda didn't look a day past thirty. Marina was both surprised and dismayed to note that Amanda reminded her of Atasha.

Now's not the time to think about her, Marina chided herself, as she extricated her hand. *Don't think about Atasha.*

Marina paused by the doorway, a beat in her chest. She shouldn't be thinking of Atasha anymore. And anyway, Atasha would have disapproved. She would never assign Marina to interview someone like Amanda, with her tropical house and predictable cars. Atasha didn't like this kind of neatness. She would find it so basic.

She followed Amanda to the living room, noting the solid teak furniture and the pebbled walls interspersed with more geometric, life-sized sculptures. There was a lightwell over a small garden enclosed in glass. Luxurious in its sparseness and space—the kind of interiors that bewildered and intimidated Marina when she first started writing for *Manila Guardian.* There had been a time when she felt like a total outsider. There had been a time when she didn't know what to say in the simplest of professional situations, even though her interviewees—entrepreneurs who wanted their businesses known, artists who needed to market themselves, celebrities promoting their films, socialites desperate to be in magazines—must have feared her more than she did them.

And then she had met Atasha and she stopped being an outsider.

She felt a movement inside her bag. Her phone had been vibrating on and off while they were going through the house. Now, as Amanda disappeared into her walk-in closet to change, Marina saw that she had three missed calls from Cecile. Her phone rang again.

'Cecile, I'm at the interview.' Marina kept her voice low.

'Giselle's back from Brazil.'

'So?' Marina craned her neck to see if Amanda had finished changing. 'We're nearly done with the issue, she won't freak.' Giselle wasn't expected until the end of the week, but it wasn't unusual for her to come back earlier from a work trip.

'She'll be making an announcement later.' There was a tremor in Cecile's voice. 'Marina, this could be it.'

'Going digital?' Marina pressed her phone closer to her ear. 'Is that it, Cecile?'

'What else could it be?' A taut panic laced Cecile's voice.

'There would have been an email,' Marina said, slowly. 'And I checked just before I came here.'

'No, no, that wouldn't happen anymore. They don't care, you see.'

'I'll be back there tomorrow,' Marina repeated. 'Then you can update me.'

* * *

They were doing the last questions out in the front yard by the swimming pool when Cecile called again. This time, Marina excused herself.

'It's done, Marina.' Cecile's voice was choked.

'What's done?' A wave of fear went through her body. 'Cecile. Listen to me. What happened?'

'There will be no more print edition. We're done.'

Cecile was crying, Marina realized, for the first time since she had met her twelve years ago.

Shopping Spree

CARMEN

Cash, because it was the easiest, came first. Somehow, Uncle Amado already had the wallet out—a simple leather two-fold that held a thousand pesos—and was emptying the front pockets of Luis's cargo shorts of a few more peso bills even before he was laid down on the bed.

And then it was the cards: Luis had two, a Visa from ING Direct and a Mastercard from Wizink Bank. Carmen could see the names in silver, glinting from the bright plastic as Uncle Amado slid them out from the tight slits of the brown leather, placing them on the dresser.

The gadgets came last—the phone that might have their pictures, the laptop that might contain passwords, the camera that Luis may have used to take photos of them when they weren't looking. It happened sometimes. Carmen thought of this as she took the backpack from Uncle Amado, extracting a MacBook Air and a Canon DSLR in a leather case. There were two sketchbooks inside, some thick Pentel pens, and a tin watercolour set.

'Put this back, please,' Uncle Amado instructed, handing over Luis's wallet, nodding towards the backpack that Carmen was still holding. There was still a card left, a driver's license. Carmen nodded after glancing at it. They would put it all back before Luis woke up.

'This, you keep.' Uncle Amado held up a yellow pencil, its sharpened lead point still intact. He tossed it on the table; hardly giving it another glance as the tip quickly broke off against the wooden surface.

'His?'

Uncle Amado nodded. 'A weapon, maybe.' He shrugged his shoulders. 'Got it from a pocket.'

Carmen knew what he was talking about. Her mother, whenever they were in an underground carpark, always chose the sharpest key in her keyring and gripped it between her fingers as they walked the dimly-lit way from the car to the mall's elevator entrance.

'There aren't any more of that, I hope,' she said, thinking of the black pen Luis had been holding when she first saw him at Luneta Park. This wasn't the first time she'd retrieved pointed things from their tourist's pockets, but she wanted to be thorough. Any failure on her part could result in the failure of the whole thing, and she still wanted to do a good job—God knows she needed that money. 'The rest are probably just in the bag,' she murmured, more to herself. She took a step towards the bed. 'I'll check again.'

A noise made Uncle Amado and her glance at Luis's bulky form on the bed, long and dark and still, like a corpse in the dim light of Uncle Amado's bedroom. He was lying on his back, just as they'd placed him there earlier, his beard looking more matted than when they had first met him that afternoon. His muscled arms lay limp and unmoving on both sides of his body. Now, his neck lolled slightly to the left, rendering his head and face away from their sight.

There it was again, soft and muffled, a sound like a grunt coming from his turned head.

'Did he—?' Carmen raised her arm, sensing a strange sensation starting behind her head. Something big and clammy, like a moist hand, felt like it was clamping down the back of her neck.

She watched as Uncle Amado stood still, cocking his ear to one side. 'He's a moaner,' he said, finally, frowning but dismissive. 'It's nothing.'

Carmen didn't say anything more, even as her eyes flicked towards the bed again. *Now*, it was nothing. But who knows what might happen later?

There was a clatter by the door as Auntie Swan burst into the room. She had changed into a different blouse, a lilac floral print with ruffled sleeves that Carmen had seen before. Shopping clothes, Carmen always thought. The pastel shades and lively print made Auntie Swan look softer, friendlier, like one of those vivacious *titas*, aunties who told you their life stories at gatherings, or set up people who were single with their friends' sons or nephews.

'We're leaving,' Auntie Swan announced, and it still both amazed and appalled Carmen how Uncle Amado and she could act as if nothing was amiss, nothing wrong was being done. As if there wasn't a man drugged and passed out in the room where Uncle Amado supposedly slept every night.

You're a part of it, too. Carmen shivered, despite the room's warm, stuffy interiors. And she, too, had gotten used to it—as Max had told her she would. The first few weeks after she'd joined Max and the gang, she'd wondered about the lack of urgency: sure, they were tense and on-edge—no, careful—at the start, while singing at the karaoke or eating with the foreigner at the restaurant. But once they secured and brought their tourist home, Auntie Swan and Uncle Amado went about their business as if they hadn't just kidnapped someone, rendered another person helpless by administering a drug. Carmen had once asked, naïvely, how everyone could be so blasé.

'What's there to panic about?' Auntie Swan, of course, had been the first to speak up. 'That tablet works every single time.' At that time, they had a Korean man who'd they walked to the ATM and who'd, earlier at the karaoke, drained his glass of Ativan-laced beer so quickly, he almost couldn't type out his ATM pin. Carmen remembered how he had crumpled to the ground after that and the dead weight of the man on her shoulders as she helped haul him to the taxi with them. They had taken him home where he had slept for more than thirty-six hours as Auntie Swan and Max went out the mall in Batangas to use his credit card.

Carmen now watched as the older woman fiddled with something on her phone, then strode over to the dresser. She picked up the credit cards, examining them with a frown before casting a disdainful glance at Luis.

'He'll be out for another day,' Auntie Swan declared, arms akimbo.

'Go soon,' Uncle Amado urged in a lower voice, motioning for all of them to leave the room. 'Go,' he repeated. 'No point in being here right now.' Turning to Auntie Swan, he said: 'Where's Max? Is he here?'

'Of course,' Auntie Swan smirked. 'My bodyguard's always ready.' She tucked the credit cards in the back pocket of her jeans, a hard cackle escaping from her mouth.

They had all been ready. Max had peeked at Luis's credit cards the moment he passed out in front of the toilet at Kabayan, then texted the tourist's name as it appeared on the card—to Kuya Fred, their contact at Recto Avenue, where every document could be reproduced. Kuya Fred manned a stall that sold used textbooks and magazines as a front but had been churning out fake documents, forging diplomas, licenses, IDs, land titles and even bank books for a decade. Max needed him to make a fake driver's licence and a passport with Max's photo and Luis's name. A quick send of Max's photo through Viber was all he needed.

Carmen had been sceptical of this, too. Was it really that easy? She knew about stolen credit cards; she also realized that shops in Manila checked IDs before granting purchase. How did the gang do it?

Simple, Max had laughed. Just produce a valid-looking ID at the cashier. In places like SM Department Store, where Auntie Swan and he mostly shopped, the ladies behind the counter were simply required to request for an ID to match the card.

'They don't have the means to actually verify them,' Max said. 'That was what we found out.' It helped that Max has had several girlfriends who'd worked as cashiers at SM, each no longer than three months.

'If things go pear-shaped, the cashiers can always tell their supervisor that they did what was required,' Max told her. 'They did their job, they ticked off what was needed on their checklist.'

Meanwhile, for the fake IDs they needed, the gang would have to learn the tourist's full name and text it immediately to Kuya Fred who would then get to work on producing a fake driver's licence or National ID with Max's photo on it, in two hours or less.

Max, it turned out, and how he looked with his pale skin and grey eyes—was crucial. A genetic accident, he always joked, but Carmen knew his father was French and his mother, a Filipina. Only he could get away with the foreign-sounding last name. Max looked like a foreigner himself. Or a half-Filipino, a balikbayan who'd decided to come home to the Philippines. No one questioned it.

Auntie Swan and Max maxed out the credit cards, mostly at the department store in SM Batangas, in a matter of hours. They bought hundreds of dollars' worth of groceries, more than enough to last them all a month. They bought laptops, phones, flat-screen TVs, and overpriced gold jewellery inside SM Department Store. Auntie Swan, having worked with some of the girls who manned the counter, took charge of that. Max, with contacts developed through the years, easily sold the appliances.

Between Auntie Swan's motherly charm and Max's mestizo looks—his irresistible flirtatious humour, too—the sales ladies and cashiers behind the counters, most on short contracts and who had rapid turnovers—didn't stand a chance. Sometimes, on a whim, Auntie Swan bought pizza from Shakey's, with an extra serving of mojo potatoes. Her favourite, she always declared, and they ate it while their tourist slept upstairs.

Drill

CARMEN

It was 7 p.m. and dark outside. People were coming home from work—or, in this part of their neighbourhood, leaving for work—but this apartment was quiet from where it stood at the very end of a tiny alley, reachable only through a confounding sprawl of narrow streets and walkways. Metro Manila was a dense city, a metropolis that insisted on growing and expanding without really knowing the meaning of urban planning. In large suburbs like Barangay Bicutan, where they all lived, it was worse: houses, made of every material imaginable—wood boards, corrugated iron, cement—seemed like they were built on top of one another, crammed in alleys so circuitous, one could get lost and wander about for hours. That is, if you weren't mugged first. Jason, who lived in the next street and who had served time in Muntinlupa Prison, used to make a living using an ice-pick.

'Can you do the thing?' Uncle Amado gestured towards Luis's phone, laptop and camera laid out beside his backpack on the table. He nodded at Carmen, hesitating by the door, then said, 'I'll leave you to it.'

Carmen nodded as Uncle Amado turned his back and closed the door. The group had come to know her ways, too. They now knew that she worked best when left alone, without any of them hovering in the background. They had come to learn that she had a tendency to linger, oddly unafraid of the tourists that they'd drugged. Maybe that was why they still kept her.

Carmen stood with her arms folded and peered out the window at the street below. She pictured Max and Auntie Swan at SM Department store, in a sprawling mall outside of Manila working quickly, efficiently, tearing through the shops. Using up Luis's credit, his money, whatever he had in those cards.

She didn't want to go to these places. They reminded her too much of her mother, and how she had loved going out, how they frequented the malls, shops, cafés, and restaurants. How her mother sometimes bought things without even looking at the price, tossing packaged food into their grocery cart or grabbing clothes from the rack and heading straight to the cashier—which both awed and terrified Carmen as a child. It made Carmen think that maybe she should care less about her things, that she shouldn't have to take such pains with her toys and clothes. Maybe her mother didn't appear to care because she thought Carmen had it together, was capable of taking care of herself. Maybe she should have let things slide, on her end, so her mother came to the rescue. Be carefree like her father, who flitted in and out of the house, and who sometimes appeared helpless, so her mother fussed over the making of his coffee, the state of his shoes.

Sometimes her father had joined them, but he was always on guard, always looking at his watch, always planning to go. 'Your mother is happy here,' he told her, before he left. Her mother appeared resentful during these times. 'Be good. Be good for your mother.'

Whenever her father had met them and then left them, her mother went on a shopping frenzy, choosing clothes for Carmen, bursting in and out of dressing rooms. And then it was dinnertime and so they needed a meal, in a buffet where her mother fetched food again and again, as if she had not eaten the whole day.

Her mother had continued going to the mall after her father died, but this time she looked carefully at the prices, her grocery cart never filling up the way it had when her father was still alive.

Quit it, Carmen. That's been—how long ago? Fourteen? Max, when they were younger, used to urge her out of her ruminations, the memories of her childhood and of her mother said out loud to Max, and only to Max. He pretended not to know how long ago it had been since her mother left her there in Barangay Bicutan, but he got the year right every time.

* * *

These days she knew better, of course. She'd been a part of it for so many times.

Carmen took Luis's phone and cradled his hand in her own. His palm felt rough, the knuckles gnarly. But there was a pulse, she could feel the faint throbbing of it as she slid her hand across his, stroking his forefinger then finally choosing his thumb. She pressed it on the button. The phone's screen slid open with a satisfying click. She'd seen him unlock his phone as she sat across him in at Kabayan Café, and Luis had made no effort to conceal it.

'*Ayan*. Bingo.' Uncle Amado was smiling. The door had been open, he'd seen the whole thing.

There were several messages, all in Spanish. Carmen didn't bother to look at them. She opened the gallery, where the pictures were, and quickly scanned it. There were no photos of any of them at all, and not even of Luis.

What if the tourist woke up? That had been one of Carmen's first questions, when Max told her about the gang. The drug was effective, Max told her. Some had woken up, yes, but each one had fallen back into a drugged stupor, too weak, too helpless to do anything but sink back into bed, craving that deep sleep. No tourist had managed to fight back.

She looked at Luis again, found herself struck by a familiar wave of pity. She knew it won't be anger he'd feel when he woke up. It would be the feeling of violation, of betrayal. He had trusted them and here they were, emptying his accounts, rifling through his things, keeping him drugged with a potent, possibly fatal toxin.

Stop making things up, she could almost hear Auntie Swan saying. You and your stories. Auntie Swan could be garrulous as hell, but had a distaste for this kind of rumination, the what ifs and what-could've-beens. She always spoke about her fraught, complicated time in Singapore in a matter-of-fact tone.

So, Carmen learned to keep things to herself, the same way she learned to refrain from divulging too much when they were out with their tourist.

Carmen removed Luis's thumb from the phone, carefully laying his hand back to his side. She watched as the icons and apps appeared on the screen, looking like little square treasures. Rewards that she was starting to feel she didn't—had never, ever—deserved.

* * *

Carmen scrolled through the most recent photos on Luis's iPhone camera roll, noting the careful way he shot the things he saw. She pulled up the Notes app, as she always did, because he might have stored his passwords there, as some people foolishly do. She swiped through the apps and opened Facebook. Luis's profile photo was a self-portrait drawing of himself, in bold lines and splashy watercolour, as if done hurriedly. She admired the studied effortlessness of the drawing. She liked that he didn't overshare.

Carmen turned her attention to Luis's blue backpack. There was a tattered Manila envelope holding some prints: a hotel booking in Ho Chi Minh City, filmy brochures on Siem Reap, a sketchbook. It had the birds that Luis had been sketching earlier at the park. Carmen thought he wasn't able to finish this sketch, but he did. She pictured his exhibition, the one he was talking about, in Barcelona. But she couldn't because she's never been to Barcelona or any other foreign city. There were loose papers stuck between the pages but before Carmen could examine each one, Uncle Amado was already calling her for the next task.

Jacket

HAI

The bottle was a million Vietnamese dong. Hai tried to keep his face neutral when he heard the offending number, but Marina seemed to know the wines listed on the fancy, leather-bound booklet the waiter had brought to their table: she didn't even blink at the price. Nothing was under five hundred thousand, and the one that Marina chose, a bottle with a shiny gold label and a thick outline of a mountain, she confidently identified as a 2014 Cabernet from Saint-Emillion, a place he'd never even heard of.

'A good year in France,' she murmured, as if it was an afterthought. 'And a steal at under fifty dollars.' Hai had nodded with purpose, though he didn't exactly know what she meant. All he could think of was that the wine she'd selected with such care wasn't even a full litre, and cost as much as a fourth of his salary. And he didn't understand why, when the waiter came over with a metal ice bucket perched smartly on a stand, Marina smiled and shook her head.

'There's no need for that,' she called out, putting out her hand as if to stop the fellow from advancing any further. Hai watched with secret glee as the waiter froze like a cartoon, eyes wide as he clutched the wine bottle in one hand and the unwieldy stand—high and precarious with its bucket of ice looking like it wanted to fall—on the other. A thick, greasy lock of hair fell like a wet leech on his forehead.

Hai fought the urge to speak to him in Vietnamese. The waiter was about twenty, smartly decked-up in the restaurant's black apron and starched whites, yet looking like he had been plucked from the remote plains of Quảng Bình. Or he could have been from the vast gum tree

fields of Quảng Trị, not unlike Hai himself. Hai sat up and pressed his
lips together, tight. The last thing he wanted was to sound dumb, or
worse, provincial. Instead, he turned to Marina and asked as softly as
he could, 'Do you need my help?'

'Oh no, it's fine,' she said. To the waiter, she asked, 'We can drink it
at room temperature, no?'

Hai shifted his gaze and couldn't help but rejoice at the waiter's
deer-in-headlights look. But when the same waiter proceeded to open
the bottle and poured what seemed to be just a tablespoon of the
expensive red liquid in his glass, Hai realized that he did not know what
to do with it. He stared, alarmed, at the tall, long-stemmed vessel in
front of him, looking like someone's leftover drink. What exactly was
he supposed to do with it?

'Taste it,' Marina piped up, a smile, both sympathetic and amused,
tugging at her lips. The waiter had stepped back, his features mirroring
Marina's expectant look.

'Ah.' Relieved, Hai promptly reached out, his fingers fully closing
on the smooth, curved glass.

'No, don't hold it like that—'

But Hai had already tipped everything down his throat, the scant
liquid barely wetting his tongue. But as he felt the alcohol graze the
insides of his throat—sweet, sour and a little spicy—his first thought
was, *this wasn't what expensive wine should taste like.*

'Well?' Marina's voice had turned curious and smooth, entitled to
an explanation. Hai stole a glance at her just as she was leaning back
languidly in her chair.

'Okay,' he declared, bristling inside, sure it wasn't the right
answer at all. He wiped his lips with the back of his hand, realizing
too late that there was nothing there. He looked down at the front
pocket of his jeans where his pack of cigarettes and keys made a bulky,
squishy outline.

'Just okay?' Marina let out one of her small, vague laughs. She
nodded at the waiter, who filled her wineglass more than halfway. 'Well,
I thought you might enjoy it.'

Hai said nothing. The waiter poured him the appropriate amount,
and as he stared at the burgundy liquid swishing in his glass, a thin

cloak of defensiveness descended on him. Of course, he knew how to drink wine. Of course, he knew what wine tasted like. He just didn't know that you had to taste it first.

* * *

He was sipping, swallowing, trying desperately to get used to the wine's sharpness and acidity, when their dinner came. One by one, plates of carefully-arranged meats in ornate, gold-rimmed plates, delicate bowls of brightly-coloured sauces, quivering little towers of carved, colourful vegetables appeared on their table. A glorious spread, though there was nothing he could recognize except for the miniscule, tear-shaped bowl of *nuoc mam*, whose garish orange hue and fishy, pungent smells announced themselves even before the waiter set it down before them. For this, he was glad. He realized he couldn't live without Vietnam's national dipping sauce, especially in times like these. He felt his stomach growl at the thought of the salty-spicy blend of fermented fish sauce, lime juice, and chili peppers— it made even the simplest, humblest spinach dish taste good. His mother liked using the strongest-smelling fish sauce she could find at the wet market; plus, she always mixed a hefty pinch of Ajinomoto in her nuoc mam.

Hai smiled inwardly at the thought of his mother's cooking, a hundred kilometres away in faraway Quảng Trị. But his thoughts turned to dismay as he surveyed the overflowing table. There were slices of fatty pork, rolls of oily *cha gio*, the deep-fried crab and pork rolls in pyramid-like piles, roasted pieces of chicken, a whole steamed fish. The soup, teeming with water spinach and some kind of crustacean, was served last. It looked like dinner for a family of six.

'Too much, *em*,' Hai blurted out, unable to stop himself even as Marina acknowledged the arrival of each dish with an eager nod and a big smile.

'Oh, Hai.' She leaned back and waved her hands, making a delicate sound, something between a snort and a laugh. 'You sound like my father.'

He kept his mouth shut after that. Hell, he sounded like his *own* father. He watched wordlessly as the waiter poured water into their glasses, tipping the pitcher as ceremoniously as he'd served the wine earlier.

'Enjoy your meal, sir, madam.' The waiter gave a small, comical bow.

Hai cringed. It could only be Manh's doing, this formal, pretentious way of serving the customer. At his new post as Orchid Hotel's assistant F&B manager, Manh must have trained his staff this way. Hai noticed the same pompous, sweeping manner that Manh put on for the diners; he'd been that way even as a waiter back in their days working together at Minh Thanh Hotel.

Hai tried to push away thoughts about his old colleague, fully aware that Manh was lurking somewhere behind the restaurant's fancy, marble-topped bar. *Waiting for me to fuck up,* Hai thought. Well, he was determined not to. He clutched his cigarette pack for a moment, then steeled himself to focus on the food. The dishes looked like sculptures on the plate, and for a moment, he wondered why Marina didn't take photos. Sinh would have posted it all, plus selfies, on Facebook.

But it was Marina in front of him right now, not Sinh. And he was with Marina, not Manh. Manh could go home to his boring Vietnamese wife tonight. Hai had been right in approaching Marina that first night in Minh Thanh. Manh may be today's hotshot, but Hai had Marina— beautiful, rich, a foreigner from Singapore. And right now, she was sitting right here, animated for and attentive to no one else but him.

* * *

Marina paid with a gold credit card and linked her arm into his as they both made their way to the elevator. They had drunk most of the wine but, as Hai had predicted, they'd only managed to go through half of the lavish dinner.

And then they were standing on the sidewalk, face to face. The yellow lights of Orchid Hotel's lobby seemed to fade away, and on the dimly-lit road, Hai could only see the outline of Marina's face as they paused in front of the hotel.

'It's a little cold.' He shook off his jacket and placed it on her shoulders, motioning for her to put the sleeves on.

She giggled. 'Nice dinner, huh?' She slipped on the bulky jacket with one quick shrug, then reached out and touched his arm. 'Shall we go to a bar?'

'A bar?' Hai repeated, feeling a sharp ache in his chest. It was almost 10 p.m.

He wanted to tell her that he would like to take her to a bar, any bar of her liking. In fact, at that very moment, he would very much like to take her wherever she wanted to go.

'Marina, I—' Hai hesitated. He thought of Manh and his big, prosperous belly. He thought of his best friend Phong and his brand-new hotel business. He even thought of Duong—cheery, naïve, forever-positive Duong. If Hai was careless, if he didn't work hard, *if he relaxed*, there was no doubt that Duong could get ahead of him not just in their daily job of securing guests for Phong Nha Hostel, but in everything.

Hai couldn't deny it any longer: all of his friends, moving forward with their lives. And him? He'd long had a growing suspicion that somehow, somewhere between working hard and trying to survive, he had let his guard down. Somehow, in all the years that he'd been working in Huế City, he had fucked up. Manh, Phong, Duong—why, they'd all started from nothing in the beginning, just like him. And look what they had now. They had *something*. He thought of the noodles he gave up every week at Minh Thanh, so he could get ten thousand dong for a pack. He thought of the half-consumed cigarette in his front pocket, carefully-saved for a later smoke. At 6 a.m. tomorrow, he had to go straight to the bus station to run after tourists and tour buses to hawk cheap rooms for a wee hostel that wasn't even his own. Hai felt a black kind of dread settle at the pit of his stomach. He was already thirty-three. He was on the verge of being left behind.

'Hai?' Marina was looking at him with earnest eyes. 'Are we going? Do you know where we can go next?'

Hai looked at the woman speaking to him, her smooth, tanned face framed like an angel with silky hair and twinkling, gold earrings on her ears. Marina—she was still here. Hai felt a flood of hope surge through his insides. He nodded mutely. *Life was still good,* he thought, and this surprised him. It had brought him Marina. She had paid for a special, expensive dinner with a gold card. She had chosen him.

'Thank you, em.' His voice came out hoarse, almost like a guttural sigh. He stepped closer, so close he could feel Marina's soft, even breath on him. He may have caused the wine fiasco earlier that evening, but right now he was sure he was saying something right.

'What?' Her face opened up to a look of pleasure and surprise. 'No, Hai,' she whispered. 'Thank *you*.'

It happened so quickly. Him, bending down to kiss her on the lips. Her, pressing into his chest and kissing him back. Her lips on his, tender and soft—and soothingly unfamiliar.

And then all Hai could think of was, *god, why didn't he do this sooner?* The newness of it felt staggering. His lips felt heavy and warm, but the rest of him was awash with something light and heady.

And then, a loud *beep-beep-beep*. Hai felt Marina stiffen in his arms.

'Shit.' His alarm, set every night at ten o'clock to signal the start of his night shift at the reception desk at Minh Thanh. He had forgotten about it. He was late for work.

'Your phone,' Marina said, pulling away. She looked at the dirty pavement, and he didn't need to see her face to know that she was disappointed. 'Someone's calling you.'

'No.' Hai fished out the phone from his pocket, quickly pressing a button. He swallowed tightly and tried to catch her eye. 'I'm sorry, I have to go to work.'

'Right.' She blew on a lock of hair on her cheek and shoved her hands inside the pockets of his jacket. 'I haven't forgotten.'

'I have to go to work now.'

'Now?' She hung her head and toed the pavement with her shoe. She coughed, still a delicate sound. 'What time does your shift end?'

'6 a.m.' For the first time in a long time, he hated saying it. Less than twelve hours, yet it felt like years. His voice softened. 'I'll see you tomorrow, em.'

'No.'

'You're busy?' He watched in alarm as she continued shaking her head, eyes downcast.

'I'm going back to Singapore tomorrow.'

There was a frightening edge to her tone and when he looked at her again, he saw that something restless and impatient and alarmingly hard had settled on her face. To his dismay, she started tugging at the jacket, unwrapping it from her shoulders.

'Em, em!' He grasped her arms, her soft flesh lost in the garment's cheap, thick padding. 'Listen to me.'

'I need to give this back—'

'Keep my jacket, please.' His hands clutched her upper arms, trying to keep the desperation from his voice. He tried to smile. 'Please.'

'What?' Marina looked bewildered. 'No, no. It's yours.'

'Please, em.' His arms fell back to his sides. It didn't matter now that that jacket had cost him over five hundred Vietnamese dong and was his best one. It was the only thing that kept him warm in the winter, the only one that kept him dry during the rains.

'Why are you giving this to me?' Marina asked, two worry lines suddenly visible on her forehead. 'Are you crazy? How will I give it back?'

Without a word, Hai gave her a hug so tight, he worried for a brief moment if he might crush her ribs.

'Please,' he said again, his voice muffled against the back of her head. 'I want you to keep the jacket.'

'But, why?' Marina's voice came through, high and baffled.

He breathed in the scent of her hair. It smelled like lilies. 'So you can return it to me the next time you come to Vietnam.'

Taxi Uncle

MARINA

The uncle had refused to lift her suitcase, complaining about a pain in his arm. Still, at the last minute, he cradled a corner of her Rimowa with his right palm as she lifted it with a laboured grunt into the trunk of the taxi.

'Why so heavy?' Taxi Uncle's voice rose above the din at Changi Airport's taxi rank and he withdrew his hand as if scalded, shooting her an injured look.

She pushed her suitcase further into the gaping space of the trunk. 'It's only fifteen kilos, uncle,' she said, ignoring his pointed glare. It was already 1 p.m. The flight from Huế to Singapore had started at 6.30 a.m. and had required a change of planes in Ho Chi Minh City, and she was tired. She was glad to be back at Changi Airport—just striding through its overly-chilly, carpeted halls almost felt like she was back in control—but the muggy midday heat that greeted her as she exited through the airport's automatic sliding doors was a mild shock.

Marina fanned herself with her hands, feeling her blouse quickly dampening with sweat. It had been cooler in Huế, for sure. It had felt like springtime, cool albeit a little wet. Huế may have looked rural, even rundown, but most times she'd felt comfortable; there was none of this oppressive, suffocating heat. Why, she'd just worn a thick jacket last night, hadn't she?

When she looked up, she saw that Taxi Uncle had whipped out his phone, forehead creased as he gingerly typed out a text, oblivious to her and the onerous smells of humidity and car exhaust.

She was overcome with a sudden longing to be back in Vietnam. To be in the midst of the messy, haphazard roads of Huế where, Marina was convinced, someone always seemed to be laughing or yelling or crying. She longed for the hodgepodge of people and stalls on the sidewalks—the life, chaos, and emotions at every turn.

She opened the cab's front door and placed her boxy Dior tote on the seat, heavy with Hai's jacket peeking from the stiff top. She felt a warm flush on her face.

'Hey—be careful your bag *ah!*' Taxi Uncle cried, stuffing his phone in a pocket and scurrying to the driver's side. 'Can scratch the dashboard!'

A flare of anger shot up in her chest, but Marina said nothing as she stepped back and slid into the back seat. It wasn't the first time that a taxi driver had yelled at her. How was it that even after twelve years in Singapore, she still hadn't gotten used to this?

This is normal, she told herself as the driver turned the air-con knob to full-blast and eased his way out of the taxi bay to join the rest of the traffic along Changi Road. At the stoplight, he pointedly glanced again at her purse on the front seat, clucking loudly.

Marina could feel her hair rising at the back of her neck. She leaned forward. 'Can you please turn down the air-con, Uncle?'

'I got heart problem, miss.' Taxi Uncle's tone was clipped. He kept his eyes on the road and both hands firmly on the steering wheel. 'Cannot be hot, *leh*. You see? I'm not young, not like you. Not sure where you come from, but I've been living in Singapore for forty-five years, what.'

Marina clenched her teeth. *This is part of it*, she told herself again. Here, she sometimes got scolded for requesting another route to and from the airport, where people in shops and restaurants appeared almost exasperated when you asked for their help. Once, a salesperson at the MAC counter didn't bother to hide her annoyance when Marina refused to buy the foundation she'd tried on—even if it was obvious that it didn't match her skin. She couldn't believe that she'd only begun to notice that there were people who, even if you did something for them, seldom said thank you.

Outside, she glimpsed the bleak edges of the pale-coloured HDBs—government housing where Singapore's eighty per cent lived. Flats, they were called, and she had one herself. Her next-door neighbours were noisy and tended daily to their abundance of potted plants along their shared corridor, but she didn't know the name of a single family member. No one said hello, even in the lifts.

Marina gazed out the window at Singapore's blindingly clean streets. Could she really belong here? She hated that this question often cropped up at the most inopportune moments. This was supposed to be home, and hadn't she'd given up her Philippine citizenship to be one of them? It was supposed to be a step up.

And yet, she knew. In moments like these, it didn't matter if she was a Singapore citizen. This Taxi Uncle was never to know unless she waved her red passport at his face. To this driver, she still looked and sounded like a Filipino.

Marina shifted in her seat and scanned the wide stretch of road ahead of them, looking scrubbed and spotless. Bright fuchsia bougainvillea bloomed at the centre islands and a solid canopy of trees, green and lush, lined the expressway leading to the city. This, too, was normal here. She wondered if she was the only one who often searched Singapore's perfect streets for something, anything that marred its smooth whiteness, its impossibly straight lines. Singapore is so *clean*, everyone kept saying. Singapore is so perfect.

She thought of the places she grew up in the Philippines, of the dense and dirty coastal villages of Carles, where her family had once lived in a bamboo house on stilts right by the sea. The water had always been thick and murky, the scores of trash underneath one of the thrilling mysteries in her childhood. She thought of the messy, traffic-clogged streets of Manila, of their rented bungalow in Project 2 with the crumbling ceilings and cracked cabinets, where things always seemed to come undone and never get fixed. Nothing was ever certain in these places, and to be in a place like Singapore—well, that was always something they always dreamed about.

'Perfection only exists on TV,' her mother used to say as she sat for hours, simmering in frustration or elation—Marina sometimes couldn't really tell—in a broken rocking chair in front of their set, surrounded by the dusty piles and towering mess of their house. What Marina knew for sure was that her mother had given up on a lot of things, and perfection was one of them.

A faint beep was coming from the dashboard. Taxi Uncle was driving too fast and had gone over the speed limit. From the back seat, Marina saw him tense for a moment before automatically slowing down until he was once again driving at Singapore's default fifty kilometres per hour.

She squinted at the other cars outside, shiny and spotless and running at uniform speed. It was mesmerizing, all this perfection. It was what had drawn her to Singapore in the first place. She tried to steady her breath as the taxi turned onto yet another neat-looking road, bringing her closer to her flat. Unless Taxi Uncle threw another fit, she would be at her door in five minutes.

But Marina couldn't relax. The thing was, she'd begun to miss things that weren't perfect. Vietnam had followed her back here, just as the Philippines had twelve years ago when she first fled the place. The country of her birth, where things were never right—and where, sometimes, she dreamed of going back.

* * *

They taxi idled at the last stop light. Marina reached inside her purse, feeling her heartbeat quicken. She didn't want to think about Hai until she reached home, completely alone and safely ensconced in her apartment. She hadn't even worn his jacket on the plane, so thick and bulky it couldn't fit in her suitcase, and so she'd stuffed it in her carry-on. She had not wanted to take it, but he'd been so insistent.

She pulled out her phone and looked at the screen, only to discover that she'd forgotten to switch it back from airplane mode. One swipe, and the messages came in immediately in a series of beeps: a missed call from Cecile. Facebook messages from friends she hadn't even seen in years, forwarding random gifs. And then the one she was reluctant to admit she'd been wanting to see: `Are you arrive?? I miss you, em . . .!!` Hai's message was in its usual needy state: messy and all wrong, with all the unnecessary punctuations. Gazing at the words glowing on her phone, Marina allowed herself a small, secret smile. Inside the harsh coldness of the taxi, its candour and warmth felt like a prize.

She closed her eyes for a moment, leaning heavily on the leather seat. Her Vietnam trip had not turned out crappy despite her predictable mistakes. It had not been the first time she'd been obsessed with someone like Vinh or had impulsive sex with strangers. She'd expected something else when Hai pressed his lips on hers. Instead, his kiss felt just like him: persistent, devoted, and eager, so willing to do things.

She'd been looking at the wrong things all along.

'Here?' Taxi Uncle broke into her thoughts. Marina snapped her head back up just in time to see him nodding to the beige building on the left.

'Yes,' Marina replied, not bothering to hide a big, noisy sigh of relief. She reached for her Dior carry-on at the front seat before sliding out of the taxi towards the trunk at the back.

To her surprise, the trunk was clicked open, but the driver remained unmoving in his seat. She remembered his faulty arm. Right. Why was she even surprised? Taxi Uncle had given up all pretentions; he saw no need to come round the back to oversee her luggage.

She walked slowly to the back of the car and lifted the lid of the trunk dutifully, the handle rough and dusty in her hand. She pulled out her suitcase, not caring if the aluminium case dragged against the taxi's enamelled finish. Then, she slammed the trunk lid shut.

I'm home, she texted Hai, as she turned away and heard the taxi speed off with a screech of the wheels. I miss you, too.

Barangay Bicutan

CARMEN

Barangay Bicutan was a district full of criminals, but it was the only place she felt safe. Carmen had been living in this suburb thirty kilometres south of Manila for fourteen years now, had grown up in its perennially wet, grimy streets with makeshift sidewalks and often dotted with dog shit—playing, walking, running, eating, drinking, even dancing in the rain—since she had been eleven.

Like most poor neighbourhoods in Manila, every sliver of space was used up. There was no order to how these homes were built or laid out. The houses were small and low, the better ones with two storeys were built with whatever material was at hand: galvanized iron and cheap plywood for walls, plastic curtains for doors, unscreened windows. Children and even adults showered at the front of their small homes, practically on the street, using pails and plastic water scoops. She had grown up seeing women hanging the laundry, men sweeping the front of their homes, children bathing outside, pouring water over themselves as they stood on plastic basins, and old men starting to gather at the sari-sari stores, sitting and smoking on the curb. It was as if they had been up for hours while Carmen was sleeping. Part of the landscape.

There was another place where Carmen had felt the same comfort and respite, a place where she was sure she had felt most herself—but that had been long ago, when she had been little. She had guarded it so meticulously in her mind—an image that only she knew: a low-ceilinged bungalow fronted by a white iron fence and low, dwarf coconut trees that sat by a watermelon field in a new subdivision, just thirty-five kilometres from where she was now.

It didn't exist anymore. Carmen may have kept it alive in her memories, but she was close to believing that it had been demolished and razed to the ground. Instead, she had this: Barangay Bicutan, the small cluster of houses packed into several small streets, one of those districts that a long-standing political dynasty had ruled over for three decades, making it one of the poorest, most neglected areas in Manila.

This was where her mother had left her fourteen years ago, when she was only eleven years old, a year after her father died.

* * *

She could still picture the evening her mother brought her to Barangay Bicutan, driving through three hours of traffic, the back seat laden with stuffed toys, a black suitcase, and her pink backpack. In the trunk was the pink bike her dad had given on her birthday just a year ago.

Her mother told her to pack for a big vacation because she was going away. 'Mama is going to the States,' she said. To America so she could buy Carmen all the toys she wanted. Didn't she want to have a Barbie doll, frilly dresses, a pink room? Mama could give her all that, except that she had to be away to work. She wouldn't be long. She would call and she would send for her and they would go and see Disneyland together. Didn't Carmen want to go to Disneyland, like she saw on TV?

They turned right from the main road, her mother having no choice but to slow to a crawl as they drove through a street lined with small houses and filled on both sides with pedestrians and street food vendors, children playing with sticks on the street, past a makeshift basketball court. When they stopped in front of a low house with grilled windows, its walls made of cement hollow blocks still unfinished, they found Nanay Luisa already outside, sitting on her haunches on a small stool.

Nanay Luisa, she would learn, was her mother's third cousin, the daughter of her mother's aunt. Nanay Luisa quickly ushered them inside, where she brought out a chipped plate laden with hard biscuits wrapped in plastic and several glasses of too-sweet, powdery orange juice. Her mother looked slightly embarrassed when they were asked to sit on the threadbare sofa.

'Here.' Her mother fished a small white envelope from her bag. 'I'll send more at the end of the month. That's when they say I'll get paid.'

Nanay Luisa took it and placed the envelope on her lap. 'You'll be earning dollars now.'

'Well, the agency said I'll get paid more when I'm legal.'

'What about your car? Your house?'

'It's already sold, I used the money to pay the agency. The house, we were just renting anyway. Nothing special. We were looking at some in Forest Village, but . . . never mind.'

'You promise to be back?' Carmen asked. She had eaten the biscuits and taken discreet sips of the juice.

'It's just a few months,' her mother said. 'We've already talked about this.'

'A year, is it?' Nanay Luisa interjected, sounding confused.

'The contract said ten months.' Her mother's tone took on a brusque edge.

'That's a long time!' Carmen cried. 'You said it's just a few months!'

'Carmen,' her mother said. 'We've talked about this. I need to go away to America so you can buy all the toys you want.'

'I don't want toys,' Carmen said. 'Dad already gave me lots.'

She saw her mother's eyes narrow. 'Really, Carmen?' Her voice was almost a sneer, but it wasn't new to Carmen. This was her mother's way of talking when she was troubled or disturbed or sad. 'You don't want the Little Twin Stars harmonica, the stamp collection, the Barbie dolls?'

Her mother was angry maybe at her or maybe not at her. Her mother was sad, like her or perhaps more than her, that her father had died. This was why her mother was grumpy all the time. This was why her mother, since they'd gone to her father's funeral, acted like Carmen was such a nuisance.

'I will buy them all for you,' her mother said. 'That's what you want, isn't it?'

Carmen had cried the next morning when she woke up at almost noon in Nanay Luisa's house, tangled in thin blankets and sweating under a whirring electric fan.

No, the sadness—extreme, debilitating, and sometimes unbearable—came after. It came weeks, months, years after—when Carmen, despite Nanay Luisa's reassurances, began to realize that her mother wasn't coming back to get her.

Facebook Mother

CARMEN

She pulled up Facebook and typed, fingers flying. Carmen knew she had entered her name in the search bar too many times. It never felt enough.

And still, she always waited with baited breath. But there was no change: today, as usual, the woman who called herself Nicole Peltier had written on her 'About' page that she was born in Manila, Philippines, was married, and living in Huế City, Vietnam.

Nicole Peltier was not Vietnamese and, from the scant family photos that were there, she didn't even have a Vietnamese husband. Instead, her husband was a blond, unsmiling man with a narrow, unshaven face who looked out of place in group pictures or standing in front of some old Vietnamese monument. They had a teenage boy who looked like his father. Carmen had zoomed in on the boy's face, looking for signs of her mother's face or her own face. She concluded that the boy must be from the husband's previous marriage. And there was a small girl, who had the same dark hair as her mother's, smiling with two front teeth missing. She was holding the boy's hand.

Carmen had scrutinized these photos for years. Nicole Peltier hardly posted, but there were precious photo updates here and there.

This was the name and face of her mother, she was sure, but with a different last name. She had married someone else. She was living somewhere else. Carmen concluded that she had married this man who was based in Huế, Vietnam, or working there. They were expats. There were no pictures of Manila or the Philippines or friends who looked Filipino. It was as if the place of her mother's birth was non-existent.

117

Nicole Peltier had disabled the 'Add Friend' function on her page, and Carmen imagined what she would have done, had she been part of Nicole's network. Would she add Nicole as her friend? Would she send her a message? So many questions were bursting out of her, all the 'whys' she'd thought of all these years growing up with Nanay Luisa and Tito Clem. It kept her up at night. It kept her typing Nicole's name on the bright white search bar over and over again.

The last time she had seen her mother was fourteen years ago, when she was eleven, the year after her father died. Mama could give Carmen everything she wanted, except that Mama had to be away to work. She wouldn't be long, that was what her mother had said. Just wait for the Barbie dolls, the dresses, Disneyland.

It was almost two decades later. There were no Barbie dolls or good dresses or pink rooms. Carmen had never seen Disneyland. There was only Nanay Luisa and Tito Clem. At first, there were carefully-spaced long-distance calls from her mother, and both Nanay Luisa and Tito Clem soothed Carmen by telling her that her mother was coming back, of course. In the next years, when there was a hardly a call every two or three months, they told her that her mother was working hard, and that she should work hard, too. She should be good for when her mother comes back. The years when they could not anymore contact or locate Nicole, despite all the numbers she had given them, were the hardest and also the most essential: these were the years Carmen knew who loved her. It was her Nanay Luisa and Tito Clem who made her feel important, loved, needed.

Was she angry? She was, for a while. After she arrived at Nanay Luisa's house, Carmen was enrolled in a public school where she saw her classmates' mothers at school events and during extracurricular activities. When she bumped into them at the minimart, they sometimes asked her why she was living with her grandparents.

And then Facebook came. She still remembered the first time she found her mother online, remembered the urge to send a message—a long, long letter. She had already thought about it in her mind and her fingers were poised on her phone. Her mother was alive, seemingly just a single click away.

In the end, Carmen logged off and buried her phone inside her bag, her insides aching. The truth was her mother was oceans away, her mother was lost, her mother was cushioned by all these years and the distance—no message could touch her, no message could even make a difference.

In the photos, Nicole Peltier wore mostly jeans and a collared blouse, just like Carmen remembered. There was a photo of her squinting in the sun, her husband and even her children steady and protected in their respective dark glasses. Her mother, she knew, never wore sunglasses, except at the wake of her father. And even then, they had not stayed for long—fifteen minutes? Carmen couldn't remember. But she remembered crying, being dragged out by her mother, who herself was in tears.

Was she bitter? Her mother had taken care of her for eleven years, then abandoned her. Growing up in Barangay Bicutan, she had come to know that worse things happened between mothers and their children. There were mothers who beat their children, mothers who were addicted to shabu, mothers who tortured their kin. There were mothers who killed their own sons and daughters. In her street, there was Mike's mother, who tied him to a chair one day when she was high and bashed him with a metal pole. There were mothers being beaten by their husbands, who, as if it was a natural domino effect, beat their children. Compared to these people, her mother had done nothing wrong, except leaving her alone.

Mr Burak

HAI

It began last year, with a guest named Burak. He appeared late one night and rang the old-fashioned bell at Minh Thanh's reception counter, rousing Hai from where he was sleeping on his cot on the floor.

'Hey, man. I need your help.' He had thick, dark curls and a red football jersey on his massive shoulders. Even from where he lay, Hai could see the dark rings underneath his eyes, which were long-lashed and rheumy. 'Anywhere I can go right now? Clubs? Bars?' The man looked about thirty-five and was chewing gum with an enthusiasm that made Hai think that it was only 9 p.m. He stared but appeared nonplussed even as Hai struggled to get up from the thin, filmy blankets of his cot, fumbling in his pockets to check the time on his phone.

It was past midnight. 'None, sir.' Hai cleared his throat. DMZ Bar closed hours ago. Also, there were three messages from Sinh. He clicked his phone shut without reading them and slipped it back into a pocket.

'No way. Really?' There was a touch of amusement in the man's tone. He squinted his eyes at the chandelier above them and continued to chew.

'Sorry, sir.' Hai stood up and smoothed his hair, his tongue still fuzzy. 'If you want to eat noodle . . .' Hai remembered a bún bò huế stall that was still open two streets away. He himself felt a slight gnawing in his stomach.

'No, I don't want noodles.' The man waved a dismissive hand, then reached into a back pocket and took out an iPhone. Hai watched as his eyes flicked rapidly up and down the screen as he started scrolling. Even if he checked TripAdvisor, Hai thought, he'd see that there would be nothing open. The man paused and looked up at Hai. 'For real, man? No more bars? Nothing?'

Hai remembered checking him in earlier. He had a Turkish passport, with a long name that ended with 'zim.' Or was it 'him'? He was alone and mostly had his head down, busy swiping on his phone while Hai photocopied his passport and activated his keycard. His handwriting was flat and barely legible, as if he couldn't be bothered, when Hai asked him to fill out the registration form.

'No, sir.' Hai stifled a small yawn. 'Everything is closed.' Maybe he should boil water and tear open one of the packets of instant noodles that Sinh gave him, precisely for hungry nights like these. Just barely two years into the relationship, and she was already acting like his mother. Still, he felt a sense of comfort at the thought. And then he wished he had sausages, chopped thin and mixed in with the salty broth the way Sinh prepared it when she stayed overnight in his rented room. Hai did not tell her that the hotel actually gave out instant noodles, and if you didn't want it, you could cash it in at 10,000 per packet. Hai got an extra 200,000 dong every month.

'Know any sexy girls?' The man's solid drawl broke into Hai's thoughts, quickly dissolving the image of a steaming bowl of instant noodles or of the money he was to collect at the end of the month.

'Sexy girls, sir?' Hai arranged his face into something neutral, though he knew what was coming. He groaned inwardly and thought of the well-worn cot he'd grown used to, and how he would again have a night with less than seven hours' sleep. Also, he needed to be up at four o'clock for another guest's early check-out.

'You know—girls.' Mr Zim-Him lowered his phone and flashed a conspiratorial smile at Hai. Hai felt his shoulders relax. Of course, he wanted girls. Hai looked at him. The guest looked patient. He looked smart, wealthy, and decent; he was not one to fuck around with a night receptionist.

'I know a girl, sir,' Hai finally said, speaking slowly. 'Her name is Nhung.'

'That's my man.' Mr Zim-Him grinned and popped a piece of gum in his mouth. He then gave the counter a triumphant slap.

'Can you wait a few minutes, sir?' Hai fished out his phone again, trying to quell a growing sense of panic. He wasn't sure if he had Nhung's number or if she even remembered him.

His mind flitted to a drunken night weeks ago with Phong and two of their friends, and a dozen glasses of *bia hoi*. Phong, of course, had dominated that night's conversation, talking about a girl from Quảng Bình who was a second-year student at the university. He described her as *ngon* and *tươi*—Phong's exact words—which directly translated to 'delicious' and 'fresh'. Phong had 'helped her buy some books', he said. Much drunken ribbing ensued, with the rest of guys accusing Phong of making it all up.

But a girl not older than twenty appeared, riding a scruffy, mud-splattered motorbike, barely ten minutes after a short phone call by Phong. When she hopped off the ghastly bike and stood on the sidewalk, all four men took in the seemingly ethereal sight of her: the abundance of hair artfully piled on top of her head, the skin that, even in the evening light, looked paler than most women in Huế, the ample bust and slim hips, enhanced by a pencil skirt and a sleeveless top that stopped just above her navel. Hai remembered how easily she sat on Phong's lap with minimal prodding, and how, in his inebriated state, he could not take his eyes off the slice of smooth, exposed skin between her waistband and blouse.

Nhung only repeated what Phong had said: that she was a student at university and that she was grateful for Phong's financial help. But she mostly talked about her penchant for shoes and fake Gucci bags, and how she was saving up for a new motorbike. She said she could mix cocktails, her specialty being something called a Long Island Iced Tea.

As it turned out, Hai did not have Nhung's number. But a quick phone call to Phong easily remedied that. *Please let her still be awake*, Hai thought, as he punched out the numbers on his ailing Nokia. His guest had retreated to one of the lobby armchairs, bopping his head to some hip-hop beat playing on his phone.

Nhung was available and asked for a million dong. 'Full sex service,' she said, something that sounded alien to Hai's ears at that time.

'That's . . . around forty-five dollars, you'd say?' said Mr Zim-Him, who finally introduced himself as Burak, when Hai told him the price.

'Yes, sir.' Hai couldn't believe it. Nhung, probably clueless that it was Hai's first time making such an arrangement, had mentioned that he was free to take his ten percent if the guest paid upfront. Hai thought she sounded so professional.

'I'll give you a tip if you can get her to do it without a condom,' Mr Burak said, his voice smooth and confident, as if he was merely requesting for a room upgrade.

'No condom,' Hai texted, as if in a daze.

'Sure.' Nhung's reply appeared a moment later. The words swam before his eyes. 'Five hundred thousand more.'

When Hai nervously relayed this bit to Mr Burak, the man threw his head back in amused laughter, as if he had known this all along. Hai watched him open a beat-up leather wallet then slide something across the counter. 'Here,' he said, 'for your time.'

Hai blinked at the folded pair of 100,000 dong bills, faded and powdery at the edges.

'Take it,' Mr Burak urged, sensing Hai's hesitation. He had one hand on his hip, the other stroking his lip as if already imagining Nhung kissing him. Or him kissing parts of Nhung.

Hai thought of Sinh, of his job as night manager. Then, he thought of the hot, dusty mornings at the bus terminal, of running after cranky, sleep-deprived tourists. And then finally of Phong, crowing about helping a girl buy her books.

'Thank you, sir,' Hai said, and closed a tight fist around the bills.

Overseas Filipino Worker (O.F.W.)

MARINA

When she first arrived in Singapore, it was as if her old self had come back: her naïve self, a part of her that she liked. Twelve years ago, Marina had come to work in this new country not as a wide-eyed, inexperienced new graduate from Manila, but as someone who'd already had years of writing for a broadsheet, someone who'd developed the skill and discipline of editing a magazine, who knew how to work a press conference. It had not been an easy route, but somehow she had become the person who knew how to conduct interviews and produce shoots, to work with models, brand managers, publicists, touchy celebrities. She had dealt with all these over and over again in publications in the Philippines like *Manila Guardian* and *Loweq*, thrown into the fire by her employers before she knew what she was getting into, but here she was. She had never been to Singapore, but she had travelled: to Asia, the United States, parts of Europe.

She said all this with confidence and sincerity—with everything that she'd got, really—to the executives who interviewed her for the lifestyle editor position at *Parcours*, twelve years ago. She had given it her all because it had been the interview of her life. She had mustered up every ounce of courage, gumption, and charm that she had in her— or what was left of it, anyway. What was, essentially, left of herself. Because it was that year twelve years ago when Marina had let herself believe that she could have everything she wanted: the love of a man, real friendship, a job she could do well so that she would never again worry about paying rent or her next meal.

At least she got one thing right. She may have lost everything else, but she had managed to save something that mattered; she had gotten a new job, she had saved her career. Or at least, with this fresh start at *Parcours,* she was about to lay the groundwork for a new one. When she told her mother that *Loweq,* the magazine she worked for in Manila, was shutting down and that she was leaving Manila, that she had found work in a magazine in Singapore, her mother appeared nonplussed. But she acted pleased that she was getting a bigger allowance, for Marina was finally getting higher pay and in Singapore dollars, no less. But she also said that it was just luck, that if Marina had not been at the right place at the right time, someone else would have gotten the job. It didn't matter, her mother said, if that next person didn't have the same level of skill and experience she did. Sometimes, especially during her loneliest moments in Singapore, Marina almost believed this to be true.

But it was during these first few weeks in Singapore, the city where she was about to live and work for the next few years, when she knew that her life was about to change, that Marina felt the old Marina coming back, albeit briefly. It was during this time at the beginning, when she let herself be her old, naïve self. It was at this time, shortly after she arrived in Singapore, that she believed that this city was where she belonged.

* * *

The immigration officers in Manila must have sensed this the day she left the Philippines because, despite her US and Schengen visas and the stamps on her passport, they had given her a hard time—asking her over and over again about the job she was about to take in Singapore and rifling repeatedly through the pages of her employment contract, almost making her miss her flight. Meanwhile, upon arriving on the island state four hours later, she was surprised at her quick passage through Singapore immigration. The petite Chinese official had not smiled at all but peered carefully at her passport, scanned her documents with a trained and thorough eye, stamped and waved her through. It had taken less than five minutes.

Changi Airport, with its thickly-carpeted halls and plethora of shops, looked better than the upscale malls in Manila. On her way to claim her luggage, she passed numerous shops, noticing that several of them were manned by Filipinas.

It made her think of Manila's overcrowded SM malls, the restaurants overflowing with cheery waiters, the clusters of sales ladies in clear stockings and black sandals who hung around the shelves complaining loudly about their boyfriends.

At Changi Airport, she followed the signs to the taxi stand, and balked at first at the long line that snaked through the bars. But she soon found that the line moved with impressive speed, and in less than ten minutes she was inside a taxi driven by a middle-aged man who instantly recognized the address she showed him.

The magazine had arranged for her to stay at a serviced apartment for three weeks. In Manila, the only serviced apartment she knew was as expensive as a five-star hotel. A real estate agent, also courtesy of *Parcours* and something she hadn't had before, had been corresponding with her to help her find a flat. A flat, for no one really said apartment here. Marina thought it sounded better, though she couldn't help but visualize a monotonous room with low ceilings.

It was a Saturday, and so she couldn't call anyone at the office. She was due to start on Monday. Her serviced apartment was near a place called Clarke Quay, and, her agent told her that if she took a bus, it would bring her to Orchard Road where all the shopping took place.

'Almost two kilometres of shopping malls,' the agent said with amusement and also, a bit of pride. 'You know us, we like to shop, shop, shop!' It sounded like chop, chop, chop and Marina thought of all the money one needed to actually buy something, but she laughed anyway.

She made it to Orchard Road, where the malls were connected. It was the day after she'd checked-in, and she felt a kind of triumph and exuberance walking along the wide sidewalk, the widest she'd ever seen. People were carrying shopping bags and walking at a faster clip; it all seemed so organized, so right. There were bus stops and pedestrian lanes that turned red and green at the right moments.

The people were dressed in mostly black, white, and grey, in expensive, sleek-looking outfits. A woman in a black gauzy skirt and a cream-coloured top that was bare at the shoulders glided past her.

I could wear that, Marina thought. *I could be that woman. I could belong here.*

Red Planet Hostel

CARMEN

They had tucked him inside a taxi, propping him up against the worn and smelly synthetic-leather back seat. Luis, with his blond hair and pale body, glowed like a sleeping angel against the taxi's dark confines.

'He'll come to when you get there,' Uncle Amado assured the driver, as he always did. 'Sorry, *pare*. These foreigners, they just love to drink, don't they?' The cabbie, who looked not older than twenty-five, was apprehensive at first. But all his anxieties seemed to vanish, replaced with a happy smile, with the extra three hundred pesos Uncle Amado pressed into his palms. Too generous for a drive that was less than three kilometres away.

Uncle Amado apologized again, as he always did, saying that he had to go home himself, back to his wife in faraway Cavite two hours away. So could he please just drop off his drunk friend at his hotel? 'Of course,' the driver said, pocketing the crisp bills. He even called Uncle Amado 'sir'.

'Yes, sir. No problem,' was what the driver said. And off he sped into the night with Luis at the back, in the direction of the Red Planet Hostel.

Manila Bay

CARMEN

There seemed to be nothing special about him, but Carmen knew he was the one. She had spotted him after walking a few hundred meters along Manila Baywalk, a two-kilometre stretch of coastline that ran parallel to Roxas Boulevard, past the Manila Yacht Club, the Cultural Centre, and the US Embassy where she saw, daily, long lines forming outside. Manila Bay's famous promenade, and the city's most popular sunset spot. Tourists were still a slow trickle this morning; except for the mainstay vendors who'd set up their wide, multi-coloured umbrellas selling soft drinks, snacks, and cold bottled water all day, there weren't very many visitors.

Carmen watched the man take his phone out, take a couple of photos of the water.

'Hi, sir, excuse me?'

'Oh, hello.' The man nodded at her.

She extended her arm, offering her phone. 'Can you please help me take my picture? I'm so tired of selfies.'

'Of course.' He took her phone and pointed it at her. 'Smile!'

Carmen felt her face stretch as she pulled her lips into what she hoped was an enthusiastic smile. 'It's for Facebook,' she said, after a few moments.

'There,' the man said, when he handed the phone back to Carmen. 'I'm sure it's going to be your next profile pic!'

Carmen nimbly scrolled through the five or so photos he had taken, not really seeing them. 'Thank you, sir! By the way, I'm Camille.'

'Stefan,' he said. 'Are you from here?'

'Yes, I'm Filipino,' Carmen said. 'But I'm not from Manila. I'm from Iloilo.' She straightened her back and smoothed the front of her blouse, which she hoped had not yet sustained any sweat marks. Max had always stressed the importance of looking well, of not looking shabby. Shabby feels needy, he said.

The man's eyes flicked at something behind Carmen. 'Are you alone?'

'Oh no,' Carmen said, looking around. 'I'm with—'

'Hello, hello! *Kamusta?*'

'Ah!' Carmen felt a tiny prickle of relief. 'They're here. My uncle and aunt, sir.'

'Call me Amado.' Uncle Amado stepped from behind her, looking shrunken next the tall foreigner. 'And my wife—'

'Swan. I'm Auntie Swan.' Auntie Swan had swiped on a touch of lipstick, the bright, pinkish coral shade like neon against her dark skin.

'He helped take my pictures while you were gone,' Carmen said, waving her phone again.

'She's crazy about pictures,' Auntie Swan told Stefan in her best English, glancing jestingly at Carmen. 'All pictures of her, of course.' Her familiar cackle rose above Uncle Amado's chuckling.

Stefan laughed with them. 'You are funny. You Filipinos, you are always smiling. A good people!' He gave them a rueful grin. 'Not too many of those where I come from.'

'Oh!' Auntie Swan's widened as her hand flew to her mouth. 'Where are you from, Stefan?' She started walking slowly, back towards the promenade.

'Belgium,' he said. 'My city is called Gent. Do you know of it? It's very cold there now.' He nodded at Uncle Amado's gestures to follow Auntie Swan.

'Belgium? Ah!' Uncle Amado said, falling in step with Stefan. 'That's very good, my friend. A beautiful place, beautiful Europe!'

'Oh, you've been there?' Stefan leaned forward, eyes lighting up. 'My town, yes, it's very beautiful, very old.'

'No, no, I haven't been there,' Uncle Amado said, with an amused shake of his head. 'But we have one thing in common.'

'Oh?' Stefan leaned closer, his crinkled, smiling eyes shifting back and forth between the two elders. 'What's that?'

'We're tourists, too!' Uncle Amado declared, then burst into laughter.

Stefan's broad shoulders relaxed, his face lighting up as Uncle Amado's hyena-like sounds floated through the promenade. 'You're not from here, either?'

'Not from Manila,' Uncle Amado said. 'We're country people. From the province. Our hometown is in Iloilo, down south. Have you been there? We flew up here to visit our grandchildren.'

Carmen hung back to let them talk. Stefan was staying in a hotel in Ermita, he revealed, and was just starting his vacation in the Philippines.

Uncle Amado's deep, melodious voice cut through her thoughts. 'Listen,' he said, pausing along the path as if an idea had just come to him. He turned to face Stefan, the waters of Manila Bay a murky blue-grey behind him. 'Can we make it up to you? You've been so kind to us.' He nodded towards Auntie Swan. 'It's her birthday today and we want to celebrate.'

'Oh, really?' Stefan's eyes widened. He spread his arms, as if about to give Auntie Swan a hug. 'Happy birthday!'

'We're having lunch to celebrate.' Auntie Swan clasped her hands together. 'Would you like to join us?'

Stefan looked regretful. 'Today?' He shook his head, his thin lips set together. 'Ah, no, sorry. I'm planning to board a bus later, so I don't think I have the time.'

Carmen's ears pricked up. 'A bus?' She cocked her head to one side. 'To where? Back home or . . .?' She let her voice trail off.

'Zambales.' This Stefan, he was so trusting, so open as they all were. A question more than a statement, and to Carmen a dead giveaway that he wasn't at all sure of where he was going. 'Have you heard of it?'

'What a coincidence!' Auntie Swan exclaimed, throwing her hands in the air. 'We're going there, too!'

Stefan looked dumbfounded. 'You are?'

'Yes, we are.' Amado's voice was smooth, his tone confident. 'How long is your stay in the Philippines?'

'Just a week,' Stefan replied. 'I'm leaving in four days, and I want to squeeze in a little beach trip.'

'Have lunch with us first,' Auntie Swan urged. 'Do you like Filipino food, hijo? We can take you to a good one!'

'Yes, yes,' Uncle Amado said. 'And it comes with a karaoke!'

Carling's Karaoke

CARMEN

They brought him to the usual place, the one on Taft Avenue where the pork dishes had too many fatty pieces and Uncle Amado knew the waiters. Carling's Karaoke always felt in want of business: it was nearly twelve noon, lunchtime, and yet only one other group was there, their table already laden with half-litre bottles of Red Horse, oily fried peanuts, and a single platter of *bopis*. It made Carmen's mouth water as they shuffled through the door: a pungent whiff of the dish's mix of minced pig's lungs, heart, onions, and tomatoes sautéed in spicy oil.

She paused by the entrance, even as she felt the others drift forward. Her 'family' was already heading to the outdoor area at back of the restaurant, Auntie Swan holding on firmly to Stefan's arm as if for support. She found them already seated in one of several *nipa* huts at the back, what was supposed to be a garden just a bare, cement-walled yard snaking with broken stone paths, dirt flooring, and a smattering of dusty Santan bushes planted like an afterthought along the edges.

'We've already ordered,' Uncle Amado declared as she squeezed her way around the bamboo table built into the hut's centre, in the usual, pre-planned arrangement: she across from Stefan, who was sandwiched in between Auntie Swan and Uncle Amado. They had moved quickly with the order, and Carmen wasn't surprised; food and drink was the most crucial here.

'You've to try the sisig, Stefan,' Auntie Swan said, her hands on the table, fingers worrying the already-broken plastic of the laminated menu. She waved it towards him. 'It's delicious.'

135

'Sisig?' Stefan said. 'What a very special name!'

'Crispy bits of pork ears, a little liver and fried chopped meat, ooh!' Auntie Swan's voice floated above them with a pointed confidence, as if she'd devised the recipe herself. 'It's what we pair with beer. What you'd call . . . local bar bites!'

Everyone laughed, but Stefan was looking beyond Carmen's shoulder, at the spot they had just passed.

'Excuse me, but—' Stefan was pointing at something by the door. 'What is that?'

He was pointing at a shelf where the food was displayed on metal trays. The trays were uncovered and deep enough to hold stews and chunky stir-fries, even soups. Carmen knew without checking that there would be *adobo, sinigang, bangus, dinuguan*—meaty, pungent stews she grew up with in Barangay Bicutan that held up all day without refrigeration or reheating.

'Why, that's the food!' Auntie Swan blurted out. 'Turo-turo! Point-point! We choose what we want and they'll serve it to us. That's what it means.'

'Local food,' Uncle Amado chimed in. 'We said we'll be treating you to authentic Filipino dishes today, didn't we?'

'Yes, yes,' Stefan murmured, eyes flicking back towards Auntie Swan and Uncle Amado. 'But is it heated?'

Carmen could see the bewildered frowns of the older couple, obviously thrown off guard. They'd never had—and she realized this just then—a tourist with them who had questioned the kind of food they were eating, or how it was prepared.

'Well, no, you just—' Auntie Swan started, face looking blank.

'We'll ask them to heat it up for you,' Carmen said, in her best assuring voice.

'No, it's all right,' Stefan said, attempting a weak smile. His Adam's apple bobbed. 'To be honest, I'm not really hungry.'

'It'll be okay, Stefan,' Carmen said, in what she hoped was a soothing tone. She tapped his arm lightly and nodded at him. 'It's perfectly safe. Just try it.'

The foreigner seemed to relent, his shoulders relaxing. He scratched at a spot behind his ear. 'We could have a drink, maybe.'

'A beer, then?' Uncle Amado's voice was caramel.

'Yes, yes,' Auntie Swan piped up, loudly. 'We can't eat without drinking beer, and we can't drink beer without eating!' As if on cue, a server appeared with several plates containing modest servings of sisig, liempo, a beef soup.

Talk about them, Max always told her, and always listen.

'Where else have you travelled, Stefan?' Carmen asked, brightly. She glanced at everyone else around the table, as if urging everyone. What was this guy's interests? What would make him stay? What would make him eat—for god's sakes. Uncle Amado and Auntie Swan had been talking too much about themselves, as they tended to, and she was reluctant to tell the Camille story. 'How many countries have you been to?'

'Ah, let's see.' The foreigner blinked then wiggled his fingers as if doing a silent count. 'Thirty, maybe thirty-five countries?'

'And where are you going next?' Uncle Amado asked.

'I was thinking Hong Kong, then Singapore.'

'Singapore?' Auntie Swan's eyes narrowed. 'Expensive city. I used to work there!'

'Oh!' Stefan's eyebrows shot up, though he smiled again. 'You did?'

'A long time ago.' Auntie Swan turned dismissive. 'But tell me, how long will you stay there? And in a hotel, right?'

'Hostels, mostly.' Stefan shrugged. 'I'm flexible. I'll see what I can find. I guess you could say that I'm also spontaneous!'

'Not me,' Auntie Swan said, making clucking noises with her tongue. 'I would need to save up. Good for you, you're prepared! Financially, I mean.'

Stefan's voice turned languid. 'Well, I'm used to travelling. I guess I've figured it out.'

Carmen murmured in approval and glanced at Uncle Amado. The conversation has turned more relaxed, more revelatory, but it was taking too long. Stefan still had not eaten anything.

Uncle Amado held her eyes and turned his head, slowly, from side to side. Carmen knew what he meant. Not yet. There was still time.

She turned back to the tourist. 'Stefan?' she asked, lightly. 'Are you really not hungry?'

Stefan was taking pictures. He had turned away from them and was holding his phone above his head, shooting the wilting, dirty garden, the shelves with the food, the screened walls of Carling's Karaoke.

And then he turned back to face them, this time raising and pointing his phone at them as if to frame a shot.

'Oops! Don't take our picture!'

It was Auntie Swan, holding up a palm with fingers splayed as if she was a traffic officer trying to stop an oncoming vehicle.

'What? Why?'

'I never take pictures when it's my birthday,' Auntie Swan declared. She was backpedalling, furiously. '*Dios ko.* Put that phone down, for goodness sakes. Stefan, please. It's—it's bad luck.'

Stefan looked confused. 'What?' He looked around the group. 'Is this true? I've never heard this thing before.'

'No. Really! It's true!' Auntie Swan was nodding her head so vigorously, babbling before any of them could say anything.

'I'll just take Camille's photo then.' Stefan started typing the code on his phone. 'Better, let's take a photo together!'

'Later.' Carmen shook her head, trying to sound calm. 'Let's give in to what my aunt wants. She's the birthday girl, after all. Let me take your photo, Stefan.'

'Enough of this picture-taking!' It was Uncle Amado. He turned to the foreigner. 'You're our guest. Let's get you a beer! You okay with that?'

'A beer?' Stefan paused, then put his phone down. 'All right. Just one, please.'

'Gio, my boy!' Uncle Amado called out to the thin guy with greasy hair covering his ears, hovering with a scuffed tray in his hand. His Carling's Karaoke T-shirt hung limp on his shoulders. Carmen thought he looked ill.

'Sir?'

'Would you get us a bucket of San Miguel, 'nak?' Uncle Amado looked up at Gio, the little folds on his chin doubling. 'Special. Okay?'

'Special.' Gio nodded. 'You got it, sir.'

The beer arrived warm, the squat, dark amber bottles of San Miguel lined up neatly on a tray. Gio placed a metal bucket with ice on the table alongside five glasses.

'*Salamat*,' Uncle Amado said, nodding approvingly at the drinks that Gio had set up on the table. He patted Gio's elbow. 'You have a nice coffee this afternoon.' Carmen knew it was code for I'll pay you later.

He turned back to them, raised a beer bottle. 'Today, we celebrate,' Uncle Amado declared, as Auntie Swan swiftly passed the glasses around the table. Uncle Amado made a big show of opening the beer and pouring it into Stefan's glass.

'Enough—I'm good, thank you,' Stefan said, holding out his palm the moment Uncle Amado paused.

'Ice?' Uncle Amado was poised with an ice cube, the tongs daintily held in his thick hand. Without waiting for an answer, he released the ice cube.

'Oh, no.' Stefan covered his glass with his hand, the ice cube slipping off the back of his palm and into the bamboo floor.

Carmen struggled to keep her face impassive, trying not to give in to the panic she was starting to feel. Uncle Amado's old tricks had worked so beautifully before. It wasn't going so well here. They should have let Stefan go when they could. But they've gone this far, and in their playbook, if someone had gone this far, they should at least get something out of it.

'Are you sure?' Uncle Amado was undeterred. 'I'm sorry, anak, the beer is not cold. We don't want you to drink warm beer.'

'It's fine.' Stefan was firm. 'No, really, I'm good!'

Carmen looked at where Gio the waiter was now serving the other customers in the next hut. It was not the first time that Uncle Amado had enlisted the young man's help, and it had been so subtle, so hidden, and so clever, no one thought that it would even work.

And it was so simple. Crushed Ativan tablets mixed with water, then frozen in plastic trays and served as cubed ice—what could be simpler? Gio was paid to put the ice trays in a hidden spot in the restaurant's freezer, a reach-in metal ice box that was rusty along the corners parked at the back of the store, then serve it at their table once he got the signal from Uncle Amado.

'We don't have to worry where to put the damn thing,' Uncle Amado had told them earlier, back at his apartment. 'There's no need to crush the tablets on the spot, sprinkle it on food, whatever.'

'Isn't Gio worried about his job?' Carmen had asked. 'If Carling's manager finds out . . .'

Uncle Amado had snorted. 'Gio? He gets nothing at Carling's. Not enough to pay anything, at least. Believe me, this boy needs the money.'

No one had said anything much after that.

Auntie Swan spoke up now. 'Camille dearest, do me a favour? Can you double check on Max? He said he'll be here fifteen minutes ago!' She turned to Stefan. 'My favourite nephew, that Max. He wouldn't want to miss this birthday lunch!'

That was when Carmen knew they weren't done. They were still keeping Stefan.

Marina's Move

MARINA

It was over before she knew it. The announcement was made on Monday, and by Friday noon she was out on the sidewalk just outside the *Parcours* offices, sweaty and burnt by Singapore's signature sunshine beating on her shoulders as she stood on the curb waiting for her Uber, two big boxes of her office things at her feet. She'd been gazing at everything around except those two boxes: twelve years' worth of stuff that she thought she needed to do her job as an editor at *Parcours*— reduced to what could fit into two brown squishy pieces of cardboard. More than half of *Parcours*'s print staff, including Cecile and her had four days to pack. It took Marina only a day to gather up her magazines, press releases, files, and books. She had been in a daze as she pulled out things from drawers, cleared out the stuff underneath her desk and handed Rosa, *Parcours Digital's* associate editor, her files on the lifestyle section.

She'd barely had time to think. The week had gone by so fast, and yet it couldn't be over fast enough. It was ruthless, this sudden change. It was like an abandonment, a betrayal—and yet they all knew it would happen, didn't they? All those long lunches spent speculating about Giselle's next move, about *Parcours*'s future.

They knew it would happen. But, not this soon. Not this quickly. There was a news item in *The Straits Times* that week, announcing the shift.

Marina had not told anyone. Not even her mother. No, not yet. *What have you done?* That would be her mother's first question. Things that went wrong were her fault, her mother would say.

She did not even tell Hai, even though he had been texting her all week. He had even emailed, saying he created an email account on Gmail just so he could email her.

She wasn't the type to spill it all out, anyway. There were twenty-two people who were laid off; it wasn't a big magazine. And strangely, she had counted on the knowledge—that it was not just her who'd been let go—as a consolation.

Somehow, the farewell emails that had to be sent out were much harder. 'Reconceptualizing the magazine', was how Giselle had put it, and that was the term that they were supposed to use in all their farewell emails. Marina had dutifully used it, though it didn't make it any easier or less humiliating. She didn't know how many times she'd copy-pasted the line, 'The magazine has chosen to publish exclusively online . . .' All week, she'd been seized with the need to email every contact she knew personally. She couldn't imagine sending out a mass email to everyone she'd been working with in some way or the other, all these years. It wasn't that she felt emotional, it simply felt automatic. It was like being in grief all over again: she needed something to keep her mind off what she had just lost.

Yet, she felt humiliated by it all. The replies had been sympathetic, even compassionate. Everyone had been so happy to have worked with her. They were just words, yes, even protocol when someone moves. Singapore's publishing industry wasn't any different from the rest of the world's: no one wanted to lose contacts, everyone still wanted to use everyone as much as they could, if they still could.

Zambales

CARMEN

They had not gone out of town for more than a year and it made Carmen nervous. But everyone else had acted so sure, even Max. After all, they had a playbook: if the tourist refused to go out with them and he had potential then they would invite him out of town. If he declined the food they offered or if he somehow spilled that he was going out of town, the entire 'family' would say that they were heading to the same town, too. Stefan, whom Carmen had befriended that morning in Manila Bay, was only just starting his week-long holiday in their country. That meant that his bank accounts were still full, and he had cash reserved just for his trip.

And now it was agreed: they were all going to Zambales, 135 kilometres away from Manila. Even Max, whom they'd called up at the last minute at Carling's Karaoke, was going.

The journey took five hours. It was past eight in the evening when the bus pulled in at the terminal in Iba, the capital town of Zambales. Like most of the towns they passed, this one was poorly-lit, the roads lined with streetlights so dim and spindly they felt like an afterthought. Most of the stores they passed were shuttered for the night, but Carmen noticed two small carinderia stalls selling cooked food, less than a kilometre away from the bus terminal.

'Where did you say your friend was?' Carmen asked Uncle Amado in Tagalog, so Stefan wouldn't understand. She took the hand that Uncle Amado offered as she jumped down the bus. The aisle was narrow and passengers were still grabbing their bags. She was the last one to alight among their small group and it felt good to stretch her legs.

143

'Botolan, the next town,' Uncle Amado replied. 'It's just seven kilometres from here, and we can take a tricycle.' He nodded towards the growing line of small vehicles similar to tuk-tuks, just outside the terminal.

It had taken some of Auntie Swan's aggressive charm, tempered with Carmen's soothing reassurances to convince Stefan to press 'Cancel' on an app in his phone where he had booked a night in Zambales—and instead stay with them in another resort, one that Uncle Amado had started arranging as soon as it was evident that they were going out of town. Why spend your holiday solo when you could be with friends like us? They had cajoled, crowding around him to look as he tapped away on his phone. And why pay a hundred dollars a night for a cookie-cutter resort when he could stay with them in a local place for free? Auntie Swan's pointed practicality had been so convincing. And Uncle Amado had already worked out the logistics; it took him a single call to a friend who owned the resort, to ask if they can have two fan rooms.

And so it was settled: Stefan would travel with them to Zambales, and they would visit the sights together.

From Carling's, they walked with him to his hotel to get his things. Stefan had not drunk much of the beer, had sipped it so slowly despite their numerous toasts amid Auntie Swan's passionate lamentations. 'It'll be bad luck if you don't eat anything on my birthday,' she'd pouted. Still, Stefan was steadfast, more stubborn than they'd thought. He had refused the rice. He had eaten some of the sisig, but that didn't count: he'd made sure that everyone has had a bite first.

* * *

The thing with going out of town was that they could get away with more, with less: more cash, more ATM withdrawals, more credit card purchases—but with far less risk. Isolating their tourist meant being away from Manila and all its hard, meticulous suspicion, its big-city zealousness. It meant being able to focus more on their target, instead of worrying that some nosy, hardened urban dweller—used to the unsavoury goings-on of a metropolitan city like Manila and who'd surely not hesitate to call the cops on them—would butt in, create a racket or worse, expose their plans. People were just different once you get out of Manila and into the outskirts; they were kinder, less suspicious, and more forgiving.

Carmen had never really thought of this until Max, sure that he'd reeled Carmen into the modus, explained that it was important to isolate their tourist and what better way to do that than to bring him to a beach town like Batangas or Baler or even further like Zambales where he'd be the lone person in a strange, new town. He would be dependent on them.

There were huge malls on the outskirts of Metro Manila, manned mostly by people in the province who had a completely different attitude from the hard-faced cynics who, used to the city's petty crimes, guarded the store counters in Manila with a stricter hand.

A few hours at the karaoke meant getting some cash, a few credit cards. Maybe an ATM withdrawal, as Auntie Swan always wanted. Going out of town, their tourist out cold in a room while they maxed out the credit cards meant that they could put everything back as if nothing had had happened. The tourist wouldn't even know that he'd been fleeced, or that his cards had already been drained useless. It had worked twice or thrice, when Carmen was already working with the group.

The last time they had gone out of town, they had taken two Swedish women. That was different, because it was well-planned. The women were in their mid-twenties and were the ones who insisted on going out of Manila. They were eager for an adventure and said yes easily. Laiya, the beach town they chose, was not much nearer but Uncle Amado, Max, and Auntie Swan knew the place. They had only to take a van and were already at a seaside resort three hours later. The two women already wanted to drink beer on the way, and were hungry once they arrived, and so it was easy to feed them. Just before the drug fully kicked in, they turned giddy, rambling incoherently in their language as Carmen led them to the ATM, carefully holding their fingers as they typed in their PINs. They were oblivious to the wads of peso bills that the machine spit out and were quickly pocketed by Auntie Swan. They laughed on the way back to the resort, only passing out once they were laid, side by side, on the double bed. They were still sleeping the next day, as Auntie Swan and Max went to the town centre mall with one of their credit cards. They were roused by evening, tucked into the van, and were sleeping once more as they drove back and returned to their hostel in the city.

* * *

'Stefan?' Carmen asked, once they've hopped out of the bus. 'Are you hungry?'

The foreigner nodded, looking wan. 'I could eat.'

'Great, man.' Max smiled, reaching out to pat Stefan on the back, his movements easy, amiable. 'I'm famished myself.' He looked nothing but refreshed.

'We can go to the resort first,' Uncle Amado said. 'It's not far. Fifteen minutes and just a tricycle ride away. Keep your eyes peeled for Tatoy's Resort.'

'We can have a little party there,' Max announced. 'A simple *salu-salo.*'

Carmen noticed that Stefan listened more to Max than to anyone else in the group. 'I guess it's too late now,' he said. 'We could check out the sights tomorrow, right?'

'For sure,' Carmen said, steeling herself to sound confident. She didn't really know what was there in Zambales, except that it was close to Subic, a more prosperous district just an hour's drive away and where Auntie Swan and Max planned to use the credit cards. She wished it would happen already.

'I've been Googling places to go,' Stefan continued. 'There's a good beach here, called Pundaquit.' A frown appeared between his brows. 'Not sure if I said that right. But we can go there to swim tomorrow morning. There are some really beautiful coves, too.'

Carmen nodded, though she had not never heard of these places. 'Sure,' she said. 'We'll do whatever you want tomorrow.' Tomorrow of course, would be a completely different day, one that Stefan could never imagine.

* * *

'Are you all just staying in one room?' Stefan stuck his head through their door. Tatoy's Resort reminded her of the ones they go to in Batangas: spartan and barracks-like, the six rooms shaped like boxy sheds, lined up one after the other.

'Why, yes we are all staying in one room,' Auntie Swan said, removing her shoes and rubbing her toes together.

Uncle Amado lit a cigarette and stood from where he was sitting at the edge of one of the twin beds. He had not brought anything. No one, really, had much to bring. Carmen felt a sparseness in the room that was even more palpable because of the lack of bags. None of them cared if they had a change of clothes or if there was soap and shampoo at the resort—details that Stefan had blabbered about as they walked with him to his hotel in Ermita so he could get his stuff.

'We're family, the more the merrier!' Uncle Amado quipped.

Max clapped his hands together. 'Let's get something to eat.' He looked steady and calm, but dark shadows had begun to appear under his eyes.

'Yes!' Stefan brightened. 'Are there any good local restaurants around?'

'It's better if we buy food outside and eat here.' Max gestured towards the trees and tables outside.

'Are you sure?' Stefan looked doubtful again. 'It's dark.'

'It's breezy out, and besides, this is Filipino style.'

* * *

The food arrived without fanfare: fried fish, pork adobo, *chicharon bulaklak*, and cold rice in small, thin plastic bags that Auntie Swan and Uncle Amado bought from one of the food stalls near the bus station, as well as three mangoes wrapped in newspaper. 'Mango season,' Uncle Amado said, simply, when he handed the crumpled package to Carmen.

Max had called them over to one of the three nipa huts, lit by a single yellow bulb.

'This is cool,' Stefan said. 'It's a staple in your country, these straw structures.'

Carmen wanted to say that it wasn't straw, it was nipa and *amakan*, a Philippine palm—but of course it was pointless. Instead, she watched as Auntie Swan swept a thick arm across the table to clear it of fallen leaves and small debris scattered on the painted plywood.

'Too bad we don't have karaoke,' Auntie Swan said. She laid out paper plates, procured from the 7-Eleven that they'd passed earlier. 'But tonight's task is to eat!'

Sketch

CARMEN

She felt the blood drain from her face, as if a colossal gust of wind, invisible and all-encompassing, was threatening to suck it all away. There she was, in black and white and brown, a combination of cleverly-drawn lines formed with such precision, as if magically representing the curving smallness of her eyes, the roundness of her nose, the fullness of her cheeks. Luis had deftly coloured-in and shadowed the contours of her face and so she looked full and fleshed-out, a three-dimensional head on a piece of paper. The reporter had not named any of them, but there was no doubt it was her, Carmen Maranan, who was up there on TV.

The photo of the sketch flashed on screen for less than a minute, but the image of her face in black ink was seared into her mind, as perhaps it would be on the thousands, maybe millions who tuned in to *Aksyon Pilipinas*, Rick Biglang-Awa's news and features show every night.

Carmen grabbed her phone and searched for the *Aksyon Pilipinas* page on Facebook. The news item was already there, livestreamed and then posted as a video. Rick's booming voice somehow sounded louder on her phone, the clip of the drawing with her face even more unnerving above a stream of comments. Nine hundred seventy-five shares. She closed the page, clicking her phone shut.

Had their neighbours seen it? Would they report her and her family to the police?

Auntie Swan immediately launched into a mini tirade about being careless while Uncle Amado made soothing sounds, something he did

149

when he was thinking hard about something, when he couldn't decide about something but wanted to stall for time.

She looked at their stained ceiling, then closed her eyes, the chatter receding to a blur. Carmen thought of her mother. Would Nicole Peltier recognize her if she saw Carmen now, fourteen years later?

It was odd that she thought of her mother at a time like this. It was odd that she thought of another person at a time when she should have been feeling afraid for her life.

It was not right that she felt this longing when she should have been feeling fear. But then wasn't that what scared people did, turn to their family? And didn't she have a family right here, right now, who had taken care of her for fourteen years? She had Nanay Luisa, Tito Clem, and Max. They had been there for her. Why was she still thinking of someone who had already forgotten her? Who people said had abandoned her?

She should be thinking of how to hide—worrying, as her family was surely doing now—how to remain inconspicuous and undiscovered. How to escape.

Escape seemed to be on top of Auntie Swan's list. 'What should we do? Should we go back to the province?' Auntie Swan's words tripped over each other, and Carmen opened her eyes to see Auntie Swan's puffy face now crumpled like a deflated pandesal, her eyes wide and panicked in a way that made Carmen feel sad.

Uncle Amado was calmer, but his usually round cheeks were drawn. 'We do nothing of the sort. Where will we go, aber?' He looked around the room, as if searching for a hiding spot. 'They only showed Carmen's face,' he said. 'And that's just a stupid drawing by that stupid Luis. They didn't name names. They didn't say *our* names.'

'I don't know.' Auntie Swan buried her head in her hands. 'We can go to one of your contacts. To my brother in La Union.'

'We stay here.' Uncle Amado stood up and steadied himself with the back of the sofa. 'We stay put.' His head swivelled back to the TV, still playing its peppy commercials.

'I thought we'd taken care of Luis,' Auntie Swan said. 'Didn't we drop him off at that hostel? Bastard reported us to the police!'

'They won't find us.' Uncle Amado's voice was gruff. 'Rick's show isn't even popular. This channel isn't even the number one. Who watches this, except us? This will be forgotten tomorrow, even tonight when everyone tunes in to that telenovela you always talk about.'

Carmen thought of the almost one-thousand shares on Facebook. She had no desire to check it again or open her phone.

'The neighbours,' Carmen blurted out, thinking of the years she'd passed through their little alley, lit by the glow of their neighbours' TV. There were always the faint sounds of someone speaking or singing, was it Rick Biglang-Awa in *Aksyon Pilipinas* or something else? She hadn't thought of peering through the neighbours' open windows, she had never thought what other people watched on TV would ever be of any concern to her.

And now it was. She prayed that her family's long friendship with the neighbours would be put to good use. God knows they need the support right now.

It was as if the faint sounds of the news, of Rick Biglang-Awa's voice, were always present at some point, at every corner of their alley. 'Do you think *they'll* tell the police?'

'No need.' Auntie Swan looked like she was going to throw up. 'Sgt Aguilar will come looking for you first thing tomorrow.'

There was a sound on the door that made them all jump up. The doorknob jiggled and in burst Max, his face grim.

'I saw it,' he said, beside her in an instant. Carmen knew that he knew what she was already thinking.

She felt his shoulders brush against hers but she kept her eyes on Auntie Swan and Uncle Amado. Both had fallen into a defeated, resigned silence, now staring absently, seemingly deep in thought, at the TV.

'What about your food business dream?' Max's voice was soft and calm, as if the likeness of Carmen's face had not just been tagged criminal and flashed on TV just minutes ago.

She knew he was going to ask her this because she was asking herself the same thing. Was it possible? To just go and leave everything behind? And, could she even leave?

'You can leave, you know.'

There it was. Max, in one whisper and a single breath, had voiced her thoughts loud and clear. He eyes darted back to Uncle Amado and Auntie Swan, alarmed that they had heard. But they had their backs turned, oblivious to the present conversation.

Carmen closed her eyes, took a deep, shaky breath. She knew where she had to go, and when. She thought of the long nights she'd spent studying the photos of Nicole, of her and her foreigner husband, of her mother's new family. She pictured her half-siblings, pale and long-limbed, with eyes the colour of light tea. Her mind shifted to the rusted box in her closet, to the stacks of crumbly peso bills that she'd kept for years. She thought of the food stall she'd once dreamed of, of all the new street food snacks she had been planning to cook for her neighbours and for anyone who was passing through their alley in the afternoons.

There would be no cooking happening tomorrow. No trips to Luneta Park, no stealthy people-watching along Manila Bay.

Somewhere across the ocean was Huế City, where her mother was waiting.

Disappointment at St Regis

MARINA

It was past noon when she got up, not looking at the clock on the kitchen wall. Marina only knew too well that she had nowhere to go; it had been like this for the past three days. She realized, with slight horror, that the later the day came, the worse she felt. She had a hangover in reverse.

But Marina opened her laptop, and out of habit, checked her email. She saw Frances Yee's message immediately among the short list in her inbox, one of the few who'd replied to her goodbye email from *Parcours*. Not a surprise: Frances, who had been with *XYZ* Magazine as associate editor for over a decade, was one of Marina's first few friends in the industry.

'Sorry for what happened, babe. But I have good news. Call me! I was lunching with the Fendi people when I saw your email. So sorry! Did you know that our Serene Chan is on the way out? We need a new deputy managing editor and of course I told Zi about you. If you can make it to the St Regis for high tea today then that would be smashing.'

Relief flooded over her. Thank god for kind, smart souls like Frances. Her editor, Zi Hong, she wrote, was open to meeting Marina for an interview today at the St Regis. Nothing formal, and Frances would be there.

Marina finally looked at the clock—it was a half-past noon—then she looked at the email timestamp; it was sent past nine o'clock last night while she was having dinner and eventually getting drunk.

* * *

It was ten minutes before three o'clock when Marina walked through the hushed lobby of the St Regis. The soft smell of lilies of the valley hung in the air, of expensive perfume lined with padded walls and artwork in rich, deep colours. She'd been in and out of hotels for more than a decade, and yet she always felt this odd mix of trepidation, comfort, and awe. Before she worked in media, she used to think it was foolish of people to spend hundreds—if not thousands—of dollars for a night, *a single night*, in a hotel, to sleep in a fancy bed and an air-conditioned room that wasn't their own but that they would have to give up in twenty-four hours anyway.

That was before, when she had been unexposed and inexperienced, struggling and hard-up, and hadn't known any better.

Now, of course, she understood.

That noontime she'd pulled herself together immediately, shooting a text and an email to Frances confirming her attendance for the interview, despite the pain that felt like a ball hitting a wall in the back of her head. The last thing she wanted was to be teased, pointedly, about arriving on 'Filipino time' as she had been the first months she'd started working here.

But Frances was already there, clad in a tailored grey shift and outrageously tall heels, her legs extended gracefully on the thick carpet as her lean figure curled over the phone in her hands. Marina could see the stack of thick charms piled on her wrists, glinting under the hotel's chandeliers and wondered if she would ever feel the same level of true comfort, of *belonging* in places like this as Frances did.

'Hey, Fran.'

Frances's head snapped up, and she dropped her phone decisively on her lap. 'Marina!' She sat up and extended a slender arm with such exaggeration that Marina instinctively leaned down for the requisite kiss on the cheek.

'God, it's been crazy.' Frances gestured towards the other seat then nodded for a waiter. A glass of iced water was laid down on the table in an instant.

'How are you—and Zi?' Marina tried to keep the anxiety out of her voice.

'He's coming,' Frances said, picking up her phone again. 'We were meeting here anyway, so I had that brilliant idea of inviting you over.'

Marina sank down on the soft chair. 'Thanks again for setting this up.'

Frances waved her hand dismissively. 'Don't thank me yet. I may be desperate to have you as our deputy managing editor, but it's still Zi's call.'

'I know.'

Frances burst out laughing. 'Don't look so worried!'

'Honestly, I am. After *Parcours*, I don't know what other surprises are in store for me . . .'

'You're funny, Marina. You've been in the industry as long as I have and you're such a good writer. One of the best editors. Everybody knows that. You didn't deserve that from *Parcours*. Advertisers—we, everybody—just *adored* your lifestyle pages. Anyway, you're practically a shoo-in.'

'That's really kind, Frances, but—'

'Oof, he's here.' Frances waved gaily to a man being led by a waiter to their table.

Zi Wijaya, editor-in-chief of *XYZ*, was kitted out in a white linen shirt, white slacks, and espadrilles, looking like he was on his way to a vacation somewhere in France. A thick lock of hair fell on his forehead that he kept brushing aside, *meant to be that way*, Marina thought. The thick, white glasses were also meant to be ironic.

'Ah, here you are lovelies! Glad you could make it in such oppressive weather. I mean, this bloody heat, right?' Zi spoke in a startlingly heavy British accent and appeared to be in high spirits. And despite the strange accent, Marina admired his enthusiasm. She'd met Zi several times and he was always so enthusiastic, so optimistic, always had something positive and uplifting to say to others. She could work with this man. No, she *wanted* to work with this man.

'We've seen your work,' Zi was saying now, warmly. 'Impeccable writing. Tight editing. We've always wanted to have lifestyle pages like yours. And your style profiles! We read them, you know. I particularly appreciate the in-depth interviews.

'We know you're the reason why *Parcours's* lifestyle pages are tightly edited. Such a shame there won't be any print editions anymore. We've truly gone online. But, it's the way to be sustainable in these times,' Zi continued. 'As you know, the work of deputy managing editor at *XYZ* involves a ton of liaising—with the team you manage, with advertisers, and with our digital group as well.

'We need to be relevant. Our tried and true brands—advertisers are upping their spend, but strongly considering putting a large chunk of that in digital. Still print, but with a strong digital presence. So, the deputy managing editor works closely with the digital team in terms of online presence, SEO relevance—well, you know those things.'

Marina's head swam at the terms.

Immigration

She had been in line for more than forty minutes, willing the queue that snaked in two twisty lines to go faster. She had seen the insides of Manila's NAIA airport, had seen lines like this once or twice in the news. It felt so different, being in the thick of it now.

There were metal posts strung with flat ropes that told people where to line up, and for a moment, all Carmen could see were the tops of heads and bodies in colourful clothes mashed up, shoulder-to-shoulder. Everyone seemed to be leaning forward, as if that would bring them closer to the windowed cubicles in the front. She herself was trying to inch her way forward in an attempt to escape the heavy breathing and occasional tongue-clicking of the person behind her, whose elaborately-cased phone had been accidentally brushing against her back.

Carmen willed herself not to be terrified: of the queue, of the immigration officer, of the thought of boarding an actual plane that would take her far and away from the Philippines. Away from her family.

Last night, she had stood frozen in front of the TV as the show flashed her face. She had gazed at it as if her body, or her breath, weren't her own, as if she had been hovering above everyone in the room. She had thought of herself. And then she had thought of her mother.

She had packed, calmly. Quietly. Nanay Luisa still thought she was crazy, but what she really was, was frightened.

She had left 8,000 pesos under one of the reused jar bottles that Nanay Luisa liked keeping. It was the only amount she could spare. The rest, she took with her. For this trip, she needed everything that she had.

* * *

Carmen felt the woman behind her lurch against her back, heard the delicate pings of her phone as she typed. Or was she playing a game? Carmen closed her eyes for a moment. She could do this. She wanted to, and most of all she needed to. She had followed Uncle Amado's instructions to the letter: arrive early, head to the travel tax counter, pay the 1,620-peso travel tax, then proceed to the check-in counter. Then immigration, the most important part.

Her nerves had been in tatters, and she had felt incredible relief after walking away from each counter. Every time the person behind the counter looked up, her maroon passport open in their hands, Carmen half-expected them to say that something was wrong, that she was not supposed to be there and worse, that the police was being called and she was, finally, under arrest.

Don't think about that, Carmen, she told herself, even as she saw a woman, close to her height and age, being questioned, her passport and papers checked, then taken out of the queue. Just think of your mother, she told herself, and how everything will somehow fall into place.

Rebirth

MARINA

She didn't know how long she sat there, staring at the cars, Frances Yee's silky voice still echoing in her ears. She was aware of a rising buzz around her as the café started filling up with people. Those who knew better than to work all afternoon were getting coffee—or a beer, maybe.

She put her cup to her lips, an automatic gesture. How could she think that she would get hired, just like that, at another magazine as prestigious and important as the one she had just left? How could she think that once she slipped, it would be easy for her? That for once, opportunities would fall in a neat, effortless trajectory onto her wide, waiting palms? No, such things happened naturally to other people, other people who were not Marina. People like Frances and Zi, her colleagues at *Parcours*, the socialites she interviewed who were born in the right family, with the right passport and *the right things*, and so didn't have to claw their way up and try until it was barely bearable.

She had genuinely yet foolishly thought that she tried her best, that she gave so much sweat and tears or at least utilized a large part of her brain, to be where she was now—but it was not enough. She missed one important thing and that was how to grow in a digital world, to work with its new formulas and rules. She blatantly refused to learn.

You've used up your luck, her mother would say.

Maybe Marina was tired. Maybe she'd had enough or too much. There were times when she thought she couldn't bear to write about yet another socialite's luxury brand closet or travelling style. There were times when she used a formula in her head to conceal her outrage at the lifestyles and characters of some of the people she interviewed. She relied so much on the things she knew, and on what she had gone through, that she forgot what it was like to be out of her comfort zone.

It wasn't too late. She knew this. She could take a course, perhaps. She didn't know. Create a website. Start something that was creative, explosive, impactful—but paperless.

Yes, maybe she could. She slid out her laptop from her bag and opened it. The answers were all there, online, one just needed to type in the right search words. Where would she start? And how?

She would have to start at the bottom. From the beginning.

Something in her seemed to deflate. The bottom had been in Manila twenty years ago and it was a hard, scary place—would she still have the energy for that? To learn and relearn things, to network, to say and write the right things. The *new*, right things. In that moment, at that very second, every cell in her body was resisting.

She closed her laptop on the table and sat stiffly with her hands at her sides, watching the cars slow down before the wide hump on the road in front of her. She felt irrelevant, small. Zi had talked about content strategies and asked her about data monitoring, social media algorithms. 'Your thoughts on these, Marina?' Zi asked her casually because, after all, it was supposed to be just high tea, a non-interview. 'Surely, you've witnessed your audience changing, getting more impatient, with suddenly-shortened attention spans.' They all laughed at this remark, because it sounded so phonetically ridiculous and because it was so obvious. Everyone in the industry could see how readership could be so fickle now, Zi kept saying. 'Don't you see it, how quickly the landscape has changed, how readers have morphed into something else?'

She didn't. Or maybe she did and was too stubborn to adjust. She didn't say that out loud to Zi and Frances, of course. Instead, she cobbled out an answer that she hoped wouldn't belie the truth dawning on her just then: that she was confounded by how things were done online, that she'd kept to her ways for so long, she didn't have a feel for these things anymore. That she'd lost touch and didn't know that her readers now wanted other things. She didn't know—or maybe refused to acknowledge—that her readers preferred reading shorter articles with outrageous, out-of-context headlines on their laptops or their phones.

She remembered Frances Yee asking her for a series of links to see the other projects she'd done. Her head swam just thinking of it. She didn't even know how to start. And how could she when now it was clear that no one would give her a chance? She would have to do it all over again. Yes, start from the beginning—or somewhere close to it. Just the thought made her stomach seize up.

Zi had been pleasant and smooth until the very end of their meeting, of their lovely 'tête-à-tête' as he called it, which lasted all of forty minutes. He popped those cucumber sandwiches and egg tarts with gusto, sipped all of his white tea, but he listened to her with the care of a concerned friend. If Zi was displeased or disappointed at Marina's obvious lack of digital savvy, he was careful not to show it.

But Marina knew she wouldn't make it. She had been given a special pass at an opportunity and she was not prepared. Because of her position, because of what she had achieved, she'd been given access to an express lane to a position that other journalists would take years to reach. And she failed. She pictured herself as they saw her: a forty-two-year-old woman who, at first glance, seemed almost overqualified for the position, and yet didn't possess the one skill that had emerged so quickly and was suddenly deemed essential. She knew she had just confirmed Zi and Frances's inklings that what they really needed for *XYZ* Magazine was someone who had grown up in that kind of digital environment, living and thriving with that kind of media.

Zi and Frances would simply move on to the next applicant. One who could produce a whole digital issue in a week or so. Not her.

Her phone rang. Frances. Marina's heart jumped, a mix of fear, surprise, and hope rippling through her so quickly that she reached for her water and gulped everything in an instant. Had she been too hasty, judging herself like this? Maybe this was just one big pity party she was allowed to have before—before what? Her reinstallation into the magazine world.

'Babe, it was so nice to see you!' Frances's tone was as warm as it had been earlier. 'We appreciate that you came to see us, truly. We've been at our wit's end looking for a replacement for Serene. But—' She paused and took a breath.

'But?' Marina pressed her phone closer to her ear.

Frances let out a sound, kind of like a sheepish, nervous chuckle. 'You know we love you. And as Zi said, there's a real appetite for the glossies in Singapore. But we have to be sustainable. We need someone who can write *and* work with the website, Marina.'

'Oh.' Marina's face burned. 'I see.' She nodded, even though Frances couldn't see her. 'I see,' she repeated. 'I completely understand, Fran. Thanks so much to Zi and you for even thinking of me.'

It's just work, she told herself, as they said exchanged goodbyes. Nothing personal.

You've ruined it, her mother would say. Marina for a second thought of calling her just to hear her say these terrible words again. At least she was someone who could be honest with her, who could tell her how it really was, and who she really was.

And she was someone who had just fucked it up. Again.

She had fucked it up because she didn't really belong in this world in the first place. She was just Marina who grew up in Manila and who knew how to string words together. She was just a nobody who thought she had achieved relative success.

The truth was, she wasn't successful at all. Because if she was, she wouldn't be sitting in this café by the road with suddenly nothing to do and nowhere to go, wondering what she needed to get a job while the rest of Singapore toiled away in their high-rise offices in the CBD.

She covered her face with her hands, willing her face to stay dry, for that gigantic fist to stop pressing against her chest, for her throat to stop feeling like there was something hard and sharp lodged in it.

Breathe, Marina, breathe.

Don't let them see you cry, her mother told her. And her mother never did. Her mother never had her face wet with sticky, useless tears. Her mother never broke down—even though something horrific was happening to her every day. *Don't let them see you weak.*

She probably deserved it, all this mess. For thinking that print was forever and that sex was a painkiller. In the end, she was still Marina who grew up with nothing, who knew nothing.

She emptied her glass, drinking the cold liquid in big, forceful gulps before placing the glass back on the table. There was a heavy, dirty smudge at the bottom that wasn't supposed to be there and probably needed taking up with the waiter or manager, but she didn't care. Hadn't she made do with scuffed, plastic glasses, with utensils that weren't—couldn't—be washed in days? For years, she had eaten off paper plates because there was no running water at all, she had washed herself with half a pail of water.

The waiter was refilling her glass. She looked up.

'Day off, ma'am?' He was smiling as he lifted the sweating water pitcher, and she was surprised to see a pale, pinkish face and a big, long nose, one that didn't seem to belong in Singapore. He couldn't be more than thirty.

'Yes,' she said, hoping he wouldn't really notice how she paused, how startled she was at the glaring awkwardness that jolted her when she realized what he was asking her.

'Good day so far?'

'It's fine,' she said, even though this day was one of her worst. 'I'm fine.'

'Awesome.' The waiter chirped before turning his attention to the next table.

She wanted this pain to go away. She craved comfort, company, someone to tell her she was great, she did it, she was fine.

It's all your fault. She could almost hear her mother saying. Just as it was her fault that her father had not come back. *You're not trying hard enough.*

Someone swept by in a yellow caftan, smelling of lavender and vanilla. The scent still lingering under her nose, Marina from the side of her eye could see the bright hem being dragged on the café's cement screed flooring, as if its owner didn't care if it was dirtied or not.

She fiddled with the rim of her water glass, thinking: it could've been Atasha.

It wasn't. It was a half-Asian beauty with super-straight blondish hair who smiled at her unsurely as she passed by and took a seat a few tables away. Marina watched as another server laid down a croissant on a plate, watched the woman dive into it with contrived gusto, cutting it into pieces.

As with everything else, Atasha wouldn't treat food so inelegantly.

There was pressure on her back molars and Marina thought of the pill her dentist had prescribed to relax her jaw so she wouldn't grind her teeth.

She sat up.

You've had it worse, Marina told herself. You were in this same position twelve years ago. Except that you had been poorer and it felt like you wouldn't last another day in Manila. Except that you had no savings, that you worried about stretching what money you had left. Except that you were ten times more scared because you didn't know if the money you had in your bank account would last you the month. Or the week, even.

Except that you had been heartbroken and felt like you couldn't function without the man you loved and who you thought loved you back. Except that you felt like the most unloved, undesirable person in the world.

It had felt like she wouldn't last another day, living. If it had not been for her mother, who needed her financial support, what would she have done?

This was not the first time something like this had happened. This was not the first time that Marina had been rejected, discarded, turned away. It sounded melodramatic even in her own head, but that was what she had felt then, and this was what she was feeling now. Not chosen.

Marina had been the chosen one, once. A long time ago, Atasha had chosen her. Atasha had chosen Marina to be her associate at work, and then she had chosen Marina to be her best friend.

That is, until she wasn't, and everything went crashing down.

Part Two

Arrival

CARMEN

The flight was delayed by three hours. The plane had stayed parked on the runway for more than two hours so that Carmen wondered if she would even get out of the Philippines.

The plane had touched down in Huế, Vietnam at 2.30 a.m. Carmen watched the flight attendants walk up and down the aisle, fresh and energetic even though it was early morning. 'Welcome to Phu Bai Airport,' the announcement said, the soothing voice in perfectly enunciated English floating above the plane cabin. Before that, there was a recorded announcement in chirpy-sounding Vietnamese.

Carmen was in the middle seat and so she could only partly see through the oval window of the plane. Beside her, a quiet man also felt compelled to look out at the dark. She caught a glimpse of lights and thought that it didn't look like anything different. It could be Manila, though, how would she know? The last airplane ride she'd been on with her mother was almost two decades ago. She could not recall seeing her city from so high above.

The other passengers were quiet. Many had put their bare and socked feet up on their seats. They were tired, like Carmen. She did not know if staying put and not moving on that runway was normal or not, but it was better than the anxiety she had felt while lining up in immigration.

'Taxi? Taxi? *Chi, oi*!' Several men called out to her as she went through the exit doors at arrivals. 'You need taxi?'

She thought she had chosen the kindest-looking one, a lanky man with a cropped haircut and delicate features who smiled hesitantly at her when she handed him her suitcase and the piece of paper that had the name of a hostel.

He did not say anything at all during the trip but kept looking at her from the rear-view mirror.

And then she didn't know what happened—if it was the hours of waiting and travelling, the fear of getting out of the airport, the awful realization that she was now far from the only city she had known, the stress and adrenaline of being somewhere she had never been, the trauma and excitement of it all—but Carmen felt her stomach lurch, and she felt dizzy every time the taxi slowed down and accelerated.

They were on a dark road, not too far from Phu Bai Airport when she felt she couldn't take it anymore.

'Stop,' she told the driver, who did not understand her at first and continued driving.

She tapped him on the shoulder. 'Stop,' she said again. 'I'm sick. I need to get out.'

The driver muttered something in Vietnamese under his breath, the car slowly coming to a halt as he pressed the brakes. Carmen was out of the vehicle in less than a minute, bending down over the grassy side of the road, the raw smell of grass and of something else making her insides churn even more. She puked, her vomit—what little she ate since the flight—appearing white and sticky on the grass.

She was still heaving, feeling weak in the knees, when she heard a door slam. The driver, she thought.

The last thing she expected was his fingers on her shoulder. She stiffened. There was a hand on her waist, then her buttocks—tightening into a grip. She could feel his chest against her torso, something hard against the small of her back.

Carmen wriggled out of his grip and spun around, slapping him hard on the face. The force of her hand had been so strong that he reeled backwards, touching his jaw and gaping at her with wild eyes as if unable to believe what had just happened.

'*Putang ina*! Putang ina *ka*! *Punyeta*!' Carmen felt the spittle and vomit dribbling from the sides of her mouth. She could hear her own voice, ragged and hoarse, animal-like. She was not this person. She had turned into an animal. No, she had turned into some creature that was worse than an animal.

'What are you doing?'

She screamed and screamed, until the driver backed into the car and opened the door. She was still screaming when he slammed the door and sped off.

She only stopped when she saw the tail lights get smaller and smaller as the vehicle receded from sight.

In the ensuing silence, she stood alone on that road, a million thoughts swirling inside her head like a raging, pent-up dam that had burst, they threatened to spill out of her head and drown her.

Because she did not know anything about travelling. Because it was her first time travelling out of the Philippines. Because it was her first time doing something like this. Because she was scared and sad and still confused about whether it had been the right thing to do, to leave Manila—and feeling as if it had been for the best—because she was actually, operating from grief, fear, and desperation. Because she was operating with just a little hope and because her grief and fear and desperation were greater than anything she'd experienced in a long time—she was robbed in Huế.

Maybe it was because of this that she had let her guard down, for a moment. She had not felt this kind of debilitating, nerve-wracking exhaustion even at the end of a complicated MO in Manila.

She sniffed at the air. It was drizzling so it was a wet kind of smell, a mix of earth, grass, asphalt, and dung. She was in the strangest place she'd ever been, not knowing where to go, *how* to go. She felt for her backpack, grateful for a split second that she'd dragged it with her when she alighted, that she'd had enough sense to bring her money and her passport, and the fake papers with her.

She knew deep down that it was plain ignorance. It was just that she didn't know anything. At this, she felt even angrier with herself. In less than a day, she had turned into one of those hapless tourists she had always taken advantage of.

Did staying in Barangay Bicutan—her comfort zone—all these years make her this soft, weak? Did it take just a change of scenery across the oceans to unnerve her, to unravel her?

No, she must be more than this. She should be more than this. She did not come all the way here to be abused, the way she knew people were abused back home. She was not about to waste this gift from the universe that allowed her to escape the wrath, cruelty, and judgement of the Philippine police. She shoved the image of her in a dirty jail cell, rotting with criminals like herself, with a force and vengeance that made her head spin all over again. She still had her money. She would pick herself up and walk and look for help.

Under the waning moonlight, she undid the backpack from her shoulders, dropped to her knees, and cried.

This Man Called Hai

CARMEN

She thought she saw a house in the distance, and she found herself running. The sky was still grey but the rain had reduced to a soft drizzle and she could feel her backpack slapping against her shoulders as she ran. Drops of sweat flew as she moved forward, sweat mixing with the raindrops running down her face, her neck, the front of her body. She heard the muffled thuds of her feet against the hard pavement, felt her already-soaked sneakers splashing in the puddles she didn't care to avoid. The lots on both side of the road were vacant and teeming with overgrown grass, shrubs, and clusters of banana trees. The house was getting closer, and she ran faster; never mind if the windows looked dark and unlit and she saw no movement, no people outside.

Her racing thoughts were interrupted as she felt a hard, sharp rock press against the thin soles of her sneakers and jut into her right foot as she took her next step. Carmen cried out, pitching backward and then forward until she completely lost balance and stumbled, landing heavily on all fours.

She cursed under her breath, knees on fire. Her palms had saved her but the force had been too great and they had hit hard against the rough pavement. The pain was searing for a moment.

Carmen heard the faint sound of a motor, and she looked up. There, coming up further from the house, was someone. Someone was coming. Eyes never leaving the motorist, she struggled into a sitting position, lifted her arms with effort, and started waving. She opened her mouth but at first, no sound came out.

It was a man on a motorbike. She didn't know if he saw her, but to her alarm she watched him slow down, make a U-turn, and head in the other direction.

'Hey!' She could not let this person go away. She pushed her feet on the ground, willed her knees to straighten until she was finally standing, and then ran. She didn't know where she got the energy, the strength. Her voice—loud, wild, hoarse—sounded like it belonged to someone else. 'Hello! Hey, you!'

She kept shouting until she saw the motorist stop abruptly, and she came to a gradual stop. He had a raincoat on, thin and light blue and covering him to the knees. She saw him twist his body and his head to look at her.

He deftly turned his motorbike back around and headed towards her. She stood still in the middle of the road, half-bent with her hands on her knees, gasping for air. Her hair had escaped her ponytail and was stuck to her face and neck. She felt as if her chest was about to burst; she had never been this out of breath in her life.

Carmen straightened up and moved to the side of the road, where the man had finally come to a stop. A small, dark, bony face was peering out from beneath the hood of the blue raincoat and Carmen saw that the man was wearing a helmet underneath. In another day, another place, another time—she would have found this sight comical. He didn't alight from his bike and instead balanced the vehicle between his legs as he half stood, half sat, his hands still on the handlebars. He looked ready to go at any moment.

'Chi oi,' he called out in a twangy, loud voice. Then, he spoke rapidly in Vietnamese.

She wiped her nose and pushed back the hair from her face. 'Excuse me? What? Please, please help me!'

He spoke again, his voice rising and falling, but she shook her head in protest. 'No, no sorry.'

She swallowed, her throat dry, and took in another huge breath of air. Sweat felt like it was gushing down her chest and armpits. 'Please help me,' she repeated.

'You're not Vietnamese?' The man looked surprised.

'What?' Carmen asked again. She shook her head, trying not to show her impatience, her anger, her tiredness. She suddenly didn't know where to begin for this man to understand what she needed right now. She had never thought she'd come to a place where English could not be spoken or understood. How foolish and ignorant and so utterly clueless she'd been to assume that everyone spoke and understood English all over the world.

She took a deep breath, her heart still pounding. There was something inside her that had stretched taut and was now threatening to break. 'Please. Help. Me.'

'Everything is okay?'

No, everything is not okay, she wanted to scream. She threw her head back and let out a groan, loud and guttural—only to stop just as quickly to look at the man again, suddenly afraid that he would drive away. The flight, the shock, the groping of the taxi driver, her things! No—the only big, bright, persistent thing she had in her mind right now was that she couldn't walk any further.

'I mean, you are okay?' The man realized his gaffe and looked apologetic. He looked around, as if fearful someone might see them. Here, on this deserted road.

'No,' she said. Her sentences spilled out, the words tripping over each another. 'The taxi driver, he left me on the road. He stole my things. He just drove away. He left me.'

The man had gone silent, listening intently. And then, he said: 'Okay, we call police.' He reached in his back pocket, presumably for his phone.

Panic rose in her chest. 'No!' she said, instinctively lunging at him and grabbing his arm. The look of surprise on his face was so palpable, Carmen thought that she had finally scared him off. Her voice was so loud, the man's head whipped up in surprise, eyes wide. The very people she was running from, and here she was about to hand herself to them.

No, she didn't want the police involved. She had managed to escape the police in Manila. She didn't want anything to do with them here.

'But you said—' The man blinked, looking bewildered. 'The taxi driver. He stole your things. Your bag. Do you know the taxi company? Was it a blue and white taxi? A green and white taxi?'

She tried hard to picture the vehicle, but she couldn't tell if it had been the colours that the man was saying. She shook her head. 'No. No, I don't know.'

They both looked up. It had started raining again.

'Here.' The man hopped off the motorbike and slipped off his raincoat. He wrapped it loosely around her, stepping away as soon as he did as if afraid to get too close.

It didn't seem to make any difference in her already wet state, but she placed the hood over her wet hair and buttoned the plastic fabric at the collar. 'I need to go to my hostel. Can you—?'

'We should go,' the man said, sighing audibly. He was back on the bike in an instant and patted the seat behind him. 'Which hostel are you staying?'

Carmen paused. 'Hostel Vy Vy.'

The man nodded, gripping the handlebars fully once more. 'I'm Hai,' he said. 'I will bring you there.'

* * *

They couldn't find Hostel Vy Vy. 'Are you sure that's the name?' Hai kept asking her.

Carmen felt a flash of fear. Was this man losing their way on purpose? She wasn't sure if she was just too tired, too resigned, or too desperate—but there was a kindness in his voice and in the way that he spoke that she somehow trusted.

She coughed but held on to Hai's shoulders. Even with the raincoat, it was cold, riding through the wind.

He drove through several narrow alleys—narrower than the ones in Barangay Bicutan. There were hostels and massage parlours, a bevy of painted signs advertising them. She saw the back of his head look right and left, muttering something. They drove through another narrow alley, then emerged back onto the main road.

'It's not there?'

'There's another one, over there.' They entered another narrow street, with a warren of buildings. It was light now, the morning sky bleak and grey, and Carmen guessed it was about 6 a.m. A lady was selling fruits on the side of the road, and Hai stopped to ask her something in Vietnamese. After a short exchange, he showed her the paper.

'There is no hotel with this name.'

She saw the back of his head turn slightly as he looked at her jeans, soiled at the knees. A small, fuzzy-edged bloodstain, brown and drying, had formed on the light denim fabric.

'You need to go to hospital.'

'What?' Carmen jerked so sharply, she felt the motorbike jerk to the side. 'No! No need for hospital. I'm okay, I'm fine.' Her head and joints throbbed, and the skin on her knees and palms stung. She was not injured seriously, though.

He didn't say anything after that, and just kept driving. For a split-second, she was afraid that he was heading to the police or the hospital, but she quickly squashed the thought. She had frightened herself enough today with so much catastrophic thinking. She just wanted to find the hostel, call Max and her family, and then be by herself, sleep. Maybe after she'd wake up, she'd know better what to do next.

Hai was slowing down to a stop in front of another alley. 'Look,' he said, steadying the bike. 'My rent room is just over there. I need to change and go to work soon. Do you want to rest there?'

Carmen shook her head. 'I'll just go to another hostel. Do you know a cheap one?'

'My hostel, the one I work for. Phong Nha Hostel. It's 11 US dollars for one night.' Hai jerked his head towards the other direction. 'I just came from my shift at Minh Thanh Hotel—my other job—but that's too expensive.'

Carmen hesitated, her mind converting the dollars to the amount in pesos. She was suddenly grateful to Max for telling her to check the exchange rate before she left and at the airports.

It was almost 600 pesos. Back home, she could have bought triple the ingredients she needed for her afternoon food stall. She sucked in her breath, careful not to move the motorbike further. Not now, she thought. She couldn't appear more vulnerable than she already was. She'd trusted this stranger, Hai, too much already.

No, she thought, she had to be practical. She needed to get some clothes and other essentials, and what other else she needed to get started here. She couldn't spare that much.

And then Hai spoke. 'Just go to my rent room. It's free. Keep your money.'

* * *

'Did he hurt you?'

'No, no,' she said, firmly. She didn't want to think of the taxi driver anymore. 'He just stole everything from me.'

'Your luggage?' Hai asked, a frown between his thick brows. 'Anything important?' His question sounded guarded and tentative, as if he wasn't sure it was the right thing to ask.

She realized that he had a voice that didn't seem to match his body. The sound that came out of his mouth was deep and strong and modulated, reminding Carmen of a radio announcer's voice. In contrast, everything about his physical appearance felt sparse and thin and wanting: his sunken face, his beady eyes, his sharp elbows and bony shoulders. He had a wide forehead and thinning, very black hair.

'No,' Carmen said again. Her thoughts flew to the suitcase she had lost, its contents meagre but essential to her. In this strange new city, they had been the only ones she had left: the two pairs of jeans, good slacks from Auntie Swan, some blouses and T-shirts, her underwear, slippers, a pair of flat shoes. Her old toothbrush and a packet of toothpaste. Upon Max's advice she had also packed soap and shampoo in small sachets, the ones that cost less than ten pesos at the minimart back home.

'Nothing important,' she said, her eyes landing on the backpack on Hai's desk, and an image of Max flashed in her head. She mentally sifted through its contents: save for her money and passport, there was nothing important in there, too. She leaned forward and grabbed it.

'Okay.' Hai paced around the room, looking uncomfortable for the first time since they had arrived in his room.

Carmen sat up straight, clutching her backpack. It occurred to her that Hai was a stranger, and this was his room, his territory. As with the taxi driver, he could do anything to her.

She shifted and heard the slight rustle of something inside her bag. Her mind flew to the small packet wrapped many times over with newspaper, and several layers of plastic bag. She had brought a stash of Ativan pills, had not told even Max that she had packed it. No one had inspected her bag at the airport, no one had stopped her.

'I need to go to work,' Hai was saying now. 'At the bus station.'

Carmen stared at him, uncomprehending.

'I can't leave you here.' Perhaps it was his voice and accent, but he didn't sound apologetic. Hai paused, then scratched the side of his nose. 'My landlady, she's coming over. She'll give me trouble if she knew I had, ah, someone here.'

Her first thought was: Did he sense it? Did he know who she really was?

The tourist buses from Ho Chi Minh, Dalat, and Hanoi were all due to arrive in an hour, Hai said, so his work at the bus terminal would start soon. Carmen was smart enough to sense that he was lying about the landlady. But she knew that, like her, he couldn't trust a stranger inside his room, with his belongings.

Room

CARMEN

They drove along another road, this time with hipster-looking cafés, many with low tables and plastic chairs. They turned in an alley, and then they were looking up at a slim, four-storey house with small windows, an elevated porch, and peeling paint in light yellow.

'This one.' Hai cut the engine and nodded sharply for her to get off. 'Wait for me.' He parked the motorbike on one side, then climbed the short steps leading to the front door.

When he came back, his face was serious. 'It's 180,000 Vietnamese dong,' he announced.

'How much is that?'

'Eight dollars.' He didn't look happy. 'But it's very bad.'

'Can I see the room?'

Hai shook his head. 'The lady is so bad. She said they're occupied and there's one they're still cleaning. But I know this place is cheap.'

'Okay,' Carmen said, 'I'll take it.'

They went inside a sparse, dark, garage-like living room. In a corner sat a woman behind a small table in a light brown fleece jacket zipped-up fully to her chin. Her eyes looked hard, even in the dim interiors, and Carmen could see her lips pressed tightly, a look of expectancy on her face.

Carmen took out the bills, counted 180,000 dong. The woman pocketed the money immediately and stood up, motioning for them to follow her up the stairs.

The room was at the end of the hall. She produced a key from her pocket, opening the flimsy door easily. Once in, Carmen ran her eyes over the single bed covered with a thin, threadbare blanket and the flattish pillow. There was only room for a bed, and a small hanging cabinet above it. It was a narrow room, like a closet.

'Okay?' Without waiting for an answer, the lady laid the key on the bed, brushing past them as she left. Carmen placed her bag on the floor, then moved towards the bed to retrieve the key.

'I will leave you,' Hai said.

She heard the door click. When she looked behind her, Hai was gone. She opened the door and ran out the corridor, caught a glimpse of Hai's retreating back. She opened her mouth to say thank you but closed it again. He was already disappearing down the stairs.

The sudden exit was bewildering, but Carmen realized that she was too exhausted to care. She went back to her room, making sure it was locked once she was inside. Then she crawled into the bed and cried.

Phu Bai

MARINA

There was a thick crowd, sweaty and restless, waiting at arrivals in Ho Chi Minh City's Tan Son Nhat Airport. Marina could feel them pressing forward as she walked through the sliding exit doors, watching them as they watched—breathless and hawk-like and with a restless anticipation reserved for important occasions—passengers from all over the world trickling out from the gate, dazed and loaded with their luggage. It felt like Manila, where entire *barangays*, whole jeepney loads came to send you off or meet you at the airport.

Saigon, however, wasn't yet her final destination. It was Huế. Marina wended her way through the crowd that had started to spill over the metal barricades. She clumsily slipped on her sunglasses, suddenly unnerved by the open, curious stares of those trying to determine if she was the one they'd been waiting for.

At this, she remembered her mother and she looked down and away. She was not anyone's family here. She still had another flight to catch and needed to go to the domestic airport just beside.

A sharp pain shot up from the balls of her feet, just as she went past the crowd to the waiting area. She stopped in front of a booth selling smoothies and sim cards, pawing at her feet. 'Shit.'

A Vietnamese man with a paper sign came up to her, said something in Vietnamese. 'Ms Bernadette Tran' was the name printed on his paper.

She shook her head no, and as the man retreated, she looked out at the crowd again and loosened her grip on her suitcase. On a whim, she'd worn her wedge shoes—and yes, she should have known better.

She'd felt inspired when she was in Singapore, where it was easy, too easy to hop on a taxi that took her straight to Changi Airport. She did not break a sweat; it was as physically stress-free as it always was when moving about in Singapore.

A cold shudder passed through her, thinking of what she'd just left behind. And now, here she was in Vietnam, the messy vibe and febrile crowds already a sharp contrast even just at the point of entry at the airport. She felt for her tote, checking yet again that Atasha's folder was still where she'd placed it in her bag. She had dug out this folder from where it had been lying at the bottom of her bedside drawer for years, and she'd made sure she didn't forget to bring it.

The crowd, the noise, and the heat was disconcerting, distracting—so much like Manila that she couldn't decide whether to rejoice or recoil that this was the place she'd chosen to start something, to start again—after what had happened at *Parcours*.

What had she done? Why hadn't she worn her flats and then put on her heels just before she landed in Huế? What made her think that trying this out would work? This was not just another press junket. This was her life.

She grabbed her suitcase again and started walking to the domestic terminal. Tan Son Nhat Airport consisted of two separate buildings with a 500-metre gap between the terminals, connected by a covered walkway. She winced as pain still shot up with every other step. She would need to queue up again, check-in her luggage, and go through security before boarding her flight to Huế. But Hai had told her that he would pick her up at the airport, and for a moment, she basked in the anticipation. Things were just starting, and she had many days to go. This was what she wanted, wasn't it? Just the thought made the seemingly never-ending checks she had to go through worth all the trouble. She imagined Hai among the faces in the crowd. Would he be smiling? Would he be serious? Would he be front and centre, wanting to be the first one to spot her? Or would he have changed from how he was the last time?

She felt her phone vibrate inside her bag. A text. It was from Hai, saying: See you soon.

It frightened her that a single, simple text could not only calm her down but also dictate how she'd feel in the next few hours that they would still be apart.

* * *

She didn't see Hai at first, just the bouquet of bright red roses that he held, so ridiculously big it covered his head and most of his upper torso.

It took her breath away—this half-man, half-bouquet sight of him amid the waiting crowd at Huế's Phu Bai Airport. She had to skid to a stop in the middle of the exit hall at arrivals.

'Sorry,' she murmured, as she felt the other arriving passengers brush past her. She found herself staring at the retreating figure of a petite Vietnamese woman in patent heels pulling a raggedy suitcase, then at a child clawing desperately at her mother's gold-bangled wrist as they both toddled out ahead of her.

And then she was striding forward again, in a way feeling rejuvenated despite the two flights. Less old. She was nine years older than Hai and she could feel it, even if she didn't look it. She should just be thankful that she didn't get a cramp—mid-flight or when she was hauling her suitcase off the conveyor belt.

Hai was in a pale, long-sleeved shirt that Marina couldn't decide was white or beige. 'Welcome, em,' he said, when Marina finally reached him. He thrust the flowers towards her, and Marina saw that he had combed back his hair and slicked on some sort of gel. He looked darker than she remembered him, even thinner and slighter as if he had been sick. But his eyes were sharp and beady, his thin mouth firm.

'My god.' Her hands felt the scratchy pot the flowers were in. Now it was her whose upper half body that was blocked with roses.

'I'll call the taxi.' Hai pressed a button on his phone and raised it up to his ear. She looked at the crowd already starting to dissipate. People were carrying bags and children, streaming out to the exit. Onto the street, then their motorbikes.

She had a month to stay in Huế. So what if she'd just lost her job? The sun was shining, and there were banana trees along the road. This day was just the beginning.

Floating Restaurant

MARINA

She had expected to eat at a simple roadside stall but instead they stopped by a lake, the water wide and still against a silhouette of mountains that faded in layers into the distance. Marina looked past the few small fishing boats moored along the edge at the wood-and-bamboo house on stilts that stood on the water a few hundred meters away from the shore.

'Wow,' Marina breathed, the weariness from the early morning flight fading away, the airport transfers, security, and its slow-moving, clunky queues already feeling like a minor inconvenience. She rolled down the car windows and felt herself smiling as cool air surged inside. Turning to Hai, she asked, 'You've been here?'

'No.' His shoulders seemed to sag, but Hai gave her a small, lopsided smile. 'I mean, not during winter. But it's not cold today. I always pass by this restaurant on the way to pick up guests from the airport.' He straightened up. 'This is okay?'

Marina reached out and squeezed his hand, gratefulness surging through her. Maybe it was the relief of finally arriving in Vietnam, the promise of rest after a day's journey, but she felt moved that he had brought her here. 'It's so peaceful,' she said, quietly. 'It's just what I need.' She glanced out the window again at the postcard view of the fading mountains, soothed for a moment by her own simple statement of certainty and contentment.

But then she lurched forward as a cry went up from the driver. The car had fallen into a deep pothole. Instinctively, Marina grabbed the back of the seat for support as Hai chuckled, speaking to the driver in Vietnamese.

Yes, this was what she needed—today. But what about the rest of her days? Did she really know?

You're just on vacation, her mother's voice, clipped and derisive, echoed in her head. *You're just running away from your problems. Look at me, I stayed in this marriage because of you.* Her mother, who saw things in black and white. Of course, she would say this about Marina's trip to Huế.

* * *

They walked the slim footpath bridge towards the entrance, past the restaurant's painted blue-and-white sign that said Nha Hang Be Than in red. The air seemed laced with the scent of moss and dung—or was it rot, Marina wasn't sure. But she didn't mind; the breeze was constant enough to mask whatever unfavourable smells were there, the landscape a statement of its own. The afternoon sky was a thin, icy blue sheet and she told herself it felt good to be out in the open, to be able to look up without a high-rise building or a crane marring the view.

The restaurant was open on three sides, crammed artlessly with long tables and chairs. Marina chose a table at the far edge overlooking the water.

'So much space,' she murmured, as they sat down. The restaurant was empty except for two men who'd already stood up at their table and were making their way out. So much sky, so much water, so many mountains. She took in the scenery with a hunger and neediness that surprised even her. She had grown up by the sea, crossing rice and coconut fields, looking up at mountains and had thought nothing of them. Taken them for granted as if they would always be there, as if they would never go away. She hadn't taken into account that it was she who would leave, that it was her who would lose them. That it would be her who would feel abandoned even if she was the one who'd left. Now, she was here in a place that wasn't her home and she wanted to preserve this moment forever.

'How long are you staying?' Hai had lit up and was blowing smoke towards the water.

'Three weeks.' Her mind flew to Atasha's folder, still in her carry-on. This was an ocular, a recce for her future business. 'I might stay longer.'

She saw his eyebrows lift slightly in surprise. 'What about your job? It's okay?'

She found that she couldn't bring herself to talk about what had happened at *Parcours*—not yet, not at this time. She didn't have the nerve to say it out loud, to express it even in the simplest of terms: that she had lost her job, that her magazine had gone digital and that there was no need for dinosaurs like her.

'I'm thinking of starting a business.'

'Ah?' Hai leaned forward, elbows on the table. 'A business, where? Singapore?'

'Here. In Huế.' Marina frowned. 'I'm planning to organize a creative retreat. It's like a gathering of creative people—a place for writers and artists. They can take classes, workshops—you know, learn from each other.'

How would Atasha explain it? How had she explained this dream to Marina, years ago? She looked out onto the water, surprised to find an ache in her. She missed Atasha. She had long realized that she missed Atasha more than she did Denis.

'I don't understand,' Hai was saying now.

'I'll bring a group of writers here from all over the world and connect them with other writers.'

'Like a tour group?'

'Like a class.' Now that she'd had to simplify it, it sounded plain and clinical. How was she to explain her vision to him?

Hai nodded. 'Do you know that I want to start a business, too? A small hotel.'

'You want to build a hotel?'

'No.' He took a short drag. 'My friend, he's with me. We'll rent a small hotel.'

'You mean you'll lease a hotel and manage it?'

'Yes, yes.' Hai was smiling. 'So, I could be my own boss.'

She saw his temples relax, the lines underneath his cheek soften. Marina thought of the money it would take, how that kind of venture needed so much capital. Not like the little creative retreat she was planning. Sure, the workshops entailed a lot of work—she could already foresee all the arranging and coordinating she would have to do—but it would not cost as much.

Despite the loftiness of his entrepreneurial plans, she felt admiration for him. She found that she liked this kind of ambition.

Living with Sinh

HAI

Sinh and Hai texted each other every day, talked over the phone on some days and met for a meal or coffee once or twice a week before going back to his rented room to have sex. Sinh worked as a waitress at Jasmine Hotel six days a week and lived with a strict aunt on Hyunh Street at the opposite side of the city, a little less than twenty minutes away from where he was staying. Because of this, they hardly saw each other during the week, and for this Hai was grateful.

Today was one of those days, but Hai didn't feel like seeing the shabby insides of his room. He had taken four nights off from Minh Thanh, something he had not done in a long time, and he'd been feeling a strange ripple of excitement all day. He hadn't told Sinh, of course. He hadn't told anyone, in fact—not even Phong—of his little plan: one night for Sinh, the rest were all for Marina. Three nights were reserved for Marina. The first night was obligatory. The next three involved something he wanted to do, and it felt dangerous yet worthwhile. He felt heady with the possibilities.

'It's good that you picked me up today,' Sinh said as she positioned herself behind him on the motorbike.

Hai was taken aback by her cold tone but didn't turn around. 'Of course,' he said, his voice amiable. He could feel her hot breath on the back of his neck.

She didn't say anything so he started his engine and backed out, heading towards the main road. Earlier that morning, they'd agreed to have an early dinner at one of the roadside restaurants they frequented.

'Someone saw you with a woman. On your motorbike.'

So that was it. 'It was a guest, em.' He tried to keep his voice smooth. They were riding slowly, and there was no traffic, so he didn't have to raise his voice. 'I have many different guests, you know that.' He sighed. Sinh was often like this when she was tired. He wanted to smoke a stick, at that very moment.

'She didn't look like a foreigner.' Sinh sounded accusing.

'So?'

'So why are you going about with another Vietnamese woman?'

She must have been talking about Carmen. That day when he met her and drove her around, looking for that stupid hostel that didn't even exist.

'It was nothing.'

'Nothing, really?' Sinh's voice reached a pitch he didn't like.

He continued riding, but instead of heading to the coffee shop, he turned in the direction of his room. He wanted to lay down in bed, not exchange niceties with some server.

'What can I tell you? She's just a guest. She's from the Philippines— that's why you think she's Vietnamese.'

Sinh didn't say anything for a moment after that. And then: 'Where are you going?'

'To my room!'

'Anh!' He felt a pinch on his waist but didn't turn his head. Sinh did this when she was annoyed with him or when she was tense. 'Aren't we going to eat?'

Sinh went about their relationship with such confidence, surety, and perhaps even entitlement—as if nothing could shake the coupledom that they had built in the last two years. She acted as if everything was a given and as it should be.

Sinh was shaking her head. 'It can't be this way. We need to get married soon.'

Hai didn't say anything. With Sinh, he had always felt that there was an invisible checklist that he had to tick.

They went inside his room, undressing quietly. Hai had wanted to sleep, but from the way Sinh was stroking his arm, he knew she wanted sex.

'I'm tired,' he said, as they laid down. But he still got on top of her, sliding his hand inside her panties before pulling them down. He tried to imagine their first time together.

'Anh.' Sinh's voice pierced through his blissful bubble.

He was shocked to see that his dick lay there limp and unresponsive. Without a word, he gathered himself up, and rolled off.

Atasha

MARINA

She wasn't craving coffee, but she decided to go to a coffee shop anyway. The cafés in Huế were quaint, old, industrial, and modern at the same time and felt different from the ones in Saigon or Hanoi. The attention to detail was impressive: stamped cement, textured walls, copper coverings for lamps, grillwork that was fitted perfectly. She had loved going to cafés and writing when she started working for the newspaper. When she came to Singapore, the time had disappeared, and the city did not encourage it.

But she was here now. She ordered at the counter, which was manned by young men and women, their faces smooth and taut. She knew she should organize herself and look through Atasha's folder soon. She was just throwing her savings away if she didn't act fast. She wanted this, right?

She took out Atasha's folder. It was a C-folder made of translucent plastic, so everything inside was protected. There were clippings on Central Vietnam, which included Huế. A packet that contained a disposable wet towel, now dried up. There were pieces of folded paper that served as chopstick holders and had addresses of restaurants. A brochure on the Imperial City, Khai Dinh's Tomb, the pagodas. There was a piece of paper with gridlines, which Atasha had always liked, even though she didn't use it for drawing, just for notes. Marina stared at Atasha's elegant handwriting, done with a thick pen. Atasha had listed hotel names, a loose list of things to do. Ten or twelve participants, she had written. Need a boutique hotel. Rent out ten rooms.

Marina rummaged through her own files, then pulled up a list she'd been working on occasionally during her spare time while working at *Parcours*. Organizing a destination writing workshop was a matter of putting things together.

First, she needed a website. She opened an account on Wix, chose a template, wrote a few words off the top of her head, and saved it as a draft. She bought an email address. She would work on that later, and maybe she should send call-out emails for a web designer and a social media person to streamline it further.

She created an account on Instagram. That was easy. Trickier was finding a place to stay for her writers and artists. A good hotel or better yet, a beautiful resort where they could all wake up inspired and invigorated by nature.

She would have to dig into her contacts for tutors and resource people, but that wasn't an issue at all.

The last part that she worked on was her favourite. It was organizing the activities the writers would do between the lectures. This was where the tours would come in, perhaps cooking lessons or a tour to a tea factory. She would have to immerse herself in the offerings of Huế.

A Small Hotel

HAI

He dropped Sinh at her aunt's house before heading to a small store that offered beer, along Ha Noi street, near Vinh Pearl Hotel. Sinh had asked him if he wanted to go out for a drink, but he said no. In reality, he wanted one but he wanted to be alone or be with anyone but Sinh. He was still reeling from what had happened, smarting from his non-performance.

Something had formed in his mind while he was waiting for Marina to come back to Huế. He'd already begun to feel a certain restlessness, months before he met Marina. He went to the bus terminal in the mornings, worked there until noon, slept in the afternoons, then stayed up nearly all night, working the reception counter at Minh Thanh. His body was used to this, but lately he'd begun to crave even more sleep and the waistband of his pants had become looser. He had the occasional tips from guests, the bigger ones from those who requested girls. And still, he made a pittance. He sent a big part of his salary to his parents through a cousin who worked in Huế but travelled back to Quảng Trị every last day of the month.

It wasn't even enough. He was paying for his father's medical bills. And even if his father wasn't sick, it was expected of him. It was just the thing to do.

Meanwhile, his colleagues were buying new motorbikes, throwing parties, eating and drinking at various restaurants during the week. Except for his manager, his colleagues at Minh Thanh were all younger than him, some living at home and supported by their parents. Unlike Hai, they had money to spend on themselves.

Surely, there must be another way?

Because no, he wasn't just stuck or stagnating—he was backtracking, pushed backwards and down. If he wanted to earn, he first needed to invest.

It was true what Phong had always been saying: 'If you want to earn big money then be prepared to invest even bigger money.'

If you want to catch a big fish, you need a bigger net.

If there was something that was getting clearer each day, it was that he was getting left behind.

* * *

Every year for the last five years, Phong and he had talked about saving and coming up with the money to finally do it: find a small hotel to lease and run it well. Every year for the last five years, Hai had asked to postpone. He was never ready with the money. He just never had enough. And because he'd known Phong for so long, he had taken it for granted that he would understand. He thought Phong would understand that his father was in and out of the hospital, and his mother didn't work outside the home.

He didn't show it, but Hai knew his friend well and long enough to sense that Phong was getting tired of waiting. Phong wouldn't do something duplicitous to him. But Hai knew he was losing patience. If he went ahead with the plan without Hai, perhaps he expected Hai to understand.

He was turning thirty-four in a few months. It was getting hard to ignore the boys in their twenties running alongside him, chasing tourists at the bus terminal. And he was one of the oldest at Minh Thanh—yet no doubt receiving the same measly salary of four million dong each month.

This is where he imagined Marina. Some force, more than physical attraction, had drawn him to her. She was reachable, available, pliable. She had potential. He wasn't quite sure, and he didn't want to admit what he had been feeling all along. She could help him in so many ways, and not just with money.

* * *

There was no one else at the small store except the owner, a man in his seventies who was always in a thin singlet, khaki slacks, and slippers. The store was tucked in the corner of an overlooked, inconspicuous alley, overshadowed by the more flamboyant souvenir shops and street coffee stalls.

'Just you?' The old man served him a can of Huda along with a small glass filled with ice. He had a strong, amiable voice that contrasted with his frail body.

'Everyone's busy tonight.' Hai lit a cigarette.

The old man raised his shoulders in a clumsy shrug. 'Not me,' he said, still smiling. He retreated to the back of the store.

Hai took his time, watching the few motorbikes that passed by on the street. He stretched his arms up, felt the looseness of his pants. Sinh and his mother may be right: he was getting too thin. He needed to fatten up.

He had told Marina earlier that because he was taking some days off, he needed to finalize some stuff at Minh Thanh. The lie had rolled off his tongue easily, as it did when he sometimes told Sinh that he was tired and would spend the afternoon and evening in his room, when actually, he'd go drinking at the beach with Phong.

He was about to finish his beer when he saw a familiar figure walking along the sidewalk across the street, coming from the direction of Minh Thanh Hotel. It was the Filipino girl, the one who said she had been robbed by her taxi driver.

'Hey!' He waved his arms. 'Hey, you there!'

Hai saw the girl freeze, her head whipping in his direction. She hesitated, then crossed the nearly empty road.

She wasn't smiling when she came up. 'Hi,' she said, her voice polite but tentative. She held out her hand awkwardly.

'How are you?' Hai took her hand. He bent down and grabbed his half-smoked stick then sat down and pulled up another chair. 'What are you doing here?'

The girl—Carmen something, yes, that was her name—sank down in the small chair. Unlike him, she had to squeeze into its tight confines. He glanced at her face. She didn't look sick or unhealthy; her face was as round and full as he had found her more than a week ago. But under the store's fluorescent lighting he could see that there were dark, puffy circles under her eyes and her cheeks sagged a little.

'I'm, um—' the girl stammered then seemed to catch herself. She straightened up. 'I was walking around. Trying to see what's here, in the city.'

Hai marvelled at the smooth clarity of her English but was astonished that she was out walking this late. It was already 9.30 p.m. If she'd been riding on a motorbike, it would have been a different story.

'Isn't your room far from here?' Hai asked.

'It's not that far.' She shrugged. She looked tired but at least she didn't look like she was about to cry. 'I already know the way.'

He paused again, the deep drawl of her voice still echoing in his ears. 'Have you eaten?' It was just the question he asked people, his way of being polite. A habit.

She nodded, curling her back and hugging herself as she looked around and further into the alley. She still didn't say anything.

The old man had emerged from his post behind the shelves. He glanced down at Carmen, smiling his yellow smile. 'Chao, em. Do you want anything?'

'She's not Vietnamese,' Hai said, slipping a fresh stick between his lips.

'Oh!' The old man looked at Hai then threw his head back, laughing. 'I thought she was your girlfriend!'

'What did he say?' Carmen was leaning towards him, the chair firmly stuck to her butt.

'He thought you were Vietnamese,' Hai said, omitting the girlfriend remark, which he didn't find amusing.

Carmen looked up and gave the old man a small smile but didn't say anything.

'Where is she from?' The old man was still there.

'Philippine,' Hai said, nodding at Carmen.

'Philippines,' Carmen piped in, 'with an "s".'

'Philippines,' Hai repeated, exaggerating the last syllable, feeling more embarrassed than annoyed.

'Ask your Philippine friend if she would like something.'

Hai turned to Carmen. 'Do you drink beer?'

'Yes,' she said, without hesitation. But she paused, then peered at the shelves. 'Wait. How much is it?'

'Don't worry,' Hai said, as the old man reappeared and gently laid down two more cans of Huda on the plastic table, along with another ice-filled glass for Carmen. 'The beer here is cheap. One dollar.'

Carmen's eyes took on a distant look, as if she was calculating the cost in her own country's money. Her eyes widened. 'That's almost fifty pesos! For one can of beer?'

'She said the beer here is too expensive,' Hai said to the old man. 'It's cheaper in the Philippines.'

'Is that so?' The old man chuckled amiably and raised his eyebrows, multiple wrinkle lines appearing on his wide forehead. He ambled back inside.

Hai turned to Carmen and sighed. 'Don't worry,' he said again, for lack of anything more to say. 'I'll pay.'

'No, no.' Carmen shook her head vehemently. 'I'll pay for my beer. Sorry.'

'Are you meeting someone?' Hai asked. It flew out of his mouth before he could stop himself. It was a little forward, asking that question—but *troi oi,* this girl was acting so reticent and secretive. He gulped down his drink, suddenly convinced it was the beer that was making him curious.

He tried again. 'So you've toured Huế?' She was a tourist, after all. For a moment, he wondered if he should refer her to Duong or Rin, who made a good living from paid guided tours in and around Huế. 'You've seen the citadel?'

She shook her head. 'No, no.' She averted her eyes as she raised the glass to her lips and took a sip. 'Um, not yet. Maybe tomorrow.'

'You want a guided tour? My friend, he can bring you to the citadel and the royal tombs. Huế has seven. If you want, you can go to the DMZ—'

The girl seemed to think, then said, 'Okay, you can give me their number.'

'I can call my friend right now, to book it for you if you want.' Shit again. He wasn't even on duty but here he was unable to stop hustling. He told himself that service was in his blood and that he was merely being efficient. The truth was, he couldn't pass up a single opportunity to earn even the smallest amount of money. Money was money.

He wasn't surprised to see that Carmen looked a little shocked. 'I'm not sure about tomorrow,' she hedged. 'I'm not sure about anything yet. I can be the one to call them.'

'Duong is my friend. Or you can go with Rin, he can bring you to the—'

'I'm here because I'm looking for someone.'

'Oh?' Hai didn't bother to hide the surprise on his face. 'Who?'

Carmen looked as if she regretted saying it but she set her shoulders and said, 'I'm looking for my mother.'

For a moment, Hai was speechless. 'Your mother is Vietnamese?' His voice sounded like a croak.

'No!' Carmen's shoulders relaxed. Her face took on something that resembled exasperation. 'She's Filipina. But she lives here.'

'In Vietnam? In Huế City?' Suddenly, Hai felt like he had a million questions to ask. 'Where?'

'I don't know,' Carmen said, simply. 'I don't know. It's just that—well, you know I don't have much money, and . . .' Her voice trailed off.

The money thing again. All this was confusing him. Carmen had told him that she wasn't here as a tourist, and now here she was saying that she was looking for her lost mother.

He wanted to ask more questions, but it was getting late. Carmen's story was as intriguing as it was mystifying for him, but Hai was more interested in getting some sleep. The beer was making him feel sleepy and he wanted to be ready for Marina tomorrow. Also, he needed to think of excuses to give Sinh.

Moving

HAI

Hai would have gladly stayed in one of the rooms in Chi Hanh's apartments, if only they had not been for women only. A room there was only 500 Vietnamese dong for the month.

'How much was your friend paying in that hotel?' Chi Hanh asked him.

'Too much, that's for sure,' Hai replied. 'Anyway, you know I'd rather bring business to you.'

'See, over here,' Hai said, waving Carmen over. 'It's just like my rent-room.' He opened the door. 'And you will be safe. It's a girls-only apartment.'

'How long do you think you'll stay?' Hai asked.

Carmen looked at him. 'Some months. Two or three . . .' The girl looked crestfallen.

Hai was brisk. 'She'll stay for six months, at least,' he told Chi Hanh in Vietnamese. 'She's very quiet. You'll have no problem. Filipinos are good clients. I know, I've had them in Minh Thanh. Funny, but really warm people.'

'Oh?' Chi Hanh raised an eyebrow, openly sizing Carmen up and down.

Hai laughed. 'Believe me.'

'Is she working here in Huế? What's her job?' Chi Hanh's eyes narrowed slightly, lips pursed. 'How is she going to pay every month after this?'

'She helps me with my English guests during tours,' Hai lied. 'You know me. I'm so bad at that. I can never pronounce their complicated words. Sometimes, I can't even get what they're saying.'

Chi Hanh grunted, though she nodded in agreement.

'But of course, if anything happens, you can always call me. I can take care of it. But what would happen, huh? She's no problem.'

Beginnings

MARINA

She had chosen to start over, so she let herself remain open. Huế City, Marina had decided, would be the big reset of her life where she could try to pursue a dream, and to find love that was different from what she had always known it to be. So, she had told herself to say yes to anything that would help her discover what it was like to live and, if she was lucky, to thrive in this city.

Just thinking about this made her feel better. Things have already happened—signs, surely—that there was a world beyond the one she'd built for herself in Singapore. Another world where she could belong.

Hai had been the first sign. And then it was the memory of Atasha.

She would let herself trust. She had let Hai, the ultimate Huế local, decide. After all, she had told herself this was a recce. She had told herself that finally, after a very long time, she had time and the mental space to feel things out. It applied to this creative retreat and to the life change she was planning.

It was late afternoon by the time they made their way back, but the heat that accosted them in An Thuan seemed to stay on Marina's skin, even as the wind that whipped against them grew cool as they drove back on Hai's motorbike towards Huế.

'Did you like the beach?' Hai asked, picking up the remote from the side table and turning on the TV. It was the first thing he did when he entered a room that had one, Marina noticed.

Marina switched on the air-con, her insides feeling wilted. 'It was nice,' she said. 'Hot.' She felt sweat trickle down her back and she fanned herself with her hands, willing the room to grow cooler.

She was still trying to make sense of what happened and so she watched him closely, though she didn't really know what she was looking for. 'It was interesting to finally meet Carmen.'

'Yes.' Hai placed the remote back on the side table, eyes still glued to the TV.

She leaned against the headboard and watched as he removed his shirt over his head, placing it carefully against the back of the chair by the dresser.

Now shirtless, wearing only his jeans, he folded a pillow in half and lay down on the space beside her. 'Are you tired?' He asked, grabbing the remote from the side table. He touched her arm briefly, then turned back to the TV, turning it on and changing the channel to HBO.

'No,' Marina said. Hai's touch had been so fleeting, it was over before it even started.

Marina saw the Vietnamese subtitles, then noticed the time on the clock on the wall. It was 4.30.

'So you're helping Carmen find an apartment?'

Hai's gaze was still trained on HBO. 'Room. Just a room.'

'What's wrong with her hotel now?'

Hai looked at her, twisting his neck so the pillow was squished behind his head. 'Too expensive.' He glanced back at the TV. 'Too ugly. Dirty.'

'How much?'

'Eight dollars for a night.'

Marina didn't say anything, mainly because she hadn't forgotten how it felt to count every single peso and cent as if your life depended on it. And there were times when she felt that her life depended on whether she had that extra hundred peso.

Instead, she studied his profile as he watched, mesmerized by the movie in front of them. How intent, how focused, and how silent this man could be. Perhaps he wasn't being evasive, giving those short answers; it could be that he wasn't even interested in the subject of Carmen. The girl had gone through a traumatic encounter on her first day in Vietnam, and was here to find a mother whom she had not seen for—how long was it?

Fourteen years. Yes, that was the number. A long time, but not unheard of with overseas workers in the Philippines. How many stories had Marina heard and read growing up in her small town and in Manila about Filipinas who left their children to take care of another person's children? Mothers and wives spending more than a decade in Milan, Dubai, London, or any state in the United States, remitting money and sending balikbayan boxes to the Philippines, boxes as big as refrigerators filled with everything from clothes and bedsheets to shoes and appliances. One of her roommates in their bedspace near *Manila Guardian,* the first newspaper she had worked for, had a mother who was a domestic worker in Hong Kong, an hour-and-a-half plane ride to Manila but who only came home every five years. And Marina herself had once been an OFW before she gave up her Philippine citizenship.

But Carmen had mentioned that her mother was living here as an expat. Vietnam was not the place for OFWs.

That wasn't her concern. What disturbed her was Hai's involvement in all this. Why was he close with Carmen, why was he solving all her problems?

Perhaps she should just let it go, stop asking questions. She had things to do, a workshop to organize.

'Give me her number,' Marina said to Hai now. A flash of inspiration. 'Maybe I can talk to her. Maybe I can help, too.'

Notes by Atasha

MARINA

She had not expected to remember Atasha so strongly and so vividly in Huế, a city Marina knew Atasha had never been to. But Atasha was here, tugging at Marina's mind when she woke up in her hotel, swirling along with her questions about Hai and Carmen.

Perhaps, she thought as she threw off the covers and gingerly got up, *I should stop resisting it*. Atasha was here, even after all these years. She was all over the stack of papers and notes she had about the workshop, in the folder she'd left with Marina, forgotten through the years. Atasha was—*is*—in this whole project because it had been her dream, a creative project she would have no doubt pursued, had she lived. Had she chosen to live. Now, conveniently, it had become Marina's. This was her solution, her way out of her personal rut.

She started making the bed, making sure that the corners were tucked in, the top part smooth, the pillows fluffed back and positioned just right.

How convenient, a part of her was saying. The guilty part of her, the one that'd been haunting her for years. Another part of her had given herself permission to use all these ideas, to do everything she could to make them work, to make them into something Atasha would have wanted.

How convenient, she thought again echoing a small voice inside her. Not Atasha's, but her own. Or maybe it was her mother's voice, which always managed to worm its way into even the minutest decisions in her life.

Was she wrong for doing this? Was she hurting herself further by being here—dredging up the memory of Atasha and all that came with it, by reviving an old dream and trying to make it come to life?

Life happened in cycles, and with this recent job loss, Marina felt that she'd already gone around twice. She may have had a terrible childhood, but this was her life now. As long as she was breathing and not dead, it wasn't too late.

She forced herself to come back to the present. She'd been successful for years, keeping all this down. Like Atasha's folder, she had kept her impoverished past, her broken relationship with her parents, and her casual sex habit safely locked away in a drawer in an unused guest room, buried deep and unable to wreak havoc. Well, it got out sometimes and still caused trouble.

And so, was she giving permission for her past to create chaos in her life now? There was a meditation guru she had caught by accident on YouTube just before the new year last year, who said that one should write down the things one wants to leave behind on a piece of paper and burn it. Maybe she should have done that with Atasha's folder. But she knew that she couldn't. Never.

The casual sex, she wanted to forget. She had Hai.

Without Atasha, she would not have learned how to or strived to improve herself. Without Atasha, she wouldn't have fallen back into her old pattern of sleeping with men. Without Atasha, she wouldn't have been here today. Without Atasha, she would still have been in Singapore, caught in a working routine—lucrative, perhaps, but also soulless and stultifying.

For years, she had been haunted, torn about whether Atasha had been the best or worst thing that happened in her life during that period. When she learned that Atasha killed herself, she still did not know the answer to that.

No, she had to continue. It could be her way out of Singapore. Or at least, out of herself.

* * *

Atasha had liked old-fashioned things. So, maybe, that was another trait that drew Marina to her. In the weeks, months, and years following

Atasha's death, Marina often found herself thinking of Atasha's ways, which seemed to belong to a different time.

Today, she allowed herself to think of Atasha's old, thrifted shelf, Marina's favourite piece of furniture in her apartment, the one crammed with her travel folders. When she had learned of Atasha's suicide, Marina hadn't even been in Manila. She was not there when she died. Was that special shelf sold, like her apartment? Probably sold and the folders, labelled as junk and thrown away. Because who would keep papers and clippings and old little notes?

She wouldn't. Except that moment when she had discovered Denis's writing on the chocolate wrapper in the Qatar and Dubai folder and, on a whim, she'd taken the Huế folder, too.

She opened the folder and spread its contents on the table.

In the 'Huế, Vietnam' file, there were pages torn from magazines that were not at all related to Vietnam. There were photos of villas in Sicily, a farmhouse in a place called Miradoux. Atasha must have saved these as pegs for the creative retreat.

There was a thin, soft-bound notebook small enough to fit into a pocket, labelled 'Creative Huế'—the kind of notebooks Marina knew Atasha favoured and which she hoarded from a shop in Tokyo.

It could be done, as Atasha kept telling her back when they were friends. Back when Atasha was still in her life.

Did Marina really want this? To do something that Atasha wanted? *It was what Atasha wanted for them both, remember?* A voice kept telling her. Was it defeatist that Marina wanted to fulfil that?

The thing was, it could be her own. And now, it was her own project. Atasha's idea, Marina's execution. Atasha had simply planted the seed. Marina was to make it grow into a tree—trees.

That wasn't really the issue, she knew that. There was absolutely nothing wrong with organizing the writing retreat. The problem was her, Marina.

Meeting Nina

HAI

There was a missed call from Chi Hanh. Hai glanced at Carmen, sipping her coffee quietly across from him, in the noisy café he'd chosen along Nguyen Huế street. He'd wanted to check up on the girl, but now he worried for a moment that she'd done something not to the landlady's liking. Chi Hanh was a rational, reasonable woman, Hai knew that; it was Carmen he was worried about. He'd already collected his unofficial commission and god knows he didn't want to give it back, no matter how measly the amount had been.

She picked up on the third ring. 'Chao, chi!' Hai kept his voice upbeat and sat up. He saw Carmen's eyes flick up, startled by the change in his voice.

'What are you doing?' Chi Hanh's tone was friendly but brisk.

'Having coffee, chi,' Hai replied, automatically. 'The usual. What can I do for you? Is there a problem?' He knew he was saying too much, but he couldn't help himself.

'Troi oi,' Chi Hanh let out a big, guttural sigh. 'I do have a problem on my hands right now.'

'With Carmen?' Hai asked.

'Carmen? No.' She sounded surprised. 'I called because one of my tenants has been pestering me day and night if I know someone who can take care of their kids. You know their nanny-tutor disappeared, right? Word is that the woman got pregnant—by another man! Her husband is in Dong Ha. Dong Ha! How far. And still . . .' Her voice trailed off.

Hai cleared his throat. 'So the nanny took off? This family—they have no one else working for them?'

'Right. The woman is Vietnamese married to a foreigner,' Chi Hanh said, her voice crisp. 'French.'

'Oh? Well, then.'

'Their lease will be up in five months, and if they don't get a tutor, they would probably want to move near the school, rent one of the villas there. As if that would help.'

Hai made a sound, as if agreeing with Chi Hanh. He was itching to get off the phone. This wasn't his business at all.

'Do you know someone? Someone who speaks perfect English? Who can take care of kids and teach them this perfect English? And who can also help around the house? A housekeeper.'

'I'll ask my colleagues in the hotel. I'll ask everyone I know,' Hai said, intending to do nothing of the sort. He already had too much to do as it is. He was just relieved there was no problem with Carmen.

'*Cam on,* em,' Chi Hanh said, hanging up before Hai could even say goodbye. It was fine. Chi Hanh was never profuse with her thank yous.

'What was that all about?'

'What?' Hai frowned as his phone beeped. A message from Chi Hanh still, saying that the mother will be calling him. He slid the phone into his pocket. He needed to go to the bus station. 'It was just Chi Hanh, your landlady.'

'You mentioned my name,' Carmen said. 'What did she say?'

'She asked if you were happy with the room,' Hai lied, his mind already on the arriving buses from Hanoi and Saigon. He was hoping he could get more tourists for the hostel.

'That's all?' Carmen raised her eyebrows again. 'You mentioned my name twice.'

Hai looked at her in surprise. 'Really? It was nothing.' He didn't have time for this. He stood up. The morning crowd at the café was starting to thin. 'Some problem with her tenant.'

'What was the problem?'

'She needed a housekeeper.' Hai looked at the time on his phone. 'For her friend. Let's go.'

'Hai? What if I apply for the position?'

'What position?' He was going to be late if they keep talking like this.

'The housekeeper of Chi Hanh's friend.'

* * *

The call came in less than ten minutes, just as Hai and Carmen were about to leave and go their separate ways.

'Alo, Anh Hai,' said a silky voice from the other line. '*Khoe khong?* How are you?'

The voice sounded familiar, though the way the caller spoke in accented English wasn't. 'Fine,' Hai replied, his voice coming out automatic and artificial.

'I hear you're going to help me again.'

'Who is this?' He tried to keep the confusion from his voice. 'Nina?' He asked, remembering the English name that Chi Hanh had texted him.

'That's me.' A tinkle of laughter.

Hai clucked his tongue. 'No, you're—'

'What a small world. Chi Hanh said you have someone for me. A foreigner? Not Vietnamese, right?' Hai was taken aback by the tinge of contempt in her tone, because she herself was Vietnamese, despite this new name. 'Whoever that is, she'll do. Come over tomorrow, yeah? Chi Hanh has my address.'

'Yes, but—'

'Ah, then good! I know how you work.' Nina lowered her voice. 'And I have to thank you.'

'Listen—'

'I need to go now. *Nhan-nhan.* Everything is busy for me now, and I really am so tired.'

Hai knew the line was dead even as he opened his mouth to say something that wouldn't be heard, well, right now. Tomorrow, she said. Of all the surprising things. For a moment, he could only stare out at the distance, frowning and unable to speak. He fished out a stick and lit it.

'Hai?' Carmen broke into his thoughts. 'So? I can go to the interview? To that French family?'

Hai blinked. 'We,' he said, grimly. '*We* will go to the interview.'

'But I thought you said you were busy tomorrow?' Carmen cocked her head to the side. Glancing at his furrowed brows, she bit her lower lip.

'No. Yes.'

'You know them,' she said, her voice cutting through the air, an annoying mix of smugness and surprise.

'Her,' Hai corrected, taking a shallow puff. 'I know her.'

'Oh no.' For a moment, Carmen looked concerned. 'Ex-girlfriend?'

Ex-prostitute, was what he wanted to tell Carmen, but no good could possibly come out of that kind of reply, could it? Because how else could he refer to Nhung a.k.a. Nina, former ca ve and once most requested by his horny regulars at Minh Thanh Hotel—now married to a rich foreigner and willing to pay 600 dollars for a fucking tutor?

The Citadel

CARMEN

The room was bare and a little dusty, but it was better than the one she'd stayed in when she first arrived in Huế—the claustrophobic, closet-like quarters where Carmen had begun to feel drowned and suffocated, as if smothered by the walls and ceiling every time she woke up in the morning. Her new room at Chi Hanh's apartments had two decent-sized square windows with thick grills in the front, yellowing walls, a wooden single bed, and a simple dresser pushed against one corner. The bathroom, shared between two tenants, was as dank as the toilet that Carmen had used in Hai's rented room. But Hai was enthusiastic, and Carmen said yes hoping that maybe, maybe she'd stop feeling like the room and everything else in it was about to fall in on her. Also, it was cheaper than paying on a day-to-day basis at the previous hotel.

But she was oblivious to these details now. There was one thing she needed to do and it clawed at her mind all morning, even as everything was finally settled and she'd handed over the first month's rent to Chi Hanh and said goodbye to Hai: she had to check if there was anything new on Nicole Peltier's Facebook account. The room and everything else in it fell away as Carmen took out her phone and sat down on the edge of the bed, keying in the WiFi password that Hai had gotten from Chi Hanh. She had her mother's name on the search bar in an instant, waiting for the page to load with bated breath, as usual. The connection lagged slightly, and Carmen felt the familiar sadness and terror creeping and coating the insides of her chest even as her heart thumped faster. This was the only connection she had with her mother and she lived in fear of one day discovering she could not anymore access it.

The photo was so vivid, so new and different from what she was used to seeing on her mother's account that Carmen thought she had the wrong Facebook page. But there it was: Nicole Peltier standing casually on a small, low bridge clad in a bright blue Vietnamese dress, the collar up to her neck, the silky fabric hugging her arms, the hem flowy around her ankles as if lifted by an invisible wind or a sudden animated movement. Carmen recognized the traditional costume from photos she'd seen online of Vietnam. She was smiling and relaxed, flanked by two other women in the same cut of dress, but in different colours, one in pink, and the other in red. They were standing on a small, old bridge with intricate mouldings and carvings, the river a pale greyish green behind them. An ancient bridge, on ancient grounds. There must be a palace or temple nearby, but the photo only caught the bridge and the river. The weather was overcast as it was that day; it could be any day in Huế.

Carmen's eyes flew to the time it was uploaded: one hour ago. She gave out a little gasp, jumping off the bed so quickly that she knocked down her backpack on the dusty floor. A tangled mix of hope, regret, and frustration squeezed at her as she thought of how while she had been taking her time, checking out this new place with Hai, her mother had been out and could have been within reach—perhaps she had even been somewhere nearby.

'*Dios ko*,' Carmen muttered, pressing her fingers on her temple as her breathing shifted to something rapid and shallow. All she could think of was that she needed to go to that place where her mother was—wherever that was in Huế—right now.

But where was that place? Where would she start? She could hardly feel her fingers as she quickly pressed 'Save' and stored the photo on her phone. And then, she reached for the keys Chi Hanh had placed on the dresser, gathering her fallen backpack from the floor. She was out of the gate in less than five minutes, trying to remember which direction Hai had told her led to the main road. She started walking, turned left and passed a small coffee shop filled with men sitting on low plastic chairs, staring at a TV that had been fixed on the wall. English was a problem, she knew, but she was desperate to know where that photo had been taken.

'Hello,' she said, walking up to them and clicking her phone open so her mother's photo was on the screen. Two of the men stood up. She knew they may not understand, but she asked the question anyway. 'Do you know where this is?' she asked, tapping the photo on her phone.

One of the men nodded. 'I know,' he said. 'That's the Citadel.'

* * *

Carmen stood in front of the gates of the Citadel, feeling the energy flow back into her bones for the first time since her arrival in Huế. Her mother had been here, she thought, as she gazed up at the tall, thick walls of the Imperial City. Possibly, even just this morning. And she could still be here. Carmen held onto this thought, hopeful and almost giddy, as she squinted and caught sight of the ancient city's wide courtyard in the distance, its size dwarfing the visitors inside.

And if she wasn't? A tiny voice inside was warning her, not for the first time since she left Manila, of the scale of what she'd decided to do.

Even if Nicole Peltier wasn't there, people who could still recognize her from the photo might be there.

She walked briskly under the gate and towards the spacious courtyard, spotting the few tourists roaming around, only to stop in their tracks every few meters to take a photo with their phone.

Seeing them only intensified her desperation. *Where was that picture taken?*

The river, just look for the river, Carmen thought. She could do this. She would do this.

Banh Mi Lady

CARMEN

It was the smell that led her closer: a smoky-sour mixture of cured meat and pickled vegetables wafting from a small, boxy cart topped with a glass shelf with 'BANH MI OPLA' painted on one side in bold, bright red. Carmen had not eaten since last night.

Behind, a slim woman in a floppy hat and a T-shirt dress was rearranging thick rolls of processed meat and sliced pork, tubs of pickled cucumbers, a small tray of eggs. Fat pieces of half-baguettes were crammed inside the glass box, one on top of the other and a makeshift oven lay blackened but unlit on the ground. Beside her was a girl who looked about sixteen, her dark hair gathered in a high pony, sitting on her haunches as she tapped away at her phone.

'Hello,' Carmen said, inching to the side of the small cart. Then, as Hai had taught her, she said, 'Xin chao.'

'*Banh mi*, em?' The woman looked up from her meats and smiled brightly, wiping her hands on the sides of her blouse. Carmen saw that the foundation she'd applied, which looked like it was three shades lighter than her skin, had settled on the lines of her face. 'One, two?'

Carmen shook her head, ignoring the gnawing in her stomach. 'Sorry.' She tried what she hoped was an apologetic smile and held out her phone, Nicole Peltier in bright blue. 'Have you seen her?' She tapped on her mother's image, sliding her fingers on the screen until Nicole's smiling face was bigger than her thumb.

'Oh!' Banh mi lady bent down to peer at her phone, so close that her nose seemed to touch the screen.

'Is she—was she around here?' Without waiting for an answer, Carmen gestured towards the wide expanse of the grounds.

Banh mi lady looked up and nodded approvingly. '*Ao dai, dep. Xinh dep!*' she said, her face splitting into a smile.

Carmen felt a rush inside her. What was it that the woman was saying? She had no clue but it sounded positive, as if she recognized Nicole or at least, knew something.

'Beautiful,' the young girl piped up. She was still on her haunches but had looked up from her phone. 'She said the dress'—the girl pointed a finger at Carmen's phone—'the dress of that woman is so beautiful.'

'She's here?' Hand trembling, she gestured at the bridge again, almost half-expecting Nicole Peltier to stroll by in her blue dress. The cart couldn't have been more than a couple of hundred metres away.

The woman nodded. 'Same-same.' As if looking for affirmation, she turned and barked out something to the girl on the ground.

Carmen was too busy to figure what it was. All she could think of was that Nicole Peltier was—or had just been—here. Of course, they'd seen her. How could they not? From where they were stationed, they had a clear view of visitors going to and from the old bridge. Nicole may have even bought a sandwich from them. For a moment Carmen thought of the meats the lady was selling at her stall. It wasn't hunger she was feeling, she told herself, it was the longing—raw and permeating—to see her mother.

'She's—' Carmen's breath caught, and she swallowed hard to keep her voice from shaking. 'She's—she's my mother.'

'Oh!' Understanding flooded the banh mi lady's face as her eyebrows shot up, her mouth forming into a delicate 'O'. She regarded Carmen for a moment. 'No,' she said finally, shaking her head. 'There!' To Carmen's surprise, she whirled around and pointed towards a tree-lined park in the distance, across the road and away from the Citadel.

Something inside her seized, even as she begun to feel lightheaded, her head feeling as if it were about to float high above and beyond this ancient, majestic sprawl.

'Are you—?' Carmen struggled to find the words, the simplest ones she knew. 'What did you say?' Was she even making sense?

The woman pointed, more vigorously this time, towards the park.

'Are you sure?' *Don't shout*, Carmen told herself. *Don't yell or frighten them with your relief, your desperation, your happiness.* Because this, so far, had turned out to be the most important moment since she arrived here in Huế. Be calm, like how you used to be, all those years with all those strangers in Luneta Park.

'Sure.' The woman was nodding. 'Linh,' she said. 'My name is Linh.'

Carmen nodded and said her own name, but her voice, as well as Linh's, sounded muffled and faint, as if murmured from a distance. It was as if she'd entered a tunnel and could see nothing else but that circle of light at the end, hazy and glowing and full of images of her and her mother. She shifted her backpack and felt her legs tense up, ready to spring forward in the direction of the road. The thought of seeing her mother's face again close, so close that she could reach out and touch her, hold her hand the way she used to when she was little—

'We go.'

The woman's heavy, hard-edged English sliced into her thoughts, a thick knife coming down on a flimsy little bubble, jarring and incongruent. Linh reached out to tap her on the shoulder. Then, a hand on her arm, moist and warm.

Carmen paused, looked at her in confusion. What was Linh doing? Why was she holding her back, now, when there wasn't time?

'I have to go,' Carmen said, taking a step back.

Pointing again into the distance, Linh threw out in clipped English, crunching her syllables: 'We go by motorbike.'

Carmen stopped. Motorbike. Of course, that would be faster. 'Yes,' she said. 'Hurry, please.'

Linh barked out something to the girl who leapt to attention and stood behind the cart, as Linh gave instructions. Or at least, that was what she looked like she was doing from her frantic hand gestures towards the meats and the bread.

'We go,' she said, disappearing behind a tree. She emerged, wheeling a slim, rusty motorbike. The seat was grey and fraying, the remaining side mirror cracked.

Something inside Carmen clicked. 'Wait.' She looked at her phone again, surprised that at that moment, she thought of Hai. 'I want to call my friend,' she said, already scrolling through her contacts. She stopped abruptly. There was only 11 percent battery left. *Shit*. She shook her backpack. Her extra battery must have fallen out when she knocked it down. 'I'll call my friend.'

'No,' Linh said. 'We go.' From out of nowhere came a yellow helmet with a lip that made it look more like a plastic hat than protective gear. In one swoosh, Carmen felt the top of her head encased in it, Linh's fingers working the thin straps under her chin.

'Uhm.' Linh nodded approvingly, patting Carmen's shoulders. She didn't have one for herself but she straddled the motorbike and pulled at Carmen's arm.

The sound came out muffled. Carmen felt her ears being squashed by the stiff padding. 'It's too tight,' she said, both hands instinctively coming up to the side of her head, fingers grappling with the helmet's smooth surface.

'Okay.' Linh pulled again at Carmen's arm until she was closer. '*Nhan-nhan!*'

'Follow me,' she repeated, patting the seat behind her.

Carmen climbed up the motorbike.

Loweq

MARINA

Manila, 2000

People in *Loweq* magazine liked to say they know Atasha Magsaysay, but Marina always felt she knew Atasha first: they attended the same creative writing class at the University of the Philippines.

Back then, Atasha had already stood out. She floated into class smelling like fresh lavender and draped in well-pressed blouses and flowy pants, her hair always in a neat, wavy bob. Everyone liked her because she listened and took everyone's comments seriously and without fuss.

'True class,' one of her classmates had remarked, as they watched Atasha getting into the back seat of a box-type Mercedes, ready to be driven to her next class.

Marina had shrugged. She got into the Philippines' state university on a full scholarship. Years after, she put her Journalism degree to use as a reporter at a national broadsheet, *Manila Guardian*. After a year, she decided to apply at *Loweq,* a boutique magazine owned by a wealthy family in Manila with several corporations that decided publishing was another way to make money.

Marina applied for the position because of the money, which— between the usual expenses of rent, food, and transportation plus a tiny allowance for her mother—always seemed to run short. But she was used to that. *Loweq*'s pay was as good as the other glossies, which was still higher than any broadsheet salary. And also, Marina was vying for a higher position of associate editor, as compared to being a lifestyle writer, a staff writer, technically, at *Manila Guardian*.

223

Atasha was *Loweq's* editor-in-chief and she had recognized Marina from that creative writing class in UP Diliman. 'Marina Bellosillo,' Atasha said, not even glancing at Marina's resumé on the table in the conference room where they had the interview. 'I remember you. Professor Ava's class, right? You wrote the stories that made everyone laugh. Lots of dry humour.'

Marina got the job after that and doubled her take home pay. She could finally move out of the house and be away from her mother.

* * *

The *Loweq* editorial staff went out in groups at lunch, but Atasha stayed at her desk most weekdays in her cubicle at the far end of their floor. Marina stayed back, too, because she was unsure what the rules in this new magazine office were: Should she go and have lunch with the rest of the staff and leave Atasha as they all did? Or should she stay and ask Atasha to lunch? She was, after all, the one mainly responsible for why Marina, now *Loweq's* new associate editor and second-in-command, was here. And why did Atasha stay behind and not eat lunch? After three days of observing Atasha from her desk, Marina rapped lightly on the cubicle wall.

'Atasha,' she said, her body not quite inside the office, 'are you not having lunch?'

'Ah,' Atasha said, delicately. 'I usually just grab a sandwich after. It gets crowded at the places downstairs. Have you seen the cafés? They're miniscule.' She sat up. 'Have you eaten lunch? Why didn't you go with the girls?'

'It's okay,' Marina said quickly. 'I'm fine, I had a big breakfast, so I'm not hungry yet.'

Atasha stood up, hoisting her expensive-looking leather handbag on her shoulder. 'Come,' she said, 'let's grab a sandwich together. There's a Reuben sandwich that I really like and maybe we can eat it somewhere else . . .'

'That would be nice.' Marina had never eaten a Reuben sandwich, but she'd read about it in the magazines.

Atasha gave her desk, which was littered with printed layouts and press kits, one last look. Then she looked up again. 'Oh my god,' she said, her hand flying to her mouth, 'I'm so sorry. Did you want rice?'

'No,' Marina said, with a vigorous shake of her head. She ate rice every day. 'A sandwich is fine. Totally fine.'

It was true. Atasha was having lunch with her. At the time, it felt like that was all Marina needed.

Atasha's Tbilisi

MARINA

Tbilisi, 2002

The idea came, aptly, as they were sipping strange-coloured wine in an old writers' residence in Tbilisi. The day before, they had peered down clay vessels buried underground, half-listening to a well-dressed Georgian oenologist explain how these wines got their amber–orange hue. The day before that, they had ridden horses down twisting roads to see a canyon, viewed the snowy tips of the Caucasus mountains from the top of a thousand-year-old monastery, clambered up ruins to reach a former king's quarters carved out of stone. And they drank more of the local vino, the blackest brew they'd ever encountered, this time from gigantic horns.

They were on a press junket to the Republic of Georgia, and Atasha was clearly inspired. Marina was, too—chiming in with the other journalists as they marvelled at the former Soviet republic's baroque doors, vintage sinks in the bathrooms, and wabi-sabi arrangements of the dining spaces. It was 2002 and she'd been working at *Loweq* and with Atasha for two years. She appreciated these things now, truly. Such had been Atasha's influence on her. Still, she found herself distracted by the local men, who were sloe-eyed and thickly-bearded, and dragged their words when they spoke English.

'Isn't it amazing,' Atasha was saying now, 'that they have *this* at a writers' residence!' She made a sweeping gesture at the lush garden before them, where century-old firs provided thick, leafy shade to the little tables nestled against ivy-covered walls. It was a restaurant, hidden far back behind the building. They themselves were at a corner table laden with Georgian *phkali* and a bottle of the amber wine, flanked on each side by a green sea of pothos. There had been a lull in the press activities that afternoon, so they'd set out to see the writers' house. But they ended up staying when they discovered the garden restaurant hidden at the back.

Marina herself still couldn't get over Tbilisi's stylish spaces, the majestic mountains, the creative restaurants, the unique cafés. And she couldn't believe she was here, thousands of miles from Manila, in this utterly unique city that no one seemed to have heard of—with Atasha Magsaysay. Even after two years, she was still fascinated, she was still enthralled.

'We should do something creative,' Atasha was saying now, fiddling with her wine glass and eyeing the tall, Georgian women who'd just sauntered in, decked in jewel-toned skirts and casual sneakers. 'We should be like these locals.'

Marina nodded, not exactly sure where this was going. Atasha had a way of noticing the smallest of details, of glorifying the ordinary. But her eyes followed Atasha's gaze. The Georgian women had lit cigarettes, never taking off their narrow, pointy Sixties-style sunglasses.

'Cool,' Marina replied. Over the years, she'd devised ways to express her wholehearted agreement. 'They look like they belong in Berlin,' she added, the words rolling off her mouth easily because they were true: she *had* been to Berlin and to some other places in the world she had never even dreamed of going. Like Tbilisi, for instance.

Two years of working with Atasha had transformed her. She was not the Marina Bellosillo of before, no. The old Marina slept in dinghy bedspaces and wore limp blouses and jeans to work and everywhere else. The old Marina didn't care about style or beauty or nuance. There had been a time when she was perfectly okay with ugliness, with ordinariness.

It was Atasha who taught her the importance of presentation, though Atasha herself never looked like she ever needed to pretend to be someone that she was not. It was Atasha who told her that it was better to be overdressed than underdressed, better to stand out than to be swept back into the sidelines. You need to make an impact, no matter how small.

Marina thought at first that it was being part of a monthly glossy, of *Loweq* and how it was as a magazine—fashion-forward, avant-garde, niche yet celebrity-driven—that had made her change her tastes, made her want to elevate herself. She had, after all, come from a staid, old-fashioned lifestyle section of a daily broadsheet, where her editors were in their late fifties and more interested in garden clubs and kids' programmes than what was pop culture-ish and current. *Manila Guardian* had paid the bills and imparted to her the discipline of turning in stories on tight deadlines. But like the broadsheet that it was, her feature stories were practical and no-nonsense. It lacked style, aspiration, indulgence.

Had it been only just two years? Atasha had remained the same—outrageous, charismatic, and fabulous. It was Marina who had changed.

Two years crammed with creative ideas, press trips, celebrity collaborations, and writing—always, the writing. Because of Atasha's standards, Marina felt it was during these two years that she had written her best lifestyle articles, her best cover stories. There was none of *Manila Guardian's* hobbling, broadsheet-style feature articles. Atasha transformed *Loweq* into the cool, niche magazine it was meant to be and brought Marina along for the ride.

Atasha was still the boss, yes. But because she was Atasha's associate editor, they often stayed late looking at proofs, discussing themes and next issues. At first, Marina was after the small overtime pay—god knows she needed it at that time. Eventually, it was her fascination with Atasha that made her want to stay. They started going out for drinks, Marina always shocked at Atasha's expensive appetite: she wanted *cochinillo*, sushi, champagne—food that Marina only had the chance to eat at posh press conferences and during travel junkets. And yet, here was Atasha treating these things as normal and everyday. That was one of Atasha's specialties: turning the extraordinary into the ordinary, and vice versa.

'I'm super inspired.' This was also one of Atasha's favourite lines. She was unapologetic about being moved by certain things: she saw the beauty in the mundane, she saw the little things. She was inspired by the colours on supermarket shelves, the lines in concrete floors, spilled sauces that created patterns. Only Atasha would say that a dilapidated junkyard was beautiful. She was an artist at heart, and she poured this creativity into *Loweq's* covers, its lifestyle features, and occasional fashion spreads.

'We should organize a creative retreat,' Atasha was saying now. 'You know, a destination thing where writers can meet other writers. It should be an inspiring place where they can all share their ideas.' She was always, always about the creative process. 'Create everyday' was one of her favourite adages.

'What do you mean?' Marina was used to Atasha's impulsive, out-of-nowhere ideas and this sounded like one of them, spurred for sure by Tbilisi's artistic vibe. This time, though, it seemed more serious than the others.

'Imagine yourself going to a city and meeting new people—your people,' Atasha said. 'Like a conference. But it should be small, a select number.'

'Here?'

'No, no,' Atasha said, 'It's too far. Somewhere closer. Asia.'

'An island in the Philippines? Palawan?'

Atasha made a face. 'It's so hard to get there.' Her face turned pensive. 'Somewhere more accessible. Somewhere I would like to go to, too.'

'Bali, then.' Marina had been there once, and she knew that Atasha liked it.

'Too touristy. I'm so over Ubud!'

'Where else, then?'

'Definitely not Singapore. Or Thailand—it's too chaotic for me,' Atasha was murmuring. 'Maybe Krabi?'

'Too remote.'

'I know,' Atasha said. 'Vietnam!'

Marina looked at her doubtfully. 'That's overexposed too. And touristy.'

'There's a place I've been wanting to go to there,' Atasha grabbed her arm. 'Huế City.'

'Where?'

'Central Vietnam,' Atasha said, looking more sure than ever. 'We can have the creative workshop in Huế City. Oh, Marina. This is exciting!'

Marina stared at her, mind racing to know how best to respond.

'We must do it, the two of us.' Atasha's eyes were bright. They had that steely light that Marina recognized when Atasha was truly determined about something. Marina also knew that Atasha could do whatever she sought because Atasha had everything.

'What about *Loweq?*'

'We can do it at the same time, it's not a conflict of interest.'

Marina felt a tiny ruffling in her insides. Panic, she thought at first, but she later identified it as annoyance. It meant more work for her, Marina, and she was already feeling swamped at the moment. And she was still perennially on her toes when writing, styling, and putting together the magazine. Marina didn't want to slip and be accused of stagnating. No, that wasn't her. It wasn't easy to sustain Atasha's standards.

'I'll finance it,' Atasha said, her voice smooth and assuring. 'You just need to help me organize it. Come on, it will be fun.'

'We can think about it.' Marina tried not to sound doubtful. 'But yeah, it could work.'

'We can even move there.' Atasha wasn't letting up. 'You and I. We could have a villa, we could each have our own villa!'

Marina was beginning to feel thrilled. Moving abroad, to Vietnam, sounded exotic and exciting. With Atasha, it would be blissful, artistic, maybe even comfortable. Two best friends living together, running a successful business.

'There would be no problem promoting it,' Atasha was saying now. 'No problem at all.' She waved her phone. 'I can be the social media manager all the way.'

Before long, it became Marina's dream too.

Scammer

CARMEN

If the slight, nondescript waiter saw the thin, long gash on her arm that had started to bloom a bright pink, bleeding ever-so-slightly at the sides—or sensed that anything was amiss—he didn't show it. After all, aside from the very visible but superficial wound that Carmen couldn't hide under her short-sleeved blouse, nothing else seemed out of the ordinary. She was merely one of his patrons who'd chosen to sit in the furthest, darkest corner of the café where the chances of seeing passersby—and being seen—was almost nil.

It was not the type of café that Carmen would choose. Like the cafés in Huế City that she'd caught a glimpse of from the road in the week that she'd been here, this one was crammed with tables and chairs but was also replete with lush, artfully-placed leafy plants and colourful, oversized lanterns that hung like bright candy from the ceiling. A stylish café, some would call it, but not one that Carmen Maranan would normally choose to sip an overpriced iced tea at—because it would be, for sure, too expensive—but she did because it was the first café she saw after darting through the many twists and turns, through the confounding alleys of that part of Huế, just so she could get as far away as possible from Linh and the petrol vendor.

She didn't ask herself why she didn't just go home. She did not go straight home because she did not know her way home. And also, she didn't want to want to cry or wail or whine as she had when the taxi driver had stolen her luggage.

No, Carmen had walked herself numb by the time she pushed open the door to the café, her body crying for some comfort, some relief—whatever it took to expel the roiling anger, betrayal, and confusion threatening, it seemed, to burst out of her as she went from alley to alley, turned corner after corner determined to put as much distance as she could between Linh and her. By then, more than an hour had passed, and she wanted whatever was on hand: cool, air-conditioned air for her too-hot body, a chair for her too-tired feet, a public but safe place where she wouldn't be able to break down and cry as she would, for sure, if she were in the privacy of her own room.

No, she could not allow her feelings to run away with her, as they had with Linh, the banh mi lady. She could not allow herself to feel, to let go; a tear, a loose thought, a single wrong move, no matter how slight or fleeting, could tip her over and cause every ounce of fear, grief, and frustration to spill out like a tsunami.

She was not a gullible person. Unlike Uncle Amado and Auntie Swan, Carmen didn't think that the tourists that they stole from were gullible. It was just that they were unfortunate.

And yet, how could she not have seen through what Linh had pulled off?

A bell tinkled by the door and she looked up, peering at the café entrance through the leaves. A well-dressed Vietnamese couple was scanning the room, looking for a suitable table. The woman was poured in tight jeans and a fire-engine red tank top, her head encased in a big floppy hat, similar to Linh's, but in neatly-woven straw. The man's crisp sport shirt glowed a bright white, a nifty pair of dark shades hanging placidly in the front pocket, his collar defiantly turned up. He stroked the girl's arm.

Carmen looked down at her dead phone and thought of Max.

She would not cry.

* * *

Four hundred fifty thousand dong, Linh had declared, when the three litres of petrol had already been poured into the gas tank. The man selling it by the litre was placing the cap back with a final twist.

'Four hundred fifty thousand? I thought you said—' Carmen stopped. What was it that Linh had said? Right after she climbed aboard Linh's motorbike, clutching gingerly at the Vietnamese woman's shoulders for support, they zoomed out of the Citadel grounds, onto the road and towards the park that Linh had pointed out to her, which was further than she realized. Linh twisted her neck to the side and barked out something in English, a number or a price because she remembered hearing 'Vietnamese dong'. But Carmen couldn't remember the amount that Linh initially said. Was it really 450,000 dong? She was so caught up in the scenes that were playing in her mind, one after the other, that she completely missed the amount that Linh was telling her.

She had been lulled by the wind on her face, the fast forward movement of Linh's motorbike, each turn and traffic light they passed made her feel as if she was moving closer to her mother at last. She did not pay attention to anything else.

The possibility, the closeness of seeing her mother had so consumed Carmen that she did not listen at all. She let the steady whine of the motorbike's engine fill her ears and filtered out what Linh was asking her just before they stopped at this stall selling gasoline.

'Gas. We need gas,' was all she remembered Linh saying as she had finally manoeuvred the motorbike into a tight alley, the road filled with long cracks. She slowed down to stop at a roadside shed where a man was sitting behind a row of one-litre plastic bottles filled with red liquid. Diesel gas.

'Four hundred fifty thousand,' Linh had repeated, as Carmen's mind raced to convert it into Philippine pesos.

'That's more than a thousand pesos!' Carmen's eyes had widened in disbelief. 'For—for three litres of gas?' Ignoring Linh and the gas vendor, she fumbled for her phone so she could double check with the calculator. The zeros must have confused her again. Surely, she must have computed it wrong?

Even in the outdoor sun, the numbers had glowed true on her phone calculator. Carmen looked up at Linh, who turned silent and immobile, her lips clamped in a resolute line, eyes looking away.

'No,' Carmen had said, though the Vietnamese woman remained stoic, staring at a point down the road, still not meeting her eyes. 'That's too much. That's not right.'

'You caused her to abandon her stall.' The young man at the gas station had taken a step closer. 'That's why she charges you that much. And so now she has lost customers for the afternoon.'

She could not understand what had happened. And yet, she did.

Carmen had struggled to get off the motorbike, but Linh was quicker. The Vietnamese woman was on her feet in an instant, grabbing her arm before uttering something in Vietnamese and then, yelling, 'You pay, you pay!'

Carmen had wrested her arm free, but not before the motorbike fell on its side with a clatter and she felt a stinging pain as Linh's nails dug into the thin skin of her forearm. Mustering every ounce of energy she had, Carmen extricated herself from her grip.

They had stood facing each other and, to her surprise, she saw that Linh was in tears. Her ponytail had come off and her hair fell in damp chunks around her wet face.

Chest heaving, Carmen had thrown a folded 100,000 dong note on the ground. Linh had charged her almost five times more.

What was she doing, handing over this much money to someone who'd told her she could help her find her mother?

Where, even, was Nicole Peltier?

Carmen had no idea.

She was angry at Linh about what happened, but she was angrier at herself for letting it happen.

With a turn of her heel, Carmen had run back to the main road.

* * *

It was late afternoon when she left the café and finally reached the small road that led to her rented room. Chi Hanh's apartment wasn't far from the Citadel, Carmen realized. Due to her tiredness and disorientation after the incident with Linh, she had gone around in circles.

The sounds of lively conversation in Vietnamese brought her out of her reverie. Not far from the corner, a small, temporary food stall had set up shop. With a pang, it reminded her of her own makeshift *merienda* stall in the afternoons in Barangay Bicutan, when she hadn't been talking to tourists in Luneta Park. She longed to call Max, but her phone was dead. And it didn't matter now, anyway.

She had left the café a different person. She arrived at the door frightened, angry, literally lost. She departed with a newfound resolve, as stoic as Linh had been when she was insisting on getting her money.

There were two things she realized: Hai had become the only person she trusted. And, she could not do it alone.

'*Em oi*!' The stall vendor called out, waving her over as if she'd been expecting Carmen all along. Carmen saw that the vendor had set up a tarpaulin sheet under which low plastic tables and chairs were arranged, ready to receive customers hungry for a bowl of hot noodle soup.

There was a metal vat of something spicy and steaming, a few globs of orange-coloured oil, tubs of round, translucent noodles, a plastic cylinder holding a bouquet of bamboo chopsticks.

Carmen went in and ordered a big bowl of bún bò huế.

Parents

MARINA

They were lying in bed, smoking, when he asked the question.

'Em, I have a favour to ask.' Hai twisted towards the bedside table and put out his stick on the makeshift ashtray Marina had fashioned out of a bottle cover and a wet tissue.

Marina was on her back, her eyes on him. She watched him slip back under the covers and pull the blanket higher over their bare bodies, until it reached their chins and she felt, once again, the warmth of his torso and his legs beside her. His clothes were draped over a chair by the dresser, carefully removed when he arrived earlier, just before noon, from the bus station. He had sat on the bed, reached for her in a way that was becoming familiar to her.

Thorough, she decided, was how she would describe sex with Hai. Better than most, and surprising because there was an absence of frills or drama. Like how he did and went about his things, there was a certain conscientiousness in the way he kissed, as if following a certain order or formula. And because it was thorough, it was satisfying.

But she wasn't here for the sex.

'What is it, Hai?' She clutched the edge of the blanket tighter and turned on her side to face him.

'I have a problem with my motorbike.' Hai's voice was soft. 'It's very old.'

'Oh?' Marina brought up the image of Hai's scruffy motorbike in her mind. She had ridden on it several times.

'I need to buy a new one. Can you loan me some money?'

Marina's breath caught. The directness of it. 'What?' She sputtered out.

Hai was now lying on his side too, stretched out again like a languid animal, his skin brown, smooth, and glistening. His eyes were steady, relaxed. 'Can I borrow three million dong from you?'

For a split second, Marina marvelled at how he could say it so unapologetically without sounding entitled or demanding. But she had not expected this. Not this soon.

An old, familiar feeling rose in her chest. 'Hai, I . . . I'm—' She couldn't breathe.

'What's wrong?'

The words, the words. They were running so fast in her brain, one after the other, mashed up against each other, like an unfortunate car pile-up along a speeding highway. She was suddenly aware of her naked body, of the blanket that was brushing the top of her breasts, of her crotch feeling bare and exposed despite the thin fabric draped on top of it.

Trembling, she tucked the blanket under her buttocks and thighs, like a burrito or a *lumpia* roll. She could not tuck it tight enough.

'Is it okay?' Hai's voice was plaintive.

She should appreciate this honesty. Hai's calm candour, as if he were only asking to borrow a pen. Instead, she felt stung. Had it all been about money, all this time?

She willed herself to look normal. But what was normal? As calm and as unperturbed as him? Not shocked or embarrassed or humiliated as she was starting to feel right now? It was not about the money— she knew how it was to need it, and how close she'd come to losing her dignity over a couple thousand pesos back in Manila. Her mother always said that the women who went with her father wanted his stability, what little money he had, as if her father himself had been unworthy of love.

You're overreacting, her mother would say. This should have been something she already knew: people saw something other than you. That people sometimes didn't really see you, they just chose to see what you can be to them. That people sometimes didn't see you as you, they just chose to see you in relation to themselves.

She pushed this thought from her mind. She might be overreacting, but it wasn't true.

'I don't know,' she said, finally.

'I already tried to borrow from my friends. But,' Hai took a small breath, as if puffing one of his half-finished cigarettes, 'nothing. They can't. They don't have the money.'

She stared at him, eyes bright, then looked up at the ceiling, something hard lodged tight in her throat. Something wet pooled in her ears. She realized, to her dismay, that she was crying.

She shifted her head away from Hai and towards the wall, her cheek landing on the pillow.

'Hey.' Hai moved closer to her, until their bodies were touching again. He shook her shoulder. 'Are you crying?'

'Hai,' Marina said, straining because she knew her voice was muffled in the pillow. 'What are we?'

'What do you mean?'

'Are we together?' She remained motionless.

A pause. 'Yes.'

'Why are we doing this?'

'Because . . .' She strained to hear, but his voice trailed off.

He was silent for a moment. Then he said, 'It's okay, em. I understand.'

He hugged her tightly, so tightly she thought her shoulders would break from his tensile strength.

'Don't worry,' he said. 'I'm sorry.'

'No.'

'Tomorrow,' Hai said, rocking her back and forth like a baby. 'Tomorrow, we will go to my parents in Quảng Trị.'

A Mistake

HAI

A mistake, that's what it was. He shouldn't have asked her. He should have known better. But really, how could he have known? How was he supposed to know that she'd break down in tears when he merely asked his question? He'd never gotten that kind of reaction, ever, from any of his friends. Or from Sinh, from whom he borrowed money too sometimes.

However which way you saw it, he had offended Marina and made her cry.

He had panicked when he saw her sobbing, and only then did he feel the belated embarrassment. So, he said the first thing that came to his head: let's go to Quảng Trị to see his parents.

Honestly, he didn't know why he had done that. It had been on his mind all week, and who could really blame him? He was sending money to his parents every month but he had not gone back to see them for almost a year.

But still—why had he decided to be his crass, impatient self and push his luck yet again? It did not feel that way when he was in bed with Marina. And now it was too late. He and Marina were already on their way to Quảng Trị, tucked in the back seat of a taxi. It was a ride that Hai had arranged so hastily that he wasn't even able to book his friend—as he usually did with tourists going out town. He asked Duong to cover for him at the bus station, he told Madame Beo and Ms Le, his supervisor in Minh Thanh, that his father was sick and needed to be brought to the hospital.

'Hai? Your house—where is it again?' Marina asked him now, her finger poised above her phone as the taxi drove through the main highway leading north. They had only been on the road for almost an hour. 'Which street in Quảng Trị?'

'No street,' Hai replied, distracted by the other motorbikes zooming past. Had he gone alone, he would have been one of those motorists.

'What?' Marina gave a small, nervous laugh. 'What do you mean?'

'I mean, there's no road going to my house. It's in the middle of the field,' he said. He glanced at her. 'It's the countryside, em.'

'So, we need to park the car somewhere?' The taxi driver spoke up, a tall guy in his mid-thirties with big, hooded eyes. He had been pleasant but not chatty.

'I'm not sure,' Hai replied. 'Sorry, *anh nhe*. I've always gone by motorbike.'

'Ah,' the driver said, good-naturedly. 'We'll tackle that problem when we get there, then.'

'Exactly!' Hai relaxed, stole a sideways glance at Marina. She was sitting back but intent on gazing out the window. He was well aware that this was the first time he was going to his parents' home in a taxi. He had always taken his motorbike, even with Sinh. He decided that it was not a total bungle, this spur-of-the-moment decision to go to Quảng Trị. It was just that he'd panicked, said the first thing that came to mind. He would have liked to plan these things, but he hadn't and now it felt—even though it was just the beginning—like it was coming together. Now, if he could only convince his parents that this visit was just business, and Marina, just his guest. A very important guest.

'Your girlfriend, anh?' The taxi driver broke into his thoughts.

'No.'

Hai looked out the window again, not caring to elaborate. Already, the questions were starting. Had he had time to book his friend Phuc, there would be none of this awkwardness and he could have focused on what he would say to his parents when they'd arrive.

'What did the driver say?' Marina asked him now, eyes curious and alert. She was especially lovely this morning, her skin creamy in a pink blouse, her hair falling in a smooth wave. There was a soft spot under her jaw that he liked to kiss. But her skirt was too short, too fancy and too high above the knees. He hadn't had the heart to tell her to change.

Sinh always came in her button-down shirts and jeans—plain and not exactly flattering or exciting, but it never elicited any bad comments from his mother. Or from whoever, because his mother wasn't even strict or judgemental. His mother, in fact, was the sweetest and quietest among his family. In the end, he thought it was for the best: even if his parents would suspect that Marina was his girlfriend, they would never think it was a serious relationship.

'He was asking about the way to my parent's house,' Hai said, 'like you.'

* * *

He was pleased to see his mother dressed in an outfit she'd wear to somewhere special—like a wedding or when she'd come down to Huế to visit him. But as with every visit Hai made in the last few years, it was as if his mother had shrunk just a little bit more. His mother was diminutive, but she looked tinier today. Darker and more stooped, as if she was shrivelling up by the year. His father had greeted them, too, but immediately disappeared to the back of the house.

'Who's this visitor you brought here?' His mother asked, after Marina and he went through the front door.

'My guest.' Hai busied himself with setting down the presents in the corner. He had asked the driver to stop along the way so he could buy packets of biscuits. 'You know how I meet so many foreigners at the hotel.'

'And Sinh?'

'Busy with her shift,' he replied, promptly. 'She knows I'm out here with a tourist.' He looked at the ceiling of their house, dismayed to see that the wood was rotting in some parts. 'Are you having the roof repaired soon? The ceiling looks like it's about to fall off.'

'I know.' His mother glanced up too. 'I didn't think you'd notice, but well, here you are. I'll remind your father to have it repaired.'

'I'll send you the money at the end of this month,' Hai said, his mind already on his shift schedule at Minh Thanh, his side projects. He glanced up again. 'It doesn't look safe.'

They both turned as Marina wandered into the living room, stopping to look at the big wedding photo of his parents on one wall.

'Thanks for having me in your home,' Marina said. 'I'm glad to be here.'

Hai turned back to his mother. 'Don't mind her,' he said. 'She's been to Vietnam many times. She books me for tours. Now she's curious about the countryside—our countryside. Just think of this as part of a tour I'm doing.'

'Are you staying the night?'

Hai frowned. 'No, not at all. We're going back to Huế in the afternoon.'

'You said that she's from the Philippines.' His mother spoke quietly, as usual. 'So she's not Viet *kieu*?'

Hai stifled a laugh. 'No, ma,' he replied. It'd been a while since he'd handled Viet kieu, Vietnamese who grew up abroad and who returned to Vietnam, to the villages of their ancestors. The term some used was *nguoi Viet hai ngoai,* overseas Vietnamese. 'She's not Vietnamese at all. But she lives in Singapore.'

His mother's eyebrows rose ever so slightly as did the corners of her lips. She gave Hai a tired, slightly confused smile, as if resigned to her son's stories. 'Let's get the food going, then,' she said, as she always did whenever Hai was there.

As expected, Marina didn't help out. How could she? She barely knew Vietnamese, and his family didn't speak a word of English.

Quảng Trị

MARINA

The house was a bungalow painted a bright blue with concrete columns and a terraced front, the corners of which were piled with the house's odds and ends: rubber slippers, a sack of cement, spare bicycle parts. There was a short cement driveway meant for motorbikes, which stopped abruptly a few metres from the entrance.

Marina looked around and saw that the house was standing by itself on a green field, peppered with a few thin trees. The taxi had driven through the grass, and then it couldn't and so they had to walk a few hundred metres to reach the house. Hai was right, this was in the middle of nowhere.

'Ma, Pa,' Hai greeted the older couple who had emerged from the already-open front door, so quick and casual as if he was saying hello to friends.

She waited for him to introduce her. To her surprise, he didn't. And then, they were ushered in so quickly that she didn't know anymore how to nudge him to do some sort of introduction.

The first thing she saw was a carved wooden dining table littered with several unwashed tea glasses, an altar, and wooden cabinets pushed back against the wall. There was a bright red calendar that said Chúc Mừng Năm Mới. A black-and-white photo of his parents hung awkwardly above a shelf, as did a big, wedding photo of them on the wall. She took a picture on her phone, then watched as Hai's mother took out dishes from the kitchen—plates piled high with leafy vegetables, a whole raw fish, and bowls of half-soaked glass noodles.

His father arranged a small stove on the living room floor laid down with woven plastic mats.

Afraid to make a gaffe, Marina didn't offer any help.

Instead, she stood in one corner, clearly out of the way until the dishes were complete and Hai motioned for her to sit down. There was something about the profusion of dishes and the way the food was laid out on the floor that reminded Marina of fiestas and birthday parties, but Hai's family ate with a quiet reserve, murmuring whatever it was that they wanted to say to each other. Hai acted as translator and volunteered basic information: that she was from the Philippines, and that she lived in Singapore.

She had been watching Hai closely since they'd arrived, a little moved to witness that he spoke to his mother in the same gentle, soft way he spoke to her in Huế. It was the same tone he had used last night when he was asking to borrow money from her: innocuous and naïve, like a child mouthing words he didn't really understand, or requesting to do a task he wasn't yet old enough to do.

Maybe it had been just that, an innocent request. All morning, during the taxi ride to Quảng Trị, she had tried telling herself it wasn't a big deal. That it was normal. Boyfriends borrowed money from their girlfriends all the time. What should be a big deal was meeting Hai's parents—and so, this was where she should focus.

Detective Service

CARMEN

The private investigator, Hai said, wanted them to wear a different set of clothes going in, and a different set going out.

'For the CCTVs,' Hai quipped, when she emerged from her room and found him smoking outside. Mr Binh Duc Ngo, private investigator, had told him of this request only that morning.

'What CCTV?' Carmen frowned, as she shut her door and double-checked the padlock. It sounded futile and simplistic, like something ripped off a bad TV show. And after yesterday's incident at the Citadel with Linh, she'd become suspicious of anyone who claimed that they knew something that she didn't; she was now wary of strange requests like these. It was what she'd failed to factor in when she'd decided to go to Vietnam, instead of just riding out that scare in the depths of Manila: the culture shock of arriving in a city you've never been to before, and more so, when you've never even travelled anywhere before.

Hai shrugged. 'It's not my fault.' He stuck the cigarette in the side of his mouth, took out a crushed pack from his pocket, and peered inside, counting the contents. He raised his head. 'You ready?'

'Yes,' Carmen said, looking at the row of shut doors. She had finally mustered the courage to leave her backpack inside her room, the money and Ativan tablets buried at the bottom, wrapped in several plastic bags. Chi Hanh's apartment was finally beginning to feel safe, the tenants seemingly on a routine where they left early in the morning and came back at night.

Hai had come to pick her up and, for this, she was grateful. She did not tell him about the incident with Linh at the Citadel, just that she'd decided to go with Hai's idea of consulting with a private investigator to find her mother. Was his friend, Phong's contact still available? She had asked him. Hai had responded with surprise, and then with his usual briskness.

'So, you gave up,' he had told her over the phone, the day she called him.

'No,' Carmen said. 'It's not that.' She was too tired to explain. How could she tell him in a way that he would really understand? That she had not given up, only that she could not do it alone anymore?

'What happened?' Hai was saying now, staring at the long, thin gash on her arm.

'Accident,' Carmen replied promptly. She had vowed to be honest, but today, she gave herself permission to lie about this. There was no need to tell Hai what happened. 'While cleaning.'

'Cleaning? Cleaning what?'

'Something.' Carmen avoided his eyes. Instead, she said, 'How much would it cost, do you think? The detective?' It was better to stick to the practical matters. They were still standing on the corridor outside her room, the smell of smoke lingering heavy and harsh. Suddenly, conscious of the wound on her arm, she resisted the urge to fan the air with her hands.

'Expensive,' Hai said, almost instantly. Glancing at the alarmed look on her face, he said with less confidence, 'I don't know. Maybe we can get a discount. It depends.'

'You'll help me talk to him, right?' Carmen asked, as they walked towards his motorbike parked by the gate. 'I mean, to get a discount, if ever?' She knew she was already pushing her luck as it is, asking Hai for every little thing. And she wondered why he was willing to help her. She tried not to think of the times he'd helped her. Carmen thought of the money she had with her; she would worry about that later.

'Yes, em,' Hai said, looking left and right at the road as he always did. He opened the seat of his motorbike and handed her the helmet. 'Let's go. Be quick. I still have work at the bus station.'

* * *

'It could be a small hotel,' Hai remarked, almost to himself, as they turned the corner and slowed to a stop under an old, gnarly tree with low-hanging branches and aerial roots. 'But the location is not good.'

Across from them stood a slim, three-story building with simple jalousie windows and raw cement walls, thick ivy creeping on some parts. Hai gestured vaguely towards one of the windows on the top floor. 'This is the office building of Mr Binh.'

Carmen didn't say anything as she hopped off the motorbike and quickly but reluctantly shrugged on Hai's raincoat, feeling foolish. Hai had insisted that they go by Mr Binh's rules; he himself wore a puffy jacket even if felt like thirty degrees out.

'Wear this,' Hai said now, putting away the helmets and handing her a pair of wire-framed Ray Bans, its lenses badly-scratched.

'Shades?' Carmen let out a tired sigh but took them anyway. 'Do I really need this? For what?' She knew she sounded childish. The suspense mixed with her anxiety and curiosity was starting to feel torturous and rendering her impatient. How she wanted this to be done and over with, to just go in, meet the private investigator who would assure her that yes, she could be reunited with her mother very, very soon.

Hai shook his head and made a clucking sound. 'Never mind. Just wear it.' He sounded exasperated. He nodded at the sunglasses in her hand. 'Be careful with that. A tourist gave it to me at the bus station.' He proceeded to don an olive-green baseball cap.

Carmen was startled to see that he looked younger with the cap on, and then caught sight of his hands. While the rest of his fingers were neatly trimmed, the ones on his pinkies were nearly a half-inch long. She looked away and shoved the sunglasses on her face, feeling oddly embarrassed.

After Hai parked his motorbike with a group of others on the adjacent vacant lot, they stood outside for several minutes and watched as several people came out of the building. Carmen then followed him when he slipped through a metal door at the side of the building, up three flights of stairs.

Mr Binh was waiting for them on the third floor, and Carmen was surprised that he was standing right outside his door. When he led them in, his office looked sparse but neat. He had a dark, wooden desk, four foldable metal chairs lined neatly to the side, and an extra table with a plastic kettle and tea bags. The windows were wide open.

Detective Binh looked like he was in his late thirties and was a stocky man, not much taller than Carmen. He had a wide, serious face, his jaw as pronounced as his cheekbones.

'Call me Mr Binh,' he said, nodding at Hai and extending a thick hand to Carmen. It felt fleshy but callused.

'I'm licensed, as you can see,' Mr Binh continued, taking out an ID from his pocket. He gestured towards a framed certificate on the wall, which reminded Carmen of the homes in the Philippines, where parents framed diplomas to go with their children's graduation portrait. 'You can also check my Google reviews. They're not fake.'

He gestured for Carmen and Hai to sit on the chairs in front of the desk. And then Hai leaned forward, saying something in Vietnamese.

'Yes, Mr Hai was asking a question.' Mr Binh remained standing. 'I used to be part of a larger agency. But I decided to start my own, with fewer staff. Actually, just one or two people is enough.'

He spoke with such confidence and a slight air of superiority that Carmen found both mesmerizing and repulsive.

'I don't do love triangles,' Mr Binh continued. 'Sometimes, I verify adultery.'

'Verify?'

Mr Binh looked at her loftily. 'Yes, verify,' he said. 'We check the loyalty of husband or wife. What people ask me to do is track the routine of their lovers or husbands or wives. We monitor.'

'I see.' Carmen smiled tightly.

He finally sat, nimbly, on the chair behind his desk. 'So, how can I help you today?'

Carmen glanced at Hai, then leaned forward, resting her hands on the table. 'I want to find my mother. She's here in Huế.'

'You're sure?'

Carmen nodded, then pulled up the screenshot of Nicole Peltier's Facebook page. 'Here, it says Huế City is where she lives.' She handed her phone to Mr Binh. 'Also, this new photo shows her at the Citadel.'

'Ah.' Mr Binh's eyes surveyed the photo for a moment. 'You've contacted her?'

Carmen felt her face grow warm. 'No. Yes. Many times. Why?'

'If you're still messaging her, you need to stop,' Mr Binh declared, with a vehemence that startled Carmen. 'Right now.'

A tinge of guilt passed through her as if she'd been caught red-handed. She nodded, 'Yes, okay.'

'You need to write down everything you know about this person. Your mother. Her name?'

'Nicole. Nicole Maranan Peltier.'

They watched as Mr Binh used his own phone and searched through Facebook. 'Yes. So her account is still searchable.'

'Do you need me to write about myself, too?' Carmen asked, waiting with bated breath.

To her relief, Mr Binh shook his head and said, 'No, no. We focus on the person.' He sat back on his seat. 'What we can do is this—skip tracing. Your mother has chosen to be here, I believe, because she doesn't want to be found. We'll use database searches like property records, utility bills. Those things. Public records, like her marriage certificate. We'll discover her friends, I'll establish contact. And then social media, of course.'

He turned to Hai and started speaking to him in Vietnamese. Carmen shifted uncomfortably in her seat, willing the conversation to go back to English.

'What did he say?' she asked, when there was a pause.

'I had a similar case like yours,' Mr Binh said. 'Yes, the same,' he continued, almost to himself. He looked up, lips pursed. 'That one, the father was in Da Nang, the child in Hanoi.'

He regarded her with pensive eyes. 'This is the first time I've met someone who has come all the way here from another country.'

'It's not a crime to locate someone.' Carmen gave a small shrug.

'What is your job in Manila?' Mr Binh asked.

'I have a small food business.' Carmen had already thought about this.

'An entrepreneur.' Mr Binh gave a knowing nod. He turned to Hai again and started speaking to him in Vietnamese.

'Excuse me,' Carmen interrupted, turning to Hai. 'Why is he—why is he asking about my job in the Philippines? Isn't he supposed to focus on my mother, and her job?'

Hai gave her a small, patient smile. '*Bình tĩnh,* Carmen,' he said.

'What?' She was getting tired of not understanding some things.

'Calm down,' Mr Binh translated. He was as matter-of-fact as Hai. 'So, miss. You don't speak Vietnamese?'

Carmen shook her head. 'No.' After a pause, she asked. 'Why, should I learn? Will it help?'

'No, no,' Mr Binh said. 'There's no need.'

'He just wants to make sure that you can pay him,' Hai said. 'It's simple like that.'

'And the cost?' Carmen held her breath as she glanced from one man to the other.

'Nineteen million dong,' Mr Binh announced. 'It can go up to twenty, twenty-five if the case drags on.'

'Nineteen million?' It felt like a rock had dropped at the bottom of her stomach, it sounded so ridiculous. 'How much—how much is that?'

'Eight hundred US dollars,' Hai said. 'For him to start, you need to give at least thirty percent down payment.'

Carmen grew quiet, mentally reviewing the money she had in the backpack she left in her room. She took her phone from the table and opened the calculator. She didn't have enough.

'Carmen?'

A mix of dismay, anger, and frustration was once again starting to bubble inside her. Of course her money wasn't enough. Why had she even tried to come to this meeting? It had been a waste of time. She was back to square one.

'I need more time,' Carmen said. *I need more money,* was what she wanted to say but she couldn't bear to be as direct as these Vietnamese, both of whom she was aware were simply trying to help her, a stranger.

Mr Binh was as effusive as he had been at the start of the meeting. 'Yes, yes, yes,' he said. Still smiling amiably, he clasped her hands with both of his. Oddly comforting but not enough to raise Carmen's flagging spirits.

* * *

They stopped at a roadside coffee shop where Hai ordered a coffee for her. The drinks came iced and in thick, squat glasses, a milky one for her and a black coffee for Hai.

She watched him take out his phone, punch some numbers in the old Nokia, and converse with someone in Vietnamese. She listened to the lilting, singsong sounds, the rising and dropping of Hai's voice, the funny sounds which to Carmen seemed to come from his nose. This time, she had no desire to comprehend it.

'The bus is late,' he announced briskly after he pocketed his phone. 'I don't have to be at the bus station right now.' His shoulders relaxed and he lit a cigarette, casting a glance at her. 'Don't look sad. I told you it would be expensive.'

Carmen nodded wordlessly, her throat thick. 'I know.' She *did* know, but why did she still feel surprised and, more disturbingly, such hopeless disappointment? When she had finally decided to try and consult with a private investigator, she had worked herself up to believe that she'd finally found a workable solution to finding Nicole. She had felt renewed hope at the possibility of hiring a professional to locate her mother, only to have it dashed again with a price she could not afford.

A glimmer of something crossed her mind. Something faint but persistent, a thought and possibility that had always been at the back of her head but one that she'd successfully kept at bay since arriving in Vietnam.

'Hai,' she said now, 'Are there really a lot of tourists at the bus station?'

Hai nodded, clamping down on his stick. 'Yeah.' He looked out on the street. It was not busy, with just a few cars and motorbikes on the road, a smattering of pedestrians.

'I mean, how many tourists do you meet every day?'

Hai had taken out his phone again. But he appeared to be listening, his answers sure and direct. 'More than a hundred each day. I have my guests in Minh Thanh, too.'

She thought of the Ativan tablets she had in her backpack. What if she just did what she had done before? Befriend some tourists, put something in their food? As far as anyone knew, she was just another traveller. Instead of playing the local, she could be just another tourist looking for company in Vietnam.

Yes, it would be so easy. Carmen blinked, thinking of Uncle Amado and Auntie Swan. She thought of Max. It was doable, even if this was Vietnam.

Her mind was still working, thinking of possibilities. She was already seeing herself in a café, a restaurant, the Citadel where she would say, 'Hello, can you take my picture?'

And the money. These tourists were like all tourists in the Philippines and all over the world—with cash, credit cards, phones, expensive cameras. And here was Hai, neck-deep in tourists every single day. What could be so wrong if she asked him, casually, about them, their plans and whereabouts?

'Carmen?' Hai broke into her thoughts. He had stood up and was patting his pockets, looking ready to go.

'What, Hai?'

'Don't ask me to lend you money.' His tone wasn't unkind but matter-of-fact. 'Okay? I don't have much. Sorry, em.'

Carmen stared at him, startled by his directness, but more surprised by the feeling of amusement and sympathy she had for this man. For a moment, she forgot that she needed an obscene amount to find her mother, pronto.

She started laughing. And then, she put her hands on her face, feeling her eyes fill up and sticky tears streaming down her cheeks.

Hai dropped his hands and sat back down, his face a mix of sympathy and shock. 'Em oi! Don't cry.'

Carmen shook her head, her face still wet. 'I'm fine, I'm fine,' she mumbled, swiping both palms across her face and wiping them on the back of her jeans.

Had she really been thinking of going back to her old ways?

No, she couldn't do that to Hai. More importantly, she could not do that to herself.

Madame Fabuleux

HAI

The house was grander than he'd imagined and reminded him of the overpriced boutique resorts already beginning to take over Hội An, a tourist town just two hours away from Huế.

'Villa' was the term Nhung had used when she ushered them in, past a small lawn and a landscaped garden with extra-tall foxtail palms out front, through the high-ceilinged living room and into a terrace that led to a narrow, blue-green swimming pool at the back. The water sparkled like tiny gems under the morning sun, showing off the spoils of this expensive location. Because the house sat on a hilly plot of land in the south of Huế, it overlooked a forested area so peaceful and lush that Hai couldn't decide whether to feel awed or just plain annoyed. Adding to his annoyance was Nhung's postponement of the meeting; she had insisted on meeting the day after their phone call, only to move it more than a week after.

'We redesigned the whole place. The interiors, Andre wanted it to be more comfortable, more French,' Nhung said, as if the house was theirs and not leased from Chi Hanh. She flitted about her little terrace, pale and ethereal like a child showing off a new dollhouse. Hai had to remind himself, again, that this house was owned by Chi Hanh, not by Nhung, and the rent must be astronomical.

'How nice,' Carmen was murmuring. 'It's all very nice.' Hai shot her a look, but the woman was too preoccupied nodding and smiling at Nhung, at the pool, at the stupidly breathtaking view.

Carmen could have come here for the interview on her own, but Hai knew he had to see for himself how Nhung was living, and how she'd manage to pull herself out from the ugly business of peddling her body and into this beautiful oasis of a life. Nhung, now Mrs Nina Blanchet had, just months ago, been scurrying in and out of Minh Thanh Hotel from midnight to the wee hours of the morning with his male guests. No wonder he'd been unable to contact her in the recent months. It was low season and there weren't too many requests for girls lately, but it all made sense now. The other girls, he realized, had been mum all this while and now he knew why: it was painful to talk about someone who'd gotten what they had all wanted all these years.

'Call me Nina,' Nhung said, casting a pointed look at Hai before turning to smile gaily at Carmen. 'Or Madame Blanchet, whichever you want,' she added with a coy shrug, her new French last name rolling off her tongue with a practised ease.

Blan-shey. She must have said that over and over again in front of a mirror, Hai thought, *to get it sounding right like that.* And she must have taken English lessons—because gone was the broken, tentative English she'd used during all those nights at Minh Thanh's reception, waiting for her clients or wrangling them for a higher fee. Nhung now spoke it better than him.

'*Chuc mung*,' Hai said, not meaning it. 'Congratulations.' Switching back to Vietnamese, he said: 'I was surprised to know that you got married. Imagine, em.' He shook his head in a way that suggested that they'd gone through something together—something harder, something more complex and messy but certainly more substantial before she arrived at this tidy state in life. Hadn't it just been just months ago that he was negotiating with her the price for no-condom sex?

Nhung pursed her delicate lips and stared at him for a second, a thoughtful look in her eyes, as if she herself was remembering those moments. 'Yes,' she finally said in a soft voice, sheepishly, lowering her eyes just like the old Nhung. 'Cam on, thank you.' Then her eyes flicked up and she was back to being the airy Mrs Blanchet, clapping her palms together in front of her chest as if in exaggerated prayer.

'All is good!' She crowed in English, eyes flitting from him to Carmen. 'Andre, my husband, will be home soon. I'm excited for you to meet him.'

They passed by a framed engagement photo placed front and centre on one wall. Nhung looking tiny despite her full-length, frilly gown, clearly a full head shorter beside a man with a longish, pale face posing in front of the Eiffel Tower. The foreigner looked trim in a grey suit and had an easy, sincere smile and a receding hairline. He certainly didn't resemble any of Hai's guests, the ones who harangued him at past midnight for girls. The Eiffel in the background looked like it was from a postcard, exactly the kind of photo his colleague at Minh Thanh, Thuong, now and then showed him whenever she spoke about getting married to her boyfriend. This was what they *all* wanted. Nhung was radiant, smiling easily as if she'd lived in Paris all her life, as if she hadn't travelled ten thousand kilometres to have that photo taken.

'Sorry I didn't invite you to the wedding,' Nhung was saying now. 'It was so fast—Andre wanted to be married so our passports—mine and the kids'—could be processed immediately.'

'And your children?' Hai tried to soften the judgemental edge in his voice.

'Oh, they had no problem calling him Papa!' Nhung exclaimed. 'Isn't that great?'

'Married to a foreigner. And you've stopped . . . of course, you have—'

'I have a YouTube channel now,' Nhung declared as if Hai hadn't spoken. She raised her chin again. 'That's why I'm very busy these days.' She whipped out an iPhone from her pocket—*the latest version*, Hai thought, with envy—studded with some kind of diamond-like crystals and pulled up an episode. She held up the screen for all of them to see.

'Madame Fabuleux, that's me,' she announced, pointing a pale-pink manicured finger at her miniature self on the small screen. They watched, rapt, as Madame Fabuleux proceeded to open a jar of cream and pat it on her face. 'I test and review beauty products,' she said. 'I love the Korean ones.'

'You're a beauty vlogger,' Carmen piped up, nodding. 'I see.'

'That's why I'm very busy these days,' Nhung repeated, clicking the phone shut. She tossed it on the white, plump couch then looked at them both earnestly. 'It's not easy filming an episode, you know. And I have to plan what else I can put there. I need that time. Andre works at his office in the city the whole day, so he's no help. It's vacation time for my children, so they don't have classes right now. They're home and we need someone who can take care of them, teach them English, clean after them. We need someone very, very quickly.'

'That's why we're here, ma'am,' Carmen said, politely.

Ma'am? Hai wanted to retch. He didn't like how Carmen was being so agreeable. He looked balefully at the two women.

'You have a beautiful home,' Carmen said, gazing at the glass-walled kitchen, which opened to the pool. Hai groaned inwardly. Of course, she too was rubbing it in his face. Hai thought she didn't have to state the obvious.

'*Merci*!' Nhung sang out, to Hai's annoyance. Turning to him, she said, 'What a coincidence, isn't it?' To Carmen, she said: 'Anh Hai, he's helped me before.'

Hai wished she would shut up about their previous connection. Nhung had been his first ca ve, and she was professional. True, she was a breeze to work with, never giving him trouble with his guests. Some guests, the businessmen from Saigon, always requested for her. In the rare times he thought about her situation, he always believed that she'd marry someone good. But this—this was another level. He had never actually known anyone who had gone from rock bottom to high heavens in such a short time. He wondered what Nhung had to go through to get to this.

The physical transformation was subtle: pixie face, wide eyes, creamy pale skin and that delicate, almost demure laugh—Nhung had always been beautiful. It was the attitude change that was stunning. Whereas Nhung was pleasant before, she was now overconfident and smug. The more she spoke to them and the longer they stayed—it felt to Hai as if she couldn't stop herself from rubbing her newfound success in the faces of anyone who would listen. No wonder the other girls had been reluctant to talk.

They went back into the kitchen, where she gestured for them to sit on the stools around the granite island. Nhung's children were there too. The girl looked about seven or eight and was intently colouring in a notebook. The boy was a toddler and was bouncing a small ball by himself.

'You're from the Philippines, Carmen?'

'Yes,' Carmen said. 'Filipinos are good in English.'

Nhung was nodding. 'This will just be a temporary arrangement, nothing permanent.' She waved her manicured fingers. 'We just need to be prepared when we go to London and Paris in September.'

'But Miss Nina,' Carmen interjected. 'Why don't you teach your kids French instead?'

Nhung looked aghast. 'What? So they can just talk to Andre?' she said in Vietnamese. 'What about me? After I've learned all these fucking English words.'

'Sorry?' Carmen cut in, her face anxious.

Nhung's gaze swivelled back to Carmen. 'English,' she panted out, still breathless from her mini rant. 'You have to teach my children good English. English is classy.'

Carmen blinked, then nodded. 'Of course,' she said. 'That's no problem.' She shook the folder with papers she'd been clutching. 'As you can see, I'm qualified for the position.'

Hearing how formal she was, Hai wanted to laugh. Poor Carmen putting her best foot forward for silly old Nhung. How desperate, really. But something told him that he wasn't in an unsimilar situation. He, too, was desperate to find a way—not just to keep the money coming in but also to earn it. He needed to keep his curiosity, his outrage, his contempt, and whatever else in check. For now. Carmen, this unfortunate girl, needed this money to pay Mr Binh.

'Yes, yes,' Nhung said, taking the folder from Carmen but not opening it. 'I believe Mr Hai and Chi Hanh. They say you're very good, and that's all I need.'

'Aren't you going to ask her if she has work experience?' Hai asked in English, flashing a sly grin at Carmen. She was in, he knew this because he also knew Nhung and how, even though she'd bagged a rich foreigner and this cushy new lifestyle, she didn't really know anything. He needed a little relief from his shock. Anyway, Carmen owed him big time.

'It's all there,' Carmen said, quickly, tapping the folder she had just handed over, a tight smile on her lips. 'My work experience as a tutor.'

'Then we have no problem, do we?' Nhung was smiling her beautiful smile.

'What do you need Carmen to do?' Hai asked, regretting it as soon as he said it; his English sounded stunted and contrived. Switching to Vietnamese, he asked Nhung, 'Tell me now—everything you need Carmen to do, so she can do a good job and we won't have a problem.'

Nhung just laughed. 'My kids, they can be super *quai*,' Nhung told Carmen. 'Anh Hai, what's the English word for it again?'

'Naughty,' was Hai's prompt reply. He suppressed a smile, pleased that he knew the right word this time. The kids weren't that bad. They appeared quiet and seemed able to entertain themselves. But perhaps they were mellow and well behaved because there were visitors.

'I work in that studio over there,' Nhung said, pointing to the squarish building they had seen at the side earlier.

Hai's eyes bulged. What studio? All he could see was a room, given some fancy name by a newly-pretentious person.

'Do not, and I repeat, do not disturb me,' she told Carmen. 'No one else goes into the studio except me. It's off limits for the kids because I don't like them touching the lights or my make-up. The one who was here before you, she let Chloe in there and I still feel a little angry.'

'What if there's an emergency?' Carmen asked. 'I can go in and knock, right?'

Nhung frowned, then cocked her head. 'Emergency? Like what?'

'Ma'am,' Carmen spoke up again, 'what if the children need you?'

Nhung pressed her thin, delicate lips together. 'It's better if you call me first,' she said, reluctance heavy in her voice.

They were on their way out when they heard the crash.

'My grandmother,' Nhung said. They all turned and stared at the elderly woman, now holding the base of a broken vase. Hai rushed forward, feeling the need to help her pick up the ragged ceramic pieces on the floor as Nhung let out a litany in Vietnamese.

'I hope she's okay,' Carmen said.

Nhung sighed. 'See?' she said. 'This is why I need you to be with the children.'

* * *

Hai left Nhung's house feeling disturbed. He'd seen his colleagues at Minh Thanh Hotel or Phong Nha Hostel come and go, had witnessed them get better positions at better hotels. But this? Somehow, despite his and Nhung's vastly different professions, he had always thought that they were on the same side, and that they had the same struggles. Nhung and the other prostitutes were forever chasing something better, always on the lookout for something else and always hustling, always hungry— the very same thing Hai found himself doing every single day living in Huế City. How had it never occurred to him that Nhung would shoot up to rich-girl status, just like that? It seemed like a fairy tale. Meanwhile, he'd cut work at the bus station just to see this abomination with his own eyes and would have to work the night shift that night.

He wished there was someone he could tell these things to.

The Blanchets

CARMEN

The kids were beautiful: sweet-faced and angelic with prominent plump cheeks, curly lashes, and fine, wispy hair—but they looked nothing like their father. Chloe and Sam—whose real names were Thuong and Diep—were, Carmen learned, Nina's children from an old boyfriend and were now Andre Blanchet's stepchildren. Nina Blanchet, Carmen also learned, was formerly Nhung Nguyen and Hai's old colleague—not ex-girlfriend as she had initially assumed—though he had been strangely vague about the connection. Not that that was her business. All that mattered to her right now was doing this job right, getting the money, and giving Mr Binh the first down payment so he could start his search for Nicole Peltier. Her first pay would be at the end of the month.

She was grateful to Hai for finding her this job. She had always known, at the back of her mind, that she needed to find one in Huế. And she had always known that she would find work. But she had hoped that her savings would help sustain her as she tried to settle into this new city. She was still overcome with the enormity of what had happened in Manila and what she had decided to do. At that time, going to Huế City had felt like an opportunity, a way to safety. The ultimate sign for her desire to change her life, the first step of which was to find her mother.

The job was for three months, meant to prepare Chloe and Sam to go to France and London, though part of Carmen's job was to keep the house in order. 'The kids want to see snow,' Nina had declared yesterday, when they were all sitting in her kitchen. 'If only the documents for our visas would get done sooner. We're still waiting.' An arduous process, she said, as with everything that goes with a Vietnamese passport.

Carmen believed that Nicole Peltier would be found well before that, but she agreed to it anyway. It was an informal arrangement, after all—one of the very few options she had and she was desperate. She said a silent prayer that everything would go quickly because, in truth, there was an urgency that she felt every day, that the sooner she found Nicole, the sooner she would be reunited with her mother, the sooner her life could truly be better.

Being at Nina's house, oddly, made her think of Barangay Bicutan. Most people there worked some kind of factory job in Cavite and Laguna in the south of Manila, but they had neighbours whose daughters worked for families in other parts of the city. They stayed with the family in their homes for months, even years, and went home on holidays.

* * *

Nina listed down what Carmen needed to do, chores she'd have to complete after she'd spent time teaching English to the children.

It didn't matter. What was important was that this job was full of possibilities for her. For one, it would bring Carmen the money she so desperately needed not just to find her mother but also to sustain herself. Second, Nina's husband was French—was it possible that they would know Nicole Peltier and her family? Finally, it felt odd in a way to not lie about herself, to not make up elaborate stories about who she was, where she worked, why she was there. Sure, she had told no one about what had happened in Manila. But she was not leading someone to think something else, and more importantly, she was not helping drug someone so that she could take their money and things. She thought of the Ativan tablets buried at the bottom of her bag, wrapped in so many layers of paper. She hadn't unwrapped them since she arrived in Huế.

Sure, she had shown fake papers to Nina, who hadn't even given them a glance so it wasn't counted, was it? Nina Blanchet was more preoccupied with telling her own story than listening to Carmen's or anybody else's.

Carmen was fine with that. More than fine—in fact, she was beginning to feel that she'd finally done one right thing since arriving in Huế City: Carmen Maranan, ex-Ativan Gang member, had found herself a somewhat honest job.

* * *

The first person she saw when she came in that morning was the grandmother. The elderly woman was sitting at the kitchen table in a loose housedress and cardigan, her head turned towards the small TV on the kitchen counter. She was watching a Vietnamese show with disinterest.

'Xin chao,' Carmen said, dipping her head in a half-hearted bow. 'Hello.' The old woman turned and looked balefully at Carmen but said nothing. Carmen remembered yesterday's mishap and quickly glanced at her hands, wondering if, perhaps, she had arthritis, which had caused her to lose her grip and break the vase she was holding at that time. They didn't look swollen or red. The grandmother turned towards the TV again.

Carmen could see the sink piled high with dirty dishes, about a dozen used glasses scattered on the counter. *Did they have a party last night?* she wondered. It was obvious that they had been left for her to clear, and she would need to do that.

She placed her backpack on a stool in one corner, then went around to check out the mess in the sink. Then, she turned back to the older woman. 'Where are the children?' She laid her palms out and made as if searching the room. 'Chloe? Sam?'

The grandmother said nothing. She didn't even turn her head.

'*Lola,*' Carmen said, a little louder this time, using the Filipino word for 'grandma', 'where are Chloe and Sam?'

Still, the older lady said nothing. Instead, she looked down and busied herself picking at something off the edge of her cardigan.

Before Carmen could ask her again, a man in a bright blue sports T-shirt and running shorts strode into the kitchen. Carmen recognized him as the man with Nina in the framed wedding picture along the hall.

'*Bonjour,* 'ello,' he said to nobody in particular, heading straight to the refrigerator and fishing out a glass bottle of cold water. He didn't give either of the women in the room more than a perfunctory glance.

He tipped his head and drank quickly, wiping his mouth with the back of his hand.

'Carmen, right?' He had a loud, grating voice. 'I'm Andre.' He extended a hand, a thin line of sweat dripping from his forearm. The tiny moustache above this lip was also glistening with sweat.

'I need to go to work,' he said. 'Nina is still sleeping.' He refilled the glass bottle in the sink, carefully manoeuvring it so that it didn't touch any of the unclean dishes.

'Okay,' Carmen nodded. 'But where are Chloe and Sam?'

Andre was already making his way out through the kitchen door. He paused to look at her, shrugging as he raised and twirled his forefinger in a round motion. 'Somewhere,' he said, before finally turning away. '*Bonne journée.*'

* * *

The children took after Nina and whoever her old boyfriend was. Nina's beauty was startling; she resembled celebrities at home. But there was a roughness, an unrefined quality about her. A swagger. There was a tough strength underneath that delicate exterior. Carmen could, strangely, imagine Nina walking the dinghy streets of Manila and remaining unfazed.

Nina wanted her to brush up the children's conversational English—'so they would know what to say when people asked them in English'—and to pay close attention to pronunciation. She also wanted Carmen to feed them lunch and a snack in the afternoon, to pick up after them, and tidy the house.

* * *

Carmen downloaded a syllabus from the internet called 'Teaching English to Young Learners', all the while feeling guilty that she wasn't a real English tutor. She spent three hours trying to decipher the terms and eventually concluded that what Nina wanted her to do was to help develop the kids' speaking and listening skills. Armed with this focused goal, she spent another hour listing down a sort of lesson plan, a list of exercises, and simple songs she found on YouTube. In the end,

Carmen resolved to teach them as if she was teaching a young sibling how to speak English. She was not an expert at all, but even she had to admit that she spoke better English than Nina and the kids—maybe even Hai—and so maybe she could appear as an authority. In any case, she told herself, she could still teach the kids things like being kind, being polite. Unlike Nina, Carmen didn't believe that everything hinged on being able to speak good English.

Atasha's Apartment

MARINA

Manila, 2002

Atasha's apartment was like her closet: colourful, overflowing with texture, a little bewildering. The walls were painted an indeterminate shade of deep green, which made the living space feel as if it were perennially late afternoon. A puffy velvet sofa in sapphire blue that seemed straight out of a magazine was flanked by rough, driftwood side tables that looked like they had been salvaged from a beach. The skull of a horned onyx was displayed on a metal stand in a lighted corner while modern art pieces by Atasha's preferred list of mostly unknown artists dotted the walls though they were not the usual framed paintings: one wall had a triptych made of mixed media. In another, a full-length macramé hanging bulged with round and cylinder shapes fashioned out of yarn and rope. There was a tree, which Marina would later learn was called a fiddle leaf fig, which dominated a corner, its broad, paddle-like leaves fanning out like giant green petals, its branches curving like an umbrella along the ceiling.

The apartment was along Salcedo Street in the posh district of Makati, two condominium units merged into one, Atasha told her. The first time Marina went to visit, she tried to imagine where the big wall had been knocked down to make way for all this glorious, art-filled space Atasha retired to every night.

'Please don't be shy,' Atasha told her that first time, as if apologizing for her fabulous interiors. 'You're always welcome here.' They had closed what Atasha deemed a particularly inspired issue of *Loweq*, and so right after they'd approved the final layout, Atasha insisted they eat *cochinillo* tacos at this late-night place somewhere in Makati's red light district. Afterwards, they had cocktails at a bespoke bar called Lantern all the way in Ortigas. It had been no problem; Atasha's driver was there to ferry them to wherever Atasha decided they would go. By the time they were done celebrating, it was past 2 a.m., and Atasha suggested that Marina just sleep over and go back to her place in the morning.

'It's no problem at all,' Atasha said. 'I have a guest bedroom badly missing a guest.'

Marina was too tired to survey her surroundings when they arrived but felt rested when she woke up in the morning and padded out of the cozy, air-conditioned guest room and into the quiet sala. Peeking through a window that showed the tall, grey buildings of Makati, the tops of houses in their exclusive subdivisions, the traffic and cars parked along the road now looking neat and miniscule, she marvelled at the thought of being so high up and above, hidden and cushioned from the sticky, messy, chaotic world that existed down below.

And then, Marina thought of her own place, in a street-level apartment that she didn't own, a room that wasn't hers and which she couldn't even afford to rent alone: she was merely renting bedspace, a common option among single people in Manila who wanted a cheap place to stay long term. What was hers, for now, was just a single bed in the bottom bunk of a double decker, and a small plywood cabinet that she, like the other three women she shared the room with, kept secure with a padlock. That apartment was a narrow, two-storey in Cubao, its four bedrooms converted into rented bedspaces for working professionals like her. She shared a bathroom with six other people. The only one who had her own en suite toilet and bath was Gracie, the girlfriend of the owner's son who acted as their supervisor.

Before that, she had lived with her parents in their rented house in one of the poorer districts in Quezon City. There was hardly a clean surface in their home and the dust settled so thick on surfaces that one could sweep it with their hand and have a small pile of it on their palms, like super fine, light grey sand. Her mother, who cleaned sporadically, complained a lot about this.

Marina wondered how Atasha kept her apartment tidy and dust-free. There was someone who cleaned for her for sure, someone who remained invisible and perhaps only came in during the day when Atasha was in the office or travelling.

* * *

By the time several months rolled by, Marina was a regular at Atasha's apartment. It was easier to reach from *Loweq's* office or that was what Marina told herself every time she found herself craving to be somewhere private and quiet, beautiful and comfortable. It was like being in a museum that was also your home or a favourite café that was still empty at seven in the morning. An escape, which was what Atasha's apartment meant most to her. For a few hours most days, as she sat on the plush couch and looked at the Makati skyline and down at the street traffic from the cool silence of Atasha's living room, Marina could pretend that she had all that Atasha had. And it gave her hope—that one day, just like Atasha, she would have it all, too.

Everything always seemed to be in order in Atasha's apartment except for one thing. The antique-looking shelf in one corner made of solid but very old teakwood, scruffy and shiny in all the right places. Instead of Atasha's usual ironic sculptures and tongue-in-cheek displays, the shelf was bulging with translucent plastic C-folders filed upright. So many of them were squeezed into such a small space that they looked ready to fall out any minute. Each folder was labelled with a certain country's name and crammed—with postcards and brochures, handwritten notes, articles and photos torn from magazines, colourful wrappers and tags, each one looking like an artwork in itself. A pressed rose, its petals rendered crepe-y and dark by time, dangled like a fancy bookmark from one.

'What's this?' Marina shook out one of the folders from the shelf, careful so the others wouldn't come tumbling down. It was a humid evening, a rare night after work when Atasha invited Marina to eat dinner at home, instead of checking out a new bistro or bar. Her cook was preparing osso bucco.

Atasha shrugged. 'I'm not sure, really. Junk? Would you really call it that?' She used a forefinger to tuck in a folded brochure that was threatening to fall off further into a folder. 'Instead of fridge magnets, I keep tickets and wrappers and stickers. I don't know. But every time I open one, it's like the trip is happening all over again. That feeling, Marina!'

'How can you save all these?' Marina took out the contents from the folder she was holding, then ran her hands along the messy files. She had never seen anything like it. 'I'd lose them all.' At that time, she had not yet travelled extensively. She had not known anyone who kept so many odds and ends from a trip, much more anyone who had gone to as many trips as Atasha.

'Oh, I just stick whatever paper bits, like museum or train tickets, there.' Atasha was breezy, non-committal. 'I know a guy who did a whole textured collage using machine receipts from his travels.'

Marina pulled out another folder, thinner than the others. 'And this?' It was unmarked. 'Nothing happened here?' She slid her fingers inside and pulled out a couple of handwritten notes, a magazine clipping of an old temple, a scrap of paper used to cover chopsticks printed with: 'Nam Bo BBQ, Huế, Vietnam'.

Atasha's face lit up with recognition. 'You found it!' she said, carefully taking the folder from her hands. She rifled through the thin stack, then looked up at Marina. 'I've been looking for this. I knew it must have been caught between those thick ones.' She held up the chopstick wrapper. 'This is from Huế, Vietnam! It's not mine, though. I got it from someone, I can't remember.'

Marina recalled, vaguely, Atasha mentioning something about this city in Vietnam.

'I told you, everybody goes to Saigon and Hanoi,' Atasha continued. 'Huế is different. Central Vietnam is different, unexplored!' She sighed and ran her hands over the smooth surface of the plastic. 'I've been wanting to go, so I just collected little things and clippings about it.'

Marina nodded. 'So that's why there's not much there.' Her gaze went back to the rest of the folders, thick and overflowing, vying for space on the shelf.

Atasha smiled. 'Not yet,' she said, running a finger along the photo of a pagoda. 'Huế City. Soon.'

'Can I look at them?'

'Of course!' Atasha tossed the folder back. 'Go through them anytime. I've already forgotten about some of them, though I've started updating again. Remember my trip to Sao Paolo?' She laughed and pointed to a folder with a hot-pink post-it. 'Voila! It's still here!'

'If only Manny could see this,' Marina said. Manny was *Loweq's* art director and was always trumpeting the convenience of going paperless. 'He would tell you to just scan these and put them in a file.'

Atasha looked horrified. 'And rob me of my hoarding mess?'

'You're so old-fashioned!'

Atasha played with the edges of the folders. 'I love modern art but yeah, maybe I am old-fashioned.' Her face lifted into a smile, her teeth looking even and wide and bright as her shoulders rose up in a cute shrug. 'I like the touch and the smell of things. How can I do that when I'm just opening a computer file?'

'That's exactly how I feel too,' Marina said, and she meant it with her whole heart.

Hypochondriac

MARINA

Manila, 2002

He was a hypochondriac. It had only been their second date when
Denis took her blood pressure, rattling off numbers that she didn't
understand. But after a while he nodded, satisfied, and said, 'You're
all right.'

He complained of back pains, rashes, headaches.

One night, he woke up, complaining of an ache in his back. 'It's
this bed,' he told her. 'I can't stand another minute lying in this bed.'
The misery was evident on his face.

They had to call a taxi at 3 a.m. so he could go home and sleep in
his own bed.

'I *am* odd, aren't I?' Denis asked her one day, in that rueful way
of his. He looked out onto the passing view. 'Maybe I've been living
alone for too long.' He looked at her, eyes softening. 'I should change.
Do better.'

'No, don't,' Marina said, placing her cheek against his, feeling the
thinness of his skin as she breathed in his smell. 'Odd things make me
love you.'

Denis

MARINA

Manila, 2002

The first time she had sex with Denis, she discovered he didn't have a shower in his apartment. She stayed the night, then crept out of bed at six the next morning with her usual urge to clean up. With Denis still sleeping, she went around in circles in his rented loft, bewildered at the absence of a bath or cubicle where she could wash off the previous night's sweat and all the other fluids that clung to her body. Instead, Marina found an old bathtub full of bikes and a stiff wire stretched above where Denis hung his laundry.

'You must think I'm a little boy,' Denis said when he got up and prepared breakfast, and she told him this. He didn't particularly sound like he cared. 'Maybe I am.'

They laughed, then devoured the eggs and rice he had cooked. Instant black coffee for her, sweet, milky coffee for him. He told her he took his showers at the gym, where he worked out, or at work—he was a game developer. In a way, he did look like a little boy, with soft, imploring eyes and unusually smooth skin, especially the parts of his body that the sun didn't hit when he was out biking, which, Marina learned, he did almost every day. He was ten years older than her but his buttocks felt supple, the skin silky like that of a baby's. He had a scar in the middle of his stomach. 'From an operation,' Denis said, and she thought about the slow, uneven curve of his abs as she sat at his table in her day-old clothes, her own nether regions feeling oily. Before she left, she decided it was no big deal. When you're in your late

279

twenties (she was twenty-eight, almost twenty-nine), things like these are minor hassles. They don't yet feel like poor decisions that have the power to ruin your day or make you question your judgement of people. And this was what she liked about Denis, in the first place: his self-deprecation, his weirdness.

They met so simply and, also, so oddly. On her day off from work one Wednesday, Marina was riding inside an 'FX'—a convenient, popular form of public transport in Manila where a small group— usually a dozen to sixteen—passengers were ferried from a single origin and to a single destination in Toyota FX vans with hardly any stops. This was the draw, the direct route, a contrast to the ubiquitous jeepneys that plied countless routes in the city but also made the most stops. Marina queued and boarded at the starting point in Taft Avenue, heading to a sprawling mall called SM North. But because it was only after lunch and not rush hour, the van slowed to a stop after ten minutes near the end of Taft and just before EDSA to pick up passengers. Marina had just opened her compact and was checking her reflection when Denis clambered in beside her.

'Miss,' he said, as he carefully arranged his long limbs on the van's torn, faux-leather seat, 'can you please move a bit? My legs, they can't fit.' He had a low, muffled voice, soft and almost melodious, so the request didn't sound demanding or unkind.

Marina glanced up from her reflection and automatically scooted an inch to the left. The man had a pale, longish face, thin lips, a narrow nose and the beginnings of a stubble. He wore a short ponytail low at the nape of his neck, topped snugly with a black Nike cap worn backwards. He wore cargo pants. He looked like a Spanish mestizo, a half-mix. Despite this, Marina's first thought was that of *holdapers* armed with knives who demanded everyone's possessions inside jeepneys or FX vans like the one they were riding in—and she felt a flare of fear then anger at the van driver who still insisted on picking up passengers even though it was against the rules.

But the man caught her eye again and she felt her anxiety dissipate as he smiled slightly and proceeded to talk to her, even as every one of the van's eleven passengers pressed forward to listen. He was going to the mall, he said in that soft, muffled voice. To a bike shop at the annex of SM North where he was planning to buy a spare part for his bike. Marina nodded politely and told him she was meeting a group of friends to window-shop and eat Chicken Joy at Jollibee. The truth was she was getting off at the bus terminal from where she planned to take a taxi to meet another man. A married man. She knew this because he had a thick, gold band on his ring finger the day she met him at an afternoon wine-tasting event at the Peninsula Hotel the day before. He had a cellar of wines that he wanted to show her, he had said.

'Jollibee?' Denis said, smiling slightly. Unflinching. 'I could use something to eat.'

Marina frowned and didn't say anything. *What a weird guy*, was her initial thought. Filipinos were friendly to each other, sure, but they didn't invite themselves this way. He wasn't creepy or sleazy—just odd in a naïve, guileless way. 'Next time,' Marina replied, mildly, as if she was talking to a friend and not some stranger she had just met.

When he finally fell silent, she saw him looking out the window as the van inched its way along Quezon City's traffic-clogged streets. The weak sun made an outline of his profile and lit up his short, gossamer lashes. She thought there was something pure and peaceful about the way he looked at the throbbing grit and mess of the people and traffic outside.

He didn't even look at her after that, but she asked for his number. Being a reporter, even if for the lifestyle section of a newspaper, taught her to not let anyone go without getting their details. This stranger could be her next man-on-the-street, a future source. He could also be her next lover, and that Marina also knew was possible. Then she got off at the busy terminal at SM North and as planned, took a taxi to have sex with the married man.

* * *

She called Denis the next day after work. The meeting with the married man had been exciting at first, but she found him too self-assured, too predictable even in bed. Afterwards, when she took the FX again to head home, she thought of Denis, of their odd encounter.

He answered on the second ring. 'Let's eat at Jollibee,' Marina blurted out, not really knowing what to say.

'I know better places,' Denis replied.

The day after that, over drinks after work, she told Atasha about both.

'Did you at least drink his wine?' Atasha, cultured as ever, wanted to know if the married man had organic ones.

Marina wondered if she should be telling Atasha, but she did anyway. It had only been a year and a half since she was hired at *Loweq*, and Atasha was still, after all, her boss. But she was also, now, a friend. The closest friend she'd had since college. She often thought of how it would have been had Atasha and she been friends in university. Would Marina still be as fascinated with her as she is now? Or would Atasha be demystified, brought down from where Marina had placed her high up there, among the unreachables?

Marina knew that she loved Denis that first date, and they spent most of the evening walking around in Cubao, trying to find a bar or an eatery that suited their different needs: she wanted a place that was cheap, he wanted one that was empty.

She stopped sleeping with other men after that. She was faithful, even when Denis had to move to Dubai for work. 'Just for a year,' he said, and so they were unfazed. Marina, especially. Except towards the end, and she made the mistake of telling Atasha. That was when Atasha swooped in.

How was she supposed to know that Atasha had been taking connecting flights to Dubai, and that all this time, she had been travelling there just to be with Denis? How many times had Marina witnessed Atasha just flying off to somewhere, saying she was just on leave or had to be with her family somewhere in Europe? It sickened her to think that Atasha was there with him during the times when Denis and she had been on a call. In the weeks and months after Marina discovered that Denis was having an affair with Atasha and her own relationship with Denis came crashing down, Marina walked about her city in a shock, unable to process or even just decide who she was and what she was feeling. Disgust, rage, betrayal—they all seemed too tame for what was going on inside her.

She had never known this level of deception. That it was possible to pursue someone far away, to go through all that trouble and spend all that money to be with a person who was your best friend's boyfriend.

It was the biggest mind-fuck Marina had ever experienced, and the hardest experience she had ever been through.

And then, just like that, Atasha shut off all her social media and disappeared. It wasn't long before Marina learned that Atasha moved to Dubai to live with Denis. *Of course,* Marina thought bitterly then. *Because Atasha can. Because Atasha can get anything she wants.* Atasha Magsaysay didn't have to work to support herself. That was what inheritances or trust funds or, simply, money in the bank provided for by your parents were for.

Left without their charismatic editor-in-chief, *Loweq* folded after a few months, leaving Marina jobless—and still reeling from the break-up. It was probably grief, but it was at that time that she felt most undesirable—the mix of emotions still so raw and palpable that the only stop-gap solution she could think of then was to go back to sleeping with other men. Sex, her good old pain reliever.

It was easy to fall back into old patterns after that. Sleeping with different men, attached or unattached—she didn't care. But it was hard to forget Denis. Just when Marina thought she had it together, when she had stopped thinking of what could have been or how great they could still have been together, the image of Denis would pop up in her head, squeeze at her chest.

And then came a man who told her she could work abroad, so why didn't she? It made her pause and think because she had always thought that working abroad was for talented, conscientious people like Denis and for rich people, like Atasha. Did she see herself somewhere in the lukewarm middle, neither here nor there? Working abroad felt like too high an ambition; she knew her limitations. She had always told herself that having a good job, like the ones she held in *Manila Guardian* and *Loweq* were good enough, and that she was lucky that her editors hired her, that they somehow recognized her skills and talent. Because of where she came from, it did not occur to her to venture out abroad. It just seemed too much to ask.

She wasn't looking for rich men, so maybe that was why she didn't meet many of them. She just wanted sex with men who appealed to her, she didn't really care what they did. During those times, she just wanted someone who would tell her that she was good, she was great, she was perfect and desirable because those were the things she didn't think of about herself.

Invitation

MARINA

Marina felt a tender fondness for Singapore, one she hadn't felt for a while, when she read the email glowing on her screen. Her application for sole proprietorship from ACRA Singapore had been approved unexpectedly early. Everything was in order, it stated, except one more document that was needed; if she could send a scanned copy of it, then everything would be complete. She could legally set up a business in Singapore. The deadline was in five working days.

Her thoughts flew back to her apartment in Singapore. She had that document, tucked away in a drawer in her desk at home. A document that wasn't with her right now and so she couldn't scan it and send it by email as the rep from ACRA had instructed her to do. That meant that she had to leave Huế City and go back home for a few days. Talk to her agent about leasing her apartment in Singapore, which could also be an extra source of income. People moved in and out of that city. There would not be a shortage of renters.

She closed her eyes for a moment, allowing the sweet mix of relief, triumph, and a sense of accomplishment to run through her. It was a relief, this approval. And it felt good that there was this one sure thing.

She had been café-hopping with her laptop around Huế, developing a fondness for the terraced area of the Saigon Morin Hotel where she'd been having coffee or a glass of wine some days, working in between sips. She found that she didn't mind the constant stream of motorbikes and she liked that it was just right across the promenade that ran along the Perfume River. There were often couples doing their prenup photo shoots and she observed them with a mixture of amusement and mild envy. It made her think of the times she'd supervised a shoot for *Parcours*, and wasn't that just weeks ago? Some had taken until the wee hours and been tense affairs, some had been pure, campy entertainment. She had ceased being star-struck by celebrities in Singapore and Manila.

Marina turned back to her screen. She had been drafting a sample website, but a clunky one was all that she could manage. She had been in a kind of frenzy the past few days, drafting and sending out emails. In between, she had gathered as many of her contacts as she could and looked for more. Today, she decided to scrutinize websites that offered workshops similar to the one she was planning to organize. And the internet was teeming with creative retreats: writing workshops, yoga retreats, art residencies. How would her—and Atasha's—creative retreat turn out? It all depended on her now.

But it was hard for her to focus. She was still reeling from what happened with Hai, trying to make sense of the trip to his hometown, his actions, her feeling, their relationship. She had been observing him closely, and it wasn't that she wasn't happy—it was that she wasn't *sure* at all of what she was seeing.

She felt a rising panic in her chest. A longing, too. How she wanted this to work. She needed this to work. She was afraid of losing Hai.

Lately, it had become easier to admit that she *was* lonely, that she was not just an introvert who craved some time alone. She had found herself with so much longing when she was in Singapore, where she had never really felt connected to someone. What was connection, anyway? Being yourself? Trusting someone? She had lost Denis and Atasha, she had distanced herself from her family. But maybe that could change. Maybe she could make friends here. A family, even.

She reached for her phone and texted. Hi, Hai, where are you?

The reply came a minute later: In my room, sleeping.

Marina smiled. Can you meet me in Saigon Morin before dinner? She knew he had free time between five to nine o'clock before his shift started at Minh Thanh. But he didn't reply for at least ten minutes so she had to call him.

Hai arrived in half an hour.

'Where's your motorbike?'

He jerked his thumb towards the corner. 'I parked it over there, in the next building.' He sat down, laid his pack on the table and immediately lit one. He'd had a shower, since the tips of his hair were still very wet.

'I met you in my dream last night,' Hai said.

'Oh?' Marina watched his face carefully, but it intrigued her, this meeting in dreams. This was not the first time a man she'd gone out with had told her that he'd dreamed of her, but they had never put it this way. They 'saw' her in their dreams, no one had said that they 'met' her, like Hai was telling her now. 'What happened?'

'You were in Singapore and I was still here, in Huế. You told me that you will be leaving for a while, that you need to go back to Singapore—just for two days.' Hai perched his cigarette on the ashtray. Then, he flicked his eyes at her and said, 'I thought that you would only be gone for two days.'

'Oh?' Marina felt her eyebrows shoot up. 'And?'

'But you were gone for a long time. In my dream, two days had turned into two years, and I'd nearly lost hope. And then you came back.' He gave her a tender look. 'I never thought that I would see you again only after two years.'

Marina gave a small laugh, unable to decide if Hai was making this up or not. It was too close to what was happening.

'Why did you take me to your parents' house, Hai?'

Hai looked out across the street, then shifted his gaze downwards. 'It's simple, em.' His hand crept again towards the cigarette on the ashtray, a thin trail of smoke floating from its tip. 'You're important. I haven't taken anyone to my parents, except you.'

Hai Goes to Singapore

HAI

Hai pressed his nose against the window, aware that he had just added another greasy mark to the thick glass already made sticky by previous passengers who've sat in the same seat. He didn't care. The clouds from the plane's miniscule round window looked like cottony mountains, the sky an infinite expanse of light blue that made him drowsy yet resolute. He was still in Vietnam but soon he would be flying above and between countries—a dream that had once seemed outrageous. It made him feel alive as if he were finally living, not just subsisting on whatever was thrown at him.

He knew he was not sitting on the right seat but that didn't matter. It belonged to the passenger now relegated to the aisle, a balding man in his fifties dressed in a thin, fraying polo shirt and matte grey trousers who had not uttered a word since he boarded, even when he saw that Hai had already occupied the window seat. Marina was beside him in the middle, his correct seat according to the boarding pass that she'd printed out for him. Earlier, she had told him to move and give way to the man.

'It's okay, em,' Hai said, not budging from his window spot. He'd already sized up the other passenger and concluded that he was Vietnamese and, judging from his accent, from Huế. When Marina looked as if she was about to say something more, Hai leaned sideways so that their shoulders bumped and said, 'I'm so happy we're going somewhere.'

It was his first time going anywhere on a plane. It was his first time on a plane, period. When he gazed down at the dense, messy sprawl of Huế's flat rooftops becoming smaller and smaller as the aircraft climbed higher in the air, he thought again of how wise it had been to have listened, just a few months ago, when his younger colleagues had been talking about getting their passports. How serendipitous it had been to have allowed himself to be swept up in the flurry of the application and the promise of going somewhere, someday: compiling IDs and documents, producing the correctly-sized passport photo, riding together on their motorbikes to the embassy on Han Thiet street to submit their papers, regrouping after at a popular roadside restaurant for spicy snails and celebratory beers. There had been seven of them in the group: five receptionists, including Hai, and two people who worked in the hotel restaurant. As they clinked their glasses, Hai felt something he hadn't felt in a long time: that he belonged. That he wasn't out of place or that different or lesser. For once, he felt sincerely glad he was part of this little Minh Thanh family.

He should have known that that feeling was fleeting, perhaps even imagined. In the succeeding months, it was his colleagues—yes, even the waiters at the hotel restaurant—who travelled, not him. He saw their pictures, an alarming deluge of them, bursting through his newsfeed on Facebook: posing under the cherry blossoms in Japan, jumping shots in a street full of skyscrapers in China, kooky poses in the famous Merlion Park in Singapore where a couple of them pretended to be drinking the water shooting out of the statue's fountain. It was silly, and he thought they looked stupid but even that couldn't stop the pangs of envy or the anger or the confusion. Why were they there and not him?

But he was here now. Or getting there. He had been to Phu Bai Airport countless times to pick up and drop off guests. It was just that he had never gone past those gates where uniformed officers checked your passports one by one.

He had never even thought about it until Marina had asked him, and it was only in that moment that he remembered he had a passport. When he said yes, he couldn't believe it himself.

* * *

He would only be in Singapore for four days. Well, three and a half. His manager wouldn't give him leave any longer than that. Not that he wanted to stay that long. There would be time for a longer stay next time. He knew it in his gut.

He told Sinh that he was going to Saigon for a training seminar. That it was just him and his manager who had been assigned to go. As he'd expected, Sinh had heard this news with hardly any reaction nor any detailed questions except the date he'd be back. That made him thank the fact that she was employed in the hotel industry, which had regular shifts that ran like clockwork. Work this kind of job long enough and the whole routine, no matter how stultifying it may seem, feels like a constant assurance that life was moving, that something in the world still works. That you are, somehow, going forward—even if you don't really know where exactly you end up. He should know. He lived for the moment the clock turned six the morning after his night shift and for his afternoon naps after working at the bus terminal, before he started his shift again at Minh Thanh.

'You okay?' Marina's voice rose above the plane's buzzy drone. Hai turned slightly when he felt her hand slide into his left palm, her fingers awkwardly interlocking with his.

'Yes,' he said softly, smiling briefly and giving her hand a squeeze before turning back to the clouds.

'Don't forget to show your return ticket to the immigration officer.'

'Hmm,' he murmured, tearing himself away from the view and shifting so he faced the front, not curled and hunched at the side as if he wanted to be sucked out of the little window. 'Yes. Of course.' The last two words came out as an airy whisper, as if he had lost his breath. He cleared his throat.

'Hai, don't forget to tell them what I told you.'

'What? Who?'

'Immigration. When they ask why you're travelling to Singapore, just tell them you're visiting your girlfriend, who's a citizen.' Her face softened as she said this, and she smiled, though her lips remained closed. 'I'll be right behind you in the queue anyway, so I don't think there will be a problem.'

She spoke gently but firmly, as if he were a child, and he nodded dutifully, surprised at the warmth he felt at this new feeling of being told exactly what to do. Maybe because it was Singapore: something completely new, something unknown to him and thus, so terribly exciting. It would not be inaccurate to say that he felt like a child. He felt adventurous. And with Marina, he felt safe, carefully guided through this adventure.

* * *

'This is your apartment?' He realized the moment the words were out how stupid they sounded. She was someone important here—why wouldn't she be living in this impressive place?

The taxi had dropped them off at a simple lobby with a roofed waiting area, past a landscaped entrance with trimmed hedges, vines with orange flowers curling thickly on the fence that delineated the property from yet another towering building.

'Please, come in!' Marina was effusive. 'You can rest here.'

He saw that she was sweating. He felt warm the moment the automatic sliding doors opened so they could walk the few steps to the waiting taxi. As a thick blanket of heat hit him, he felt nauseous for a moment. Marina had warned him that it was hotter in Singapore. Still, he wasn't prepared for the sharp contrast of a chilly air-conditioned airport with the humid heat wave outside.

* * *

Marina went out the next day. Hai wandered about in the small apartment, his eyes glossing over the things that didn't interest him, like the plants she kept in the bedroom and the living room, the colourful small canisters in the kitchen that Marina said contained all her favourite teas. He went to the living room and stepped on the thin rug, rubbing his toes into the nubby texture, noticing the dark print for the first time. He opened the balcony door, carefully unlatching the small lock on the frame, nearly jumping out of his skin when the glass door emitted a high squeak as he slid it open. He did not want to break things.

He was not into disturbing other people's privacy. Even with Sinh, he had little interest in her past relationships, had never even checked her phone. Standing in the middle of that clean, quiet apartment, he felt a sudden intimacy with Marina, one that was different from when they were in bed, naked and close. He simply wanted to get a feel of how she lived. Of how to be her or be someone who was close to her.

There was a spare bedroom with a bulky armchair piled with purses, books stacked on the floor. The room felt musty and unused, a storeroom of sorts. There was a desk against the wall by the window and when Hai walked over, he saw that a space had been cleared among the items, as if a laptop had suddenly been taken and there hadn't been time for the other things to be placed back.

He found a stack of unlined pad paper on her desk, then spotted a clear pen holder bursting with markers and coloured pens. The ballpen he chose skipped, but he forged on; choosing another one felt like too much trouble.

'Dear Marina,' he wrote.

* * *

'Hai? Wake up. I'm here, I'm back.' Marina's face was over his. 'How long have you been sleeping? Have you eaten something?'

'Coke,' Hai croaked, rubbing his eyes with one hand. He sat up and blinked. He had fallen asleep. He hadn't even begun the letter he had wanted to write. 'I drank Coke.'

He stood up, shrugged into his shirt and jeans.

'Hai?' Marina was calling him. 'Hai, what's this?'

Marina had seen the note without a message, and it amazed him that instead of being disappointed, she looked so happy with it.

Marina's Singapore

MARINA

She could tell Hai was impressed when he started taking pictures with her phone. He who never seemed to be concerned about capturing a moment back when they were in Hué. Hai could be so transparent when it came to some things. Marina felt a strange wave of satisfaction as they sat at the back of another roomy Comfort taxi, which smelled like pomade mixed with scalp sweat. They were zooming past Changi's familiar bougainvillea, pink and lush as ever, before the taxi hopped onto the wide length of the TPE that would soon lead them to her flat.

'The roads—they're so clean,' Hai murmured, raising the phone by the window and tapping on the screen button. The trees came out a blur, but Hai was already training the phone towards the windshield to catch a full view of the road ahead, his fingers clumsy and almost trembling, as if he suddenly didn't know how to hold a phone.

Hai had been silent for most part of the flight, peering and squinting through the plane's tiny oval window. He had borrowed her phone and taken pictures of the clouds, of the flat roofs of Hué after take-off, as the plane climbed higher into the air. He had gone to the bathroom just as the announcement to fasten seatbelts came on, earning a disapproving look from the flight attendant who ushered him back to his seat.

She pushed open the door of her flat, guiding her old door stopper with her foot to hold it in place so Hai could bring in their bags. 'Yes, of course, this is my apartment,' she said. She understood why he had asked. They had to walk through a small garden to get to her unit, and he had remarked that it looked like a resort. That it was, in fact, better than the resorts in Vietnam. From the entrance, the white walls looked as pristine as when she had bought it five years ago. The tile floor had issues, but Hai wasn't paying attention to that. And the living room smelled musty, so she hurried over to open her balcony doors. The high-rises from afar looked grey and fuzzy, probably covered in haze.

'But why do you want to live in Vietnam?' He was murmuring again, dragging his bag.

That question again. 'I already told you.' Marina walked into the kitchen, fetched two glasses and a plastic container of cold water from the fridge.

'Hai, I need to go to ACRA to submit a document,' she told him. 'It's for the business I'm starting, the creative retreat. I need to do it first thing tomorrow, so I'll be out by noontime.'

Hai nodded without saying anything, as if still in a daze.

* * *

It was windy when she slipped out of her flat and stood along the hallway in front of the elevator. She watched the red numbers slowly change, then glanced out at the clouds, today an off-white blanket that covered the whole sky. It made her feel like it was early morning—when things are just starting—instead of just after lunch. She felt calm when the weather was this way, when she could move around the city and do chores at home sans sweat because it wasn't scorching and humid. It reminded her of Huế again and she took this as another sign. She was only staying in Singapore for a week, and then she would be back again in Huế.

The appointment at ACRA was smooth and unremarkable, perhaps a little too brisk as with most things in Singapore. As she stood on the escalators descending into Newton Station, she stared at the email on her phone, the email the officer had told her she would be sending already lodged into her inbox. After being in Huế, everything in Singapore felt startlingly quick.

So here it was, a little business she had started for herself. Singapore had made it easy for her, but she didn't know if she could make it here. If she could last here.

She wanted to go back to the flat and check on Hai. He had told her he was fine, nothing to worry about, when she texted him on Viber. The message was short and awkward-sounding as usual, but what did she really expect? She expected more, that was it. The last two weeks in Huế, she had noticed that he had been distant, getting quieter, trying less. She hated to admit it, but it scared her and so she had come up with the idea that he could come to Singapore with her, because why not? Couples travelled together. She didn't want to admit that she wanted him to see that there was a world more sophisticated that his, and that she had once belonged there and so she was valuable. She wanted that power. She couldn't believe she was playing this game again, but she was short on ideas. Besides, there was the creative retreat she was organizing, the business she was building.

He doesn't really love you, her mother would say, if she knew about this. Her mother, sensitive to the slightest of slights when it came to the men she went out with, who measured love strictly via certain actions—or non-actions. And so, Marina had stopped telling her a long time ago about the men she went out with. She had kept men from visiting their house, even those that she felt wouldn't judge her.

A New Plan

HAI

There was a sharp, thin sting across the back of his neck, and Hai thought at first it was just the sun beating down on his skin. It had hit him when he was in Singapore just a couple of days ago when he was with Marina, strolling along one of those elevated, tree-lined walkways, the ones he found so wondrous, where he could see the cars below and Singapore's trademark high-rises above. There was one that was his favourite, which led up to the Marina Bay Sands, that colossal, oddly-shaped landmark everyone recognized, looking like it had a long, gleaming metal boat about to float or fly from atop three wide, thick columns. It was just a hotel, he had already known that before he came, but he couldn't tear his eyes away each time it showed up between the buildings as he trailed after Marina on their daily outings in the city. He had nodded meekly as Marina bought tickets (at an outrageous 800,000 dong per person, he computed in his head) and they went up to see the view from the fifty-seventh floor. He didn't say no when Marina instructed him to pose for a picture. And then it rained, just as they stepped off the elevator. Marina had to get a taxi to take them to lunch, and they joined a fast-moving queue in front of the hotel lobby.

There were none of those in Huế—no shining high-rises or well-dressed people or smooth highways that looked brand-new, and certainly no quiet, orderly queues. He was well aware of what he'd be coming back to, of course, once he'd get off the plane at Phu Bai Airport. It was just that he'd been plagued with a feeling of—what, really? A disturbing disappointment because Marina didn't want to lend him the money? Discontent because he wasn't living in the kind of place, the kind of life that Marina and well, the fortunate people of this world, were living? He couldn't tell them apart. He knew he wanted things he didn't yet have but was it possible to want something you didn't know you needed?

There were only old, dusty things like the Citadel, the kings' tombs, and the bus station. Right now there was dust flying, like thin cloudbursts, seemingly every which way he turned amid this jostling group of touts who for sure would love to edge him out of his job from day one. They were standing shoulder-to-shoulder by the doors of the bus, calling out, like him, in English at the passengers who were just starting to alight.

'Ow!' There it was again. It was Lau, the guy from Ngan Thien Inn, a few hostels away from Phong Nha.

'Watch it,' Hai said, grimly. 'You're hurting people.' The man was younger than him by at least ten years and talked too much.

'Hurting?' Lau grinned, then bit down on what was left of his cigarette before deftly flicking it away and above their heads. 'Don't be crazy. We're all working here.'

Had he really been enduring this for four years? Four years of the same crap, the same rude colleagues, the same tourists—because, really, weren't they all just the same? Demanding and entitled and privileged, not recognizing what they had been enjoying all their lives.

And yet, four days ago, he had been on a plane on his way to a different place, where he had, unexpectedly, had a glimpse of a different life. Singapore had been exhilarating, yes. But he had refused to let it affect his work, once he came back. He had striven to go back to his work schedule, his routine. Singapore had been a blip, a stroke of luck.

Several of the other touts were already sitting on the tables under the tents, having yet another coffee and smoke.

'This one's no good,' one of them said, waving towards the bus that they'd approached earlier. Trails of smoke flew from a cigarette lodged between his fingers. 'Too many organized tourists.'

'Hey,' Lau said. 'I heard you were in Singapore.'

'Singapore, really?' Ngoc said. 'Big time, man.'

'Do they get winter over there?' Duong asked. 'Does it really look like it does in the pictures?'

Hai shook his head no, just as his phone started ringing. It was Phong.

'Good, I caught you,' Phong's voice was animated, alert. 'I found our hotel.'

'What? Where?' A rush of excitement shot through his head like a too-cold drink. And then came the dread. 'A hotel?'

'We need to view it today. The owner is flying to Buon Ma Tout early morning tomorrow.'

Hai scanned the parking area where the buses were and saw that the crowd had thinned. Most of the newly-arrived passengers had gone through the exit and into the streets. Over the years, he'd seen how tourists had smartened up: these days, they knew better than to get into a waiting taxi or *xe om* right at the station, which would likely charge them more. Now, he knew they would most likely be hailing cabs further from the bus station.

He didn't ask Phong about the money. He would deal with that when they met in person.

'Okay,' Hai said, willing his voice to sound firm and in control, his fingers already itching again for the cigarettes in his pocket. 'I'll be there.'

* * *

The hotel for lease was on Thi Bui street, close to a small market and several local cafés. 'See?' The agent gestured towards nothing in particular at the first room they viewed, steering them quickly towards the en suite bathroom. 'Western style.'

Hai didn't think it was but it looked more modern than the tired spaces of Phong Nha Hostel. The agent looked slick, in manner and appearance, and had a quick smile and pinkish skin, which looked like a girl's. He had an energetic way about him as he took them from room to room, describing the spaces as if he were peddling a plush, modern, and upscale resort.

The hotel had fifteen rooms. 'Seven apartments and eight studios,' the agent said, with a grand sweep of his arms. The owner, he said, would need a deposit of six months.

But they are not apartments, Hai thought. They were hotel rooms. The studios were just smaller rooms. He made a mental note to bring this up with Phong.

'You see now.' The agent had pulled open the curtains of the window in one of the rooms, gesturing for Hai and Phong to peer through the opening. 'See the market? The shops? There are restaurants on the next street, local ones. You can't go wrong with this area.'

After the meeting, Hai and Phong rode side-by-side on their respective motorbikes on the way back. They did this from time to time—riding slowly through the streets of Huế, talking as they manoeuvred through the old roads.

Hai was the first to say something. 'I don't know,' he said. 'It seems expensive to me.'

'Are you kidding? It's a steal if you look at the location!' Phong's voice rose above the noise of the other motorbikes. 'Come on! Haven't we seen enough crap hotels?'

'Maybe we can still look at other hotels.'

'You really want to do that?' Phong was shaking his head. 'This is a good time. We need to get ahead. The tourists, we don't want them going anywhere else, do we? And I know you, Anh Hai. Everything is expensive for you. Don't do this to us!'

It *was* a good spot. It seemed like a good hotel, better than the ones they'd viewed in the past. This happening, it was something he both dreaded and rejoiced in: the hotel was exactly what they were looking for.

They stopped at a traffic light as Phong started making noises about going for a drink. Hai knew Phong wanted to dive into the details of the lease, perhaps make a timeline, figure out a budget.

But Hai dreaded having to talk about the money, to think of where he would get it. And that was always the problem, wasn't it?

Loaning Quảng Trị

HAI

He saw that the ceiling had been repaired, just as he had told his mother. Hai could see where the old wood ended and the new one, looking raw and lighter in colour, had been installed.

'It's good you did the roof,' he told her, which was what he usually talked about with his mother: practical matters, neutral topics. Nothing too personal or deep that would require an excavation of feelings or a hard, uncomfortable review of what had been or what was right and wrong in their relationship.

'We had to. If not, the ceiling would have fallen down on us.' His mother may have meant to be matter-of-fact, but her words came out slow, relaxed. He could tell she was happy with the work.

Hai had lived at home until he was past twenty, leaving for military service and then university. He felt closer to his mother than his father, but this was as close to a conversation they have ever had.

The sight of the new ceiling and his mother's contentment caused a fresh wave of doubt but he had to do something big, as Phong said, if he wanted to move forward—no, if he wanted something bigger. The more Phong spoke about the home equity loan, the more convincing it sounded. It was a way out and a way through.

Hai knew nothing about this, but he felt he had control when he secured the special power of attorney that would allow him authority over this property, this house and lot that was his mother's. He had the papers in a brown envelope stashed underneath his motorbike's seat.

He looked at the dark corners of the house, tried to remember how it had been when his brother and he were younger. But he couldn't drum up the memory—maybe they spent most of the time playing outside? He could only picture his brother's children sprawled about, sleeping. Some birthday parties were held there, with the cake on the floor, some shiny things on the wall. He vaguely recalled the photo session where his brother shot pictures of his nephew, propped up by his sister-in-law. Everybody sitting on the floor, with the food and the cake in front of them. He saw the pictures on Facebook.

'You want tea?' His mother's quiet voice again. She was looking at him with that neutral expression he knew so well, as if he was merely someone who had dropped by.

'I'll do it,' he said, turning in the direction of their kitchen at the side of the house. 'I'll make tea.'

'No,' his mother said and slipped in through the door before he could say anything more. When she came out, less than two minutes later, she was carrying a small wooden tray with an old ceramic teapot and the tiny glasses he knew so well from childhood. Now, as then, each one felt no bigger than a thimble between his fingers.

'Ma, I need to ask you something,' he said, looking at the light yellow–green liquid his mother was pouring into the small glasses.

'Your father's still out.'

'I need money for the hotel. Around five hundred million.' At least he could be direct.

His mother looked up, startled. 'Five hundred million?' She sat back on the floor, clutching a tea cup with one hand. 'I thought a business would make you more money, not need more of it.'

The remark felt short-sighted and it confirmed what he had feared the most of his life about remaining in Quảng Trị: staying here wouldn't just limit your opportunities for work but also your knowledge of what was going on in the world.

Still, Hai didn't feel any resentment towards his mother. 'I need to get a loan from the bank,' he said, barrelling on. 'And I have to list the house and land as collateral.'

His mother bristled. 'Your salary isn't enough as a guarantee that you can pay it back?' The thimble-sized tea cup was still in her hand. 'Have you asked your friends to help you?'

'My salary's not big enough,' Hai replied, and it was at this that he felt angry. The low pay, the rigid hours, the daily grind, the various kinds of bullshit he had to do or put up with from his manager and colleagues. And, they would never make him manager anyway. Even if Duc, his current manager, left—or died—upper management would probably choose an outsider. They would not choose Hai.

His mother remained silent.

'With the house, I can get the loan approved in ten days.'

'And to pay back? How long will that take us?'

'Five years.' Hai realized that he, too, was still holding the small glass. He downed his tea in a second. 'Not you. Me. I'll be paying it back in five years. Even less, if the hotel does well.' The lawyer had said he could choose a ten-year plan, but he didn't want that. He wouldn't let that happen.

'This house needs a lot of repairs,' his mother said. 'But it was given to me by my father, your grandfather. The title is still in my name. I feared it would be too complicated to have your father's name included in it.'

'I'll pay it back, Ma.' Hai tried to keep the desperation out of his voice. 'I told you, it can take less than five years.'

His mother didn't say anything, but she stood up and disappeared into the kitchen again, taking the teapot with her.

When she emerged, there was steam coming out of the old pot. She had refreshed the tea.

'Where will we live?' Her voice was quiet. 'I can't go through that. We can't lose our home.'

'I won't let that happen.'

'Oh?' His mother sighed. 'How can you be so sure?'

'Because Huế is booming,' Hai said, matter-of-factly. 'They need hotels. And we—Phong and I—well, we've found the perfect one.'

She shook her head, firm this time. 'No. It's too much. It's too risky.' And then: 'Children will never really understand their parents unless they become parents themselves.'

'Don't be like that.' Hai had always avoided smoking in front of his mother, but today he couldn't help himself. He lit up.

She was looking at him with tired eyes. 'As a mother, there's nothing more I want in this world than to give you everything that you need, and everything you want. I've seen your room in Huế. But once I'm back here, I still worry about how you live. Are you getting enough food? Rest? Are you working too much? Are people being unkind to you?'

'Ma, I'm not a child anymore.'

'That's the funny thing.' His mother gave a small, rueful smile. 'Somehow, I still think you're no older than fifteen.'

'I can take care of myself.'

'Remember the typhoon that happened two . . . three years ago? When you were here in the countryside with us because you said you had a few days off?'

'Of course,' Hai replied. 'We had to put sandbags on the roof. I remember that.'

'It wasn't the roof that blew off,' his mother said. 'It was one of the windows at the back.'

'Nothing serious.' Hai shook his head. 'It didn't even last the whole day, that storm. By nighttime, everything had died down.'

'Yes, and you know what I remember?' His mother looked straight at him, and he saw that her face was small and thin, her jaw sagging.

'What?'

'The winds may have been very strong. I can still remember the sounds it made, like a bulldozer in the distance. I remember thinking how lucky I was that day that you were here with us. Not in Huế, but here, in this house.'

* * *

It was past four when he emerged from the house.

Hai walked to his motorbike, eyeing the seat. The special power of attorney, that very important document he had stashed there would be of no use now.

'Hai!'

He turned and there was his mother, half walking and half running towards him. She was clutching the ceramic teapot that they had used that afternoon.

'Ma,' Hai said. He was tired. Discouraged, more than he wanted to admit. He dreaded the ride back to Huế, where his problems were waiting. 'I don't need tea.'

His mother reached him and stopped, panting. 'No,' she huffed, tucking the teapot into her armpit. 'No, no, not tea.'

She was still catching her breath as she reached for her pocket with her free hand and produced a plastic ballpen, gnawed badly at the end. 'Where is it?' She waved the pen in the air.

'Where's what, Ma?'

'The—the paper. Whatever it is you need me to sign. To put the property up as collateral.'

His mother didn't even ask about the special power of attorney, of course, she didn't. She didn't know any of those things. She had not been near a lawyer or a government office in years, maybe for more than a decade. What she knew—and he knew this—was that she trusted him. And he knew that after all these years of sending money to the family, helping out with the expenses, coming home during Tết, following almost everything they had told him to do, that he had certainly earned this trust.

Loaner's Remorse

HAI

It had been a week since he had gone to the bank to process the home loan, and today, as he was coming home from the bus terminal, he received a call: the money would be ready in two days. He just needed to come to the bank with his IDs.

He had expected to feel relieved. Settled and assured. He'd managed to find a means to produce the money that was needed, money that had long been due him and the very thing that had been holding him back from fulfilling his goal of running his own hotel. He was awash with a lot of feelings—overwhelmed with so much—but nothing that, he was sorry to note, even resembled relief. Instead, he had felt disturbingly unsettled since signing the papers. He had not slept well at all the past few days, his afternoon naps turning into some kind of dreadful loneliness. He found himself waking up each morning entangled in his thin sheets, the skin on his back chafing against the bed's rattan underside. He had not done his laundry for a week, and so he slept on the bare bed. He had taken to spending more time with Marina; at least there the air-con in her room was a brief respite, and the TV was certainly a necessary distraction. In the past week, he had only slept four to five hours. And he had missed things at Minh Thanh. The requests for girls had almost been nil, he wondered if someone had ratted on him about his little side hustle. It was as if one big thing had worked out, but everything else had gone awry. Some nights he found himself angry again at how things were.

They would need 500 million dong to pay just the deposit at the very least. Three thousand US dollars every month. That meant he needed to cough up 250 million dong.

But he knew what was weighing him down, despite the knowledge that Phong would be off his back, finally, and that he was closer to his goal. It was the house that he had offered as collateral. His mother's property. And yet, people in Vietnam did it all the time—pawned their property off as collateral, so what was he afraid of? Did he really know someone who had their home snatched by the bank? He had to admit that he didn't. There had been stories, but he couldn't be sure if they were even true.

What bothered him was the thought of his mother who had trusted him all the way through. Because the thing was, did he really trust himself to do this?

Had he really done the right thing? *You'll get over it*, he kept telling himself, even as visions of his mother's property being foreclosed seemed to crowd his brain, more than visions of the new hotel he would soon be managing with Phong.

But the meeting with the bank manager had unnerved him. *A month's default, and we'll pull the house*—not his exact words, but something to that effect. Hai was increasingly getting the feeling that he had not thought this through, that he had failed in threshing out the next steps. He'd been so caught up in coming up with the money and saving face that he'd neglected to think beyond it.

Hai was also scared to admit that he may have a handle on running a hotel, but he had no idea how to turn in a profit. And he had not admitted this to anyone, not even to Sinh, who knew all about this new venture. But she didn't know about the loan.

What had he gotten himself into?

But there was still Marina. She would help him. She'd balked at the money he'd asked for the motorbike, but she had given in at the end. She had paid for his trip to Singapore, all their meals, the little things. She would be there for him.

Hotel Hai

HAI

It didn't look that much different from the other hotels in town, with its white and blue façade and boxy, aluminium-framed glass windows lining all floors of the three-storey building. Narrow and tall, it was no gleaming five-star hotel like Saigon Morin or La Residence—it couldn't even begin to compete with places of that level. But Hotel Hong Thien was just ten minutes from the Perfume River, still with some trees and a small garden at the back, built by the owners eight years ago in a quiet alley while being close to a cluster of restaurants and shops—an important selling point. The agent hadn't let them forget about that. The hotel was old but still better than most, and now it was special— because it was his. Well, part of it, anyway, and only for a number of years. But still.

It was sandwiched between a local restaurant selling *banh loc* and a handicrafts shop that sold handmade things from different parts of Vietnam. In the mornings, he knew there were people selling vegetables, meat, and fish on basins they laid out on the sidewalk. He didn't have the heart to tell them to stop. He would just do what he had always done, all these years interacting with the tourists in his city: point them out to his guests with a laugh, maybe throw in a little joke—and hope that they might find the sight charming.

He parked his motorbike by the road, slipping through the door at the side of the small lobby. He had gone straight from his shift at Minh Thanh, even though a guest had woken him at 3 a.m. asking to replace a lost key. He didn't even think of stopping by the noodle stand he usually went to grab a quick breakfast.

It had only been a week since they'd signed the contract and handed the keys. But to Hai, it felt like time slowing down for once. He could have this hotel forever.

There were fifteen rooms in this hotel, a number that felt right.

He walked silently through the empty lobby, scattered with loose boards and bags of cement. The workers were repairing a part of the room that was already old and rotting. A small renovation, though Phong and he hadn't expected it to be this complicated, tedious, and detail-oriented. Hai was not a carpenter, had not really built anything with his hands. What did he know about putting a room back together?

It was not perfect. And it had cost him so much, too much.

He should feel lucky. He should have just believed Phong when he said that this was a steal, that the lease for this was nearly a third of the price of the other hotels that they'd looked at.

Still, Hai had balked at the amount of money they had to pay just for the six-month deposit alone. The lease was for three years, which still made him uneasy. It was a significant investment, the biggest investment he'd done in his whole life. Did he see his mother's house in this hotel? No, in his mind, he only saw it getting bigger and brighter, filled with people whom he didn't have to cajole, fight tooth and nail into booking a room, like he was still doing for Phong Nha Hostel.

This was the beginning of his dream.

He took a key from the reception counter and climbed the stairs to the second floor. The hotel didn't have an elevator, as with most two-star hotels. The walls were plain, the dark wood beams on the ceiling and the heavy wooden furniture in the lobby left by the previous managers the only traditional touch. Sinh could probably do something, make it prettier, but he was reluctant to go all-out in discussing this hotel. He didn't yet want to reveal that this hotel felt like the culmination of what he'd worked for. Sinh would get what he meant but then she would most likely suggest that they get married as soon as possible and he didn't want that right now, not at this time.

He looked at his phone. It was only 6.30 a.m., early enough. He wasn't needed at the bus station until 8.30 a.m. today and the buses from Hội An and Hanoi would surely be delayed. The couple of guys repairing the lobby wouldn't be here until 7.30 a.m.

He opened the first room nearest the staircase.

He slid open a window; the view was just the wall of the next hotel, grimy and unkempt. He turned towards the double bed, slipping out of his shoes. When he laid down, the bare mattress felt prickly and warm.

He remembered how he had longed for this. To sign a lease contract, to have this hotel. No, it wasn't just longing. It was anger. Rage. How angry he was at having to go through this tortuous process of reaching his dream while others seemed to float into theirs so effortlessly. There was nothing romantic about it, nothing funny or amusing about his suffering—his anguish—at all. It had not been easy and so he was determined to get it all back. Make it up to himself and to his family. Pay back for all his hardships with all the money he could get.

The hotel had three floors and fifteen rooms. It was no nonsense: five rooms on each floor, connected by a stairway, no elevator. The hallways looked stark and felt warm, almost stuffy, but Hai wasn't really worried about that. He had told Phong that they just needed to replace the lights to make it brighter. People wouldn't care how hot the hallway was as long as their rooms had fans and air-conditioners.

A hotel that was functional, whose rooms he could rent for cheap; no one wanted an expensive hotel when they were mostly out touring the city. And he would make sure that they would be touring. It would feel authentic for tourists and backpackers and affordable enough for the Vietnamese. Value for money.

There was no café in the hotel, but Hai could see that the space could be made at the lobby reception—a tiny lobby café. Only drinks would be available—they'd have a proper cooler; he'll make sure of that—but food could be bought from the vendors outside. He was not new to this. When he had been working as a bellboy in Orchid Hotel, he worried about the guests arriving in the middle of the night or at 5 or 6 a.m. He'd ask them if they needed any food, and he would offer to buy it for them. 'Any food you want,' he'd say. He didn't exactly know why he did this—it wasn't required of him by his manager then, and he didn't even skim money off what the guests gave him. It made him feel a little ashamed that he might do this right now, to get what he could. Well, he did try, in the succeeding years, but it always came up short. One guest had been so surprised, she gave him a tip of

100,000 dong—he tried to return it, thinking she made a mistake but she shooed him away.

Phong had been complaining about all the little things that needed to be fixed, of the million details to consider but, to Hai, it felt simple. Doable. He had not felt this alive in a long time, not even when Sinh agreed to be his girlfriend. Or when he got the job at Minh Thanh, his first job at a four-star hotel.

And there was Marina, of course.

There was still his work at Phong Nha, his receptionist job at Minh Thanh, the occasional deals with his guests and the girls. Maybe soon he could be free of that. Not yet, though. He needed to be sure.

Chloe and Sam

CARMEN

It had been more than a week since Carmen started, and she was exhausted. The work was cooking, cleaning, minding the kids, and tutoring them. It did not help that Grandma Ba was always there, on the periphery, seemingly watching over her in disapproving silence. She had her own spot in the living room and the kitchen, always sitting in the same chair in one corner of the dining table. Often, she would whisper to one of the kids and Chloe or sometimes even Sam would go up to her with instructions on some mundane task: take out the trash, wash her tumbler, wipe a damp spot on a corner of the table that Carmen had missed.

That morning, the stove was on when Carmen arrived.

'I want to be a chef!'

'Is that so?' Carmen took three big strides and turned the stove knob, snuffing out the flame. Then she bent down to eye-level with the young girl and said, 'I like cooking, too.'

'No, not like you,' Chloe said, frowning. 'I want to be a famous chef. Like on TV or YouTube.'

Carmen nodded, straightening up. 'Then maybe we can learn some English vocabulary about chef things.' She was just winging it, she knew. But then wouldn't it still be helpful, to know the English words for these things?

Chloe brightened visibly. 'Let's go cook something! Rice!'

'Good idea.' Carmen scooped out two cups of rice from the dispenser, grabbed the rice cooker container, and opened the tap.

'I just want to be with Me,' Sam said mournfully.

'Mummy!' Chloe yelled. 'She wants us to call her Mummy!'

The little boy shrugged and looked longingly in the direction of the studio.

Grandma Ba came in, stared at the three of them rooting around in the kitchen, and said something to Chloe. Carmen watched the loose skin on her jaw work up and down as she spoke in Vietnamese.

'What did she say, Chloe?'

'She said we should continue our lesson in the living room, not play here in the kitchen.'

'We're not playing.' Carmen glanced at the elderly lady. 'Could you please tell her we're still doing our lesson? You're still learning here.'

Chloe stood with arms akimbo. 'I already told her that, but she said we shouldn't stay here.' She shrugged and looked away in that detached way that kids do.

Carmen sighed. 'All right.' She had washed the rice. She pressed the button of the rice cooker. 'Let's get your iPad and look at pictures instead.'

* * *

After starting an easy lesson on the iPad, Carmen read them the picture books that Nina had bought. And then she read them some more from short books that she'd downloaded from the internet. She had watched some simple English children's songs on YouTube, and she sang one with them, something about morning routines. Sam had taken particularly to the song, demanding to repeat it at least three more times.

Now, both Chloe and Sam were sprawled on the floor in the living room, busy with their colouring books. Carmen had written the English words under some of the line drawings that they were filling in with colour.

She pulled out her phone and opened Facebook, pressed on Nicole Peltier's name that was already at the top of her search list. She felt an immediate calm as the face of her smiling mother came up. Soon, she thought, she will be smiling at the thought of being with her daughter. She clicked on the photo so she could see the comments, but there were none except for a GIF that showed a funny cartoon holding an oversized trembling heart. Or at least, that was what it looked like. She had never been enthralled with Facebook or any kind of social media up until the time she discovered that her mother was on it. Otherwise, it had always felt like a betrayal of privacy, of things she never wished the world to know.

She left the kids in the living room and went into the kitchen. There was the usual pile in the sink that was beginning to feel like it would always be there. But for the first time since she had arrived in this city, she felt confident. Perhaps it was having this job. Perhaps it was the thought of earning money from this kind of work, one that didn't require her to take something from someone. Work that felt good because it was about giving. She remembered telling Max about being a nurse, something she could never be—no, it was too late for that.

Carmen had been mulling over her new job with the Blanchets, trying to make sense and tamp down the fearful, doubtful voice that was telling her that she didn't know what she was really doing. That voice that told her that it may feel good right now, but everything could take a horrible turn tomorrow.

She felt a tug on the hem of her shirt. It was Chloe. 'What is it? You were supposed to stay in the living room.'

'Her clothes. Wash her clothes. Ba's clothes.'

Carmen grabbed the sponge. The counter was still sticky. 'Yes, yes of course I'll wash her clothes. Later.'

'No, no.' Chloe's voice was stubborn. 'She means now.'

'I'm still doing something, dear. I will do it after this.' Carmen had learned in the past week that the kids responded well once you assured them that you will be doing it after your present task.

Chloe flung the soft doll she was carrying and started crying. 'She means now! She's—she's . . .' Snot had started coming out of her nose.

'Chloe!' Carmen dropped the sponge in the sink and knelt down. 'What is it?'

The child didn't answer, tears still streaming down her cheeks. Carmen wiped her face with a washcloth and handed her back the discarded doll. 'Okay. Go back to the living room and watch your brother. Only for a little while, I promise. I'll be back.' Then, she hurried towards Grandma Ba's room.

The air was heavy and stale when she slipped through the door after a knock. Grandma Ba was sitting on her bed, instead of the chair where she usually sat, and looked as if she had been waiting for Carmen.

There was a pile of clothes on the floor, just by the side of her chair.

'Xin chao, Ba,' Carmen said softly. 'Sorry—you want to me wash this?' She berated herself for not listening to Chloe and not doing this right away. She should have said yes at the start; Nina had showed her a big washing machine at the back that looked like it had never been used. It would be no problem to load the clothes there.

The elderly woman looked at her with the same stony expression she'd always had since Carmen had started working there. Not an issue at all with Carmen, since Grandma Ba couldn't—or didn't want to—speak English.

Carmen took a few steps towards her and the pile of clothes. 'I'll just take this and wash them, okay?' She picked up the few pieces of clothing and noticed just then that the pile smelled of something putrid. It reminded her of the odours of the canal she used to play in Barangay Bicutan. Could it be what she thought it was? She looked down, not wanting to look at the older woman *looking* at her as she slipped out of the room and through the door, her heart pounding.

Chloe was nowhere to be found when she went back to the kitchen, but she could hear both the kids' murmurs and squeals in the living room. The kids had been a pleasant surprise to her and were actually the least problematic part of this job.

Good, Carmen thought, quickly opening the narrow back door that led to the backyard. She stepped into the small, three-walled shed connected to the house that Nina had showed her. Inside was a washing machine and a dryer, as well as a makeshift, dirty kitchen with a single burner stove.

Only then did she lay down Grandma Ba's clothes on the rough cement floor, peeling away layers of the colourful clothing. Some were slightly damp—the cardigans, some towels, a housedress and blouse, several pieces of underwear . . .

She picked up the underwear, meaning to place the delicates in a separate pile. And there it was, on one of the panties: a brown pile of human waste, runny and wet. Grandma Ba had defecated in her underpants.

Carmen dropped the clothes, feeling her stomach turn. Inside the shed, the smell seemed to have intensified. She had been in less-than-sanitary conditions before—Manila was full of dirty, grimy places—but she had never cleaned up anyone's shit, and it repulsed her to touch this stranger's waste.

She felt her breath coming in short, shallow spurts, images of Barangay Bicutan playing in her mind, her tasks of going up to strangers, telling all those lies, watching her 'family' strip a helpless, unconscious stranger of his belongings. She had wanted to be far away from all that. She had not really known it when she was still in Barangay Bicutan, doing the jobs for Uncle Amado, Auntie Swan and Max—but the speed and velocity of her departure and arrival in Huế City told her that she was, in fact, desperate to leave. And then she thought of the Facebook photos of Nicole Peltier who was here, in this very same city. The thing is, she was desperate for her mother. Was she going to give up now? She had been in harder situations.

'Chi oi?'

It was Chloe again, peeking her head through the open door. 'What are you doing?'

'Stay back! Don't come here, it's hot and dirty.' Carmen struggled to keep her voice calm. 'Chloe, where's Sam?'

'Still colouring.'

'I need you to take care of your brother for a few minutes more, okay?' She prayed the little girl would understand her fully.

Chloe nodded then frowned and wrinkled her nose. '*Hoi qua*, chi oi!'

Carmen didn't need a translator to know what she was talking about. She fanned her hands. 'I know, I know. It smells bad. Go inside! I'll be there soon, and we will sing again, okay?'

The girl darted back into the kitchen, and Carmen heard the back door closing with a soft bang.

She looked down at the fallen clothes, suddenly worried that she had now soiled the floor. She went back into the kitchen to wash her hands. She knew that Grandma Ba wouldn't be able to forgive her if she threw away a perfectly functional piece of underwear. In the kitchen, she took a roll of toilet paper, the bottle of handwash by the sink, and found a small wash basin under the sink of the dirty kitchen. She boiled some water in the plastic electric kettle. Once it was done, she poured it on the basin she'd half-filled with lukewarm, water and detergent she'd found near the washing machine, along with bleach. She wiped away the shit as much as she could, then dunked it into the water. Only then did she step back, heaving a sigh of relief as she gathered the rest of the clothes and placed them inside the washer.

Her phone beeped. It was Hai, asking if everything was okay in his usual stunted texts. His messages sounded just like him in real life. And then, because of this, she remembered Marina again who was here on a business trip—her own business trip—and whatever workshop that she was organizing.

Marina, who could afford to do anything she wanted. Carmen had no desire at all to talk or be with the woman. And where was she staying? Probably in some high-class hotel. It occurred to Carmen that she had been so wrapped up in her own problems, she hadn't even cared to ask. In any case, Marina couldn't have been farther from Carmen's situation. What did Marina know about cleaning toilets and other people's shit?

She wanted to resent Marina, she really did. But there was a certain sadness, a sort of desperation about the woman that she couldn't really pinpoint—though Carmen felt she had no time or business to ponder on other people's problems—but which she suspected had something to do with Marina's relationship with Hai. As for that, she was not surprised that Marina and Hai were together, although the match seemed so contradictory. No, it didn't feel like a good match at all. But what did she know?

Hai had become her only friend, following the intense events of the past weeks. And yet, she realized that she really didn't know much about Hai at all, that all her impressions had been just those—impressions. Speculations. She didn't know why she was surprised that Hai preferred foreigners, that he didn't have a girlfriend here in Huế. He acted like such an old man sometimes, a strict older brother who could at times be rigid and inflexible. She wasn't even sure if Hai was that. No, she wasn't sure of anything at all.

Wanting more of the things he couldn't give. Maybe it was a culture thing. She had complained before about him being too quiet. What could he do? What else could he say? She wasn't Vietnamese, how could she understand everything that was going on? How could she know that some things are just the way they should be?

'The hotel is doing well,' he said, the words slipping easily out of his mouth. He didn't pause to think if he regretted saying it. Why did he say that? Two rooms out of fifteen were occupied. One was a guest checking out tomorrow after staying for only two days. Marina didn't have to know that. He felt tired just thinking of explaining the hotel to her, the English that it would require.

'Oh? Wow, well—that's great!' Marina looked genuinely pleased, and he was glad that she didn't know anything about hotels except what was offered to the guests. 'I'm happy.'

'You know that we only have fifteen rooms, right?' he said. 'We're expecting so many more guests, especially in the high season.' He took another stick from his pack on the table, rolling it between his thumb and forefinger. He tried not to think how he'd just finished one less than a minute ago or how his voice sounded alien, even to himself.

'A boutique hotel,' Marina was saying now, nodding. 'Your hotel could be that if you want it to be.'

Indeed, he would have wanted it to be a boutique hotel, Hai thought bitterly, if only that didn't cost more, perhaps double of what Phong and he had had to shell out for the lease. A boutique hotel entailed tricky renovations and fancy concepts he couldn't even begin to think about, a whole separate budget for a designer—no, that wasn't for him at all. He wanted a hotel that was simple, clean, and functional. A hotel that was affordable and did the job of housing foreigners and local travellers. And that is what his was, only it was off to a slow start.

He remembered when he had brought Marina there, how they didn't stay long because he had things to do and didn't think at that time that there was much use showing off to Marina—Marina, who wouldn't understand it, anyway, just because she wasn't from Huế.

'A small hotel,' he said finally, shrugging his shoulders and taking a long drag. 'It's very small.'

'At least you have your own business,' Marina said. 'I'm hoping to have a business of mine too.' There was a light, mischievous tone in her voice that told him that that business had already been done, easily. Everything was in place for this foreigner who had just arrived in Vietnam because she had the very thing he didn't have: money.

'Marina,' he said, as softly and as gently as he could. He leaned back in his chair, lowered his hand on his lap. This was important, and it would be better if he was relaxed, flexible, nimble. He raised his hand and took a deep, delicate drag, carefully blowing the smoke to his side so the thin cloud of white wouldn't float over to her.

'You remember the *nha nghi* beside Hong Thien? Beside my hotel.' He watched as she nodded, unable to stop herself from smiling, signalling that she recognized the words nha nghi, a small hotel. 'The owner is going to America.'

'Is that so?' Marina raised her eyebrows languidly. 'For a vacation?'

'No,' Hai said, trying to remember the words. 'Not for a vacation. He will live there, in California, as an immigrant. His children are there.' He congratulated himself for coming up with this piece of information. He placed his stick carefully on the ashtray, raised his head. All of a sudden, he felt bold and gazed openly at Marina. He wanted to see how she would take this.

'And you know what, em? It's for sale now, the property and the hotel. They're selling it for cheap. Very, very cheap.'

'Really?' Marina appeared non-committal, distracted. 'How much?'

'Fifty thousand dollars,' he said, feeling lightheaded even as he said the amount. 'US dollars. I heard he can still lower the price to forty-eight.' That was 700 million dong and that was something.

'Oh?' Marina, for the first time that day, looked sceptical. 'Just fifty thousand, for a hotel? And the land, too?' She fiddled with the edge of the menu. 'How big is it?'

'More than a thousand square metres,' he answered, the numbers jumping in his head. 'The hotel has twenty-two rooms.'

'A thousand square metres? That's big,' Marina said. 'And all that for fifty thousand dollars?'

'The owner is desperate,' Hai said, quickly, alarmed at Marina's reaction. Was the price too low? He steeled himself. 'The man and his wife are desperate to leave,' he said again, keeping his voice even, 'and so he really needs the money.' He shrugged his shoulders. 'Amazing, isn't it? I think, soon, when Hong Thien Hotel starts doing well, I will think of expanding.'

He barrelled on, even if she didn't say anything. 'Can you imagine, em, if we got that hotel? We could have a bigger business. We can build more rooms, have more guests. This is an opportunity.'

'Yes,' Marina nodded. 'It's an opportunity.'

'This is for our future.'

'Do you need money?' Marina's voice was soft, non-threatening as usual. In the months that he had known her, he noticed that she was like this when sensitive topics came up, like money, illness, and even salaries. Hai knew it had more to do with her sensitivity to other people and less about not wanting to offend someone. And he knew this because he had witnessed, first-hand, that she was just good like that.

Yes, Marina may be right in some things and perhaps it really was the polite thing to do, but Hai was long past this walking-on-eggshells kind of politeness. He had long been over bending backwards for other people out of consideration for others. No, he'd been pummelled enough; he wanted things for himself, without being scared, without needing to apologize.

'Hai? I asked, do you need money?'

Hai shook his head vigorously. 'Oh no, no. I couldn't even think of having that much money. It's just a dream, you know?'

'I know.'

'I'm just telling you, em. I was just so amazed. I mean, if I had the money . . . I wouldn't let this slip by. I don't know if I'll ever come across a deal as good as this.'

'Well,' Marina shrugged. 'In the future—'

'I want you to be my wife,' he blurted out. 'Do you know that?'

Hai saw her pause, eyes widening, the corners of her mouth going slack.

He held his breath but only for a split second—allowing that tiny fear he'd been holding on to, the fear that told him he might regret saying it out loud, that it might be a repeat of the motorbike incident. He felt a surge of strength as the words left his mouth, as if letting them out of his system allowed new energy to flow through his body. He could do this. He would get what he needed.

'We could own this hotel. Start our own thing. The revenue would be double. It could be the site of our future house, even.' He was babbling.

'What did you say?' Marina's tone was quiet, a contrast to his frenzied noises.

Hai cleared his throat. 'I said—' This time, he made sure he enunciated his words. 'I want you to be my wife.'

Marina inhaled sharply, noisily—but said nothing at first. There was a look in her eyes that he couldn't define, something he'd seen before but couldn't really place.

'I have to check my bank,' she said, finally. 'Okay, Hai?'

Uncovering Carmen

HAI

Hai gazed at Sinh's bent head beside him, now just a head of very dark, thick hair. She was on her phone as usual, looking pleased as a clam, smiling at some inane video of a woman ranting about something he couldn't even understand. Sinh always had a thing for slapstick humour; she laughed at the silliest things. She looked happy now. And why wouldn't she be—she had in her hands the latest Samsung, freshly bought from one of those mobile phone sellers she followed on Facebook. Sinh had saved the money from her salary and had also perhaps been bumped up by the aunt she was staying with. Meanwhile, she relied on Hai to pay for her various caprices—pizzas and fake branded bags and sunglasses—as if he didn't notice.

He couldn't see Sinh's face at all, but he had a clear view of the bright, white screen of her phone, open on Facebook. Bits of dialogues and monologues flew out as she scrolled through her feed, and the multitude of clips it presented. Where did she get all these anyway? There was a time when he himself followed all these media news sites but soon tired of them. The thought of work, of earning more, and how to do it worried and preoccupied him most days.

'Look at this, anh,' Sinh was crowing now, sidling closer. He felt her hips bump against his, some button or hard metal grommet digging into his hip bone and causing him to move away involuntarily.

'Sorry,' he mumbled, throwing her a quick glance. There was a time, years ago, when he would have been on fire just from her clothed skin brushing against his. He had wanted her so much then, had always thought she was too good for him. Too pretty and too smart.

Well, people had always told him that. Now, he wondered if any of that was even true. Had he listened too much to people who didn't even care about him? People who didn't really know him.

But Sinh's eyes were still on her phone. She had never stopped looking at it. 'Look, look.' She turned the phone slightly so he could clearly see the screen.

It was a video of a woman washing dishes but facing the camera. Another silly clip where someone was lip-synching to something, saying something ridiculous. It was over in less than 30 seconds.

And then Sinh's fingers were on the screen again, scrolling and tapping on a new video. Hai watched a couple more with her. She had tapped on a third video, and it had only begun to play when Sinh made a sound.

'Well. It's so boring now.' She grunted and looked around as if woken up from some social media stupor. 'We'd better go and—'

'Wait.' He grabbed her wrist to steady her hand, which was still holding the phone.

'Ow!' Sinh cried, wriggling in her seat. But the hand with the phone was still facing him.

'This video,' Hai said, nodding at the screen. 'Wait.'

It was in another language—Filipino or English with Vietnamese subtitles—but Hai wasn't even looking at that. He was staring at the photo that was being flashed again and again in the clip, in that jarring, dizzy way people presented news on Facebook these days. No, it was a drawing—an astonishingly good ink-and-paint drawing of a woman that looked familiar.

Why, it was Carmen.

'Anh ơi!' Sinh gave his arm a hard tug, her tone impatient. 'What are you watching? I'm hungry. Let's go.'

'Wait,' he said again. Frowning, he let go of her wrist. 'Save it,' he said, referring to the video still playing. 'I need that.'

He watched as she pressed something on her Facebook and then showed him the screen. 'So,' Sinh handed him the phone. 'Happy?'

He played the video again. It was only 45 seconds long but that was just what he needed.

'Who's that?'

'Nothing,' he said.

It wasn't nothing of course. It was, in fact, everything. He had been dealing with a criminal, all this while, and he had no other thought except that it was a blessing.

Convincing Carmen

HAI

He took a certain comfort in knowing where to find her. Nhung's —Nina's—house and where it stood on a hill just outside the centre of Huế was already etched in his brain, making it feel as if he could drive up there anytime on his motorbike to see Carmen.

He needed to see her now. This was about Carmen and very possibly about him and Marina, and this couldn't wait at all. A plan had formed in his mind, and as his motorbike climbed up the steep road leading to Nina Blanchet's house, he stopped short of congratulating himself for connecting everything. For still finding a way. It was because of this that he now had a solution to his sticky dilemma.

He had saved the video on his own second hand phone, once Sinh and he had separated. He had gone to a coffee shop and watched it again and again, consuming more than five sticks of cigarettes, even after he drained his iced cà phê đen until not a drop was left.

Today, a low, steady buzz seemed to be coursing through his insides. Excitement mixed with tension, which was certainly better than the agony he'd been feeling since he had spoken with Marina about the hotel. He felt bereft of something he never had, but it was certainly something he felt he deserved. All morning, he had asked himself if this thing, this plan that had occurred to him would work. He had tried telling himself that even if the circumstances were different, it was only right that the truth about Carmen be revealed.

'Chao em,' he chirped, when Carmen opened the door for him. He was surprised at how his own voice came out louder and more forceful than he'd expected. He cleared his throat and shifted on his feet. 'Everything okay?'

'Hi, Hai.' Carmen paused, and then, as if realizing what she had just said, chuckled at her own joke. She looked so cheerful, her wide face now breaking into an easy smile. 'Yes, yes. How are you?'

He followed her into the sun-filled kitchen, trying not to gape yet again at the high ceilings, the gleaming coffee machine, the full wine rack—this whole space that he found both luxurious and deplorable. In front of him, Carmen was saying something breezy in English and Hai marvelled at the bright, innocent tone of Carmen's voice. Had this been the same fearful girl he'd encountered just a month ago? It felt like a different time. A better time. A time when he felt useful and, more importantly, in control—in a way that he sometimes couldn't when he was with Marina or even Sinh. Carmen had been so grateful—and, despite her problems, so simple. He felt his insides softening just a little.

Don't back out now, he told himself as he watched her lightly touch the heads of the kids who were parked, heads down and busy with their colouring books and iPads around the kitchen table. Carmen then proceeded to wipe the length of the kitchen counter with a folded nubby cloth, humming a low but happy tune.

Maybe Nhung—Nina—had been good to her. At the thought of Nina—oh, hell—just being inside this rented house that they had customized just because her stupid French husband wanted it to be more French, reminded him of just how unfair everything was, and how he needed to grab the opportunity, wherever and however it came to him.

And he certainly had an opportunity now.

Carmen looked happy and more relaxed, certainly less anxious. She was now done cleaning up and was mixing something on the stove. When she turned, there was something steaming and fragrant inside the pot she was holding. He watched her spoon what looked like oatmeal in two small bowls on the table, the room suddenly smelling like milk and cinnamon. He craved coffee all of a sudden.

Even the kids looked tamer than when he had last seen them a few weeks ago. Chloe was rifling through a thin picture book while Sam was swiping at an iPad. Nina was nowhere to be found.

'How are things here?' he asked again. He felt awkward standing there, so he moved to a corner and leaned against a cupboard. 'Nina is good to you? The children? They're not . . . bad?' He couldn't find the English word for that thing he didn't like about kids.

'It's okay,' Carmen said. 'I'm a little tired, but it's okay.'

'Chi oi,' Chloe's tinny voice cut through their conversation. 'I want the—the—strawberry! No, the blueberry!'

'Blueberries,' Carmen corrected her. 'Yes, we have a lot of blueberries.'

Hai watched as she ambled to the refrigerator and took out a plastic container of the dark fruit. Vietnam had a lot of local fruit—pineapples, mangoes, rambutans, watermelons, and guavas that were all so cheap, even he didn't mind buying them on a regular basis. Nina, of course, had to get something Western and expensive and so impractical, like blueberries. He was sure now that Nina shopped at the imported section at Big C or in that small, upscale supermarket just across it, the one that served tourists and foreigners in Huế and so it must be expensive. Going to the wet market, of course, was out of the question.

'Nina . . .' Hai paused and tried to search for the right words. 'She goes to the market? Or is it you?'

'The supermarket, you mean?' Carmen was emptying the packet of blueberries on the kids' bowls of oatmeal. 'No, it's her. I think she goes with the children.' She paused, then gave a small shrug. 'Maybe she does her grocery shopping on my day off, I don't know. I just use whatever is in their fridge.'

He looked around, something black and thick building up in him. Everything felt foreign in this house. It irked him that there was hardly a trace of anything Vietnamese. He didn't feel like being here.

'Let's have coffee?' He gave Carmen a brisk nod. 'Outside, it's better.' He meant out of this house and in a coffee shop that he was familiar with. Anywhere but here.

'Coffee? Who is going out?'

The door burst open. It was Nina's husband. What was his name again?

'*Bonjour*, I'm Andre,' the man said, nodding politely at him but turning to smile at Carmen as if they'd been friends for years. He was toting a green and black bike helmet by the strap, clad in tight bike shorts and a black Nike T-shirt that hugged his biceps. He did look quite handsome, even to Hai, though the clothes he wore were nothing that Hai would even be caught dead in.

'I heard someone mention coffee,' Andre said, eyes animated. 'It's a beautiful morning. *Les enfants*—kids—why don't we go out to the park? To the river? Just finish your breakfast!'

'You'll take them out?' Carmen asked, glancing at Hai. 'Now?'

Andre pursed his lips and gave a shrug. 'Why not? The weather here is so good.' He bent down and frowned at the cartoon that Sam was watching on his iPad. The child was also slowly spooning the oatmeal into his mouth. 'I don't understand why they have to be indoors.'

'What? What? I heard you, Uncle Andre!' Chloe dropped her coloured pencils with a clatter and looked up. Her English was so good, Hai wondered if that was Carmen's doing. 'Going out? Uncle Andre, are we going out?'

'*Oui, ma cherie!*' Andre grinned. 'Yes!'

Carmen blinked. 'But Nina—'

'*Alors*, I'll take care of Nina.' Andre placed the helmet on the table, as the kids started untangling themselves from their chairs and gadgets. 'She's there, in her little studio, with not a care in the world.'

* * *

'Tell me again,' Hai leaned against the wall at the back of the house, looking at the overgrown weeds in the backyard, the cement perimeter fence still rough and unpainted unlike the whitewashed one at the front. It had only been a few minutes since Andre left with the kids in tow, with Sam perched on Andre's shoulders as they went out through the front door, chattering like good friends, albeit in diversely and heavily-accented English.

The house was quiet without them, and Nina had still not emerged from her studio.

'What is it, Hai? You're so full of questions today.' Carmen's voice was chirpier than earlier that morning, before the kids had gone out. He needed to smoke, so they both agreed to hang outside at the back.

'What were you doing again in Manila? I forgot, sorry.'

Carmen frowned a little, then straightened up. 'Different things, like I said. Haven't I told you? But that doesn't matter. I'm here to look for my mother.'

Hai nodded. 'Of course, I haven't forgotten that.' He felt annoyed, but then, after a moment, he was surprised to be overcome with something that felt like lightness and freedom. Yes, he felt free. It dawned on him that he could do whatever he wanted, and Carmen would still be what she was. A criminal.

'Carmen. You know Marina?'

'You and her, you mean? You're together.'

'No, no. I mean, yes.' Hai took a deep breath. 'Let's not talk about that now.' He slipped his hand inside his pocket and stroked the smooth, cold surface of his phone. *Not yet*, he told himself.

'I need help in talking to her about something. An important thing. And since you're also from the Philippines—'

'Oh, Hai!' Carmen laughed. 'Just because we're from the same country doesn't mean that we think the same. And, look at Marina! She's rich, she has a lot of money, while I . . .' her voice trailed off.

'Yes, she has money.' Hai took a puff and breathed out the smoke, slowly. 'That's why I need you.'

Quickly, he told her about the recent events in his life, the way he had imagined it in his head that morning. He recounted how he had gotten a loan using his mother's property as collateral, how his best friend Phong and he had found the hotel they had been looking for, how he had signed the lease agreement with Phong and paid his share with every cent that he had. He told her that the hotel right beside them was on sale for cheap. Finally, he told her how they realized that the money was not enough when they started doing the renovations.

Carmen listened intently, her face inscrutable. 'Hai,' she said, when he was done, 'I don't have money. You know that.' She shook her head as if to emphasize this fact. 'Maybe Marina—'

'Marina, yes.' Hai nodded, feeling conspiratorial. 'Exact.'

'Exactly,' Carmen corrected him, and he felt his face burn. Why did she have that infuriating habit of correcting people's English? He felt like whipping out his phone right then.

But he didn't. Instead, he tried again. 'Maybe you can help me talk to Marina.'

'Talk to Marina? About what?'

'Tell her that we—she—needs to buy the hotel just beside us. You know, the one that I just told you about. The owner is selling it. He's moving to America and he needs the money so it's very cheap. Very, very cheap.' He had no plans of telling her that it was non-existent. Because, though the hotel had been there for years, it still had more guests than Hong Thien Hotel, *his* hotel.

Carmen placed a hand on her chin and didn't say anything. Hai knew she was thinking about this. It was a request, a simple favour.

'I don't know,' Carmen said, finally. 'If Marina has made up her mind, then there is no reason for her to say no.'

'So? What is it? Yes or no?'

'What?' Carmen looked exasperated. 'Look, Hai. I don't even know her at all. Why would you ask me this? What is this?'

'You won't do it? You won't help me?' Hai felt the blood rush to his head, and he grabbed his phone from his pocket. He swiped up and opened the video, trying to keep his hands steady as he handed her the phone.

'Look,' he said, through gritted teeth, 'that's you.'

He watched as she took the phone and watched, wordlessly, the forty-five-second-long clip. He had played and replayed the video so often the previous night that he almost knew when the voice-over paused and at which part the image of Carmen's drawing appeared.

'So?'

Carmen slowly turned her head towards him, still without saying anything. Typical Carmen.

He wanted to see the usual signs of shock and fear, though what were they anyway? Was it a widening of the eyes, a shortness of breath, Carmen begging him to not tell? It incensed him that Carmen appeared composed, almost indifferent to what she just saw.

Because there was hardly a flicker in her eyelids. There was no nervous breathing, no tremble or quiver on her lips that suggested that she'd been affected at all by what he had just shown her, by what she had just seen about herself, up close and first-hand. No. When she turned to fully face him, her expression was flat and impassive.

It infuriated him. Had she always been like this? True, he had not paid much attention to her since they met, but now he thought that maybe he had missed something important about this strange, reclusive woman from the Philippines who claimed to be looking for her mother in Huế, of all places. Maybe he had been wrong all this time and Carmen wasn't helpless or hard up or scared of anything, at all.

He tried again. 'It is you, right?' He tried to keep his voice even. She didn't answer.

'You're wanted by the police in Manila.'

She shook her head slightly, the movement barely perceptible.

'Well,' he said. 'Even if you're not wanted, I know they're looking for you. I can report you to the police here. Remember, this is Vietnam.'

There must have been something compelling in the way he said the name of his country, because Carmen opened her mouth, as if to speak.

He barrelled on. 'It's been done before, you know. How easy. Vietnamese police can ban you from this country—'

'Why would you do that?' Carmen's voice rang out, high and questioning, which seemed to echo across the empty backyard. 'Why would you—' She gave an exasperated sigh, the most emotion she'd shown Hai since seeing the video. 'Hai, I thought you were my friend. Why are you doing this? Threatening me this way . . .' Her voice trailed off in what Hai thought was a choking sound.

He avoided her eyes and instead searched his pockets for the matchbox he'd taken from the café earlier. He lit another stick. 'I don't know. Like you, I also have a problem.'

'What problem?' This time, Carmen frowned. 'Marina? Is that it?'

'No, not Marina.' He didn't want to talk about that right now. He kept on taking drags from the stick, tilting his head up as he released the smoke from his throat and lungs. 'You don't understand.'

'Then what is it, Hai? What's your problem?'

'I don't have—I'm losing—' Troi oi, he couldn't say it. *He couldn't say it.* He took a shallow puff and tried again. 'My hotel is . . . not good.'

'Not good? What do you mean? Has something happened, Hai? Your hotel is not earning and is losing money, is that what you mean?'

It was only morning, but Hai felt a tiredness in his bones. He wanted to go back to his room, lie down on the comforting flatness of his bed. He had been sleeping in that bed for years. He knew its uneven bumps and depressions, all its nicks on the wooden frame edges, the parts that splintered. He didn't want to be in this big, arrogant house. He didn't want to be doing this to Carmen.

'No, it's not good,' he repeated. But he couldn't forgive himself if he didn't do this one last thing for himself. He could be a wall, too, like Carmen. 'Talk to her, Carmen.'

Carmen looked pained. 'Andre and the kids will be back soon. And Nina—'

'Never mind. Do whatever you want.' With that, Hai threw his cigarette stub on the grass, jangled his motorbike keys, and headed back towards the kitchen door.

Carmen's Choice

CARMEN

This time, she went alone. When she messaged Mr Binh, the private investigator that Hai and she had met with, he immediately texted her back. First was a message with a list of reminders about being discreet.

'Use sunglasses,' was one of his instructions. The second text was a more personal one, asking her how she was and if she was ready. Carmen knew what it meant. She had gone ahead, taking a xe om to Mr Binh's office. When she clambered up to the third floor, she couldn't help but feel amused with Mr Binh's incognito games. She didn't even own a pair of sunglasses the detective had wanted her to wear.

What she had was 400 US dollars, more than enough for the deposit that Mr Binh required for him to start the search for her mother.

And now it was done. Carmen emerged from the grey building with a feeling of accomplishment, oddly not caring if she had trusted a stranger with all the money she had at that time, a combination of the cash she had brought from Manila and the salary she got from Nina. Mr Binh had given her a rough timetable, and repeated the steps of the skip tracing process he was planning to do, all the avenues he would try so that he could locate Nicole Peltier.

'How long do you think it would take?' Carmen had asked.

'Give me a week or two.' Mr Binh had sounded confident. He paused when he saw her face. 'Or not. Some cases take months. But, don't worry. I'll be talking to people today.'

And so she had felt reckless, and also hopeful. She walked the narrow sidewalk from the building that led to the main road, heady with the thought that it was just a matter of time before she would see

341

her mother. She had decided to walk around the city, particularly the streets around the Citadel. The Blanchets were in Dalat for a vacation, and so she was not needed for three days. A luxury, but it had not felt as luxurious as daydreaming of the day when she would finally meet Nicole Peltier.

It had been more than two weeks since she had spoken to Hai. Two weeks since that day when he came to see her at the Blanchets' house and shown her the video. She had not texted Hai anymore—how could she, after what had happened at Nina's house? After what Hai had shown her that day. What he had *done* to her. It was only right that he walked out and left her there.

Carmen had felt shame at first, and then nothing, except that she had no desire to see him, had nothing more to say. She had been shocked by the video, had felt frightened, violated, and humiliated as she had the last time, when she saw the news report about her and the Ativan Gang on TV that terrible, fateful evening in Barangay Bicutan.

But wasn't that what their tourists had felt when they woke up? The way she felt when the taxi driver had touched her. The way she felt after being unapologetically labelled a criminal on national TV.

She pushed the thoughts away. That was done. All of it: the driver, the gang, her old life, Max, and Hai. All that damage. All that mess and hurt.

Her mother had left her fourteen years ago. That was the biggest damage of it all. And yet here she was, still alive.

* * *

Carmen was not surprised that, in a way, she understood what Hai was doing. He had always seemed cunning and smart, and yet he did not seem like a man who had money. He didn't feel like someone who could have money and keep it, sustain it. She didn't know if she could fully forgive Hai for what he had done to her—and how he had done it: a betrayal that was such a low blow, there were still moments when Carmen felt that what he'd done was as humiliating for him as it was for her. But then who was she in his life, anyway? The only thing she could believe about Hai right now was that his hotel was going bankrupt.

She, too, had decided on something. And she had done it. It had not been a problem calling Marina and setting up a meeting. And it had not just been one meeting but several. It had been her decision, fully.

It would be the last, she told herself. Here she was, befriending people again. And it was not hard to work on being Marina's new friend, to ask her out on casual coffee dates as she had learned the Vietnamese were wont to do. She had been prepping their relationship, imagining it as a canvas that was being prepared, not yet knowing if it would be painted on. Yes, this was sometimes how she saw her relationship with Marina. Not exactly a con, but one that wasn't fully upfront and honest. Carmen didn't know exactly what to call the things she'd been telling Marina—second-hand information, assumptions, lies? Whatever they were, they had been effortless. Whatever they were, they had all been to help Hai get what he had told Carmen he needed.

He didn't have to know what she had done.

Marina's Huế

MARINA

Marina stared at the screen of her phone, for a moment a jumble of black and red, little numbers in grey that at first she couldn't find. She had spent the last fifteen minutes opening and closing the app that was her online bank account, and now she didn't want to see it again.

She had always been reluctant to look at how much money she had in the bank. No, she was reluctant to look at the transactions she'd made. Online banking made it so much easier to keep track of what you had, but she had a feeling it also made it easier for her to lose what she had.

If there was one thing she feared, it was losing something.

Why did she have the feeling that if she said no, she would lose Hai, in some way? *He just said he wanted you to be his wife,* a voice inside her said. Right. It all made sense, didn't it?

But then why did she have a feeling that even if she gave the money, she would still lose Hai?

They could get married. Not that Marina was really interested in getting married. It was the thought of being together that she wanted. Or maybe it was being in Huế that was stirring up this yearning in her, whetting her appetite, in a way, for another go at coupledom. It was seeing up close and every day, how everyone just seemed to have *someone.* One taxi driver who'd chatted gamely with her revealed that he was already married with two kids and that he was only twenty-three.

When she asked why he had gotten married so early, he only smiled and said, 'For love.'

The words had echoed in her, long after she alighted and said goodbye to the driver.

Marina sat up and adjusted herself in the café's rattan seat, taking a controlled sip of her iced coffee. She had been a tea drinker for years, but had given way to the fragrant, creamy coffees of Huế, a different one in every café. A relapse.

* * *

The café that Carmen had chosen wasn't a café at all. It was a tea shop. Another tea shop, and it was another meeting she was having with Carmen today, their third get-together in a little more than two weeks.

But it felt good. She felt supported because Carmen was also a Filipina navigating her way in and around a city that wasn't her own. It was different being with another person who had come from the same place, who understood first-hand where she came from, what had happened to their country, who knew how marvellous and terrible Filipinos could be.

The week after Hai told her about the property for sale next door, she ran into Carmen again. When Marina asked about her mother, Carmen reacted with a hopeful smile, saying that she'd asked a private investigator to help her, and that she was still working to get the money. She appeared settled and confident.

At the most recent one, Carmen invited her to the home of her employer, a Vietnamese woman named Nina Blanchet who herself had been eager to meet someone like Marina. Carmen told Marina that Nina was married to a French man, and that he had adopted her kids.

'She used to be a sex worker,' Carmen told Marina in Tagalog. 'Now she's turned her life around. She works all day, shooting videos for YouTube. That's what I realized about the Vietnamese—they're hard workers.'

* * *

Carmen was already there, giving Marina a short wave as she slipped off her shoes at the entrance. The teahouse was called An Nhien, a sprawling room with low tables and shelves neatly-lined with packages of loose-leaf tea, their labels handwritten in thick blue ink. Marina walked past the tea displays and headed to where Carmen was sitting cross-legged on the floor, a glass tumbler of light brown tea on the table in front of her.

'Hai's not with you?' Carmen asked, as Marina settled on the floor cushion across from her.

'He's at the hotel right now,' Marina said. 'His new hotel, with Phong.' She told Carmen about the property for sale next door and how Hai had told her that he wanted to buy it.

Carmen was nodding. 'I think that's good—that he's expanding.' She motioned for the server—then paused mid-wave as if remembering something. 'Wait,' she said, frowning as she lowered her arm. 'I think they already have a buyer. Poor Hai.'

'Oh?' Marina felt a flash of guilt. 'Is it too late? Hai—well, he's still looking for the money.' She didn't want to tell Carmen that Hai had asked her. And that she had not yet decided.

'Are you marrying Hai?'

'What?' Marina stared at Carmen, a little taken aback. 'No,' she said. But she realized that she was smiling. 'Did Hai tell you that?'

'I know how he feels about you.' Carmen hesitated, then gave her a knowing look. 'Do you know what? He told me he wants you to be his wife someday.'

That was exactly what Hai had told her.

'Marina.' Carmen reaching across the table to tap her hand. 'If you get married, will you live in Huế? Or in Singapore?'

'If, Carmen. *If* we get married.' Marina laughed and shook her head. 'No,' she said, turning serious. 'I would like to live here, in Huế.'

Carmen nodded. 'Hai's hotel is doing so good. You know that, right?'

Marina gave her a rueful smile. 'I don't really know anything about hotel operations, Carmen,' she said. 'Or doing that kind of business.'

'Well, I do,' Carmen said. 'My uncles in Manila used to run a hotel. They were businessmen, good ones.'

'Oh, really? And their business was hotels?'

'Small ones. Two-star ones.' Carmen narrowed her eyes. 'I think if they saw that hotel next door—the one that Hai wants—they wouldn't think twice. They would buy it. It just makes sense.'

'Really? I don't know.' Marina tried to keep the doubt out of her voice.

'What was it that Hai told me?' Carmen blinked and looked up, brow furrowing. 'Ah! That it could be life-changing, this kind of expansion.' Then, she gazed directly at Marina, her eyes steady. 'The same way, he said, that you've changed his life.'

The Simple Part

MARINA

She felt frightened at first, and then she felt flattered. Power, really, was what she should have been feeling, but it wasn't that.

Chosen. That was what Marina felt. Something akin to being included. Included, finally, in Hai's life.

She told herself she didn't need a marriage proposal. She did not need to be asked. Hai had said something about her being his wife. If she was not asked, had she been told?

She could see herself in Huế. There was now even the possibility of owning property. Huế was where she felt free and anonymous, unencumbered by the need to get everything exactly right. Here, she was okay to take it slow, to not be the first—or even the best.

You just need one person who cares for you, she had always told herself. One person, that's all it takes. Maybe that person was Hai.

She just needed to go online. A few swipes and taps and the fifty thousand US dollars that Hai was asking would be sent in an instant.

The money, that was the simple part. Marina had checked her bank account, and it wasn't as if she didn't have enough. Why, then, was she still thinking of saying no?

And what would it mean if she said yes?

Closure

MARINA

The hotel she'd chosen for the creative retreat turned out to not be in the city. Marina knew this when she booked it, ignoring the reviews that said it was too far. It was beside an abandoned waterpark, and it stood on a corner where the perpendicular streets were lined with local houses, not souvenir shops or cafés.

She stayed in the rooftop room that had floor-to-ceiling glass walls, a vegetable garden, and a view of the hills. Below was a small pool clad in rustic grey-green tiles and surrounded by plants considered designer in Singapore, and maybe even Manila. The airy lobby served as a dining room, lounge area, and bar, kitted out with tables built from roughly-cut trunks of trees.

It was a relaxing space. It felt private, removed from the frenzied bustle of the city. Marina started imagining people wanting to stay there, to write, to create. She imagined them waking up and writing everywhere—on the rooftop, on the terrace, in the lobby. This creative retreat—this idea from Atasha—wasn't at all an illogical or impractical concept. It was plausible. It felt both straightforward and creative because Marina and Atasha had been in the industry for years. The room had cost less than fifty dollars.

Now that she knew what Atasha had been planning all along, Marina could see the potential. The possibilities. Marina knew, in her heart, that it was time to do this. For herself, for Atasha.

Was that the thing that had changed? Was it her decision to stop distancing herself from what happened between Atasha and her?

Was it her resolve to finally face what had been there all these years, just waiting for her acknowledgement?

Or was it just because she'd lost her job? Her mother would have said this for sure, insisting on the simple, practical, and mundane. *You've just been fired,* her mother would say, *and now desperate for something different, something less humiliating, a way out.*

Marina closed her eyes, tried to take a breath. *This is why you're here,* she told herself. This was the voice she needed, not her mother's. *Here is where you can discern what's for you. Here is where you can discover what you need.*

She pictured Hai. Sweet and strange and unlike anyone she had met before.

* * *

Could she start thinking of Atasha again? Could she start living with what had happened twelve years ago? She knew she should do the right thing. But what was the right thing to do? Go back to Singapore, find another job similar to what she'd been doing at *Parcours?* Her mother would say that, her mother had already said that.

She had to start living with what happened twelve years ago. She had to start working with the hurt she'd buried so well in work, in travel, in acquiring the things she thought she needed. How successful Marina Bellosillo had been! Yes, she was a success, and she had lost someone like Atasha. No one was like Atasha. There was nobody who could understand this kind of thing except Atasha.

Would she? If Atasha had understood, she would not have done what she'd done.

The thing is, now Marina would never know the answer. The thing is, maybe she didn't need it anymore.

'Huế is in your blood,' a random person had told Marina during one of her errands, when she chatted about coming to Huế. 'There must be something coursing through you that led you back here,' that person said.

Marina doubted it, of course. There was no other blood running through her except her own: alone, weak, maybe defeated—but still alive. Still throbbing, still running.

We die as we live.

She wasn't dead yet. She wasn't dead yet like Atasha.

Blood

MARINA

People say you can't expect everything from just one friend. You get something from each one. But for Marina, Atasha was everything.

What was it like to idolize someone, only to have them betray you in a way you could never imagine? 'I have only committed the mistake of believing in you,' Prince Sisowath Sirik Matak had said to US Ambassador John Gunther Jean in 1975, refusing his offer of escape.

There were four hundred reported suicides in Singapore that year, and more than three thousand in the Philippines. Some of them she'd read about in the news, some she'd heard whispered about among the journalists and writers she'd worked with, back when she had still been with *Manila Guardian* and *Loweq*. Marina could still remember the outpouring of shock and condolences for the Filipina model who threw herself six floors down, the author who was a scion of Manila's wealthiest intellectuals, ten floors down. The actress-turned-restaurant owner who hung herself in the bathroom.

She knew about them. In Manila or Singapore, it didn't matter, because she could only think of one: Atasha's.

Atasha had swallowed sleeping pills.

When she learned that Atasha had killed herself, Marina was ashamed to think that after that initial shock, the next emotion that engulfed her was fear. Because her first thought was, it couldn't have been because of her.

Fifty Thousand

HAI

It all came back to money, didn't it? Fifty thousand dollars—why, that was nothing to Marina. Not to him, never. Fifty thousand US dollars was 700 million dong and Hai's head swam at the thought that it would be in his bank account soon.

He was still angry at Carmen even when he learned, belatedly, that she had contacted Marina. All that drama, when Carmen did what Hai had asked her to do, after all.

Carmen talked to Marina about him and for him. If she did that out of pity or fear, Hai didn't care anymore. Now that things were moving into place, he didn't have time to ponder or ruminate—or worry. Marina may not have said yes yet, but she was still on his side—Hai was so sure of that—and for now, that was all that mattered. Nothing would have to change. If it had to, it would be for the better.

He was waiting for Sinh at his usual spot outside Jasmine Hotel, but she had not emerged from the side door that was the employees' entrance. Hai looked at his phone. He had been waiting for twenty minutes. He had already smoked three sticks. It was the end of her shift, and he'd already seen some of her colleagues leave.

'Em oi,' he called out to one of the girls who'd just emerged out of the basement parking on her motorbike. 'Is Sinh still there?'

'Sinh?' The girl's face was drawn and unsmiling, a smattering of red pimples on her cheeks. 'She went home. Said she wasn't feeling well.'

Hai thanked her as she sped off. Frowning, he lit another stick and took his phone out. Why didn't Sinh tell him that she had gone home?

He could have gone to his room and slept. He hadn't been sleeping well since renovations started at Hong Thien Hotel.

Sinh answered on the second ring. '*Alo*.'

'Where are you?' Hai asked, annoyed, even though he knew that Sinh and he had no real plans that day. He'd assumed they would ride back to his room, stop and eat at one of the sidewalk stalls along the way. The usual.

'Are you okay? They told me here that you were sick.'

'I'm fine.' Sinh's voice was unusually subdued. 'I'm at the doctor's.'

'Why?' A sudden worry replaced his annoyance. 'What happened? Is it something serious?' Naïvely, he had imagined a headache or menstrual cramps, something simple like that.

'I'm pregnant,' Sinh said.

'What?'

'A baby, *anh yeu*,' Sinh said. 'We're going to have a baby.'

* * *

Hai was still standing in the same spot by the side of Jasmine Hotel after Sinh and he got off the phone, and he agreed to pick her up from the doctor's. He smoked stick after stick.

When his pack ran out, he took out his phone again. He pressed Marina's number, listening to the continuous ring on the other line.

When he was sure that there was no answer, he pressed her number again. He would tell Marina that he loved her, that he would marry her, that they would travel again to Singapore, that they would live together in Huế.

He was still thinking of this, and what else he could promise her on the third call, and the fourth, and fifth, even as Marina's phone kept ringing.

Vong Canh Hill

MARINA

Marina stood still under a pine tree at the edge of the hill, unable to believe the sky. The soft pinks and purple tinged with orange, all these colours reflected on the water of the Perfume River below. In the distance, the delicate grey silhouettes of the mountains overlapped and faded out like a shadowy, monochromatic painting. It was sunset at Vong Canh Hill—the eye of Huế, as it was often referred to by the locals—and she was just in time.

Marina had read about this place. The kings felt inspired here, had painted and written poetry on the very ground she was standing. No wonder the emperors Tu Duc, Dong Khanh, and Thieu Tri had all built their tombs around this hill.

It had been two days since she'd seen Hai. They would be meeting again that evening, and she knew it would be their last. Marina thought of the emails that had started coming in, of the people who've expressed their interest in the retreat, of the writers who'd been eager to join, of the tutors she'd asked to come and had said yes. She had six participants who had sent the deposit to reserve their slot. She had been introduced to a poet in Huế, whom she asked to give a talk. The Instagram page she'd started was growing slowly with followers increasing every day.

She was almost done. She would soon be done with the arrangements. Atasha's idea, Marina's execution. What was it that Atasha had wanted? Writers and artists like her who could explore a new city like Huế, find their tribe, discover the divine in the mundane—even if just for a few days.

Freedom and happiness were what Atasha wanted, too. And love, always love. It had taken Marina all these years to realize that she and Atasha had always sought out the same things. That they had both wanted—no, *needed*—the same things. What had changed was that Marina was still here, breathing and alive and able to do it all differently. She could still choose to believe that what she needed wasn't Hai or Huế City or anything else. That what she, Marina Bellosillo, only ever needed was herself.

Her phone started vibrating. A call—one of many—but she made no move to answer it. She didn't need to.

Instead, she soaked in the soft purple and peach hues of the waning sun over Vong Canh Hill and thought of the kings and their tombs.

Marina prayed that she would still be alive tomorrow. And the next day. The next weeks, months, years. *Let me live for the next twenty years, please,* she prayed. Two more decades, and even that felt short.

Campfire 88

CARMEN

Three days after she had gone to Mr Binh, Carmen was back at the Blanchet house. Nina could not stop talking about their Dalat holiday, and in the afternoon announced that they were going to eat at a barbecue restaurant near Vong Canh Hill.

'Good for Madame Fabuleux,' Nina declared. She had gained nearly a thousand new followers on her YouTube channel, she said, and she wanted to celebrate, go to a new spot, take more videos. Maybe she'd even do a whole vlog about this barbecue place, just because it was all over her feed. 'I'm very motivated,' she said the last word deliberately, looking pleased with her pronunciation.

'It looks like something you would find in Dalat, which Andre likes,' Nina said. 'Come with us, Carmen.'

The property was called Campfire 88 and looked like it had been built for Instagram. Most visible from the road were the teepee-like structures in pastel colours, hung with dried flowers and bunting. A vintage Volkswagen Kombi van in bright yellow was parked by the entrance, just for display. Long wooden picnic tables with built-in benches were neatly arranged outside, surrounding an all-wood bungalow that had open louvres instead of walls. It housed the kitchen and more seating area. Fairy lights, strung above and everywhere, had already been turned on when Carmen and the Blanchets arrived there at 5 p.m.

'If you go straight there, you will see a beautiful hill with a beautiful view,' Andre told her, as he looked for a parking spot in the space

just outside the restaurant. He gestured towards the road ahead, framed
by a canopy of pine trees. Carmen was not surprised that he knew
these sites. The French man had been working and living in Huế for six
years before he met Nina.

All the teepees had already been reserved, to Nina's disappointment.
Andre led them to one of the long tables outside, just by the
bungalow. A stand-alone grill had been placed right beside their
table and was lit as soon as they all sat down. Soon, Andre and the
kids were preoccupied handling and cooking the cut pieces of meat,
vegetables, and shellfish on the grill. They had vehemently declined
offers from Carmen to help.

Nina was still pouting about the teepees. She had brought her
camera, of course—a small black Canon with a little furry mike
that looked like a cute, quirky accessory, which Sam kept stroking
during the ride.

'Oh, this smoke!' Nina exclaimed, flapping her slender, pale arms to
fan out the fumes coming from the hot grill. She mumbled something
in Vietnamese as she stood up, positioned herself so her back was
facing the entrance.

'Carmen,' she called out, holding out her camera. 'Take my
picture—no, a video! I'm tired of taking my own. Make sure you get
the . . . the . . .' She gestured towards the teepees and tables.

Carmen held up the camera and pointed it in her direction, swinging
it slowly upwards and slightly to the right so the charming picnic tables
and the bright yellow van showed up behind her. As Nina fell out of
the camera's tiny screen and the tables came into view, Carmen took
a step back to avoid filming a family of four who were occupying one
of the tables. They must have arrived at the restaurant when Nina and
Andre were ordering, and Carmen was busy holding the kids down.

'Wait,' Carmen said, slowly lowering the camera. She had stopped
recording. And she hardly felt it snatched from out of her hands by
Nina, eager to see the clip that Carmen had just taken. She turned
towards the wooden bungalow.

'Where are you going?''

'Toilet,' Carmen replied, surprised at the steadiness of her voice. It had never sounded as strong and well-modulated as it did in that moment.

A violent roiling had started in her stomach, but she was inside the airy building in less than a minute, avoiding the open kitchen and standing in a spot behind the wooden louvres. No one was eating indoors at that moment, and she angled herself so she was sure she wasn't seen from the outside.

Seen by whom?

Carmen felt a crazy bubble of laughter rise inside her, and she clamped a palm on her mouth as a choking cough, broken and rough, shot out of her throat. Carmen had spent the last fourteen years apart and out of sight from her mother and here she was, not wanting to be seen by the very same person she'd been longing for.

Because it *was* her mother who was out there. Nicole Maranan Peltier was part of the family of four that had just arrived for a barbecue dinner at the very Instagrammable Campfire 88. Carmen knew it was her, the moment Nina's camera captured her mother's profile: the gentle sloping of her wide forehead, the straightness of her nose, the narrow shoulders, the quiet stillness about her even though the other members of her family seemed raucous and talkative.

The people with Nicole Peltier were the ones Carmen had seen on Facebook. The Caucasian husband. The two kids, a boy who looked about sixteen and a little girl who couldn't be more than ten years old.

Only her mother was sitting still. The rest of her family were buoyant and animated, constantly moving, talking, gesturing, fiddling with the utensils, poking at each other. There was an upbeat energy about Nicole Peltier's family that she didn't seem to share, but from where Carmen could see her, Nicole looked well, healthy, and younger than her forty-seven years. Carmen knew her mother's birthday by heart.

Nicole was gazing at something in the distance, but no one seemed to be noticing. *It's me,* Carmen wanted to shout, the voice inside her head back to sounding like her eleven-year-old self. But her mind blanked on the numerous scenarios she had composed for years in her head, on the many ways she thought she would act and react when she finally saw her mother. And so, Carmen remained where she was at that very moment: hidden, safe, steeping in agony and anticipation at what could be next. It was all up to her, she knew.

Certainly, it would not be as simple as hurrying over and saying: 'Excuse me, are you Nicole Peltier? I'm your daughter, Carmen.'

But if it were, would her mother hug her? Would she cry? Would she be silent yet moved at the sight of her daughter? Would she break down and hold her, just like she used to when Carmen was small? Whatever her reaction would be, Carmen had always imagined that it would be one filled with gratefulness, with wonder at having found her.

Up until this moment, the possibilities had been endless. It was the hope of being with her mother again that had kept Carmen going, somehow, all these years. Her mother had left her, that was true. Carmen knew what they—Nanay Luisa and Max and whoever else in Barangay Bicutan had come to know the story of a certain woman named Nicole Maranan—thought of the woman who had driven in one evening and left without her daughter and then never come back again.

If her mother was as evil and as bad as people thought her to be, then why couldn't Carmen, whom they said she had done the most damage to, forget her? Didn't they know that it was the *thought* of her mother that had kept her believing that life could still be good? Didn't they know that as long one was breathing, nothing was too late?

A thick drowsiness overcame her, and she closed her eyes for a moment, the clanging of the grills, the shouts of the servers, the buzz of the people outside faded out and sounded as if they were far, far away.

When Carmen opened her eyes, Andre was there. He had come for her. The Blanchet family were seated on the other side of the property, the part Carmen could see from where she stood. She turned her back from the window.

'Carmen, Nina is looking for you.'

She nodded. 'And the kids?'

Andre's face relaxed, the corners of his thin mouth easily curving up. 'They're all right,' he said. 'We are all playing.'

Carmen paused for a moment, then looked over to where her mother was still sitting with her family, her profile now looking fuzzy in the heat and smoke of the barbecue grill fires that were being lit around her.

Her mother was alive. Her mother was here and she was real. She had all limbs on her, and something more: she had peace. If Carmen wanted to be surer than she was right now, it would only take her twenty feet and three long strides to prove what she had already seen.

She turned to Andre. 'Where is that place again that you were talking about? The one with the beautiful view?'

'Vong Canh Hill, yes.' Andre gestured towards the entrance. 'Just go that way and follow the road. It will lead you straight up there.'

'Thank you,' Carmen said, stepping outside. Without turning her head, she walked out of the restaurant, heading towards the hill.

Acknowledgments

It takes multiple people to make a story.

I am incredibly grateful to my publisher, Nora Nazarene Abu Bakar, for her generous belief in me.

Thank you to editor Sneha Bhagwat of Penguin Random House SEA, for the thoughtful and thorough editing of *Huế City*.

To my writing sisters at Migrant Writers of Singapore—Jane, Jenelyn, Julie Ann, Ate Ellen, Stephanie, Sonia, Laila, Nelie, Naicy, Cristina, Susie, Ayu, Siti, Indah, Rochelle, and Fitri—whose creativity and compassion inspire me.

To Meg Nones Tongio, for the gift of real friendship full of wisdom, strength, and support.

To Joanne Ongkeko, for sharing her vast creativity, company, and counsel in writing, art, and life.

Thank you to the hardworking folks at The Philippine Embassy in Singapore for their dedication to uplifting Filipino talent.

To friends An, Chi Tam, Na, Mino, and Giang whose elegance and eye for beauty brought me closer to Huế's soul and grace.

Cảm ơn rất nhiều to Vo Minh Tuan, with whom I began this adventure in Huế.

To my talented community of writers and poets in my two homes, Singapore and the Philippines, who've let me share myself and my work.

To the marketing team: Chai Srivastava, Simran Singh, and Almira, for their support in bringing this book to readers.

To my amazing readers, for honouring me with their trust and their time.

My deepest love and gratitude to my family, Alfred and Ulric, for their unmatched selflessness, magnanimity, and patience. Thank you for this life of writing, and the laughter in between.